ARCHMAGOS

More great Warhammer 40,000 fiction from Black Library

BELISARIUS CAWL: THE GREAT WORK
A novel by Guy Haley

GENEFATHER
A novel by Guy Haley

THE INFINITE AND THE DIVINE
A novel by Robert Rath

DOMINION GENESIS
A novel by Jonathan D Beer

LEVIATHAN
A novel by Darius Hinks

• DARK IMPERIUM •
by Guy Haley

BOOK 1: DARK IMPERIUM
BOOK 2: PLAGUE WAR
BOOK 3: GODBLIGHT

• DAWN OF FIRE •
BOOK 1: AVENGING SON
by Guy Haley
BOOK 2: THE GATE OF BONES
by Andy Clark
BOOK 3: THE WOLFTIME
by Gav Thorpe
BOOK 4: THRONE OF LIGHT
by Guy Haley
BOOK 5: THE IRON KINGDOM
by Nick Kyme
BOOK 6: THE MARTYR'S TOMB
by Marc Collins
BOOK 7: SEA OF SOULS
by Chris Wraight
BOOK 8: HAND OF ABADDON
by Nick Kyme
BOOK 9: THE SILENT KING
by Guy Haley

ARCHMAGOS

GUY HALEY

BLACK LIBRARY

A BLACK LIBRARY PUBLICATION

First published in 2025.
This edition published in Great Britain in 2026 by
Black Library, Games Workshop Ltd., Willow Road,
Nottingham, NG7 2WS, UK.

Represented by: Games Workshop Limited – Irish branch,
Unit 3, Lower Liffey Street, Dublin 1,
D01 K199, Ireland.

10 9 8 7 6 5 4 3 2 1

Produced by Games Workshop in Nottingham.
Cover illustration by Lorenzo Mastroianni.

A CIP record for this book is available from the British Library.

ISBN 13: 978-1-83609-401-2

Printed and bound in the UK.

For more than a hundred centuries the Emperor has sat immobile on the Golden Throne of Earth. He is the Master of Mankind. By the might of his inexhaustible armies a million worlds stand against the dark.

Yet, he is a rotting carcass, the Carrion Lord of the Imperium held in life by marvels from the Dark Age of Technology and the thousand souls sacrificed each day so his may continue to burn.

To be a man in such times is to be one amongst untold billions. It is to live in the cruelest and most bloody regime imaginable. It is to suffer an eternity of carnage and slaughter. It is to have cries of anguish and sorrow drowned by the thirsting laughter of dark gods.

This is a dark and terrible era where you will find little comfort or hope. Forget the power of technology and science. Forget the promise of progress and advancement. Forget any notion of common humanity or compassion.

There is no peace amongst the stars, for in the grim darkness of the far future, there is only war.

CHAPTER ONE

SOLANA OF MARS

Slitho Gallifa, the master of the *Light of Reason,* called Solana of Mars minutes after the four-hour translation bell rang. With the uncanny prescience that dogged her in the warp, she knew it was the captain the moment the hardline vox-unit bolted to the wall of her quarters started to squawk, and if she didn't exactly intuit it, she could guess what he wanted. She resented the intrusion. She was lying on her bunk. She didn't want to go anywhere. She should have risen hours ago, but was too worn out by the psychic pressures of traversing the immaterium to do much of anything. She wished to stay where she was, and she just knew he was going to ask her to leave.

'Mistress? Mistress, are you going to receive this communication?' Eremenitas asked. *More urged,* she thought irritably. He'd been with her the whole way, lurking in the corner of her cabin, upright the whole time because he didn't need a bed. Eremenitas was a shadowed block, his heavy track unit solid as a piece of Jovian furniture. The protruding glass bulbs of his false eyes and the high dome of his silvered brain case glimmered out of the shadows. She avoided looking at him. Despite his entirely artificial face, she always had the feeling he disapproved of her, and right then, with that headache, she couldn't stomach that.

'Mistress historitor?' he said. He was trying to be gentle. It wasn't working.

'I'm going,' she groaned, sounding far more petulant than she meant to.

Bare feet slapped onto a cold metal floor. She begrudged getting up to walk across the room, and, worst horror of all, lifting her leaden arm to depress the 'receive' rune.

The button sank into its housing with a sullen reluctance she empathised with. An amber light indicated the line was open.

Gallifa's voice crackled out of the voxmitter. The *Light of Reason* was a new ship, less than a decade old in a navy in which the average age was measured in hundreds of years. It was a novel pattern, designed to convey the regent's servants as quickly as was possible in this benighted age of warp storms and war. Many of the same type had led the torchbearer fleets in the opening years of the Indomitus Crusade.

Guilliman's return had prompted something of a renaissance in ship construction, led, of course, by the multitalented Belisarius Cawl.

'Renaissance' was such a subjective term. Solana knew many magi who preferred words like 'blasphemy' when applied to Cawl's approach to technology. Either way, the *Light* was blessed with the finest technologies. In realspace the signal over the hardline was crystal clear, almost as if the speaker was right next to her. In the warp the signal burred and popped as if it were widecast through extreme magnetic turmoil, not sent a short distance down a well-insulated wire. Simple malfunction wasn't all of it. There were voices on the edge of hearing, voices which spoke words that were almost comprehensible. Voices she shouldn't listen to but strained so hard to hear it made the roots of her teeth ache.

The thought of those voices made her feel sick.

'Madam historitor, we shall be emerging from the warp within three hours, forty-nine minutes ship time.' Behind Gallifa's voice a tormented something laughed. The static roared as if frightened, obliterating the master's next words. *'...ially extend an invitation to attend both the translation and shutter-opening ceremonies upon the command deck. Might I presume you will attend?'*

Solana was too tired to sigh. Gallifa courted her favour assiduously, though that was no surprise. Nearly everyone saw her as a direct link to the primarch; it didn't matter that she was most emphatically not.

She didn't want to go among people. She wanted to be left alone. All the excitement she had felt at the start of her journey, being sent to personally report on Belisarius Cawl, the greatest mind in the galaxy, to really speak to him, to a rare man who might actually get something done... All that was gone. After the awful pressures of the warp voyage it seemed a grey duty, no more interesting than any number of other so-called vital assignments she'd fulfilled as one of the Founding Four of the Logos Historica Verita.

She didn't care about any of that. She wanted to sleep.

From the corner of her eye she caught the bottle of the pharmasomna tincture nestled between her notebooks on the chamber's single shelf. Maybe if she drank enough she'd stay unconscious until it was all over. If she were really lucky, she might not even dream.

She shook the thought away. She was already taking four times the dose prescribed by the ship's chirurgeon. Not only was that dangerous, but she felt guilty for having the pharmasomna in the first place. There were thousands of people aboard the *Light of Reason*; few of them had access to real medical care. What was their recourse when nightmares shook their sleep? Prayer? She'd seen how well that worked. The Emperor wasn't listening. He was rather busy these days.

'Mistress Solana?' Gallifa's voice was an odd blend of solicitousness, concern, and annoyance that his offer had not been taken up with alacrity.

She had to swallow twice before she could speak. Omnissiah, her mouth was so dry.

'My apologies, shipmaster. I was sleeping, and am a little dull-headed. I would be delighted to attend,' she said, which was the exact opposite of how she felt.

Too often, protocol took precedence over desire.

'Excellent. We shall expect your arrival in say… two hours?'

'I look forward to it,' she said. *Not at all*, she added to herself.

At least this all meant the journey through the warp would be over soon.

'Thank the Machine God,' she murmured.

Her hand slid off the button. The connection light flickered from green to red, then went dark.

'An unwelcome offer?' Eremenitas asked.

'Any offer would be unwelcome right now.'

She fought the urge to clamber back into bed and pull the coverlet over her head. Instead, she decided to dress, and began to unlace her nightshirt. It was a little strange having Eremenitas in there, but there was no chance of impropriety. Eremenitas wasn't a man any more. He'd carved away all those parts of himself so as to better be able to think. For many Martians, sexuality was an unwelcome distraction. She only used the masculine pronoun in Gothic to avoid confusion. Gender was a matter for more biological beings than they.

'I didn't know you were awake,' she said.

'You know I don't sleep. I was thinking.'

'That's what you do, isn't it? Cogitate, cogitate, cogitate.' She winced at the whine in her voice.

'The paths to comprehension are many.' Eremenitas' voice rose slightly with indignation. He knew what effect the warp had on her, and was usually more emollient. Maybe it was getting to him too. 'I follow mine, as you follow yours.' He paused. 'Most of the time.'

Eremenitas was a machine aesthete far down the path to the final knowing, and thus hardly human at all. For all that, she found he could be surprisingly tart.

She let the nightshirt drop around her shoulders and pool upon the floor, revealing her far more modest suite of modifications. A run of electoos down her left arm to contact points on her fingers; an interface port embedded in the right forearm, the dataspike coiled out of sight in her hollow metal radius; a steel finger, the smallest, on the same hand that held a group of molecular manipulators as feathery-fine as the arms of sessile sea creatures. There was her memcore plug gleaming low down on the shaved part of her head. She wore most of her hair long now, hiding the tattoo of the Machina Opus across the right of her skull. She couldn't remember when she'd started concealing it, or why, beyond a vague disappointment that the crusade had not gone as she had expected, and her own people had often stood in her way. The memcore was an unsurprising augmetic – no real magos went without one. Her eyes had a silvery cast, simple full-spectral range upgrades, enhanced low-light vision and an internal retinal display. Then there was the banded casing of the fibre bundles that replaced her right sternocleidomastoid muscle. Not elective, that one, but the result of a las bolt on Fhalami Delta that had come within a fraction of an inch of her carotid artery.

She'd avoided further enhancement. That was unusual for a member of the Machine Cult, but then her very unusualness was why she'd ended up in the Logos Historica Verita in the first place. She supposed her rebellion against the strictures of the Cult began there, with an instinctive rejection of body modification, long before she was hauled away for modus innovatum. She was, in her way, as big a rebel as Cawl, and yet she was celebrated as Guilliman's Martian inductee, Solana of Mars! The irony dogged her still. A rebel elevated to representative of the thing she was rebelling against. She thought, for a while, that she had won, but the Logos hadn't proven to be any more freeing than life on Mars.

For example, she had not chosen her name. It wasn't her real title. Fabian wasn't 'Fabian of Terra', Viablo hadn't been 'Viablo of Jupiter'. My, how it still smarted, to be the political choice, but at the beginning Guilliman needed someone from Mars in his nascent organisation of truth-seekers for all the obvious reasons, and she was it. After all, without a Martian in his new organisation, Guilliman would have denied himself much access to information, he would have caused offence, and in both ways he would have seemed weak.

There we are, she thought. *Politics again.* Fine for the regent, but it left her with the lingering doubt as to whether she'd been chosen for her talents or for what she was: a presentable member of the priesthood who was sufficiently opposed to its ways to be biddable to the Imperium.

'And what exactly do you mean by "most of the time", Eremenitas?'

'I mean that for you the pursuit of comprehension is of lesser importance than it is for me.'

'Because only the Omnissiah knows all, comprehends all.'

'Don't pretend your lack of application is caused by respect, madam.'

Maybe he did not mean to condemn her. Maybe he simply

spoke truthfully. Eremenitas was supremely rational. On the other hand, he spoke Gothic with her all the time. He never used the Lingua Technis, and binharic only in moments of danger. That spoke volumes about his opinion of her as a real magos.

Nevertheless, she was grateful he had ended up sharing her quarters. As the crusade had ground on and on and on, she'd found it increasingly hard to spend nights in the warp alone. Nearly two decades in, sleep was elusive.

Their quarters were generous by Naval standards, though not as generous as some she'd had on other ships. Five paces to the tiny wardrobe from her bed. Inside were the ceremonial robes of a tech-priest. A long undershift woven with thread of gold circuitry patterns, all purely decorative; a habit of heavy fibres dyed Martian crimson to go over that; then a long tabard of white and black edged with cog-tooth patterns and carrying a bronze cast of the Opus Machina in the Martian mode, a high-collared shoulder piece, chain-link belt, and more. There was always more when it came to ceremonial garb. It all looked so... heavy. She took out her undergarments – these at least were light, comfortable, and her own choice – and shrugged herself lethargically into them. She glanced over her shoulder.

'Could you help me dress, Eremenitas? It is unfair to wake my attendants. None of them have weathered this voyage well.'

'Of course, madam.'

Eremenitas trundled out of the corner. He started with a lurch she thought would topple him, so hard did it set his columnar body swaying. A number of limbs extended themselves from this central pillar. He picked up the shift and lifted it. Solana let it slide over her head and arms, grunting as the weight of the garment settled on her.

'I'll not miss this ridiculous dress-up. These aristocrats and their displays.'

'It is expected. You are a high-ranking magos, Solana.'

'I thought I'd left all that behind when I was chosen for the Logos.'

Eremenitas gave a pitying chuckle. 'Really, why do you think you were chosen?'

'I was just reflecting upon that,' she said drily.

'Arms up again!' Eremenitas helped her pull her habit on. 'Power has its own visual language. Discomfort is a key part of the syntax. You must dress as people expect. Influence comes through display.'

'Whatever. I'll be glad to be back in Logos battle dress. Ow!' She looked sharply over her shoulder. 'Watch it. Bits of this are sharp!'

'Apologies. This part is tricky.' He proceeded with more care. 'Take comfort.'

'Very amusing.'

'Take comfort,' he repeated, continuing smoothly over her interruption. 'You will not be alone. All the nobles and higher officers will be sweating in their finery, pulled in and pushed out, powdered and puffed.' He sounded amused at this human vanity.

'It's not as if the Prime Conduit is even going to care,' she said, as Eremenitas offered her the tabard. She bent for him to slide the stiff brocade over her head. Everything went over her head. She stood, then he laced the sides up. His simple pincer manipulators were surprisingly dextrous. 'And I should be exempt. I'm a historitor first, only Martian second, Omnissiah preserve me.'

'These displays are not for Cawl. As an agent of Roboute Guilliman, you must be all things to all people, and that means the right dress for the right time. It is as important as the correct selection of weapons, or the correct mathematical proofs in astrogation. You were chosen by the primarch partially because you were a member of the Cult, ergo, in times like these you must dress like one. Like it or not, madam, you are and always will be one of us.'

'I know that,' she said. She still sounded peevish. She'd better kill that.

She reached for the belt.

'Here, let me,' Eremenitas said, extending a pincer past her. It was funny, she thought, not really thinking it funny at all, how the Logos had started out with deliberately plain uniforms, yet by convoluted roads she had come to sport this gothic horror. It was emblematic of every effort Guilliman had made to simplify matters. The Imperium got in the way of making things easier, and more and more she was forced to employ the very same inefficient methods that were strangling the God-Emperor's domain. Clothes were only the start of it. She hitched the belt over her waist and held it while Eremenitas did up all the many pointlessly tiny hooks on the back.

She wondered what the rest of the Founding Four would make of that. Fabian, Mudire, Viablo... She could only guess. She'd not seen Fabian or Mudire for years, and Viablo was dead.

They got the shoulder piece on. It was moulded in a such a way it forced her shoulders further back than she was strictly comfortable with. Eremenitas helped her pull the deep hood of the habit over the top and arrange it atop the rest of the ensemble.

'There,' he said. 'Fit for the finest of forge-fanes.'

She smoothed down the various layers. 'Emperor alive, I'm going to cook in this thing.'

'Hm,' said Eremenitas. What he meant by that she had no idea.

'I can manage the rest,' she said, slapping away a handful of manipulators reaching out to make final adjustments. She tried to will a little energy into her limbs, and mostly failed. The flesh was weak. She reminded herself that in a few hours they'd be back in the materium and all this torment would go away.

If they survived translation.

Eremenitas' tracks spun in opposite directions, turning him around on the spot so he faced the other side of the wardrobe. When Solana saw what he was reaching for she snapped.

'For the Emperor's sake, spare me the hat. I'll wear my field cap and they can like it.'

The other magos dipped his head and fetched the cap. For some reason known only to himself, he'd kept the flesh assemblage of upper shoulders and neck. It was a strange biological interruption in the machine he'd made of the rest of his body. He held her cap while she did her hair, and applied an amount of makeup commensurate with the minimum expected for someone of her rank. A touch of rouge, a little black under the eye, gently impressed skull and cog on each cheek: seeing as she looked mainly human, that was the least people would expect. She drew the line there. No powdered face or gold-leaf circuitry. She took her hat, tugged it onto her head with a businesslike manner that was pretty much entirely faked.

'How do I look?'

'A fine balance of a person acquiescing to the social mores of a situation while maintaining a demonstrative amount of individuality.'

'Like one of the most influential women in the Imperium?'

'The melange of respect for the traditions of others and agency in choosing to disregard certain aspects of them as indicated by your manner of dress is appropriate for such a person, I would agree.'

She nodded briskly. Now, she was getting into the role. Being angry helped.

'That'll do. Let's go.'

CHAPTER TWO

TO THE EDGE OF FOREVER

Solana expected translation to be awful, and she was right about that.

The archmagos' rendezvous point was dangerously close to a gravitic singularity, an astronomical object known by less educated voidfarers as a 'black hole'. Though the sector was embraced fully by the Ultima Segmentum, it was in effect outside Imperial borders, deep in wilderness space, because what use was a dangerous astronomical phenomenon to the Imperium? It was called the Scorean Singularity. Why it had that name, Solana could find no clue.

Why Cawl was there was one of the things Solana had been tasked with finding out. She expected that to be difficult as well. Cawl had been predictably evasive about his whereabouts and business for years. Only a direct command from the Lord Imperial Regent to give account of himself had made the archmagos dominus cooperative, and then only barely; they could have joined his fleet somewhere safer, and travelled on together. Instead, he'd insisted on this ridiculously dangerous rendezvous.

Gravity was the problem. Large mass bodies in the materium impinged themselves upon the immaterium in some incomprehensible way, making shoals, cliffs and treacherous reefs in the sea of souls. The greater the gravity, the greater the peril. That was why ships very rarely translated in-system, and why every system had its Mandeville point where the warp could be gained in relative safety. By safety, they meant a vessel not being torn to pieces by inter-dimensional gravitic shear when the warp engines forced their portals to make the crossing. Next down the list of traversable points were the gravipauses, the calm spots within a system where the gravity of competing astronomical bodies cancelled each other out. These were dangerous.

A black hole was gravity at its most wicked. A black hole plunged itself like a dagger deep into the universe. Its influence spread far and wide around; its caresses, even softened by distance, were likely to be deadly to all but the most skilful of Navigators, the best of pilots, the most daring of crews, who attempted to translate too close.

The *Light of Reason* had been selected because of its captain's reputation. Nine years taking news of Guilliman's return across the Imperium, several more acting as a rapid courier where astrotelepathy had failed, Gallifa was not a man to be easily cowed, but as Solana watched him on his command dais, she could tell from the deep lines etched into his sallow face that he found the situation testing. The studious silence of his crew as they swapped call and response checks with each other, hunched so attentively over their instruments, only reinforced this opinion.

Solana and Eremenitas entered without anyone caring. They avoided a gaggle of diplomats off to the side, all squeezed into uncomfortable finery, makeup thick as corpse-starch porridge. It was a display put on for each other. Wherever Cawl was on the other side of the veil, it'd be days if not weeks of sailing before they had the chance to meet him, if he agreed to see them at all.

'I'll bet that Gallifa would rather they were not here.' Solana nodded at the dignitaries. Where they were each ultimately bound, she did not know. Dropping Solana off was only one of Gallifa's stops. She'd been glad they had kept their errands to themselves during the voyage.

'Rituals must be obeyed. Observances followed. As for the machine, so it is for society.'

Solana blew out dismissively.

'You original historitors were selected for your originality of thought, I understand, and there is a certain contempt for the norms as a corollary to that, but in dismissing these rituals, you dismiss human nature, and so dismiss knowledge,' Eremenitas said calmly. 'This is what I watch. This is what I am for. The pursuit of the knowledge of sentient interactions. Thinking beings as components of the Great Work.'

She gave him a sideways glance. 'For a student of human behaviour, you've given up a lot of your humanity. Why not let me abandon my small part in peace?'

'I abhor the flesh as it is a barrier to complete understanding. Only by becoming less than human can I hope to comprehend what it means to be human. You cannot observe from the inside, madam historitor. That is a limit of human nature. I chose to step beyond so I might look back and comprehend.'

'Fie on human nature,' she said. She wanted this over and done with. Once they were out, and this bloody headache was gone, then she might behave with a little more decorum.

'Fie?' He chuckled. 'You are still following both ritual and your innate humanity.'

He was right about that. She wanted to use stronger words than 'fie', which she realised, having uttered it, was far too mannered, but hadn't for fear of causing too much offence. *We all do our little part of the dance,* she thought. *Whether we tell ourselves we are taking part or not.* She wouldn't give Eremenitas the satisfaction of letting him know he was right.

'This collar itches,' she said, and stretched her neck against the pull of the collar.

A servitor drone swooped down, its contra-grav unit buzzing alarmingly. Under a cowled unit the size of a human torso a yellowed skull stared out with red glass eyes. Primitive grippers proffered a tray. Upon the tray were tall glasses full of liquid that smelled of mint, Vissellian amaranth liquor, and wood oil.

'Refreshments, Madam Solana?' it grated in a charmless machine voice.

Solana smiled wanly. 'I don't drink, nor do I indulge in other mind-altering chemicals,' she said, in case it offered her something else.

Apart from the pharmasomna, that counts, a small part of her said.

'Praise the Machine God, who made you in perfection so that you might be perfected,' said Eremenitas to the machine with rather more politesse.

The servitor dipped a grotesque bow, nearly spilling its cargo, and hummed noisily away. Of all the things on the command deck – the servitor choirs, the crew, the machines, the diplomats – only it seemed unperturbed. Even its cybernetic kin, who buzzed and flapped about the high vaulting, murmuring auto-blessings and snatches of hymn, seemed nervy somehow.

Gallifa came down to the main deck and spent the next ten minutes conferring with his senior officers, still ignoring the dignitaries as much as Solana did. He gave each man and woman his complete attention while they delivered their report. That was a rare enough quality in a commander to be remarkable, so she blinked a couple of images of him at work, and composed a quick memorio to be expanded in her journal later. Having heard his officers, Gallifa nodded gravely, and ascended the steps of the dais to his command throne. There he assumed a pose of studied calm. He gestured, and a servo-skull plated in age-darkened bronze floated down. It had a vox-thief jammed into its gaping jaws, which it presented to the shipmaster's mouth. When Gallifa spoke, his voice boomed from voxmitters hidden high up in the ceiling. The static was as heavy on them as it had been on the hardline, and behind lurked laughter.

'We begin translation. Master of the watch, sound the bell.'

A man wearing a frown that matched Gallifa's almost exactly leaned forward and with great solemnity depressed a large button. Very far above, the translation bell tolled.

The ornate door at the back of the deck to the officer's chapel slid open. Ministorum priests emerged, swinging censers and singing loudly, calling the Master of Mankind to turn His eye upon the ship, if only for long enough to guide them from the warp.

'Start the translation countdown,' Gallifa commanded.

A mindless voice rang from every quarter. This would be repeated across the ship, in every part of the vessel, from the lowest bilge to the highest tower.

'All crew. All crew. Translation in one hundred and sixty seconds. Mark. Countdown set. Countdown commencing. One five nine. One five eight. One five seven. One five six...'

A large green light illuminated at the top of the shuttered grand oculus. To look out into the warp was to be damned. Only the Navigators could do that. There was as always a small, shrill part of Solana that urged her to take a look, a maddening, cajoling voice, a voice like hers, but it was not hers. They all heard that voice from time to time, like the threats behind the static in the vox. One of the dignitaries struggled with it, she could tell. He drank quickly, sweated freely, ran fluttering fingers down tight buttons and stays.

'...one two six, one two five, one two four, one two three...'

Another bell rang, this one small and silver. *'Navigator So Fen of House Xing is ready to guide the ship from the warp,'* the Navigatorial liaison proclaimed over the vox, her words clashing with the countdown.

Solana wondered what deals had been struck to secure House Xing's involvement with this most risky of missions.

'Begin warp envelope collapse,' Gallifa ordered. 'Enginarium, prepare. Realspace drive ignition on my mark, helm. Stand ready, all hands!'

'All hands stand ready!' warrant officers shouted.

'Aye-aye, shipmaster!' the chief helmsman responded.

A hum began to build somewhere that might have been deep within the ship, or might have been somewhere else entirely, far outside, in the madness of the immaterium.

'Navigator's manse to cede piloting to main ship control in thirty-five seconds. Mark.'

'Thirty-four seconds, mark, shipmaster.' A pause. 'Mistress Lo Fen of House Xing retains control. All helm ready.' There was no change in the ship yet.

Gallifa settled back into his chair. 'May the Emperor guide her by His true light.'

His voice boomed again from the crackling vox. The laughter behind his words grew louder, more mocking. The priests raised their hymns to drown it out.

'Nine seven, nine six, nine five...'

There was an air of controlled tension everywhere. Solana imagined the lower crew praying on their knees in their workplaces and barracks. No translation in the Era Indomitus was easy. Only Guilliman, who had the blessed gaze of his father the Emperor forever upon him, could calm the tempest.

The whining grew into a howl. The ship shuddered. She imagined its iron soul quaking like a frightened beast.

'Four four, four three, four two, four one...'

A noise like loose pebbles rolled in a drum rattled over the shuttered oculus. The voices in the vox shrilled. The vox-crew worked to shut the system down. It would make no difference. At this point, when the ship moved from one side of the Great Work to the other, from the immaterial to the material, that was when they were most at risk. The voices would shout now with or without technological mediation.

'Two one, twenty, nineteen, eighteen, seventeen, sixteen...'

She wondered if this was worth it. If Cawl would see her. She'd met him four times in the past, only that, and had exchanged a meagre handful of words with him. He'd shown little interest in her, just another scribe writing down histories nobody would read. She knew he was uncooperative, dangerous, a heretic as much as a saviour. She wondered if he would obey the primarch's writ, and bow to it, or if he would simply turn her away. He'd done so before to Guilliman's emissaries.

'Nine, eight, seven, six, five, four...'

She reminded herself they had to get out into realspace first. She wondered if she'd have the chance to be disappointed.

'Three, two one. Translation! Translation! Translation! All praise the Emperor! All praise Him on Terra!'

She felt something fundamental in her unseated, a deep, spiritual pain in the vicinity of her heart. She imagined her soul as a tooth, slowly easing out of the gums, easing, easing, and then...

What then?

The voices howled. Her vision doubled, tripled, smeared with violent colours. The ship rumbled and squealed, and every alarm the vessel possessed went off at once. A horrendous, bone-shaking tremor emanated from the deck, and now it was not just her soul that felt in peril, but her body too, as if the vibrations would hit a crucial resonance, and her bones would turn to jelly.

She needed to piss, desperately.

And then, it was over. They were through. There were orders given that she did not hear, and a sudden, concentrated activity as control was passed back from the manse to the helm. The crew readied themselves to sail once more a sea of vacuum and stars, not one made of nightmares.

A different kind of vibration rumbled through the ship. More rooted in metal than spirit. Realspace engines ignited.

All of a sudden, her hearing came back. Her spirit was where it should be, though, she feared, a little looser in its socket than before.

'Mistress historitor majoris?'

'Eremenitas,' she said hoarsely. She was gripping one of his metal arms. She looked at her hands, not quite believing they were hers. The sense of dissociation was strong. Her knuckles were white.

'It is over,' he said, cool as the void outside. 'A hard passage.'

She nodded, released him, stepped away, smoothed her dress clothes down.

'Translation successful,' Gallifa announced. This time, his voice rang clearly from the voxmitters, untroubled by parasitic words. 'Master augurum, open the shutters.'

More lights, more alarms, more hymns. All the palaver of Imperial humans when they did anything, complicating and complicating it until the merest act carried unbearable weights of tradition. The shutters moved aside smoothly but slowly, disappearing into their housings either side of the three-bay window.

They were looking down the ship to the ploughshare prow and

into the blackness beyond. And it was blackness that dominated the view. Complete and utter, except at the very edges, where stars shone at the periphery of the oculus, but what was before the *Light of Reason* was so dark as to be glossy, a palpable shadow on the stars, all light sucked away by the giant mass of the singularity.

There was light at the centre of the view. A dim ring surrounded the fissure in space and time, burning low and blue, like swamp gas, and round that another ring that was warm and hot as an open flame. At the top and bottom two pillars of brilliant light vented into the void, bright spears of broken matter. Within all that, hardly visible so far away, was the black hole itself. It pulled on Solana greedily. Even a morsel as meagre as she could not escape its hunger.

'Keep position,' Gallifa commanded. 'I don't care how much fuel we burn.' He looked down at the screens embedded in his command throne's arms. 'Give me an augur sounding. Concentrate soak to the fore quadrants. Let's see if we can find our archmagos quickly.'

This took time. Augur soundings were restricted to light speed, and that speed was more sluggish than usual, thanks to the singularity dragging at its heels, slowing the signals reflected back.

Solana realised suddenly she still needed to pee. She went to relieve herself. In the finely appointed command deck ablutorial she splashed her face with water, wasting a liquid fortune, but it made her feel better. Her headache was gone, her anxieties with it. Back in the materium, the terrors of the warp seemed foolish and far away. More herself than she had been for weeks, her curiosity rekindled, she went to speak with some of the other dignitaries. They'd all met before – the voyage was long – but it seemed with some of them that she was meeting them for the first time, so different was everyone's behaviour, and her memories of earlier conversations were jagged with unreality.

An hour passed, then two, then a third. The dignitaries dawdled long past the shutter opening: all of them wanted to witness the great Cawl's ship at least. All the while the singularity watched them. The sensorium crew had their work cut out, but the Machine God provided in the end.

'Signal return!' the master augurum shouted with relief.

'Show me,' Gallifa commanded.

The primary cartolith ignited, giving them a featureless representation of space, blank except for the complex dance of energies about the singularity, depicted on the map by shivering grey lines and tagged with much information. But their interest lay not there, but in a cluster of dots far, far away, right at the edge of the *Light of Reason*'s augur range.

'Magnify,' Gallifa ordered.

The cartolith zoomed in on a flotilla, each ship appended with an icon bearing the skull and cog of the Adeptus Mechanicus. A view an hour and a half old, but accurate. Though now identified, they remained small dots in the dark.

'Magnify.'

Once more the augury field zoomed sickeningly forward, and light models of ships filled the spherical display entirely.

At the centre of the flotilla was a hulking shape so large there was no mistaking it, huge and bulbous, its sides scored with hangar slots and manufactorum delivery bays.

The *Zar Quaesitor*, the ship, forge-fane, and roving kingdom of Archmagos Dominus Belisarius Cawl, sailed towards the edge of forever.

CHAPTER THREE

A MAVERICK MAGOS

The voyage across the materium took two weeks, the *Light of Reason* only catching up with Cawl's small fleet when halted in a stable orbit around the singularity. Solana's energy returned, as did her focus upon the mission. The listless, wrung-out version of herself that had endured the warp receded into memory, and she applied herself to preparing to meet the archmagos with a species of grim enthusiasm, reading and rereading all she had regarding him and his errant ways.

Solana remained conflicted about Cawl. Some called him saviour, some called him the exact opposite. The truths were so divergent it was hard to come down in favour of one side or the other.

His reticence to speak did not help. Some communication passed back and forth between the *Light of Reason* and the *Zar Quaesitor*, not a great deal beyond the usual diplomatic pleasantries. She sent her credentials as soon as the vox-arrays were up and running. She had to ask if they had been received. A short, almost curt, response informed her they had. She then sent a list of her expectations, and again cited the orders of the primarch. This missive was acknowledged but not properly responded to for four days, so long that she came close to resending it, but she held her nerve. She could not appear flustered or overly solicitous. She was the one sent by the de facto ruler of the galaxy. Still, she came close. Eremenitas said that it did not bode well.

'Cawl is unenthusiastic, as we thought he would be,' he said. 'I fear this meeting will be unproductive, if it proceeds at all.'

'Be patient,' Solana said.

'With what, being ignored?' Eremenitas responded. 'All signs suggest Cawl is living up to his reputation as a dangerous maverick.'

Solana told him again to be patient, although privately she agreed.

A reply eventually came that Cawl would receive her. When they arrived at the flotilla a further three days passed before the archmagos finally summoned her, more days of snubbing, so Eremenitas had it. She thought it possible Cawl was indifferent. He regarded himself as the saviour of mankind. He was busy. He probably regarded her visit as unimportant.

Part of her duty was to educate him that there were greater powers than he.

Gallifa was eager to be away, and was glad when she was invited to take quarters on the ark. There was no farewell. She, Eremenitas, her few aides and her belongings were shuttled over to the *Zar Quaesitor*, and that was that.

She was informed once aboard that her first meeting with Cawl would take place immediately. A servitor took her staff to their quarters from the shuttle dock, clumping on heavy, industrial legs with painful slowness. A faster one balanced upon a fat monowheel took her the opposite direction. There was little human left to it, just the torso and the head containing a butchered brain. It did not speak, but indicated she should follow the flashing beacon set into its back.

It led her through empty halls. There would be tens of thousands of souls aboard a ship that size, but the deck was deserted. She could only think Cawl had taken her to this place for juvenile reasons of theatre; that would fit with his profile. She followed the drone for half an hour of eerie emptiness. Open doors looked on shrouded machines and huge hold spaces that smelled faintly of methanol, her footsteps echoing into extinction among inactive production lines, until finally the servitor led her down a corridor as wide as a via majoris, then through huge gates into what she first took for an inactive manufactorum, only she quickly saw that it was too big to be a manufactorum. It was a shipyard, she thought, one large enough to launch escort craft whole, and probably fabricate larger vessels if they were made in pieces to be assembled in the void. It astounded her, and she had seen more than her fair share of Imperial megastructures.

The road turned into a ramp. They reached a point where it descended fourteen levels, coming out on a huge manufacturing floor three hundred yards wide a dizzying distance below.

There the servitor stopped. The beacon blinked off. It remained silent. The main lumens were out. Everything she saw was picked out dimly by standby biolumes. Giant claws and construction cradles hung silently from chains made of links five yards long. The dock gate took up all the far side of the space, closed with doors bigger than battleship flanks. The plasteel gate could not entirely blunt the chill of the void, and her breath dropped in glittering falls of ice crystals. Why there? she wondered. She had expected a meeting in his private workshops. That was the archmagos' preferred modus operandi: welcoming his guests in some cluttered laboratorium, then working through the meeting to show how oh-so-busy he was.

The servitor lurched back into life, its blinking beacon reactivating before it wheeled down one of a dozen tiered walkways running along the back wall of the shipyard. They turned a corner round machinery hidden by tightly tied tarpaulins, and there was Cawl upon a gantry, a shadow in the lumen glow. If he was going for impact, he'd chosen the spot well.

Definitely theatrics.

'The Archmagos Dominus Belisarius Cawl, Prime Conduit of the Omnissiah,' intoned the servitor, the only words it had uttered since collecting her. It executed a delicate reverse turn, then sped away.

Cawl was as she remembered him, a massively augmented human being, his bulk hugely increased by a long, serpentine conveyor permanently bonded to his lower body. Several legs, half covered with a voluminous red robe, moved restlessly along its underside. His upper torso remained mostly humanoid. He was not wearing his war panoply, and without the high cowled back, armoured plates and weaponry, she could see he retained a surprising number of organic components. Despite this residual humanity, he was inhumanly massive, and towered over her like a sort of bizarre centaur: half arthropod, half mammal. His head was studded with additional sensors. His right eye was augmetic, but the left was organic, milky blue, and full of a surprising mischief.

Cawl activated a single lumen globe hovering nearby. In its bright halo clustered Cawl's coterie of servo-skulls, like nocturnal insects drawn to a lantern flame.

Solana mounted the steps leading up to the low gantry. Cawl spoke only when she had reached the grilled catwalk. *Another little dramatic flourish,* she thought.

'So then,' said Belisarius Cawl. 'Solana of Mars. You are the primarch's favoured representative of our glorious religion. How positively uplifting to meet you.'

He reached out a hand, a gesture she was unfamiliar with, and so looked at it dumbly. There was the warrior's grip, opposite hands grasping opposite forearms. This did not look like that.

'Am I supposed to kiss your hand?'

Cawl looked at her hand, then his own, then he smiled.

'No! A high lady such as you. No! You're supposed to take my hand and shake it. An ancient custom I favour. It shows we are equals, it shows we come unarmed.'

She bowed instead.

'Archmagos,' she said.

'No?' He looked down at his hand again, pulled a face of surprise that it was still there, then withdrew it. 'Suit yourself.'

Each word was mockingly arch. Not many magi had a sense of humour. She could already tell that this was going to be difficult.

She stood up from her bow. Rigid formality wouldn't serve her here. Respect, yes, courtly manners, no. She adjusted her approach.

'It is an honour to speak with you, Prime Conduit.'

'An honour to be sent to spy on me, you mean,' said Cawl, wagging a mechadendrite at her like a finger. He turned around, then back, his metal feet click-click-clicking. He was, she thought, fidgety.

'I'm not here to spy on you.'

'Then why are you here? Do try to be honest. I can tell when people are lying, and we have precious little time as it is.'

She thought a moment. She'd gone over her few memories of meeting Cawl over and over again. Roboute Guilliman himself had given her his own impressions one evening before she left, a large amount of time for the Imperial Regent to give anyone.

More than anything else, that was the surest sign of how important to the primarch her embassy was.

And now, she felt wrong-footed.

'What?' Cawl prompted, still amused. 'Cat got your tongue? I really don't mind if you are spying. We all have to do unpleasant things from time to time.' He laughed, just a little.

She had no idea what he meant by that.

'I really have not been sent to spy on you, oh exalted one. I swear by the three aspects of perfection,' she said. 'I am here to gather a report on how close you are to finishing your new technologies for the stabilisation of the–'

'Attilan Gap, yes, yes, yes, I do get Roboute's messages, you know,' said Cawl. He waved a number of hands irritably. 'When will he learn to trust me? He never seems to trust me to do what I've said I'm going to do. Me! Who gave him his precious Primaris and so much more besides. Well!' He clapped two hands together. 'I am glad we cleared up that you are not here to *spy*, only to *keep an eye*. Which you, being an intelligent young woman–'

'Don't patronise me. I'm not young. I'm nearly forty-five, Terran standard–' she began, not liking his tone one bit.

'And I'm nearly eleven thousand years old. I patronise everyone,' he interjected, without skipping a breath. 'As I was saying, being an intelligent young woman, you will know that *keeping an eye* is completely different to spying. Good old Roboute has been most eager to learn of my progress these last years, and I have kept him informed, I really have. I do not see the need for all this fuss.'

According to what Guilliman had told Solana, Cawl had been sparing in his reports.

'Progress is slow, you know?' Cawl went on. 'I am the galaxy's pre-eminent mind, but even for me, breaking the hyper-technologies of the necrons to our will is a difficult proposition. But it must be done, oh yes, and it will be. I assure you.'

She found the simple, straightforward way he admitted to the heresy of xenotech chilling. She expected even him to be graver about it, or at least evasive.

'I am sure once the primarch has been furnished with the full details–'

'Oh, that won't matter,' Cawl said, once more demonstrating his propensity for interruption.

'Why?'

'Because I am nearly done, do you see? You have arrived at the perfect moment, my dear. By the time your report reaches wherever the primarch has got to in Imperium Nihilus, I predict, and with great confidence, that my labours will be finished and the Gate will be open and safe enough for military traffic. Within a year, in fact, notwithstanding any warp delays, battles, or similar nonsense.'

'Then why are you here in–'

'The middle of nowhere? Very good question, a very good question indeed. We shall get to that in due course. Before I begin, let us get acquainted. Do tell me a little about yourself.' He clasped his primary hands, one pale, ancient flesh, the other a many-fingered augmetic, placing one atop the other on his stomach in a way that reminded her of an old woman getting comfortable to gossip.

'I am the emissary of Roboute Guilliman, Imperial Regent. I hold the rank of historitor majoris, one of the Founding Four of that ordo commissioned by the returned primarch and empowered…'

'Yes! Yes! Oh my goodness,' said Cawl, and he shook his wizened head vigorously. 'I have met you before, you know, and all your colleagues. Surprised I remember? You shouldn't be. Let me tell you, I remember everything!' He smiled. 'Well, technically, I have it all recorded somewhere. Now, when I say tell me about yourself, I mean tell me about *your*self. I don't want your qualifications, your powers, your achievements. Who are you? Who is Solana of Mars? What makes her tick? That sort of thing.'

'I don't…'

He waved his fleshy forefinger in the air as if he'd just had the most marvellous idea. 'Let's start with your actual name, perhaps?'

'Solana,' she said.

'And the rest. Give me your…' That smile again. 'Full Martian designation.'

She sighed. Solana of Mars served her well in the Logos Historica Verita. As much as she hated the way it reduced her to a political footnote, she'd been using the title so long it had become her name.

'Technically I am Magos Solana Fer-Verrum Chi-869-976-44, Phi 02t45. Or I was, once.'

'There we are! Not so difficult. Tharsis Manufactorum Complex, yes? I thought so. You have that look about you. Theta batch, so well made.' He paced around her. She allowed herself to be subjected to his examination. He stopped, leaned back, and leaned back in again. 'But ho ho, what's this? If I'm not mistaken, you're not vat-born!'

'I was not made,' she confirmed. 'The batch code refers only to my educational record.'

He whistled appreciatively. 'True-born and tested Phi-grade? An actual mother and an actual father? My, my, exciting!' He placed his hands upon his chest and puffed it out. 'Myself, I came out of the genevats in Mundus Planus. At least, the body that hosted my core personality did. That's this body, by the way, even now. Eleven millennia old and still going strong.' He slapped his sternum proudly. 'But one or two of the other elements of my personality were born of man and woman, I suppose, Sedayne must have been…' He trailed off a moment, his face going unnervingly slack, then started again. 'What I regard as the heart and soul of me was formed by the very hand of the Machine God Himself, not to boast about it.'

'As was I,' said Solana. Bafflement was turning to annoyance. 'True- or vat-born, He calls us to motion in ways befitting our individual creation. And does He not make us all, whether in tank or womb?'

'By the power of the Motive Force,' said Cawl, finishing the prayer. He inclined his head in acknowledgement of the correction, then peered at her with his single bright, organic eye. Solana was not sure she enjoyed such scrutiny. 'A believer, eh?'

'Aren't you?' she countered.

Cawl snorted. It echoed oddly behind his mandibular shield. 'Yes, despite what you might have heard, there's no greater believer than I.' He pointed an unnaturally long metal finger at her. The end bore a sharp metal claw. 'You, on the other hand, are the one recruited into a deliberately iconoclastic order by a man trying to circumvent all our fusty old ways. In such a case as yours, faith is not to be assumed. Why were you recruited, by the way? Where are your loyalties? The Machine God, or the primarch? Mars or Terra? Do tell. I note you wear Guilliman's uniform, not the robes of the priesthood.'

'My relationship with the Cult is a little complicated,' she admitted.

'And so it should be! The Great Work is a complicated creation.' He looked expectant. 'So then, go on.'

She hesitated only a moment before deciding honesty was probably the best course to take. In all likelihood Cawl knew everything about her already. She had the irritating feeling he was, if not exactly toying with her, deliberately prodding at her.

'I was scheduled for mind-wipe and servitorisation before I was recruited by the primarch's agent.'

'I thought so.'

'I'm sure you *know* so,' she responded, a little brusquely.

'Not at all. I am not omniscient. I assume from your simple title of magos, your arrest came early in your career.'

'Not that early. I was denied advancement because of some of my tendencies.'

'What was the nature of your modus unbecoming?'

She gritted her teeth. She still felt a flush of shame when admitting her crime.

'Unauthorised reconfiguration of manufacturing systems. Neglect of basic rites. Elision of the prayers of good function. It was not my first crime.' Now she said it out loud, it did sound bad.

'I see,' he said. His long, centipede's body rocked back and he reared up. 'Did what you do work? Was it not more efficient?'

'It was.' A rebellious upwelling of pride flushed her face further. 'It worked much better than the prescribed methods.'

He nodded enthusiastically again. 'So much quicker without all those prayers, and is not efficiency one of the greatest forms of worship?' he said with a conspiratorial wink. 'The Machine God gave us this.' He tapped his head. 'It is a sin not to use it.'

'Most magi do not agree.'

'It is the nature of gods to be poorly served by men who insist they know their god's will. I have found that only crude gods are truly knowable, Solana Fer-Verrum Chi-869-976-44, Phi 02t45, and I should know, I've met a few. Ours is not a crude god. I myself was something of an aberration. I was generated to a random factor in the Xanthe Terra flesh vats of Magos Biologis Hammareth.' He laughed. 'He did like to roll the dice, old Hammareth. I could have come out a peon. Can you imagine, me, brain-cut and fused to a laslock, trudging about in some tech-thrall cohort?' He waggled his head from side to side, slack-faced, then grinned.

Mostly, the expression was visible in his eyes. Only the top of his wrinkled, thin lips was visible above his mandibular shield. 'But I didn't. They could have swatted me down the moment I emerged from my birthing jar, but they didn't do that either. Instead, I was tested, employed, and I succeeded! So nice that in this Imperium of ours one's background is not a limiting factor on success, don't you think? Look at us, both misfits in our way, and now important. Very important!'

He spread his limbs and declaimed this last bit so pompously she had no idea if he was sincere or not. When he bowed, deeply and ridiculously, she knew with a startling clarity that he was both serious and mocking at one and the same time.

'Now,' said Cawl briskly. 'Thank you for the introduction. You'll be wondering what we're about, what we're about! Time to look into that, don't you think?'

CHAPTER FOUR

ETERNITY IMPRISONED

As Cawl turned to face the giant door covering the manufactorum access slot it was already opening. Its smooth surface broke into segments that dropped out of line one by one before sliding under each other, each contact between metal and metal booming unhindered through the empty facility. Their retraction revealed the void beyond. Atmospheric fields were in place, the blue glow of particles netting the air visible around the edges. Brilliant light flooded the shipyard, causing Solana to shield her eyes with her hand to give her a chance to adjust her vision.

'I took the liberty of clearing the rest of this fleet from our field of view, so that you could better see…' He waited for the doors to clear more of the slot. 'This,' he said, and pointed.

Solana gasped. There was nothing between her and the black hole, so awe-inspiring, and a hard reminder there were material phenomena in the galaxy just as terrifying as the warp.

The photon sphere was the brightest component of the object. That was a ring but the gravitic lensing of the singularity was so extreme she could see the whole thing bent up by gravity. From the top and bottom relativistic jets blasted high-energy radiation light years into space. This close, they were too painful too look at directly.

Inside the photonic sphere, beyond the jets, beyond the accretion disc that marked the final boundary of the event horizon, visible as a faint glow diffuse as the atmospheric field within the blaze, the singularity was a complete, velvety black. Nothing could go into that unknowable space, and nothing could come out, and yet she still felt like something was looking out at her from its fathomless reaches.

Her back shivered.

'Omnissiah.'

'Disquieting, isn't it?' said Cawl, his bombast all but gone. 'Nobody really knows what these things are. Even me!' He reached out all his limbs, and used them to frame the singularity. 'If we were to fall within, would we be destroyed, or would we emerge in some other place? I have never come across a satisfactory answer from any species. I doubt our ancestors at the height of their technology understood them. Some ancient necrontyr records I, er' – he gave a mannered laugh – 'came into possession of by completely legitimate means say they believed them to be the graves of their mightiest star gods. Maybe that is true.' He shrugged. When Cawl shrugged, it was memorable. He was so heavily augmented a shrug was a movement of remarkable complexity. 'Why not? If a star can birth something with the power of a god, then why wouldn't an astronomical body like this harbour similar secrets, hmm?'

'Is that what you're here to investigate?' She looked up at him. 'But what has that to do with your pylons?'

'Nothing,' said Cawl, 'because investigating the Scorean Singularity is not what I'm here to do. I enjoy a little metaphysical ponder now and then, that's all. No, we're here to visit that, not the singularity itself.' He stuck out his arm and unfolded his long metal finger again, so it was pointing at the very edge of the black hole.

'The accretion disc?' Solana squinted.

'Look closer,' said Cawl.

'I can see nothing.'

'Hmm, it is quite bright. Here, let me show you.' A mechadendrite popped out of his belly plating and snaked forward, lining itself up with Cawl's finger. A lens in its head displayed a small hololith in front of them. At first it overlaid a section of the accretion disc exactly, then Cawl zoomed in. The disc was too bright to look at, so Solana further adjusted her silvered eyes until the band resolved itself into a complex set of brilliant currents with their ends curling out into space. Some of the matter pulled into the hole ricocheted off the event horizon. That provided the light. The rest would be pulled around and around the hole at ever increasing speeds until it was devoured.

'You see this here?' He highlighted a darker area amid the churning currents.

'That small lacuna… I assume it is evidence of a massive object circling the rim of oblivion?'

Cawl smiled with delight. 'Exactly! A planet, to be precise. It really shouldn't be there, so you can guess it's not a normal planet. I'd magnify the view but, you know…' He steepled fingers, metal pressing into desiccated flesh.

'The informational content of whatever light one receives here will be severely lacking.'

'I was going to say it will be rather blurry, but yes, that about covers it.'

The hololith winked out. Cawl set off at a brisk scuttle towards the far end of the dormant shipyard, his metal limbs clitter-clattering.

The lumen globe glided after him silently, the skulls followed that, and Solana followed them.

'Why this planet, you are asking. Why here, why now?' Cawl was well known for asking questions on behalf of his interlocutors, so much so he could carry on an entire conversation by himself. She'd expected that. 'I will tell you,' he continued. 'I have spent a good part of the last couple of decades researching the pylon networks of the necrons, since even before the Primaris Revelation and the beginning of the Ultima Founding. This you will know.'

She did.

'I came so close to true understanding upon Cadia. So very close.' He sounded regretful, tormented even. 'To think, if I had not failed in that one crucial instance then the Rift might never have opened, and Abaddon's hordes would not have had so easy a time terrorising the galaxy.'

'Are you blaming yourself?'

Cawl sighed. There was a metallic edge to it, an air-processor's wheeze.

'It was not my fault, I know, but I still hold myself accountable. The Machine God made me for a purpose, and I sometimes wonder if I have failed Him. I had help, you know,' he said, and suddenly stopped and turned his head to look at her. They were out of the direct light of the singularity. The lumen globe shone upon him dramatically, casting his face into deep shadow and giving him a sinister aspect. From the pit of the hood his artificial eye glowed cold as a blue star. His mechanical limbs were claws. His crooked back and long, clattering train of legs dominated his form, lit so, and his humanity receded. Like that, he looked dangerous.

'The help I had was, shall we say, xenos in nature.'

'I am aware. You told the primarch. A being named Trazyn.'

'Yes! Trazyn. What do you think of that?' He leaned closer, curious.

'It is heterodox, if not blasphemous, by the tenets of our Cult, to explore the technologies of the alien, and a mark of a true heretic to traffic with them.' She had the sudden, ridiculous urge to straighten her tunic. A small defiance, but of what she was not sure.

'And your opinion?'

'I am suspicious of the wiles of xenos,' she said. 'Their technologies are unclean. One can never discount the taint of the warp, for alien species are not as wise as mankind in avoiding it.'

'But…?'

She looked into the dim blue star of his augmetic eye. His organic glinted. She thought of it as his 'remaining' eye, but being organic did not mean it was original.

'There are races that have plied the stars of this galaxy for millions of years longer than we, and others that freely innovate. Their ideas are worth exploring.' She took a deep breath before giving her next opinion, for it was a dangerous one. 'We do not know everything.'

Cawl chuckled. 'I can see why you were condemned, Solana of Mars.'

As abruptly as he had stopped walking, he set off again, ascending a set of stairs that led by multiple flights to a floating walkway.

'So, this fellow, Trazyn the Infinite, a tricky, *tricky* fellow, helped me. He was old, wise, and very dangerous, but he helped me. Why do you think he did that?'

'I would not care to speculate,' she said.

Cawl laughed. 'Very diplomatic.' He took a turn in the stair at speed. Clatter-clatter-clatter went his legs. 'I'll tell you, then. The necrons have no more desire to see the galaxy overrun by

Chaos than we do. We must cling to that knowledge, exploit it. It will come in useful soon.'

'On the planet?'

He grinned. 'You are sharp.'

They came off the stairs onto the catwalk. The plasteel mesh of the floor panels looked the perfect snare for Cawl's pointed motivators, but he strode over them without mishap. At the far end was a monumental pair of blast doors. Perspective played its tricks, making them appear close at first glance, until the rangefinders in Solana's eyes kicked in and gave her an accurate distance of half a mile. The rails of the walkway almost touched vanishing point before reaching the doors.

'I have replicated the necron contra-warp technology perfectly,' Cawl went on. 'Down to the deepest subatomic level. I was not lying to Roboute when I told him this. Test equipment has been installed at Raukos, and construction of the passage stabilisers is well underway. I can, and have, activated a small network of them already.'

'How many?'

'Ah, a magos for facts! I like it. Six, and not for long.' He said. 'More than that, and the network won't initiate. So my problem is I can't run them in a series sufficiently big and powerful enough to completely dampen down the intrusion of the warp into the materium even at a small scale.'

'You hope to find the means on the planet.'

'Tsk!' he said, and admonished her with a wave of a mechadendrite. 'I don't hope to, madam historitor, I *shall*. That world is falling into the black hole. It has been doing so for a very long time, locked into a decaying orbit since the days of the great war between the necrons and the Old Ones. This was called the War in–'

'I know of the War in Heaven. The compilation, interpretation and dissemination of little-known information was the Logos' primary role when incepted. We were not restricted to human history alone.'

'Of course, of course, my apologies. Well, that world was a necron world, attacked by their enemies millions upon millions of years ago. I surmise that actually that black hole is artificial, created by the intentional collapse of a nearby star.'

Solana looked up at him in surprise. 'They could do that? With a *weapon*?'

Cawl nodded. 'You see now why the investigation of xenotech is a worthwhile pursuit. The world has been falling into that singularity ever since. Now, this is the important part. Because of the gravitational influence of the black hole upon that world, time will have slowed to a crawl.'

'I am aware of this too,' she said, before he could go on. 'Depending on the distance of the collapsed star from the planet, then anything between minutes to a few thousand years will have passed while millions sped by outside, each second lengthening the closer the planet got to the singularity.'

'Exactly!' said Cawl. 'I actually think your lower estimate is more likely, that very little time has passed there. It is probable that the singularity was in fact this system's sun.'

'Isn't that impossible? Wouldn't the planet have fallen into the black hole almost immediately?'

'Never underestimate our metal friends, my dear. The information I have gathered gives me a substantial insight into the old necron realms before they removed themselves from galactic history. This world here is fully motive. I theorise it did not fall into the black hole because it attempted to escape – a doomed endeavour, but lucky for us they at least gave it a shot, don't you think?'

'A fully motive world?' she said.

'Oh, my dear, it's not impossible – even we managed that in our glorious past – but it is exceedingly difficult. Xenotech. Didn't I say *marvellous*?' said Cawl.

By then they were approaching the blast doors.

'Then if it is fully motive, and ancient xenos went to the trouble of collapsing a star to rid themselves of it, it must be important.'

'Haha! Smart, you are *smart*. I believe it was a battle station, a centre for the coordination of the war effort,' said Cawl. 'A whole world given over to strategic cogitation. As a strategic nexus, I anticipate there will be a cache of necron data in its systems not degraded by time, and not protected by hordes of annoyed deathless androids stirred from their epochal slumbers. Within that data, I expect to find full control coding for a pylon network of the kind we wish to construct.'

'But it's a battle station,' Solana insisted. 'It will be crawling with necrons, and if they're time-locked, then–'

Once again, Cawl interrupted her to finish her sentence. 'Somewhat friskier than the ones we're used to? Only if they can get to us. You must have faith, my dear. If not in I, Belisarius Cawl, then in the Machine God, which some people say is pretty much the same thing, though I really do not agree,' he said modestly. He held up his hand, bringing them to a halt fifty yards from the doors at a patch of yellow-and-black striping wide enough to park a lander on. 'We're stopping here. We don't want to get squashed.'

'I have so many questions, Prime Conduit,' Solana said, trying to remain as respectful as possible. 'How will you get away from the world? You will be trapped within its temporal frame. A second there will last hundreds of thousands of years out here. And the necrons there, they will attack you.'

'Hush now!' he said. 'I'm getting to that.'

The doors were a cliff of moulded plasteel, each one a single-piece construction that must have been stamped out of a machine the size of a mountain. Cawl waved a hand. Beacon lights in time-hallowed hazard orange began to rotate. There were lines of them up either side of the doors, hundreds in each line. A klaxon sounded, a raucous, pulsed blare so low half of it was in infrasound level, shivering Solana's heart and instilling a sense of dread. With puffs of released gas, locking hooks all up the zig-zag toothed centreline unclasped with grave, metallic clunks. Pistons the size of super-heavy tanks, three to each side of the door, contracted into their sleeves with a shudder, and the doors ponderously opened. Metal groaned. A seal broke. A minor equalisation of pressure sucked in air, as though the doors were drawing in breath, stirring the robes of the magi and making the lumen globe and servo-skulls bob.

A slice of bright illumination cut the floor into portions of dark and light. The light widened, the dark shrank away, and the clangour of industry hit Solana like a blow. The deep, resonant booms of heavy metallic objects hitting each other, a veritable cacophony of chatter of both the audible and noospheric sort, the honks of reversing machines, warning chimes, echoing vox-announcements, and the chanting of tech-priests sanctifying machines, initiating subprocesses, and smacking things with hammers. And the smell! Hot metal, warm valves, oil, rust, and cut steel. Like home.

When the doors had opened far enough that they would not sweep the magi off their feet, Cawl continued.

'This way, this way.'

On the far side of the portal was another manufactorum. Incredibly this one was larger than the first, built lower into the hull and extending higher into the decks above. The walkway split immediately into a dozen catwalks. Cawl took one that led them high up the wall, took her to a viewing platform, then gestured portentously down to the factory floor. Solana leaned on the rail to look over the drop at teeming clades of tech-adepts labouring over a giant instrument of nested tubes, acceleration races and thousands and thousands of yards of cabling. It had the look of a gargantuan energy cannon, tipped at the end by a square emitter dish with rounded corners. An antenna sporting stacked dishes near its bulbous tip extended from the main dish, lengthening the grand instrument by fifty additional yards. As in the deserted shipyard, an immense loading slot was open onto space. The glare of the singularity's accretion disc and the more muted, pulsing luminescence of the trapped photons reflected off everything inside, imbuing the scene with hard, brassy edges, despite every inch of the manufactorum being lit by intense flood lumens.

'By the Omnissiah,' said Solana. She made the sign of the cog over her heart.

'Oh, I think you'll find it's largely my work, not His,' said Cawl. 'Well, all right. Not just my work. It's a joint effort. You can see the acolytes of both Accatran and Tigrus down there with my own Martian followers.' He pointed them out. 'Three forge worlds of the Adeptus Mechanicus, in concert together.' He became proud. 'See what we can fashion when we put aside our dogma and our jealousies? If only this scene could be replicated across all the forge worlds, we could solve any problem.'

'What is it I am looking at, exactly?' Solana asked. She couldn't take her eyes off the enormous machine. Four walkers fitted with heavy lifting gear stomped past a procession of acolytes singing hosannas to the triple god, all tiny by the device's side. A servo-skull nosed up over the railing, played a broad scan beam over her, flashed an acceptance code, then flew away. 'Is it a weapon?'

Cawl laughed. 'Oh my, no! No, my dear historitor majoris. Not a weapon. It is a frame shift stabiliser, similar to those employed on our expeditions to the worlds of the so-called Pariah Nexus a few years ago to prevent cross-temporal ingress via necron transit gate, only this one is much, much bigger.'

'It's enormous,' she stated flatly.

'I did say bigger. Big enough to penetrate the temporal cloak surrounding the planet,' said Cawl. 'With this device, fashioned by some of the finest chronomagi in the Imperium, and employing not a little necron xenotech, I admit, we will be able to project a...' He paused to choose the correct word. 'Let's call it a tunnel, one where time runs at a regular pace, directly onto the surface of the war world. Those within its area of influence will be able to move at will within the temporal frame experienced by the rest of the fleet, even while paddling in the shallows of infinite gravitic temporal distortion.' He smiled, pleased with his metaphor. Solana thought it trite.

'Won't aiming this tunnel be impossible to that level of precision?'

'Impossible is a word I have no fondness for,' Cawl said with obvious glee. 'Of course I have taken all factors into account. The frame shift imposed on our sensors by the light's escape vector. Gravity lensing. Refraction through the cosmic medium. All that.' He gave another elaborate shrug. 'It'll be fine!'

'Let me take you at your word,' she said, 'and assuming you can make that work' – she pointed at the immense machine – 'then how do you propose you move around when you are there? Surely this thing doesn't have the precision to track you across the surface.'

'Correct again. We will be taking a mobile receiving unit with us. That will receive the chrono-tuning signal from this device here, and project a field around us, allowing us the freedom to wander at will and take what we like, no matter how deep we may have to go.'

'But the necrons...'

'Will be avoidable.' He walked his fingers in the air like legs, avoiding invisible obstacles. 'We shall go around them.'

'They have their own chronomantic technologies. How do you know they are not active under their own fields?'

'I do not, but if they are active, our unit will act as a counter,' said Cawl smugly. 'Trust me, it's very special.'

'All right, what about plasmic blowback once you tap into the photonic sphere with your tunnel? What about gravitic overpressure? What about temporal bleed? What about flying right into the path of highly energised radiation trapped in a vortex about a black hole that has been suddenly released!' She finished breathlessly, and widened her eyes in challenge.

'My my, you are well informed. You sound like something of a polymath. They really were fools to condemn you.' He looked at her with genuine curiosity. 'Do you know, I like you. I think you may interview my magi, watch the show.' He put an avuncular hand on her shoulder. 'Let's do that. While we are setting up the various machineries and stages required to pull this admittedly audacious enterprise off, I shall allow you to observe everything! It will take some time, this is no small task we are about, but a record... Yes.' He nodded. 'Yes! A fine idea. You will see and record everything, and then you can tell dear old Roboute what you have seen, and then maybe he can leave me alone so I can finally fulfil his blasted orders.'

'I don't care what you show me,' said Solana. 'It doesn't matter. You are going to die. What you're proposing...' She rarely lost her composure, but she was getting close. 'It's insane. It's impossible!' She shook her head, unable to believe it. 'You can't do it.'

'Oh, my dear,' said Cawl, and he clucked his ancient, leathery tongue. 'Haven't you heard? I am Belisarius Cawl, and I assure you, I can do anything.'

CHAPTER FIVE

GUARDIAN OF ULTRAMAR

Dawn. The tetrarch had to put down at dawn. It was too dangerous to arrive at night on Ulvheim, though he had pushed to do so. Night was when the daemons came and choked the land in their multitudes.

So Tetrarch Decimus Androdinus Felix was forced to wait for morning, though he called for clearance to land as soon as the line of night swept away from Guilliman's triumphal ground. Bjarni Arvisson and Gjarmin of the Wolfspear waited for him with daemonic ichor caked upon their pale grey armour, tired from battle. Their weariness would fade, but their souls ached from the leering hole in the sky, and that pain would not leave them.

As the supernatural terrors of the night receded, normality reasserted itself. The two Wolfspear took the masks of their helms off to feel the sun, a habit Bjarni found far more rejuvenating than any amount of Day Feasting. He breathed deeply. The night was full of daemon stink, but the sun cleansed the place, and Ulvheim's natural smells asserted themselves: sharp dust, salt pan, chill stone – solid odours that calmed him.

In low orbit, the cruiser *Lord of Vespator* was pale as a daytime moon against the pink morning. Beta-Kalapus, the system star, was dying, but it had some strength still, and the chill was lifting. The rift had sunk to the far side of the world and was thankfully no longer visible, though the skeins of predatory light linking the sun to its doom would streak the sky all through the day.

Gjarmin squinted at the ship, deepening the creases in the tanned skin around his eyes. There was, as yet, no movement around the vessel. It hung as stilly as if it were painted on the sky.

'He demands to land then takes his *vakh* time, this friend of yours,' Gjarmin said. He was old enough for the wolf-growl in his voice to have come to the fore. The tips of his canine teeth showed on his bottom lip even when his mouth was closed. Bjarni didn't know how many years of war Gjarmin had to his name – the Space Marine was peculiarly evasive on the matter – but he was not far off Long Fang status, which meant he was a hundred years old at least. 'He should have come down to fight with us. He should have joined in the slaughter.'

'You know he couldn't do that,' said Bjarni. 'Any ship that tries to put down during the hours of incursion is lost.'

Gjarmin huffed. His breath clouded the cold morning air. 'Not every time.'

'Nearly every time,' insisted Bjarni. 'Felix is too cunning a man to take needless risks, and too important to be allowed to take them.'

'Then I don't think much of his honour,' said Gjarmin. He spat on the ground near where the sand was crusted with Neverborn blood. The sun was strengthening, the blood was steaming and would soon be gone.

'If we'd have been in trouble, it would have been different, he'd have come then,' Bjarni went on. 'But we weren't in trouble. Last night was like all the rest.'

'Hnh,' Gjarmin grunted dismissively. 'You mean boring.'

They waited on the remains of the triumphal ground, built to commemorate the end of the first phase of the Indomitus Crusade some decade and a half ago. The ground was still flat and remained an ideal place for a pitched battle, but little else was whole. Not one of the statues carved into the hills either side had escaped damage. All were pocked by shell fire. Several had collapsed entirely. The grand building where Guilliman had delivered the speech that dissolved the pseudo-Legions of the Unnumbered Sons had suffered particularly badly. Only its unnatural, regular shape, the odd squared piece of masonry poking out of the cracked rubble and, on the northern side, vaulted spaces that had once been closed gave its constructed nature away. Cawl's workers had wrought further damage on the square with trenches and power lines crisscrossing parts of the outer grounds to carry energy to the pylons. Work started on them every day as soon as battle was over. Already construction cadres and tech-priest clades were on their way to look the towers over for damage, to replace ripped-up cabling outside of the pylon's null fields, and to run more of the endless calibration tests the things required. Plumes of dust kicked up by heavy crawlers followed the lighter smudges their grav-craft created.

Gjarmin narrowed his eyes further, then nudged Bjarni with his elbow. 'Snap out of it, Arvisson, they're coming.' He pointed skyward.

A bright dot detached itself from the cruiser. Bjarni's vox-beads chirruped. He listened.

'Orbital control just contacted me,' he said to Gjarmin. 'The tetrarch will be here in eight minutes.' He unclamped a smoke grenade from his thigh, crushed in the detonator, and tossed it in front of him. Crimson fumes hissed from one end, making it spin, and it sent up a twisted column of smoke.

Bjarni grunted. 'There.'

'Are you nervous, Bjarni?' Gjarmin said slyly. 'You always were nervy. What was it Wolf Priest Ulfreyr said about you that first day we met?'

'Nervous as a maid on her wedding night, as well you remember,' said Bjarni. He glanced down at his dirty armour. 'I wish we'd had time to clean this *skitja* off ourselves.'

'Best he see us this way,' said Gjarmin. 'Our allies need to know how hard we're fighting, or they won't value us.'

'That's posturing, even for Fenrisians,' said Bjarni.

'It's only the truth,' said Gjarmin. 'The Vlka Fenryka strive for truth, so should the Wolfspear. All sons of Russ should.'

'All sons of Russ,' Bjarni echoed. Truth was, he *was* nervous. He didn't take his eyes off the lander as it moved down from the void to the atmosphere, sprouting a brief umbrella of superheated, compressed air that glowed spectacularly before the prow. When that dimmed, the craft levelled out, seeming to hold the same position, but growing bigger as it approached, until it resolved itself into a twin-hulled Overlord gunship more than twice the size of a Thunderhawk.

Early sunlight glinted off its sides. The double prows and their assault ramps were scorched black by atmospheric re-entry. The Overlord roared overhead, tipping its wings as it banked back around and decelerated. Jet feathers opened, widening the hot blue flames of the six engines and slowing it further. They had a clear view of the badge of the Tetrarch of Vespator: the severed head of some mythical female monster with snakes for hair atop stylised aquilan wings, set within the inverted omega of the Ultramarines Chapter.

The ship passed directly overhead almost at a hover, buffeting Gjarmin and Bjarni, flooding the area with dust-laden vortices, and came to a stop over the landing zone. Jet wash blew away Bjarni's smoke signal. On howling contra-grav the vessel turned upon its axis, the rocket motors rumbling. Then with a final firing of plasma jets to stabilise itself, the Overlord sank towards the parade ground, blasting sand from the mosaics hidden beneath.

Landing claws spread on the paving. Huge pistons slid back into pneumatic sleeves. Abruptly, the engines and contra-grav cut out, leaving Bjarni and Gjarmin's ears ringing. The ramps gaped slowly on their pistons, not the violent, explosive opening they'd perform in an assault. As soon as their toothed edges touched the ground, two lines of Space Marines jogged out. There were five to each hull, all in differing liveries, though in common to all, their right shoulder pads and right arms were gold, with the badge of Vespator cast in relief upon the pauldron. In perfect synchronicity, they fanned out and formed semicircles around the two Wolfspear.

'Allfather alive,' said Gjarmin, taking in the differing colours of their armour. 'It's like a skitja carnival.'

The Space Marines ignored them, turning out to sweep their weapons over the landscape.

Gjarmin cupped his hand to his mouth. 'There's nothing to shoot in this place during the day! You should have come down at night.'

Bjarni touched his wrist. 'Show some respect,' he voxed privately.

Gjarmin locked eyes with him, and saw Bjarni was serious.

'Yes... captain,' he said, then muttered to himself. 'How on Terra a newborn like you came to outrank me...'

The newcomers' leader, a sergeant in the red and white of the Sons of Orar, rested his bolt rifle on his hip and signalled the others, who stood to attention. He then addressed the Wolfspear.

'I am Veteran Sergeant Cominus of the Chosen of Vespator, representative of Tetrarch Felix, and his life guard.'

'It's all right, he can come out,' said Gjarmin. 'No need to hide inside.'

Bjarni shot him a glare.

'It is my duty to ensure the tetrarch is protected at all times,' said Cominus. 'With our lives, we guard him. Do not mock our honour.'

He turned about, parade style, and went to stand by one of the ramps.

'My, he's a barrel of laughs,' muttered Gjarmin.

'Tetrarch Decimus Androdinus Felix, Lord of the Eastern Marches!' Cominus shouted.

A tall figure in heavy Gravis armour emerged. He was in Ultramarines livery, though his battlegear was so ornate and crusted in gold that Chapter blue showed only in places.

He came to a halt before Bjarni, reached up, and removed his helmet. Air hissed as the seal broke.

The face beneath was noble, olive-skinned, dark-haired. He was almost exactly as Bjarni remembered him.

'Bjarni Arvisson,' Felix said.

Bjarni bowed his head, provoking a snort of derision from Gjarmin.

'Tetrarch Decimus Felix, welcome to Ulvheim.' He held his arms wide. Felix did not hesitate, but stepped into the embrace. Gjarmin chuckled to see a member of the normally staid Ultramarines behaving so.

'So they do have hearts.'

'Ignore him, brother,' Bjarni said. 'He thinks he has a *skjald*'s wit. He's mistaken.'

'Brother,' Felix replied. 'It is good to see you.'

They stood back, hands on each other's shoulders, looking

each other up and down as if neither could really believe what they saw.

'A captain, I see,' said Felix. 'Congratulations.'

'A jarl.' Bjarni smiled, exposing sharp eye teeth much shorter than Gjarmin's, but growing day by day. 'Says the man who rules a hundred worlds as a king.'

'In all honesty, Bjarni Arvisson,' said Felix, 'I would rather be a captain than a king.'

'Do you remember that time when Sulinus… You remember Sulinus, right?' said Bjarni tipsily. 'Son of Dorn? Always barking "I shall secure…"'

'The area,' Felix finished the epithet for him.

'Exactly!' said Bjarni. 'I shall secure the area! It was practically all he said.' He elbowed Gjarmin. 'There was this one time he went stomping off, gun up, that bright yellow armour of his glaring at us, and he put his foot right through the crust on a hot spring. Went in right up to his knee.' Bjarni laughed, though his mirth wasn't completely easy. Felix smiled wider for his friend's sake. He was sorry for Bjarni. He'd been working hard to recapture their sense of comradeship, and to help him do that he'd been working just as hard on the *mjød*. Felix tried too to bridge the distance of years and experience, but it had been a long time since he and Bjarni had fought together, and Felix had never been the quickest one to jest. Not that Felix saw a problem with that. Frivolity got in the way of things. There wasn't much to laugh about in the universe.

'Sulinus, Sulinus.' Bjarni shook his head and smiled his forced smile. 'Yellow and bright. Whatever happened to him?'

'Fighting, like the rest of us.'

'Or dead,' said Bjarni, suddenly solemn. The seriousness of drunks came over him like a cloud. He looked into Felix's eyes and held up his pot of mjød. 'We're still here, we can thank the Emperor for that. It is good to see you again, brother. To Sulinus, and all the others, wherever they may be.'

'To them and to you, Bjarni,' said Felix sincerely. They touched beakers.

'Drink!' said Bjarni, and he drank deeply, as did Gjarmin and the other high-ranking Wolfspear at the high table where they sat.

Felix only sipped his mjød. The sons of Russ made a big deal about how it was potent enough to intoxicate a Space Marine. Felix did not think that was a point in its favour, and it tasted like sugar boiled up with engine oil.

Felix let his sight wander round the feast. He found the Wolfspear's ways odd. On the one hand, they were Space Wolves. The Spear Hall was full of poetry. Battle-brothers swaggered about with a braggadocio that threatened to spill over into violence with every chest bump and jolted arm. There was a lot of boasting. A lot of shouting. On the other hand, the Varghalen had the aseptic feel of a prefabricated fortress that no number of animal pelts could obscure, and they were grimmer than their Fenrisian kin, quieter.

'What do you think of our brothers, my lord?' asked Captain Linir, a golden-skinned man with level teeth that made his canines appear even more pronounced.

'They are certainly lively,' said Felix.

'They are barbarians,' muttered Cominus sourly. He did not like being out of his armour, and he was letting everyone know it. He'd refused to join them at the feast at first, citing his oath to protect Felix, that he should be fully equipped and standing guard. He had only relented when Felix, not wishing to offend his hosts or his friend, ordered him to disarm. Felix shot him a hard look. Only Cominus had been given a seat at the High Table; the rest of the Chosen of Vespator sat with the battle-brothers of the host Chapter, and Felix did not want his sergeant to disrespect this honour, but Gjarmin seemed to find the insult funny.

'You can thank us for that,' said Gjarmin, waving a leg of meat around. 'When the Vlka Fenryka arrived at Ulvheim, the feasting halls of the Wolfspear were solemn places. We brought them the delights of mjød, and now' – he grinned – 'they are less solemn.'

'You were a Space Wolf, were you not?'

Gjarmin wrinkled his nose at that name, making Felix recall the Space Wolves did not call themselves that way, but the older warrior made no comment on it.

'Was, am no longer. Now I am of the Wolfspear, and proud.'

'Gjarmin arrived with two others, Troels and a Wolf Priest named Ulfreyr Ketilsson,' said Bjarni. 'They brought much-needed reinforcements not long before Cawl's work crews arrived. The Vlka visited every Chapter derived from their gene-seed, is that not so, Gjarmin?'

'That is so.'

Felix raised his eyebrows.

'What?' said Bjarni. He set his beaker down carefully.

'Nothing.' Felix held up his hand to show he meant no offence. 'Only I'm surprised you were not reinforced more quickly if that was Grimnar's strategy. It is years since the lord regent visited Fenris and passed on the sons of Russ Greyshields to Grimnar's care. It was some years even before the triumph here.'

'Aye, there was a delay,' said Gjarmin. 'With good reason. You try assimilating thousands of half-wolves into your brotherhood and trying to contain them.'

'What do you mean by contain?' asked Felix.

'You saw them,' said Gjarmin. 'Cawl's creations were broken-minded. Soulless, heartless, lacking in decency or agency. You wouldn't have liked what would have happened if they'd been sent out by the horde.'

'They'd had plenty of combat experience.'

'Had they now? Experience of battle is only a part of being Vlka. I say a wolf with no conscience is a dangerous thing.' Gjarmin tossed his bone aside. His eyes narrowed. 'It would have helped if Guilliman had let it be known not all the sons of Russ were given over to the Rout when he visited at the Aett.'

'Only a few were kept behind. Your brothers here represent almost the entire number of those kept back. Bjarni and I were a part of the last great endeavour of the Greyshields, to build trust between lineages.'

'Ah yes, the famous mixing of the brethren.' Gjarmin's expression became challenging. 'So the Legion-breaker could better control us.'

Felix's face set. Gjarmin's attempts to get a rise out of him were becoming tiresome. 'So that we might better know one another and not fall into war as our ancestors did.'

'What a meeting that must have been!' Bjarni said. It was an obvious attempt to head off the rising tension, but welcome. 'Great Wolf Logan Grimnar and the Imperial Regent face to face. I wish I had seen it with my own eyes.'

'Huh,' said Gjarmin. He rocked back, arms full out and hands braced on the table. Like the hall with its scant primitive hangings, the table had an air of artifice. It had been made to look hewn by hand, but there were no trees on Ulvheim, so the timber would have been imported from elsewhere, and although the planks had been split from the trunk and the edges left with bark clinging to them, the top of the boards had been planed smooth by machine.

It must have been hard for Gjarmin to accept these warriors as brothers, Felix thought. The Space Wolves were honest through and through. The atmosphere at the Varghalen still rang false.

'I was there the day of that meeting,' said Gjarmin. 'A dangerous time. They almost parted enemies.'

'Then we're lucky Grimnar accepted the primarch's judgement.'

'Your primarch, not mine. What choice did the Great Wolf have?' Gjarmin said, looking around the hall himself, and when he did, Felix saw a flicker of disappointment. 'He was offered control of something he never wanted. His only other option to accepting was to let wolves run free without oversight. That would have gone badly for all of us, so he agreed. It had to be that way. Your skitja schemer of a gene-father saw to it.' His temper was rising, but suddenly he leaned in, folded his arms on the table and scowled thoughtfully, mercurial in his cups. 'Maybe it was for the best. There are thousands of us now, to stand against the darkness.' He grinned suddenly. The faint lines of the Rubicon scars on his arms and face shone whitely in the candlelight. 'You are right, Bjarni! What a meeting it was. Like the days of old, when the sons of the Allfather strode the stars together and nothing could stand in our way.'

'I wish I had seen it,' said Felix.

'I thought you might have been there. Were you not with Guilliman's fleet?'

'Our battle group was off fighting to the south.'

'Orks,' said Bjarni, nodding. 'A lot of orks.'

'Where are the others who came here with you?' Felix asked.

'Troels drinks at the Allfather's table,' said Gjarmin. 'He was never lucky, and what little luck he had ran out here in that broken parade ground, along with his blood.'

'Ulfreyr is with the High Jarl,' Bjarni said. 'On crusade. Six of seven jarldoms hunt through the stars. We of Hrossvalur Company alone garrison here.' His guard lowered by the mjød, he sounded bitter about that.

'I see no Wolf Priests.'

'Ulfreyr builds the order slowly. The rest are with the other clans. It takes time to make a Wolf Priest. It's not as simple as swearing on the first slain.' Felix's expression prompted Bjarni to explain. 'Those who died before.'

'We have no ancestors here as on Fenris,' Gjarmin added. 'The ones who died in battle early take their place. They are the first slain.' He drank with a satisfied air, as if that explained it all.

'This is everyone?'

Bjarni nodded.

'What I see here cannot amount to much more than a company's worth of warriors,' said Felix. 'How can you hold here against the infinite hordes of the warp with so few?'

Gjarmin laughed. 'Oh, that's good! A nice little compliment from our blue lord.'

'You should not be surprised,' said Bjarni proudly. 'You'll recall that after the triumph, Guilliman's standing orders to us were to guard this world and prepare it for Cawl's experiment. It doesn't take a full Chapter to do a little job like that. Once Sendavael died and High Jarl Irik Stianolf took command, he decreed we would be better concentrating our efforts elsewhere. Besides our nightly entertainment here, hellspawn and renegades slip out of the Pit from time to time, putting the worlds of this sector in danger. We hunt them down. Other jarldoms range even further.'

'I wonder what your mighty overlord would say to that,' Gjarmin said.

'So long as you may do it while maintaining your responsibility here, he would say nothing against it,' said Felix.

'It is our duty to the people. Cawl's had us waiting on this rock for years. We have to do something other than kill endless tides of Neverborn,' said Bjarni, drunk and defensive without reason.

'Yes,' said Gjarmin. 'Our brothers hunt the stars while we rot here, guarding this nowhere place.'

Felix sipped his drink without comment. It was not his place to tell an independent Chapter what to do, nor to rebuke their brothers. He was right about the drinking though. A bad idea.

Gjarmin shrugged. 'We like to hunt. Killing the enemies of the Allfather is just as important out there as it is here. It stops us from getting rusty. How do you find that, ruling so many worlds? You must spend a lot of time arguing with people. You must have to make time to train, so your skills do not decline.'

Felix ignored the jibe. 'Things look to be going well here. Perhaps your fears about we Primaris were unfounded.'

'Maybe. This is my Chapter,' said Gjarmin with an expansive gesture. 'So what if it's not the Rout, and Ulvheim isn't Fenris? Grimnar remains my lord, and here we follow some of the traditions of home. It's enough for me. Take that back to the Legion-breaker, and reassure him.'

'I'm not here to judge you,' said Felix.

Gjarmin snorted. 'You're a princeling servant of Guilliman, of course you're here to judge us.' He raised his beaker in a salute that was only half mocking.

'I am here to make sure Belisarius Cawl is good to his word,' said Felix. 'Nothing more.'

'The pylons?' Bjarni looked up. 'Then he is coming?' A shadow of disquiet passed over his face. Neither of their experiences with Cawl had been pleasant.

'He is coming. Soon,' said Felix. He looked into his cup. He had drunk more than he had thought. 'Allegedly.'

The noise in the hall was getting louder. The high table was quiet. Bjarni slapped the boards, making pots jump.

'So we feast by day, and fight by night. Sounds like something out of the sagas,' said Bjarni. 'In truth, the changelessness of it gnaws at us. It's good most of us get to hunt through the stars. Speaking of which, it's four hours until nightfall. We have time to survey the area before battle is joined again. Take a look in peace. I thought you might like to see it again, Decimus.'

'If you would escort me,' said Felix. He gave Gjarmin a rare smile. 'I am not spying on you, I am spying on the pylons. Maybe it is time I went to look at them.'

'If you say.' Gjarmin sipped his mjød.

Felix looked back to his friend. 'Bjarni, we will go out fully equipped. I and my men will fight alongside you tonight.' Felix looked Gjarmin dead in the eye. 'We would not want to get rusty.'

CHAPTER SIX

HONOUR'S BURDEN

The Rhino grunted to a halt atop the ridge. Ulvheim was an arid world like billions of others scattered through the galaxy, ancient and tired. It was not blessed with highlands. The hills where the Varghalen was situated were unusual, and at five hundred feet high the ridge the Rhino climbed was the greatest eminence for miles around. Fumes blew from the tank's quad exhaust stacks, the air over the power units shimmering hotly. The left side ramp swung down and hit the dirt. The doors behind slid open and Bjarni emerged. He went to the edge of the cliffs to look at the view while Felix got out carefully, finding the exit a tight squeeze in his Gravis armour.

'Sorry about that,' said Bjarni. 'They're bit a cramped, those old Rhinos, but we're short on Impulsors.' He pointed his thumb behind him at the tank. 'We were given a lot of legacy equipment when we were founded. There wasn't so much of the new machinery to spare. What we have we sent out with the hunting companies, and negotiations with the Adeptus Mechanicus take their time.' Bjarni looked at Felix. 'I know you, Decimus, you'll be thinking we've been here five years, and in that time we should have got our forges operating at full capacity, and should be making our own as well. But the Varghalen is not a fortress-monastery – that honour goes to the *Umbral Claw* – and we do not have many Techmarines here. Fighting every night doesn't leave a lot of time to get things accomplished, so we'll be forced to make do with what we have until some forge world or other agrees to supply us.'

The low cliffs either side of the valley were carved with statues. The Chapter's stronghold commanded the modest heights on the far side, looking new and unfinished: a fort rather than a citadel. When Felix was on Ulvheim years before, it was to take the world from a combined force of Iron Warriors and Word Bearers. There had been a substantial fortress in the valley – its curtain wall had blocked the small valley almost to the level of the hilltops – but that had been tainted, and condemned, and so thoroughly demolished no stone stood upon another when Imperial engineers had finished with it.

It was dangerous to dwell in the fastnesses of the enemy.

They couldn't see that from their current position, nor the ruins of Guilliman's stage that had taken its place.

'There are your pylons,' Bjarni said, and swept his hand around at Cawl's creations encompassing the valley and the parade ground that extended from its mouth, dotting the summits of hills like primitive beacons, then marching down to the rocky plains and out in a wide circumference. They were identical in form, being ugly, the maze of bewildering piping that made up their outer layers exemplifying the utilitarian technology the Adeptus Mechanicus saved for themselves. The black, gleaming obelisks at the heart of each were so obscured it was hard to tell the devices were derived from xenotech at all. Felix's retinal displays gave him the dimensions of the machines, but it was from the tiny specks of the work crews moving around the bases that he derived a real sense of their scale, each over a hundred feet, their metal-encased tips poking aggressively at the void, like missiles in their silos waiting for launch. He surveyed them carefully, one after the other, marking their positions, the difficulty of defence of their varied situations, and he wondered at their efficacy. Cawl had built them to close the Pit. Felix had no idea if that would be possible. Cawl's long delays in doing so suggested not.

'This is the best view on Ulvheim,' Bjarni said. He was by then quite sober, his Space Marine's gifts having purged the effects of the mjød quickly once he had stopped drinking. 'Allfather's bones, it's the only view on the planet.' His laugh came out metallically from his vox-grille, then he sighed. 'I never thought I'd come to see this place as home, but I have.'

Felix looked over the plains, the thin sky showing the brightest stars at the height of afternoon, the dun rock and sand that held a hint of pink out past the parade ground, both featureless in their own, specific way. The parade ground flat and covered with sand, the plain rough with identical boulders. He was amazed to see how much it had changed. He had helped build the parade ground himself, only five years or so ago, but it looked like it had been abandoned for a century. It was very different to singular Fenris, he thought.

'You were disappointed with this posting, I recall.'

Bjarni shrugged. His armour mechanisms whined. 'I got over it. We fight all night, then feast, drink mjød, sleep. Then we do it all over again, like heroes in the Underverse. It's not so bad.'

Bjarni couldn't hide his regret. He used to be lighter of heart. He had grown grim.

'Fighting among the stars is a privilege I am granted from

time to time, and I am captain of Hrossvalur Company now, the guardians of Ulvheim and Raukos.'

'These are well-deserved honours,' Felix said. 'For what it is worth, I am sorry you could not go home.'

Bjarni pulled a face. 'Bah. It wouldn't have been the same anyway. Too long had passed. Even places like Fenris change.' He turned away from the view to Felix. 'What choice do the likes of us get, Decimus? For my people it is the highest calling to join the Sky Warriors, and I am a Sky Warrior, so what does it matter if I am somewhere else? My path upon the star road was more crooked than most, thanks to Cawl, but it will lead me to just as glorious an end.'

'Our realm was softer, but your traditions are not so different to ours,' said Felix. 'Families compete for generations to have just one of their number become an Ultramarine. I understand.'

'Only...' Bjarni let the word hang.

'Neither of us expected to be changed the way we were. Cawl made us into something new, and we did not ask for that,' Felix finished for him. 'All Space Marines make sacrifices, but he deprived us even of the time we were born into. The Imperium that I knew, and the one that you knew, are both gone. Thousands of years. That torment....' He closed his eyes briefly. 'I sometimes think...'

Felix hesitated. There were no people he could speak to so openly. He had had few real peers since Guilliman had chosen him as his equerry, and fewer friends. Even the common experience of being the first of the Primaris Marines was slipping into history. The early generations' brotherhoods were divided, many were dead in the crusade, and since the final disbanding of the Unnumbered Sons, their numbers had been diluted by the Firstborn Space Marines that came before them and the neophytes that came after, and neither of those groups were the same as

Felix and Bjarni. So although Felix still questioned the wisdom of talking openly given his position, he decided to go on, simply because there were no others he could confide in. It had been too long since he had unburdened himself. There was no one better to talk to than Bjarni. They had been comrades once. Felix was right to call him brother.

'Cawl's actions mark us all. There are many statues in Ultramar, of heroes gone to serve the Emperor. I would have been one of them. My family would have known of my deeds. They would have shared my honour. Instead I was taken from a shuttle before it launched, hauled off in front of other recruits. Thus I vanished without a trace. Like a failure. Cawl shamed my house.'

He fell quiet. That was hard to bear.

'Do you remember your people?' Bjarni asked.

'Not really. Flashes, mostly. I wonder sometimes what happened to them, even so. I have many more memories of Cawl. Waking me. Prodding at me. Trying to be friendly as he experimented on me, as if his endeavours were some great game I was as interested in as he.' Felix clenched his fists. 'In some ways he is my father more than my blood and more than my primarch, and that…'

'That what?' Bjarni prompted.

'That makes me angry.'

Bjarni let out a deep breath. 'We have that in common. I would have watched over my tribe. I dwell here instead, thousands of years out of time. We bear many burdens, you and I, but this fight is my sacred duty, while the tetrarchy is yours.' He placed a hand on Felix's vambrace. Ceramite scraped on ceramite. 'Come on. We'll go to the summit. It's too grand a name for it, but you can see a little better from up there.'

They set off up the slight slope of the ridge.

'Tell me, how is your life? How does it feel to be the king of Eastern Ultramar?'

'I would not know where to start,' said Felix. 'The primarch commanded the Five Hundred Worlds be reconstituted. It has not been a simple order to complete.'

Bjarni grunted. 'No wonder the great lords are suspicious of him.' He looked at his friend. His eye-lenses flashed in the weak evening sun. 'You know it looks like empire building.'

'I have seen many worlds since I was given my task. Humanity lives poorly, Bjarni. I believe the regent is sincere when he says he wishes to make Ultramar an example of what the Imperium could be. You may think that misguided, but he is honest. Granted, there are strategic considerations – greater cohesion in Ultramar is the most expedient way of securing the south-eastern territories of the Imperium, and it is a solid base to wage war from, even after Mortarion's depredations.'

'Huh,' Bjarni grunted. 'Your primarch has one enormous flaw, and it's on display right there.'

'Which is?'

'He thinks he is right. About everything. And he's impatient. So that's actually two flaws.' He held up two grey-clad fingers. 'He orders others to perform a task, he's not satisfied with how it's done, so he'll seize control to do it himself. You might not like this, but thinking like that can lead only one way. I won't speak it out loud, but you know what I mean.'

'He has no designs on the Throne of Terra. I have seen him resist temptation of every kind. I trust him.'

Bjarni made a frustrated noise. 'You're too close to him. It's not about trust. It's not even about intention, it's about where the skeins of your wyrd drag you. Maybe I'm wrong. On the other hand, maybe one day you'll look back on this conversation and know I was right, because we have a new Emperor.'

'Careful, Bjarni.'

'I'm not saying he's going to do it! Maybe Ultramar will work.

Maybe the rest of humanity will cast off one hundred centuries of bad choices once the regent shows them the way. Who knows?'

'If it is possible. Reunification is difficult,' said Felix. 'Guilliman broke Ultramar up ten millennia ago. There are worlds that are proud and will not submit, others that insist they were never a part of the primarch's realm. What am I to do with them? Invade them? Devastate them when so many other worlds already burn? They pay their tithes. I'd make them rebels for the sake of lines on a chart. Talk is the only way forward.'

'Ah, so you're a diplomat now?' Bjarni chuckled. It sounded like a growl.

'Not a good one, and diplomacy is only a part of it. I have xenos of eight different strains to contend with, including magna-grade threats from the necrons, the t'au, tyranid remnants, and the orks. Chaos assails the northern reaches. The Plague Wars devastated swathes of the realm, and I am obliged to send aid that would otherwise go to redeveloping the eastern quarter. Most of my territory, that once ruled by the Sotharan League, is a waste. It is lawless, bedevilled by pirates. I sometimes question the wisdom of reclaiming it.'

'Ultramar has ten Space Marine Chapters to call upon, at least.'

'A hundred would not suffice. I can claim a fifth of the Shield Chapters' attention at best. There are three other tetrarchs and the Lord Macragge besides. Five sectors of Ultramar, and over it all Lord Calgar's will is paramount.'

'How is he?'

'He is just.'

'You mean he is still pissed off.'

'What do you mean by that?'

'Come on, don't play simple. Even we've heard about that out here, how he was... humbled.'

'His pride is still wounded, if that's what you mean. It is true he is only nominally the head of the realm now. Guilliman has eclipsed him.'

'Sounds tricky. If that's your life, I prefer mine. Simpler. Kill, drink, sleep, repeat.'

They climbed a small ledge of rock that led to the bump of the summit. A few feet beyond, the ridge made its lazy way down to the plain.

They could see the triumphal square much better. Felix looked down on rubble at the valley's mouth, all that was left of the stage where Guilliman had delivered his great address. Felix had been there with him, looking out. He imagined watching the gathering from up on the hill, how it must have looked, the colours of ten thousand Space Marines, flags at the head of Astra Militarum regiments, Titans towering at the back of a crowd that filled the plain, and yet it had been only a tiny proportion of one fleet in the crusade, a symbolic act. Felix was certain it had been entirely for show: the triumph celebrated early gains, but nothing truly decisive. Although Imperium Sanctus was much safer than it had been, calling it stable was a leap. The Primaris Marines were the real reason Guilliman had held his triumph, to disband the last of the pseudo-Legions. The balance of power had to be seen as restored. One thousand Chapters of one thousand battle-brothers. These numbers were themselves mythical, but myths were important. *Myths are the foundations to the world,* Guilliman had once said to him. *Even though they themselves are ephemeral.*

Felix had used the principle himself. He had tried to exemplify it in his person, holding as he did an office plucked from history to justify the policies of the present.

A myth had been made here, history had moved on, and now there was only broken statues. It felt false, in retrospect. Cynical.

'It's incredible,' said Bjarni. He looked upon the scene with more generous eyes. 'Even after half a decade of war, the square persists. I can still see them all. The flags. The people. The power. We made something here. It's all gone, but the memory of it is worth protecting.'

All Felix saw was sand. He did not have the heart to say so.

'What about the pylons, Bjarni? It is they I must report upon.'

'Yes, of course. I thought you might wish to see this again first, seeing as you helped build it.'

'I did, thank you,' Felix said. The ruination despaired him.

'The pylons are all finished, according to Cleontis – he's the magos in charge of the construction crews here. You were sent to see them activated, right? This will soon be over, the daemons and such?

'Yes,' said Felix. 'There has been a communication from Cawl. It was ambiguous, but it might soon be over. Are the pylons in danger?'

'Not so much,' said Bjarni. 'Since the daemons started appearing they've been obsessed with tearing down the square, and killing us, I should add. When the pylons were under construction, they forayed against them, and for a few months battle was concentrated on the pylon ring, every night. It made our mission harder. We had to split our forces. We were fortunate Lord Grimnar sent us reinforcements before Cawl's work crews turned up, or we'd have struggled to protect all the construction sites.'

'Did Cawl send any of his own troops?'

'A few.' Bjarni scuffed a fist-sized rock against the stone with the sole of his boot. 'There's a roster you can look at, if you wish. Cawl was open about his activities, and his locum here will tell you what you want. He's a good man.' He grinned. 'For someone with an engine casing for a face. They're mostly tech-priests, some are handy fighters, and all of them have a small retinue – but they're only servitors and minor automata that number a couple of hundred all told. They don't have numbers to go head to head with the daemons. But the pylons are active now, they project some sort of exclusion zone around themselves. Tech stuff. Warp stuff. The daemons don't go near them any more.'

'Then there is progress.'

'What are these things for, anyway?'

Felix looked at him silently, looked away.

'Look, I get that you can't tell me what this is really about, but I assume the regent is impatient if he's sent you. These pylons, they're some sort of test, right? That's what Fabricator-Magos KuVal said. Why?'

Impatient is an understatement, Felix thought. Guilliman had been angry the last time he had seen him. 'A demonstration of the technology is key to the fulfilment of important strategic goals,' he said, deadpan.

Bjarni snorted. 'Goals you can't tell me about.'

'I can tell you I will be remaining here until Cawl has come and finished the experiment.'

'And what if he doesn't come?'

'Then I am empowered to fetch him.'

That made Bjarni laugh.

'What's he like? I never really knew him. I mean, he woke me a few times like all of us, and I still have nightmares about that. But I don't think we ever spoke.'

'Dangerous,' said Felix. 'He's very dangerous.'

Bjarni nodded, as if that simple explanation was more than enough. They looked to the west. The sun was setting, and the long, cancerous umbilicus of stolen energy leaching from it into the warp was pulling the Pit of Raukos over the opposing horizon.

'Night's coming. We can forget about all that for a while. Time to fight.'

'Do you have any idea why they only come at night? It's not like any daemonic incursion I've ever heard of.'

'Do I look like a Rune Priest?' Bjarni said. 'I've no idea.' He snickered. 'Neither do the Rune Priests, before you ask. Symbolic, magical skitja. All we know is they come, and that we have to kill them.' He switched to *Juvjk,* and grumbled out a sentence or two to himself.

The Pit edged its way over the eastern edge of the world like a predator stalking the cowering sun. A deep, purplish black, it emitted an anti-light that consumed the glow of the stars.

'The daemons come, then they go. Their bodies evaporate in the sun. The only trace they leave is the corpses of our brothers.' Bjarni kicked the stone he'd been rolling under his sole over the cliff. It shot out seventy yards across the valley before it began to fall. He looked to the sky. 'First stars are out. We should make ready, tetrarch.'

CHAPTER SEVEN

GORAGAMAK

'You are swift, I will give you that.' Warsmith Kraverek turned the aeldari from side to side. It scrabbled at the gauntlet clamped around its throat with gaudily gloved fingers, powerless to free itself. 'Nor are your kind weak. You once ruled the stars.' Kraverek smiled, baring a cruel run of iron in place of teeth. His voice grated like a machine on the edge of failure. 'Alas, neither of these things will save you now.'

He squeezed. The corsair's panicked eyes widened. Kraverek saw himself reflected in the black of alien pupils: his skin, once a deep tan, now paled with centuries in space; the glint of metal teeth framed by thin blue lips; the augmetic band he had replaced his eyes with, the dull bronze of its casing, the sea-green of the slit lens, the result of a painful purification undergone long ago. His armour was ornate, dirty iron trimmed with bronze, heavily modified. The extended power pack looming over his head supported four twitching mechadendrites, two tipped with pincers, the other pair carrying lascutters.

'Your speed has failed you, and dead empires protect no one.'

The creature's struggles weakened. Its last breath rattled. They were apart from the battle raging around them, locked together in the most profound intimacy of all, that of murderer and victim.

'Be glad. Know that your end serves to advance the one cause that matters in all this mortal tedium. Because of you, mankind will be a step closer to ascendancy.'

One final squeeze to end the aeldari's life. Kraverek felt vertebrae separate through the ceramite of his gauntlet. The aeldari's head lolled upon its armour, eyes dulled. Its soul did not depart, only changed location, fleeing from the divine hungers of the warp into the large gem the creature bore upon its chest.

Amber light from the soul stone bathed Kraverek's face. He looked at it curiously. Such strange beings, these aeldari. He would collect it later. First, the rest of the corsairs had to be dealt with. He cast the alien aside. A whistling hail of shuriken and las beams hit the corpse several times before it bounced off the far wall of the corridor. Kraverek used the distraction to step away from the fluted wall. A few rounds hit him, to no real effect. For all the race's supposed superior technology, aeldari weapons were weak.

Corsairs sheltered behind the columns of three tall archways at the end of the corridor, filling it with sharp-edged death. Kraverek turned side-on and dropped his shoulder into the hail of monomolecular discs. His pauldron's inner machinery clunked, shifting it up to protect his face. Shurikens screeched off the moulded plate. A couple embedded themselves in the outer ceramite so deeply they cut into the mechanisms beneath. When the pauldron shifted against another flurry coming at a different angle, the edge of the lodged projectile dragged itself through the workings, and his war plate's machine spirit grumbled. Kraverek grunted, sharing its displeasure. His armour was his own work, and he disliked seeing it damaged.

All this took place in a matter of seconds, all of it logged by armour and man to be mulled over later. An Iron Warrior only became more proficient at killing through logical reflection.

'Enough of this,' he said, and drew his plasma pistol, pausing to loose a blaze of superheated gas up the hallway. Projectiles vaporised in its track. It smashed into the wraithbone with a roar, carving out a chunk of the leftmost archway. The crater billowed thick smoke that smelled like burning hair. 'Into them!' Kraverek commanded. 'I want this ship secured!'

His chosen stepped up beside him, making a wall of dull steel. Za Tso was nearby, the beacon pole mag-locked to his back. The chipped yellow-and-black stripes decorating their armour flashed in the gloom. The lumens were dying. Smoke from patches of blazing wraithbone choked the air. Bolters banged loudly, their forceful shouts of belligerence pitted against the insidious whispers and crackles of xenos weaponry.

The Iron Warriors marched with the indefatigability of the ancient Legion, a quality they had never lost in ten thousand years. While others abandoned themselves to excess and madness, the Iron Warriors remained strong. Kraverek took pride in that. Of all the Legions who had sided with Horus, only the Iron Warriors retained their essential nature. They alone were pure.

Bolts blasted the leftmost arch into smoking wreckage. Feeble alien bodies exploded. The survivors called in shrill voices and fell back. Those in the central and right arches remained steadfast, and more were coming up to reinforce them. Kraverek didn't care. Concentrating themselves like that made the aeldari all the easier to kill.

Ovoid grenades fell among his men, venting pink gases. Kraverek's machine spirits dutifully reported a potent hallucinogen.

He sneered. Such things could not affect the Iron Warriors. His breathing grille locked shut, the gases' only effect to thicken the smog of battle.

More piping shouts presaged a hail of intense fire. Shurikens clattered into the chest of Salar Domaras, breaching the thick frontal armour and destroying both his hearts. He carried on killing as he fell to his knees and toppled onto his face.

Kraverek judged him weak to die so.

There was movement in the smoke, a shimmer then a roar, the telltale report of a fusion beam connecting with Kandar. The fool was too old and addled to get out of the way. Ceramite ran like melting wax. Kandar gave out a hoarse cry of pain and collapsed, smoke pouring from every aperture in his battle plate. Kraverek shot a blaze of searing white plasma at the central arch in return. His augmetic vision darkened as the stream caught a corsair full in the chest, immolating him. Fire burst from the lenses of the alien's conical helm and he fell screaming. And yet the others held. Not only that, the lithe figures reinforcing the position were busy deploying weapons of exotically powerful type.

Kraverek cursed. This was harder than he had expected. The rendezvous was only minutes away and they were running out of time.

Heavy shurikens sliced into the wall of chosen with a noise like hail hitting sheet steel. A dark beam of unlight buzzed overhead, narrowly missing Xeseus.

'This was a bad plan, Kraverek,' he shouted.

'Be silent and take cover,' Kraverek commanded.

His men retreated to the corridor edges at the same unhurried pace that they had advanced, still firing as they pressed themselves into the alcoves between the ribs that ran all the way along the walls.

'These ones have heavier weaponry,' Kraverek voxed. He checked the numbers running in the corner of his vision. 'We are seven minutes behind schedule. It is imperative we have the beacon operative soon or our allies will be lost in the webway.'

'What do you suggest, now walking directly into their guns has failed?' said Xeseus conversationally.

Kraverek ground his metal teeth. Xeseus had always been insolent. Recently, his insubordination had grown insupportable. He would have to do something about that.

'Goragamak. He will clear the way.'

'He will likely kill us in the process,' Xeseus said, provoking a darkly mirthful laugh from Za Tso.

Kraverek ignored them both, and voxed Orios Zhask. 'Release Goragamak on my signal.'

'He is not free of the boarding torpedo, my lord,' Zhask responded.

'Then get him ready. Be quick.'

'So it shall be, my lord.'

Kraverek swore upon his primarch's name. He had hoped to avoid deploying the Helbrute. Xeseus was right, he was unstoppable, and that was the problem, for he was apt to slay his erstwhile comrades once his true foes had been scattered.

A las beam scored Kraverek's thigh plate. He pressed himself back further, and with the aid of his battle plate's targeting systems, he hunted out the sniper, found her kneeling in the shimmering cocoon of a camouflage field. She was taking aim again. Kraverek gripped his pistol double-handed, and burned her xenos life away.

The plasma pistol chirred a warning. Too many shots in too short a time. With a thought he activated the heat dump. Billows of scalding steam jetted from its cooling vents, wreathing him completely and cutting visibility down to a few feet. In a war brume like that, auto-senses only helped so much.

A green ready rune shone bright in the custom displays built into his eyes.

Zhask signalling. Goragamak was in position.

'Cease firing,' he commanded. 'The Helbrute is ready.' His men knew what that meant. Hide yourself from Goragamak. Do not distract him from the enemy, lest the ancient turn his blind rage upon you.

From down the corridor came an impatient howling.

Everything on the pirate ship was an off-white colour, like the ribcage of some gargantuan beast, its construction disgustingly organic. The fluidity of it reminded him of the vessels of warbands less strong-willed than his, who had allowed the warp too far in, and whose ships had been infected with warp-rot. It was but a passing resemblance. The alien ship was orderly, not some daemon's mad whim. The bone-like plasteks were not dangerous in themselves, and provided plenty of shelter. Still they disgusted him.

Seeing their enemy lie flat against the walls, the aliens gave out eager cries. The noise of their twittering voices grated on Kraverek. They were regrouping now, ready to advance, too short-sighted to see that the Iron Warriors were not beaten, only waiting. The aeldari were arrogant wretches, those who took up piracy among the worst.

'Now, Zhask! Now!' Kraverek commanded. The xenos sang ululating whoops; even so, they were clever enough not to race down the corridor, but went into the thick smoke slowly.

Caution wouldn't help them.

Goragamak heralded himself not with a roar, or a bellow, or a war cry, but an idiot moan, thick and phlegmy, a moan of misery and incomprehension, a moan of woe.

The Helbrute approached at a lumbering gallop, his footsteps making a noise to rival a cannonade. Targeting lasers shone sickly beams. The aeldari cried in alarm and opened fire with everything they had.

The Helbrute's broad silhouette reared out of the smoke and stopped directly in front of Kraverek, though Goragamak did not see him. What little intelligence was left to him was occupied entirely by the xenos.

'Goragamak here! Goragamak slay!' His revolting, deformed head had swollen to three times the size it had been during life. Jaundiced eyes swept hungrily from side to side, avid beneath the toothed cowl of his sarcophagus cover. The tendrils of his power scourge lashed. For a moment he did not move – Kraverek suspected the plenitude of targets confused Goragamak – then a lascannon beam burned a hole in the Helbrute's plating.

Goragamak roared in outrage, spraying drool from malformed teeth. He stamped forward, slammed an aeldari down. Kraverek leaned out a little to watch him work. A xenos tried to run up the wall, perhaps to flip over Goragamak's back and plant the egg-shaped fusion charge ready in its hand in the Helbrute's vulnerable workings. It failed spectacularly. One of the whips of the scourge wrapped itself around the alien, cutting its slight body in half with a blaze of disruption lightning. The legs and torso thumped to the deck separately, thin alien blood spraying everywhere. The fusion charge bounced towards the Helbrute, and Goragamak crushed it flat beneath his heavy foot.

'Kill, slay!' The Helbrute hooted with moronic delight. The metallic banging of the autocannon activated Kraverek's audio dampers, shutting out all noise but that coming through his vox-beads.

There were the beginnings of movement all around him. His chosen were ready to move on.

'Hold,' he commanded them. 'Hold until Goragamak is done!'

Goragamak stamped forward, his ungainly body moving with

a fluidity at odds with his rotted mind. Kraverek was in awe of the Helbrute's destructive power, almost as much as he was sickened by the machine. All the Helbrutes he had known had ended in the grip of the false-flesh corruption of the warp. Goragamak was no exception.

The Helbrute paused to swing his autocannon across the corridor, fired a burst of fist-sized rounds, gave a bubbling laugh, and moved on in his unsteady, angry child's walk.

'Now,' Kraverek said.

His chosen stepped out from the wall as smoothly as automata, firing past the warped machine. They picked their targets carefully, squeezing their triggers only when certain of missing the Helbrute. Goragamak's habit was to terminally punish friendly fire. The Helbrute waded into the xenos holding the central corridor. He swung his scourge carelessly, slicing it through the wraithbone walls. The power field enwrapping the banded alloy annihilated broad chunks of the wall and cut down the warriors behind.

Once Goragamak was in play, it was over in a few moments. Most of the aeldari were slain, the last few fled to be hunted down later. It was easy to achieve victory by unleashing Goragamak, but it could be costly in the lives of his own men should the Helbrute's fragile self-control break. Like any weapon, once drawn Goragamak must be sheathed after use lest he cut the hand of the wielder.

That duty fell to Kraverek.

He held up his arms and mechadendrites to make himself bigger, and shouted.

'Goragamak! Goragamak, heed me!'

The melding of sorcery, machine and warrior snuffled to himself, stamping with a bovine intensity upon an aeldari corpse already a smear of red and bright, tattered cloth.

'Goragamak!' Kraverek shouted. 'Heed me!'

The hulking thing turned around, exposing the fleshy cavity at the centre of its chest where Goragamak's mutated head nestled. He fixed Kraverek with a dull gaze. The meat of the nose was long gone. The exposed septum quivered at the air. Streams of mucus spilled down Goragamak's face and he frowned. Kraverek hated the way he had become. Before he was imprisoned in the Helbrute Goragamak had been bold, swaggering, a talent with directed energy weapons, both in their employment and in their crafting. The Helbrutes shared origins in the distant past with Imperial Dreadnoughts, but they were now nothing alike. Placement in a Helbrute was no honour. Goragamak had been condemned to a living hell.

Still, Kraverek had not hesitated to damn his friend. A Helbrute's strength was an asset to a warband of modest size like his.

'Back, Goragamak! Slaughter is done. The battle is over. Stand down.'

'Stand… down…?' Goragamak's frown turned to a snarl. 'Stand down? No!'

The machine swung awkwardly around his waist pivot, tearing the warp-born flesh that had grown over the joint. His scourge shivered dangerously. 'No! Slay! Goragamak slay!'

Orios Zhask approached with a coterie of mortal slaves. Kraverek waved him to stop, which Zhask duly did, but one of Zhask's forge thralls tripped, and Goragamak reacted as swiftly as a striking serpent. His autocannon chugged noisily. Heavy rounds obliterated the thrall. The Iron Warriors didn't react to the violence, just disdainfully watched the other thralls scatter.

'Enough!' the Warsmith commanded. A pulse from his comms array activated the shock matrix embedded in Goragamak's armour. Sparks skittered all over the ceramite, flesh smoked. Goragamak's head rocked back, yellowed eyes rolled up into his swollen skull, and he collapsed heavily into the wall.

Kraverek sidestepped enough to avoid the falling giant, no more.

'You shouldn't have done that. Moving him will take time and effort,' said Zhask, 'and he may wake in the process.'

'Then train your thralls better,' Kraverek said. 'It is their fault. They spooked him.'

He walked around the stunned Helbrute and went into the corridor. Dismembered aliens lay everywhere.

Behind him, Zhask shouted his thralls into action. Electro-whips cracked. Chains rattled out from drums.

Kraverek beckoned his remaining four chosen: Kallimus, Za Tso, Adnarax, and Xeseus.

'Forward,' he commanded. 'The gate is this way.'

A shadow moved in an alcove. Three bolt rounds raced from Za Tso's gun. A shattered aeldari corpse tumbled out in front of Kraverek. He stepped on it, crushing it without breaking stride. The repellent, spicy smell of its blood followed him.

'We approach,' he said. 'Kallimus, Adnarax, break and cover.'

The two chosen jogged ahead, their weapons moving with discipline to cover every potential avenue of attack. There were stores down the corridor, robing rooms, shrines to the aeldari's long-dead gods. There would be weapons, armour, food, technology. Things Kraverek could trade, but for the moment none of these things were important. Kraverek had to get the beacon active at the aeldari gateway.

Every aeldari ship of any size carried a portal into the webway, the strange under-realm that existed between immaterium and materium, linking the scattered remnants of their empire together. But their control over it was far from complete, and they were not the only ones to tread its inconstant ways.

Kallimus and Adnarax took station either side of the door

into the gate chamber. Adnarax shifted his grip on his bolter to hold it one-handed, and took out an auspex that was older than the Imperium. He activated it, examined it, then nodded at his Warsmith.

'Empty,' he said.

Kraverek strode into the chamber. It was high, gloomy where the pillar-ribs came together at the apex. The gate it housed was modestly sized, two spars that reminded him of jawbones. An aeldari rune of typical geometric form was mounted at the top.

Adnarax spoke to him, his vox-borne voice intimate in Kraverek's ears.

'I hate aeldari architecture, it reeks of complacency.'

'Za Tso,' said Kraverek. 'Deploy the beacon, set it–'

A trio of aeldari leapt out of hiding up in the ceiling, each heading in a different direction, stepping off the walls and somersaulting down right on top of the squad of chosen, grav harnesses increasing their preternatural nimbleness to superhuman levels. They wielded pistols and elegant power swords, one of which Kraverek found buzzing directly towards his head. Guns barked behind him. He blocked the blow with a mechadendrite. The sword cut its snapping pincers free, and Kraverek experienced a stab of annoyance to go with the pain he shared with his armour. He moved aside just enough that a second blow of the blade passed him by, then slammed the tip of one of his lower mechadendrites into the stomach of the aeldari.

It doubled over, the wind knocked from it. For all their vaunted superiority the damned things still needed to breathe. He ignited the lascutter on the mechadendrite tip. The thing screamed as it was gutted.

Kraverek shook the alien's corpse loose. Za Tso was down, his head cleaved open. Adnarax nursed the stump of his arm.

His hand still gripped his bolter, which was now lying on the ground. All three aeldari were dead.

'I thought you said it was empty,' Kraverek said. He strode to Za Tso's body and plucked free the beacon pole mag-locked to his power plant.

'Auspex baffles,' Adnarax said.

'You should have known.'

Adnarax held up his mangled arm. The power sword had cauterised his wrist. 'I paid my price.'

'You lost a hand, I almost lost my head,' Kraverek said. 'And Za Tso is dead.' He jerked the beacon pole. The bottom section snapped out, extending the length to more than six feet. Then he climbed all three steps of the gate platform with one stride, his feet scuffing the interlocking circles patterning the pale psychoplastic. The gate was inert. The far wall was clearly visible. If he stepped through it he would go nowhere.

'How are we to activate it?' Xeseus said. He was genuinely curious about the aeldari device. He spent too much time meddling with xenotech for Kraverek's liking.

'We are not.' Kraverek twisted the head of the pole. It looked like a simple wire-caged lantern. Active, it pulsed a steady red. He pressed a button and a gleaming spike shot out of the bottom of the pole. He slammed this into the platform, piercing it, and left the pole standing there. 'Our allies will be close, if they have kept to their schedule. They shall open the way for themselves.'

'How?' Xeseus pressed.

'Kolumbari-Enas has the secret. I do not know, and nor does it matter. We have fulfilled our part of the bargain.'

'So we have to wait?' Xeseus came up the steps and commenced examining the gate from all sides. The clattering of chains and the shouts of the master of the dead echoed down the corridor.

'Hurry! Hurry! Get those suspensors fixed! Bring up the grav-bier! Hurry, before he wakes!'

'Not long,' Kraverek said. He went back to the lower floor and plucked up his lost mechadendrite head. He turned it this way, then that. The cut was clean, the wiring sound. 'Find something to do.'

He began repairs.

CHAPTER EIGHT

FIRST-AMONG-EQUALS, AGAIN

With the aeldari dead, a menacing silence descended on the corsair ship. An unshakeable conviction took hold of Kraverek that they had killed the crew, but the ship lived. He felt its hatred. He felt its sorrow. To distract his men he ordered them to begin looting, while he busied himself with reattaching the pincer to the mechadendrite. A Chaos Space Marine warband of the size Kraverek commanded could not rely on force to provide all they needed to survive. Squads swept the vessel stem to stern for survivors. They found none. The oppressive sense of watchfulness pressed on them. Kraverek found himself turning more than once to see if something were behind him. There wasn't, but he hadn't survived so many centuries by ignoring his instincts.

'We should blast this ship to atoms when we're done,' said Xeseus. They were all feeling the ship's attention. None of them set their weapons aside.

'They're late,' said Adnarax. 'Maybe they're not coming.'

Kraverek didn't favour that with a response.

After hours of waiting the beacon confirmed a twin-lock. *So much for timeliness,* Kraverek thought. The pulsing red turned steady green. A hard sound blurted.

The Iron Warriors, still until then, moved all at once to turn their boltguns upon the gate.

Kraverek pushed himself up from the ground.

The beacon chimed again.

'They are coming,' he said.

'Finally,' said Adnarax.

'Careful, Adnarax, you'll anger our glorious leader,' said Xeseus.

'Still your tongue,' Kraverek said.

Light grew in the centre of the archway so gradually it gave the disquieting impression of something that had always been there, and had only chosen that moment to show itself. The beacon sounded again. The glow spread like fat poured onto a flat sheet, stopping precisely at the spars of wraithbone framing the gate. The more sensitive elements of Kraverek's sensorium picked up the oily patterns of electromagnetic radiation that sometimes accompanied warp phenomena. A bright line grew up the centre, then split, and spread, subsuming the faint glow. The beacon chime rang every few seconds, then quicker, until it gave out a constant tone. The light burned. His men looked away, or shielded their eyes. Only Kraverek, protected by his augmetics, was looking into the light as the skin of reality split, and so he glimpsed the non-world beyond as a shifting mist. Deceptive shadows crowded the exit, far away, then close again, then filing out onto the platform.

Without warning, one of the gate spars cracked all down its length. Silver liquid oozed from the fissures.

The gate changed colour, taking on a greasy taint that turned a sick red, as if it were polluted by the beings coming through. The wounded spar shook. The silver ran down bone, thick as blood.

There were four figures on the dais, then six.

The fissures on the wraithbone spar spread. With a noise like the grind of glacial ice, its opposite half grew its own network of injuries.

Eight misshapen beings were on the dais. Behind them came four more, so big they overtopped the Chaos Space Marines by a head's height. The last pair carried a tall shape that wavered in the ruddy glow of the polluted portal. A stasis casket.

The last figure emerged. The wraithbone spars crumbled before Kraverek's eyes. In the tunnel beyond, the mist was sent into convulsions. The spars bent, crackling loudly, and shattered. The portal winked out. Smoking wraithbone pieces skidded across the deck, the roughly textured marrow of it grey and dead, the silver fluid leaden.

On the dais were eight magi of the True Mechanicum, dark robes covered in arcane symbols hiding crooked, mechanically enhanced forms. The four larger creatures were cybernetic constructs, or perhaps Myrmidons, tech-priests who obsessively enhanced themselves to increase their combat capabilities. The line between the two was blurry.

Kraverek never trusted the True, or Dark, Mechanicum – which name you used depended on which of their twisted kind you were dealing with. Kraverek preferred the latter. His Legion retained their facility with machines, and had always despised the Mechanicum's mysticism. These fools were worse than the Martians. They steeped themselves in Chaos, quizzing daemons in exchange for paltry secrets and declaring themselves masters of creation. Their quest for knowledge delivered them only madness.

They had their uses, nonetheless.

'Magos Kolumbari-Enas,' said Kraverek. 'I see you were successful.'

Kolumbari-Enas inclined his head on a crooked neck. All Kraverek could see of his face under the hood was a metal snout and breathing tube.

'Statement of agreement. Our mission was satisfactory.'

'I assume you encountered difficulties,' said Kraverek. 'You have been gone months.' He walked over to the dais. The magi shuffled aside. He smelled oil, hot metal, and ancient, unwashed skin.

'Refutation of criticism,' said the magos. 'First, possession of subject host by Fabius Bile had to be ascertained. Then, a bargain sealed. Then, military action undertaken in support of Bile's actions in order to secure payment in form of subject host.' Spiky-sounding binharic accompanied his speech, both delivered by voxmitter.

Kraverek examined the casket. The style was archaic, though definitely human. Thousands of years old, he thought. A practical design, none of the flourishes you would see on Imperial devices, even from the early days, so therefore pre-Imperial, maybe even from the unknown eras before the Age of Strife.

'Action against whom?' he asked.

'Belisarius Cawl.'

Kraverek tensed. 'You were told not to engage with him. Not yet. You swore you would give Bile Cawl's whereabouts, nothing more. You lied to me.'

'Assertion. Kolumbari-Enas is not in the habit of delivering falsehoods.' Despite his entirely electronic voice he sounded offended. 'Bile gained what he required from the false prophet. In return for this artefact, the Disciples of Nul helped him.'

'We could not stand back. Bile is a spent force,' one of the others interjected. Female. Kraverek recalled her name: Alixia-Dyos, Enas' lieutenant in his little cult. 'We were obliged to find him allies, and guide him. To stand back would have been suspicious.'

'You didn't kill Cawl, did you?' said Kraverek. 'We need him.'

'Expression of irritation. Of course we need him. He is crucial to our plan. Battle was made to secure resources by Fabius Bile. We possessed insufficient assets to kill the archmagos. That was not our mission goal. Our mission was a success. Cawl lives.'

Kraverek rested his hand on the sarcophagus. Even through his armour, through the stasis field, it was unnaturally warm.

'Bile suspected nothing? He did not tell him of our bargain or our intentions?'

'Cawl and Bile went on their way in perfect ignorance,' Kolumbari-Enas said. The magos had never shown any trace of human emotion beyond a grasping desire for knowledge before, but Kraverek could tell he was gloating.

'Bile is irrelevant. The plan is intact,' Alixia-Dyos insisted. 'We have the vessel. Phase two may commence.'

Together, all eight of the magi gestured theatrically at the sarcophagus. The movement was replicated eerily by each one of them.

'Within this casket is a machine from the days before. It was made to house the spirit of the Neverborn. It will make a most suitable vessel for the one we shall summon.'

'It better. There's a lot riding on this,' said Kraverek. *Far too much,* he thought. *Everything.*

'Query. Kolumbari-Enas must know. Do you possess the material necessary for the summoning effort? The Disciples of Nul have fulfilled their part of the bargain. Has Kraverek of the Iron Warriors fulfilled his?'

Kraverek looked the group of magi over. His expression remained impassive. Inside he was contemptuous.

'What do you take me for?' Kraverek said.

'You have payment for his dark majesty?'

'Gathered, at great cost. I lost some of my best men.'

'Show me.'

'So you can steal it? Not a chance. I have what Va–'

The magi let out a simultaneous shriek of scrapcode-laced binharic that made Kraverek's implants fizz with painful electricity.

'Do not say his name!' Kolumbari-Enas shrieked. 'Do not draw his attention towards this vessel before we are ready! He must be taken unawares, or our efforts will come to naught. Reiteration! Do not say his name.' His voice degenerated into a squalling electronic hash of squeals and words. *'Do not say his name.'*

Kraverek turned his artificial eyes on the magos. He and Kolumbari-Enas were both altered augmetically, and he had the sudden and very unwelcome thought that they had more in common than he'd prefer. 'I have the payment. That is all you need to know.' He tried to stare the magos down. He should have known better. The glassy lenses set above Kolumbari-Enas' metal snout glinted back at him.

'You have a suitable location for the summoning?'

'A forge world. Guesan IV, close to the Rift. It should fit the requirements you gave me. It is not far. It is dead, the veil is thin there. It hosts foundries of your so-called Machine God. Everything you need.'

'Expression of satisfaction transmitted. Good. We will continue preparations for the invocation on board your ship. The host must be blessed eight times eight times, the process will be difficult. Query, certainty required. Do you have any objections to proceeding?' Kraverek thought he detected a smile in Kolumbari-Enas' voice.

'We do not.'

'Satisfaction redoubled. Excellent. We have waited a long time for this. Such secrets we shall learn.'

'Remember our bargain, magos.'

Kolumbari-Enas inclined his head. 'Understood. All parties

shall profit. Astartes and Mechanicum. Additional warning, emphasised. This is no small work we undertake, trapping an avatar majoris of the Machine God. Advise more gratitude.'

'When the invocation is complete and our plan is fulfilled, then I shall be grateful. Not before.'

Kolumbari-Enas inclined his head again. Once more moving in perfect synchronicity, the magi turned towards the casket and began checking it over ready for transit.

They departed the alien vessel for Kraverek's cruiser, the *Ferrus Indignatum*. Thrall teams finished looting what was left and salvaged the Iron Warriors' boarding torpedoes.

Before they left, Kraverek followed Xeseus' wishes, and had the aeldari ship blasted to pieces. They slipped into the warp leaving only an expanding, glittering cloud of wraithbone dust behind as evidence of their passing.

CHAPTER NINE

IMPOSSIBILITY SQUARED

A knock at the door interrupted Solana's work.

She glanced up, annoyed. A week had passed aboard the *Zar Quaesitor*. Already she had drawings, print-out scrolls, a set of data crystals carrying vid-recordings and audex captures of her interviews. They all needed organising. Currently they were in a semicircle of messy piles around her.

She liked to be thorough. Interruption prevented satisfactory completion of her task. That irked her. She was already annoyed. Too hot, too tired, because her accommodation was awful. She didn't expect to be feted everywhere she went, especially not on a Mechanicus vessel, but her quarters were overheated and cramped, souring her humours.

A skull was embedded at the apex of the door arch. It was no surprise that even the doors on Cawl's flying kingdom had vox-enabled machine spirits. She waited for it to tell her the identity of her visitor. When it gave no announcement, she went back to her work.

The knock came again. *Tink tink tink.* She ignored it.

'I believe there is someone at the door, madam historitor,' Erementias said.

Is it just me, she thought, *or is he being especially arch today?*

'So it seems,' she said. She shuffled through a pile of sketches, trying to decide on the most suitable for permanent preservation.

'Will you not answer?'

'I'm busy,' she said.

'If you will not answer, I shall,' Erementias said, and lurched into action.

'It will not be important.' Her voice rose.

'We are aboard the vessel of the Prime Conduit, madam,' Erementias droned as he trundled towards the door, 'everything is important. Even the fact that they do not announce themselves will be significant in some way.'

She scowled after him. It was not his place to tell her her job, though that didn't stop him being right, which was even more vexing. It looked like she was having this meeting whether she wanted to or not, so she stood up and tugged her tunic smooth. This was simple, grey fabric, the uniform of the Logos with Adeptus Mechanicus flashes.

Erementias slowly extended a telescopic digit to depress the door button. *His augmetics do nothing to actually augment him,* Solana thought. In most cases the original limbs would have been more efficient. Despite his supposed open-mindedness, Erementias exhibited some of the worst habits of the Machine Cult.

The door slid back. A magos waited outside hunched over, wearing an apologetic expression. His hands crossed at his waist reinforced his solicitous air.

'Good day,' he said. He was heavily altered, but like his face, his voice was almost pure human; only a slight hum betrayed its synthetic nature. 'I wondered if the historitor majoris is within? We are about to undertake an important stage of preparations to visit the necron war world, should she be interested, and the archmagos wishes to extend an invitation to her to observe.'

'She is interested, of course,' Eremenitas answered for her. One track turned backwards, pivoting him away from the door to leave the way clear. 'Pray enter. She will be delighted to accommodate you.'

Thanks, Eremenitas, Solana thought.

'Good day, magos,' she said. There was no actual day, but they were a good way into the third watch, which passed as daytime on board. At least Cawl kept to that protocol; a lot of magi didn't bother. The diurnal cycle meant nothing to them.

'Ah!' said the magos, and was more apologetic still. 'I am no magos.' He stepped into the room, and from the way his body moved beneath his robes, she could see that every part of him except his face was artificial. 'I am Qvo-89, construct companion of Belisarius Cawl.'

'Interesting,' said Eremenitas. Deep inside his innards, clicking cogitators processed this information.

'As you I see, I am not human at all,' Qvo went on.

'An abominable intelligence?' Solana said. The idea was repellent, if thrilling.

'No, no!' He held up his hands. 'If you must, regard me as a particularly sophisticated servitor.' He tapped his chest. 'In here is cranial matter. I house no silica animus. I understand your concern, however, so if it makes you feel better, think of me as an incomplete clone, which is also accurate, although I must say I dislike that particular designation.'

'Servitor it is then,' said Solana. She looked him up and down. She recalled hearing of Qvo, Cawl's strange companion, his attempt to return a long-dead friend to life. Despite the vaguely blasphemous nature of the exercise, Cawl made no secret of Qvo's existence or purpose, and both were widely known of in Guilliman's inner circles. Cawl's sentimentality was a weakness. Dark paths followed the fault lines of kindness in the human soul. She showed none of this outwardly, but saluted him politely, making a circle with her hands in front of her face and then over her heart, a representation of the Opus Machina acceptable to many sects of the Cult. He returned the gesture.

'Charmed,' he said in tone very much like the archmagos'. 'How are your accommodations?'

'Too hot and noisy,' she said. 'Do you have anything more suited to baseline human needs?'

'I like it,' Eremenitas said.

'I see,' said Qvo. 'I am so sorry. We meant to honour you. These chambers are kept for favoured magi – the suite is close to the reactor levels, the beating heart of the machine.' Qvo looked her over. 'But I see you are lightly augmented. I shall have your effects moved to quarters in the upper levels. Something with a cosmic view? We do have rooms suitable for every kind of human being, you know, every class, type and preference.' He smiled. There was something freakish about it, despite its warmth. 'The *Zar Quaesitor* is a very big ship.'

'Thank you. I would have thought the archmagos would have been aware of my needs.'

Qvo inclined his head. 'Belisarius might have meant to honour you, but he equally might have meant to test you.'

'Did I pass?'

'I have no idea,' he said. 'He baffles me, always has. And does it really matter? Now, if you are ready, please follow me. Is your servant coming?'

'Assistant,' Eremenitas said loftily. 'And yes, I am coming.'

'Give me a moment, please, Master Qvo.' She couldn't think of what else to call him. It seemed an acceptable term.

'As you wish.'

Solana gathered up her historitor's instruments, her autoquill, notebooks, dataslate, and called two servo-skulls down from their charging roosts. She fitted scribing tips to the ends of her left-hand fingers.

Qvo led her outside, where something large blocked the lumen lights. She looked up into the face of the biggest Space Marine she had ever seen.

'Alpha Primus!' she breathed. This warrior she had seen before, though only at a distance, never close.

Primus looked down at her with a dour expression. *Is there a little hatred there too?* she wondered.

'Primus is to guard you while you are with us. That *is* an honour. He is Belisarius' finest creation,' Qvo said, laying a hand on the giant's power-armoured forearm. Primus transferred his baleful glare to Qvo. The pseudo-magos didn't seem to care, but beamed with pride as if presenting a particularly talented nephew to a friend. 'He is ordinarily occupied with the grandest matters, so if you want an indication of how important you are to the archmagos, here he is, standing in front of you.'

'The first of the Primaris Space Marines,' Eremenitas said emotionlessly. Solana could tell he was impressed even so.

'An honour.' Solana bowed.

Primus turned his massive, scarred head around to stare at her again. 'This way,' he said dolefully, and turned abruptly about.

Qvo leaned in and touched her arm lightly, in exactly the same way as he had touched Primus'. *A key indicator of his falseness,* she thought, *that limits gestural repertoire.*

'What do you think of him?' he whispered.

'Him?' She watched Primus' armoured back move away down the corridor. 'He's magnificent.'

Qvo's smile widened. 'There we are, I knew I'd like her,' Qvo said to Eremenitas conspiratorially.

'Explain,' Eremenitas said.

Qvo's mouth made a little round zero of consideration. 'Oh,' he said, 'because most people find Primus terrifying.'

Qvo and Primus escorted Solana through the ship to another immense hangar. Shuttles and autonomous construction craft were coming and going through the pale, barely visible shimmer of the atmospheric field. There were thousands of people in there: Cawl's servants and peons of Tigrus and Accatran dressed in heavy void suits, comptrollers, tech-priests, and score upon score of servitors. Many were outfitted for hard vacuum work, boarding yet more craft that lifted up from the three dozen landing pads in the hangar with throaty roars, their plasma thrusters heating the air to boiling blasts that contrasted uncomfortably with the cold pressing in from deep space. It is a myth that all of the void is cold. It is a thing of extremes, not of constants. But there, far from the light of any sun and with the Scorean Singularity eating up every iota of energy, it was as cold as it could possibly get.

'We are going to witness the activation of a key part of the apparatus,' Qvo shouted over the noise. It was so noisy that Solana wondered why he didn't switch to transmitted machine speech. They were all fitted with the requisite implants for machine telepathy, yet it appeared that Qvo preferred to talk. 'We're going out! Our vessel is this way!'

Primus' imposing presence opened a path through the crowds. He led them to a large transport barque, much larger than the Arvus lighters that made up the majority of the small boats.

Two tech-priests waited for them, both heavily augmented, one to the point of inhumanity. The inhuman one wore the orange and dark steel of the forge world of Tigrus, his counterpart the predominantly black robes of Accatran. They were archmagi, masters of their own professions, which Solana saw from the sigils decorating their robes to be shipwright and macro-architect respectively.

Qvo introduced them. 'Constructor-Artisan Fidelius Hothan 32-R Demicar of Accatran, and from Tigrus we have Macro-Enginseer Lipuid Vrange.'

The archmagi bowed and made the usual pleasant noises expected when greeting someone of Solana's rank. Despite his massively augmented body, Vrange – 'Call me Lipuid,' as he said – had the more human voice and manner, while Demicar was as aloof as Eremenitas. It was clear Demicar did not prefer to use standard human speech, switching back and forth between Accatranian Lingua Technis and Eastern Fringe binharic, even when addressed in Gothic, a language he went to conspicuous lengths to avoid speaking.

'It is a great pleasure to host you here,' said Vrange's smoothly artificial voice. 'As you know, both our forge worlds are close allies of Ultramar, so it is an especial pleasure to meet one so high in the primarch's service.'

Solana's fingers danced over the scroll unit she wore on her stomach. When she noted the word 'ally' down she underlined it twice. It was an interesting interpretation. Accatran was little more than a dependency of Guilliman's realm.

'And it is therefore our privilege to show you a little of the work that shall help drive Lord Guilliman's reconquest of Imperium Nihilus,' Vrange concluded.

Another noteworthy turn of phrase. She'd heard that a lot recently. People no longer spoke of 'saving' Nihilus, but of 'reconquering' it. After a decade and a half of total war, expectations were shifting. Imperial propaganda made a great deal of Imperium Sanctus' ostensible salvation, which was questionable itself, while ignoring the fact that half the Imperium was lost to the dark.

'I concur,' was all Demicar had to add to that. 'This way, if you please, madam historitor majoris,' he said, and led them towards the dropped prow ramp of the barque. 'Our work here is nearly complete,' he went on in terse data packets – not speech as such, but edification exloads that Solana translated on the fly and input as text into a dataslate she wore on her left hip. 'Our specialities combined have furnished the archmagos dominus with the means of approaching the singularity without being rent atom from atom.' As much as anyone could who communicated chiefly via digital code, he sounded pleased with his work.

The ramp took them to an internal airlock, which led in turn to a large passenger lounge furnished solely with steel benches and transit clamps. A huge, ornate brass rendition of the Machina Opus covered the doors leading deeper into the ship. This skull and cog was the only decoration, otherwise the bay was entirely utilitarian. She had her servo-skulls sweep the room and take detailed picts she'd work up into a full plan later. It never hurt to have more information.

'What do you mean exactly?' Solana asked, wanting Demicar to elaborate on his work for Cawl.

'Sit here, please,' Demicar blurted.

Solana buckled herself into an acceleration harness. Qvo sat beside her, his completely mechanical body moving in a remarkably human way. Eremenitas and the magi stepped onto locking stations. Blunt claws snapped around their motivators, tethering them in place. Primus grunted at them with distaste. The opus emblem split, and Primus went through. Solana had a glimpse of a long corridor before the doors closed. The transport was bigger than it appeared from the outside.

'What we mean,' Vrange said pleasantly, 'is that one cannot simply penetrate the event horizon of a black hole with any sort of frame-fixing device, and not expect consequences, as I believe you mentioned yourself to the archmagos dominus? If you'll allow my colleague and I a little indulgence here, it will be easier to show you how we will get around this problem rather than explaining. Out there.' He gestured expansively with three of his left arms.

'Very well,' said Solana. 'I put myself in your hands.'

'You must forgive them their need for flourish,' Qvo confided quietly. 'It's a tendency found in a great many of Belisarius' followers. He attracts the sort.'

Primus returned and wordlessly took his place on a seat specially constructed to hold his bulk. The engines of the ship fired, and a deep vibration shivered through the passengers. The boarding ramp closed. Solana experienced a queasy shift in her guts as the grav-plating of the transport kicked in slightly at odds with the false gravity of the *Zar Quaesitor*.

The ship wheeled around, tilted and set its nose towards the open void.

Either side of the passenger compartment, the walls rose up. Large panels retracted into housings and exposed the inside of the ship to the hangar outside. They passed the atom-thin skin of the atmospheric shielding into the open void. She felt no alarm at this. The barque's own atmospheric shield emitters snapped on as soon as they left the hangar. It was not unusual for the Cult Mechanicus to rely on energy fields over crude matter.

Qvo watched Solana's skulls with interest.

'You're recording everything,' he said.

'I am. That is my remit.'

'It is not a criticism,' said Qvo.

'You're covertly sampling their exloads too. Should I take that as criticism instead?'

'I am gathering data. You are gathering data.' Qvo shrugged equivocally. 'Belisarius expected you to gather thorough data – indeed he would encourage it were you not doing so. The regent must be satisfied. He understands that.'

'Cawl has been absent so long, it will take a lot to satisfy the regent,' said Solana.

'Noted,' said Qvo. 'I am curious, who will ever see the things that you record? You will submit a report, a very thorough one I am sure, and I am equally sure that the primarch will study it, but the rest, all this raw data, the sketches I saw, your notes, your tri-d models.' He moved a metal hand through the air, as if offering his question to the void. 'Where will it go? What will be done with it?'

'It will be held in safekeeping,' said Solana. 'It is gathered by Eremenitas and then archived. That is his primary purpose. Everything I record here, all my thoughts, he safeguards them.'

'This is correct,' said Eremenitas. 'I am, in this context, an archivist,' he explained.

'Despite his need to comment on everything I say and do,' she added.

'Purely from a sociological point of view,' Eremenitas said. 'Social interactions. That was my original speciality, the science of distributed action in large group situations and the manipulation of the same.'

'Who sees it? What is the point?' Qvo pressed.

'It does not need a point,' said Solana tersely. 'We are of the Adeptus Mechanicus. We gather information as a form of worship, do we not?'

Qvo smiled in an uneasy way. It was the smile of something

trapped between two states, not quite human, not quite machine, and it caused a crawling between Solana's shoulder blades. For an instant she wished that Qvo would look away. However, when he spoke the feeling passed. His voice was too warm to warrant such terror, and she felt a little ashamed.

'I suppose we do,' he said, and patted her hand.

CHAPTER TEN

THE ARRAY

The barque raced out from the fleet in the wake of the flotilla of work craft. The chief constituents were four transit carracks of middling size mobbed by crowds of servitor ships, worker transports and control barges bristling with antennae. Qvo informed her their flight would take two hours, so in the interim Solana called up a hololithic representation of the Scorean Singularity, and became entranced by its bizarre appearance, the photonic disc burning brightly against the uttermost black, the halo over the top of the hole that was the far side of the disc made visible by the lensing effect of the singularity's enormous gravity. In the other direction, the lazy turn of the galaxy's Norma and Sagittarian arms spilled milky luminescence in broad bands, until the livid purple scar of the Great Rift cut across everything, its malevolence palpable even at a distance of tens of thousands of light years.

She recorded her thoughts, she recorded the view. She plugged herself into a data socket set next to her seat and drew in all she could from the ship's sensorium. Data, data, data, enough from that short flight to fill a whole shelf of mem-crystals. She thought back to what Qvo had asked, and could not quite dismiss his question. Then she reassured herself she was doing this for the primarch, whose hunger for information was almost as profound as the hunger of the singularity for matter.

'Look!' Vrange spoke suddenly, interrupting her train of thought. 'They are starting.'

The flotilla had come to a halt. The barque veered off and took up a position a thousand miles from the work site.

'We watch now. Come,' said Demicar. He released himself from his clamps. Solana and the others got up. Primus remained where he was, his eyes fixed on an invisible horizon, his face completely blank. Qvo was humming.

Solana looked from the Space Marine to Qvo, one so immobile his face might as well have been carved from granite, the other's expressions wavering from cunning sentience to imbecility and back again. Their ersatz humanity was troubling. She wondered if anyone in Cawl's service objected to his tendency to play Machine God, or if they were all as driven as their master, and blind to it. She could not see these habits going down well in the courts of the magisterium on Mars. No wonder they called him heretek.

'Mistress? Mistress historitor,' Vrange said, beckoning her. 'It is beginning. Be quick, or you shall miss it.'

Solana went to the port side of the ship, which offered a clear view of the event. The transit carracks fired plasma thrusters, lighting up their previously dark flanks, showing the nozzles of more primitive gas ejectors alongside them. The carracks moved up into an expanding square formation, their attendant work craft in the centre, and rolled, presenting their ventral profiles to the open void. This didn't take long, fifteen minutes maybe, and in contrast with the voyage out to the deployment point the whole operation seemed to pass very quickly. The carracks opened cavernous loading bays, and from each floated large, oblong objects identical in form. Solana estimated them to be half a mile in length apiece, for they cleared the bay doors with barely feet to spare, and so must have filled the holds completely.

The plasma thrusters shut down. Jets of low-velocity gas spurted from the carracks' nozzles, bringing them to a gradual halt, then sending them into reverse. It was a deliberately low-powered means of manoeuvre, to avoid disturbing the obelisks from their course. Inertia sent the machines out from the ships. Clearing the zone took the carracks several minutes. Once they were some way from the devices, they ignited their plasma drives and accelerated back towards the fleet.

Solana again noted exactly what happened. She ordered one of her servo-skulls to inload the data from the hololith directly so as to have an uncorrupted record, while she continued to observe from the open ship sides. Primus watched it all with disinterest, Qvo with his species of idiot acceptance.

'What is the exact purpose of these objects?' she asked.

'Deflection,' Demicar burbled. 'Is it not obvious?'

'When the frame stabiliser tunnel penetrates the accretion ring of the singularity, it will be akin to puncturing the skin of a pressurised container, precipitating the violent release of the contents,' said Vrange, more amenable to explanation. 'Imagine a promethium flask thus punctured, then imagine this eventuality again at cosmic scale. Liberated from the attraction of the black hole's mass, the photons in the ring will escape at the speed of light. You came to this conclusion yourself, correct?'

'I did.'

'Then you will know that it only is the most energetic of particles that can retain position outside the event horizon.'

'It is light,' said Solana.

'It is light,' agreed Vrange, 'but it is light compacted to a hyperfluid state, an extreme photonic plasma. We shall abruptly interrupt the gravitic conditions that allow this matter to exist in such a state.'

'The force released will be incredible,' said Solana. She looked around the magi, whose augmetic studded faces remained inscrutable. Even so, she could feel their excitement. It reminded her of the foolishness of young men about reckless adventure.

'More than incredible,' Demicar said. 'Incalculable. A material force greater than any released by mankind since the High Age of Technology.'

'The artefacts fashioned by the magi of Accatran–'

'With Archmagos Cawl's supervision,' said Vrange, magos of Tigrus.

'Yes, yes, but the labours were ours!' canted Demicar irritably. 'Our artefacts,' he stressed, 'are designed to capture and deflect the streams of liquid light that will explode from the singularity once the ring is tapped.'

'And if it does not work?' asked Qvo with a hollow, unpleasant solicitousness.

'Then we will all die! Smeared as strings of atoms several light years around,' said Demicar, speaking Gothic for once, though with a shriek of binharic overlaid. 'That will not occur. Our instruments are precisely calibrated. The machines are perfection made manifest.'

'Then you must have tested them,' said Solana.

There followed a sheepish silence.

'Not as such…' began Vrange.

'Negative,' said Demicar with impressive bluntness. 'There was nowhere we could test them.'

'Absorbing the photon shock will eventually destroy the devices, no matter that Accatran made them so well,' said Vrange.

'This has to work once, and it has to work first time, which if colleague Vrange's calculations are correct, they will.' Demicar hunched into himself, becoming crouched and sinister. 'If the devices fail, it will not be because of Accatran's error.' The implication was clear.

'Colleague Demicar,' Vrange admonished. 'Let us discuss failure when failure has occurred. This will work.' His bionic eyes glinted. 'Imagine if we could make it a weapon!'

'Exotic radiations. Unknown atomic states!' canted Demicar with excitement, now returning to his higher datacast modes. 'Power beyond the dreams of any. If Cawl dies in his attempt to reach the war world, we will still learn much. I have prepared an army of data thieves to gather all information. We shall fill the noosphere of this fleet to the brim with observations!'

'But this is… this is innovation,' said Solana. 'Original research, novel technologies.'

'Correct,' said Vrange.

'High blasphemy,' Solana pressed him.

'In ignorant circles.'

'Ignorant circles that have preserved the Imperium for thousands of years.'

'And because of that, Mistress Solana, our species stands on the brink of extinction. The Prime Conduit shows the way. Change, or die,' said Vrange.

Qvo took her hand in his. 'I am confused by your misgivings, madam historitor. You yourself were accused of modus original. Sentenced to death, so I heard.'

'She was, I have heard it too!' The magi crowded forward, metal limbs clicking, false organs whirring. Solana told herself not to retreat from them. The open void beckoned only inches from her heels.

'I did nothing like this. It is the scale of it, the scope! Xenotech, tapping the vitae of this dead star, changing the run of time itself!' She shook her head in slow amazement. 'The scale of it!' She could not believe the words, and had to say them again.

'An act of audacious brilliance that will put us on the same level as our sainted ancestors, the masters of technology!' Vrange said.

'Observe!' cast Demicar. 'The photonic deflectors are in position.'

He pointed into space. Bright lights marked the firing of plasma engines bringing the obelisks to a halt.

'And if they've moved out of alignment by some chance in the interim?' said Qvo. He sounded nervous.

'Then the fleet will be obliterated by plasmic-photonic eruption from the accretion ring, and we shall all die in the service of the Machine God,' said Vrange. 'Such is the price of experimentation.'

'I dislike it when they experiment,' said Qvo glumly.

'How do they operate?' asked Solana, wanting to change the subject.

'By creating their own mass attraction, a large-scale application of false gravity,' said Vrange. 'Electromagnetic conduits are projected also for each machine, which will help divide the photonic tsunami and guide it towards the mass attractors in each device, but it is the gravitic technology here that is doing all the heavy lifting. If you will excuse my pun.'

'Wait,' she said. 'How will Cawl go down the frame-stabilised tunnel, if it is full of hard photons coming the other way?'

'That is where the genius of Tigrus comes into play,' said Vrange. '*Our*' – he stressed the word very heavily – 'frame stabiliser contains a secondary emitter which has been designed to project a second tunnel down the inside of the first. This second tunnel will activate after the first has penetrated the temporal skin of the photon sphere. It will lock onto the planetary surface directly, so creating a safe passage for Lord Cawl to traverse.'

'Like a pipe?'

'Like a double-skinned pipe, yes, if you like.'

Solana dutifully noted all this down in her scrollbook with the ink-claws that tipped the fingers of her left hand. The autoquills mounted on her shoulder array came to life, creating detailed technical drawings of every element of the equipment shown to her upon the scroll. Ordinarily, this would have caused a great deal of trouble, for a magos protects their knowledge to the death, but she was the emissary of the Imperial Regent, and in any case, Cawl was no ordinary magos, so the autoquills darted back and forth through the interview without any objection forthcoming, each movement of their servomotors giving out a tiny purr.

'Why not envelop the entire planet, and bring it into our frame of temporal reference?' She knew the answer, but had discovered long ago playing a little ignorant often yielded additional information.

Primus spoke, dully, leadenly, the voice of a man who is weary. 'Necrons, that is why, madam historitor.'

'Cawl mentioned a portable frame projector.'

'That is correct,' Vrange said. 'Though I know little of it – that is Lord Cawl's own work.'

'So you are doing this the difficult way because of necrons?'

'We are,' said Vrange. 'But it is safer, and will not release the time-lost inmates of that temporal gaol to trouble our galaxy.'

'This will be a mission of stealth,' said Primus.

'Then in order for this scheme to work, the frame stabiliser cannon must function perfectly, the secondary emitter too, and if we're all not to die, the photonic deflectors must function as you have designed them, and be precisely placed. All of it experimental, potentially heretekal technology. Do I have this right?'

Of course Solana had it right. But she wanted them to say so. For the record.

The magi of Accatran and Tigrus shared a look, and no doubt, Solana thought, a short private binharic exchange.

'Affirmative,' Demicar said, in another rare and grudging use of speech.

'Remarkable,' she said, and continued her notes.

Primus pushed himself off the wall. 'You will have ample opportunity to judge all this at first hand,' he said. A ghostly smile played over his lips.

'How so?' she asked.

'Because you shall be accompanying the archmagos yourself.'

'He gave me unfettered access to the process, but I have heard nothing about actually going with him.'

'He intends to invite you to join the party formally at the pre-mission conclave.'

'My assistant?'

'Only you,' said Primus.

'A pity,' Eremenitas said. 'I should very much have enjoyed the opportunity to go into extreme danger for the sake of knowledge.'

Solana could not tell if he was being sarcastic or not.

CHAPTER ELEVEN

GUESAN IV

A gale of screams and dust raced over Guesan IV. Through it, Kraverek, Xeseus, Adnarax, Orios Zhask, and the sorcerer Psephalas shepherded a pair of tracked sleds stacked with crates. Ahead went the eight Disciples of Nul, dragging the sarcophagus upon a grav-bier.

Faces in the dust formed, screamed then melted away. Guesan was largely sheathed in metal. No deserts, no soil, little exposed rock. Therefore, Kraverek concluded, the dust was the remains of the population, of whose billions there was an otherwise obvious lack. Relay towers clustered like copses of dead trees, their twisted limbs thrown up in horror. This had been a thriving world, until the Rift split the sky.

Kraverek's vox-beads chimed. The notification signal buzzed with psychic interference, not a crackle of disrupted electromagnetism, but a feeling of profound unease.

'I shut the vox-net down for a reason, Xeseus,' he said before the chosen could speak. 'Can you hear the whispering? The warp seeps into everything so close to the Rift. This place is almost as bad as Medrengard.'

Xeseus could no doubt hear the whispering perfectly well. They all could – a wheedling, needling voice that alternated between promises and threats.

'What do you care for the rantings of trapped Neverborn?' said Xeseus.

'That's exactly it, Xeseus, I don't care for the rantings of trapped Neverborn. Which is why I am not listening to it.'

'It can do no harm,' said Xeseus.

'They annoy me,' Kraverek replied. 'You are annoying me. These damned priests should have landed us closer. Now what do you want?' Kraverek said.

'Forebear me a moment, my lord,' said Xeseus. 'Firstly, I do not trust these magi.'

'You think I do?' Kraverek watched the cowled figures half hidden in the storm.

'I assume you have a plan.'

'When do I not?'

'Never.'

'Then what is your point?'

'I wished to make my own misgivings known.'

Their feet crunched on bones hidden under the drifts.

Power and knowledge, power and knowledge… the thing on the wind whispered. Psychic residue, a half-formed mind. Like a shroud of plastek caught in bushes to be ripped away storm by storm, the whispering thing was dissipating, but it had enough of a hold on reality to gibber a while.

The secrets of the animus mendacem. Look inside. Find it inside. Insiiiiiiiddeeeeee… Then, with a sharp, change of tone, ***I shall feast on thine eyes! Heed me! Heed me! HEEEEEEEEEEEeeeeeeeeee…***

'Is that it, Xeseus? This daemon is testing my patience.'

'We should send parties down to the cities. We're running low on supplies. I had the *Ferrus Indignatum* run an auspex scry of the forge capital and the primary two space ports. There are good returns from all three. There will be weapons, and raw materials. Maybe food. We're short on food.'

'Fine, get on with it. Send in scouts. Put strict limits on the numbers of thralls sent to the surface. Groups of twenty at a time, no more than three hours on the ground. Have them all watched closely by one of the men.'

'I didn't know you cared,' said Xeseus. Kraverek hated that tone. If Xeseus wasn't such a useful warrior, Kraverek would have killed him years ago.

'We're running low on bodies as well as everything else. The last thing I want is this whispering bastard getting into one of the mortals and crawling out of him on board our ship. It's getting desperate. There will be more. They'll take whatever chance they can to get off the planet.'

Kraverek turned the vox off. The day was running out. The storm refracted the last of the afternoon into an orange blur. Rods of soundless lightning jousted through the soaring metal towers crowding every horizon, never striking. The wind keened around the heat vanes of their armour, hooted into the nozzles of their stabilisation jets. The dust thickened. His men became hunched ochre shapes, the tech-priests vanished. Kraverek was shut into a world delineated by his armour. His breathing and the thrum of his systems closed in on him.

Walls of sand separated him from his men, the storm a legacy of sudden planetary death. Whispers were not the only things that lingered in places like this.

Kraverek kept his sensorium open and his guard up.

* * *

Evening sidled in and finally the wind died. The dust had little purchase on the thin air without the wind to loft it, and cleared rapidly. The Rift dominated the night, curved like a knowing grin. Shining clouds of tormented matter hid the unplumbable depths of the warp for the most part, but here and there the raw stuff of it peeped through, glaring hate at reality's ordered atomic dance.

The landscape became a series of sharp and mournful silhouettes, reminding Kraverek of a shadow show he had seen when he was yet mortal. The puppeteer created the illusion of motion by moving elements of scenery on sliders past one another at different rates, so the shadow of a man ran through a forest, or a horse galloped along the road, or a chariot came down from the stars. The dead forges of this world recalled this trick, giant silos and ragged towers that slipped by only according to the laws of perspective, yet seemed unreal just the same, as if moved by a hidden hand.

Young Kraverek had thought he would like to make puppets like that. Bringing a little joy to hard lives had seemed a pleasing way to earn a living. Then a few years later the Iron Warriors came from the sky to gather their harvest of lives. The memory soured his mood. It turned out that all the universe was made of shadows, and the puppeteers who controlled them owed no love to mankind. His own world was dead, dead as this place, dead as everywhere would one day be. Death was the only gift of Chaos, and Chaos would triumph. What could he do but fight for his own power before the inevitable end?

His vox came on. The magi intruded.

'Declaration. We approach the ritual ground,' Kolumbari-Enas, the First-Among-Equals said.

'All praise the three in one, who favours the seekers of knowledge,' the others responded. The whispering was gone, but Kraverek was sure he heard a distant laugh before the vox cut out.

They turned towards a manufactorum of staggering size, crowned by hundreds of chimneys and vents, the silent tombstones of industry. They entered gates rent by claw marks so huge only Battle Titans could have made them. He expected a warren of corridors and individual facilities inside so monumental an edifice, but the interior was a single space, too vast for his armour's sensorium to detect either the far side or its ceiling.

Huge machines loomed out of the silent dark, giant gantries carrying assembly claws, gargantuan hoppers for raw materials, conveyor belts a hundred feet wide far overhead, then pits of stagnating acids whose vapours triggered environmental warnings in Kraverek's battle plate.

They came to a tall ziggurat.

'We are here,' Alixia-Dyos informed him.

Kraverek looked up the steep stairways. 'Unload the offerings,' he ordered. 'The sleds will go no further.'

His men mag-locked their weapons and dragged crates from the flatbeds. Their armour made the burden light. They would have to return. The sleds were piled high. The being they courted was greedy.

The party climbed to the summit, the magi and the sarcophagus first, Kraverek a few steps behind. He guessed this was some place of worship, there at the centre of the manufactorum. It looked to serve no practical purpose.

Whatever its original use, the summit certainly meant something to the beings who destroyed the planet. Kraverek halted at the edge of the top. Adnarax stopped at his side.

'By dead Olympia...'

A few stepped rings led down to a wide, circular plaza paved with patterned metal plating. There were pedestals around the perimeter.

New sculptures had taken the place of their shattered statues.

Blood dried to black tar glued men and women to one another in the forms of multi-armed giants. Strange transfigurations who mocked the Corpse-Emperor and his champions. They appeared to be peons as opposed to magi, for they bore few augmetics, and what shreds of clothing remained on their tortured bodies suggested simple work suits.

'You're too squeamish, Adnarax.' Psephalas pushed them aside with his crate. Kraverek had no time for conjurors and daemon-whisperers, yet Psephalas had his uses. Little shocked him. The path of sorcerer was attached intimately to atrocity.

'This place is cursed,' said Adnarax.

'Why do you think we are here?' Psephalas put his crate down.

Xeseus set his crate atop the first, then prodded the nearest body with the muzzle of his boltgun.

'Hard as stone,' he said. 'Interesting.' He swiped at a head. It broke off and landed with a gritty thud, face up, at Kraverek's feet. A man, he guessed. The face was mummified, the skin grey, the eyes shrivelled, so it was difficult to be certain, but probably a man. The look of terror on his face, however, was as clear as day.

'Fine work,' said Orios Zhask thoughtfully, laying his burden down. He too, being the warband's master of flesh, was unmoved.

'They are thralls. Is this an insult?' Kraverek asked Psephalas.

'To the Martians, yes. The Neverborn exalt the flesh over the machine in the heart of the forge to show their contempt for the Machine God. The Neverborn manifested here. This was a place of much emotion. The veil is thin.' Psephalas glanced at Kraverek. 'Does this trouble you? I sometimes think you sentimental.'

'I am not sentimental.' Kraverek stepped over the head and placed his crate upon the others. An outer ring of floor plates was clear of dust or blood, but the centre was blackened, and upon it was stamped an eight-pointed wheel, the octed of Chaos held holy by many, though not by Kraverek. He had no time for the gods.

Psephalas made to go back to the sleds, but when no one followed he turned. 'The rest of you, will you not help me with these offerings? It is not right that I, your lore master, should do the work of thralls alone.'

Psephalas' ire brought grim laughter from his comrades, and because Psephalas regarded himself with utmost seriousness, he became moody.

'Laugh all you will. The one you seek to summon is dangerous. The more powerful the daemon, the deadlier the peril, and he is among the most dangerous of all! Only my skill stands between you and damnation. Show more respect. Now come, help me with the offerings.'

'We should have brought thralls,' Adnarax grumbled.

'Thralls would die here, do you not understand?' Psephalas snarled. 'Before they could be of any use, they would become a danger to us.'

The Iron Warriors went back down the pyramid. Kraverek remained at the top. Leadership had to have some advantage.

He ignored the chatter of his men, and watched the magi walking around the branded plasteel, flicking rank-smelling oil from smoking aspergillums. They made one pass, then another, nearing the centre on a spiral path. Their chants got louder. Servo-skulls flew around them, the chittering machine speech weaving in and out of their psalms.

'So they're just another clutch of sorcerers,' Xeseus said, hefting another crate up the stairs. 'No offence,' he added, aiming this at Psephalas, who grunted back. There was no love lost between them. 'How disappointing they are. I expected a focus on the machine, the real. Not more mumbled spells.'

The rearmost of the eight magi surprised them by stopping and responding.

'The ultimate truth bridges two worlds. That of the material' – he pushed a metal palm flat towards the ground – 'and that of the immaterial.' He raised the palm up towards the dark. 'The usurpers of Mars are blind to fully half of the Great Work. The immaterium reflects the materium. They are parts of one and the same thing. An adept of the True Mechanicum must be a binder of spirits as well as of metal. That is the Machine God's will.'

Adnarax put his crate down. 'That's the last of it. I don't see what use this junk will be either. Daemons like blood.'

The magos wheezed. 'You expose your ignorance. The one we call hungers not for the vitae of mortals, but for the souls of machines. Now prepare your offerings.'

'Set the crates around the circle,' Psephalas directed. 'Open them so the contents are on display, facing inwards.'

The chosen did as they were told, dragging the crates into position and flinging open the lids. Inside each were rare technologies that had taken Kraverek much time to gather. There were eight crates, eight artefacts, xenos and human, each one irreplaceable, each one gained only after hard battle and rivers of blood spilled. Kraverek looked on them, their provenances and applications largely unknown. He wondered briefly if he were doing the right thing letting them be destroyed.

Focus, he told himself. *A greater prize awaits. These are the price.*

The magi continued their slow procession. The chosen withdrew. Outside, in the night, the Rift leered. Somehow, Kraverek could feel its regard through the millions of tons of metal hanging over his head.

CHAPTER TWELVE

INVOCATION

Kraverek bade his men stand back from the magi.

'Let them be about their work,' he said. 'Do not interrupt them.'

The chosen grumbled but obeyed. Kraverek could not hope for more than that. Times had been lean. Discipline was eroding, and so was respect for his rule. This plan had to work, or he was finished.

Arranged in a circle at the heart of the place, the magi prayed to the Machine God. To begin with the prayers were indistinguishable from those used by the usurpers of Mars, supplications for good function, purity of operation, success of operation, the usual pointless pleas. Kraverek watched the magi's preparations. His men passed the time according to their will. Adnarax meditated. Xeseus morbidly poked at the flesh sculptures. Psephalas watched the ritual attentively. Zhask was only interested in what was hidden in the casket.

After a time Kraverek grew bored, finding the rites both superstitious and naive. He let himself slip into the half-sleep of the catalepsean node. Hunting the corsairs had been enervating, and he had slept little these last weeks. Ordinarily, resting in demi-wakefulness did not bring dreams, but Kraverek was troubled by waking visions. As the priests continued their binharic chanting, the division between the then and the now dissolved, and Kraverek found himself reliving fragments of his past, unsure whether his visions or the forge-fane he dimly perceived were the reality. None of the memories were good. Past failures replayed in his head, and he recalled the thousands of people he had slain. Hundreds of battlefields in dozens of wars flickered through his memory, each one dredging up forgotten doubts.

Hours passed in this unpleasant fugue, until the touch of Psephalas' armoured hand upon his arm called him back.

'My lord, they are nearly done.'

Kraverek came to groggy. Guesan seemed unreal. The past clutched at him, unwilling to let go.

'The demigod will come,' Psephalas continued urgently. 'Remember what I told you, how risky this is. This is no mere daemon, he is a minor power. One does not trap one such as he, not completely. Be on your guard.'

Kraverek could not see the present clearly. His helm plate display was a distant neon epitaph for deeds undone. Only the past was close. He was thinking of the first man he killed, one of the ship serfs, months before his first implantation when they'd been forced to hunt to survive in the lowermost decks. He remembered Medrengard. He remembered the primarch. He remembered home, the first, terrifying glimpse of the Iron Warriors.

'Kraverek!' Psephalas hissed urgently, grabbing Kraverek's arm. 'Do you hear me? You must appear strong before him. You must gather your wits.'

Kraverek focused on the metal under his feet, the steel sky

above, the world beyond the gates. His flesh, his blood, his armour. These were real. This was now. He wrenched his arm from Psephalas' grip. 'I hear you. I will be as strong as iron.'

'See that you are,' Psephalas said, 'or you will damn us all.' The sorcerer stood away. 'I do not know why you consult me, if you will not heed my counsel.'

'You are heeded, but needs must. Abaddon's orders are clear.'

'I find it strange he reached out to you.'

'And yet he did,' Kraverek said, rounding on the sorcerer so fast that he took a step back. 'You have seen the orders yourself. He does me a great honour. Why is that so hard to believe?'

On the *Ferrus Indignatum* was a long, black scroll, inked with glowing pigments, a screaming daemon head for a case. Upon it was written Abaddon's command. All Kraverek's men had seen it. He had made sure of that, for he had revealed it at the moment of mutiny. The orders had bought some time.

Kraverek moved away, towards the edge of the plaza. Out past the open forge gates, dawn blushed the thinning sky. A stark crescent of sun licked over the horizon.

'A strange day for a summoning,' he said. 'This morning is bright.'

'The daemons do not care how they gain entry to our world, only that entrance is offered,' said Psephalas. 'A good day, a black day, it matters not to them.'

The input ports of Kraverek's augmetic eyes ached, a biting pain that gnawed at the bones of his skull. The light was not of an entirely natural sort.

There was a cry from the centre of the circle, all eight magi shouting as one, a shout that began a chant that rose to shrieking heights then fell to a malign mumbling, then back up again in hypnotic waves.

Kraverek turned his back on the sun. A broad orange tongue

of daylight lapped at the magi through the gates. The sarcophagus' lock plates disengaged and the lid opened. Chill vapours tumbled down the sides in misty falls and pooled upon the ground. Inside a gaseous murk cleared, so the occupant became visible. It was a machine so like a skeleton Kraverek first took it for a grotesque sculpture of one. Only as the sun shone deeper into the casket did he see it for an automaton, and an ugly one at that.

The face was a grinning death's head. Its arms and legs were cast to resemble bones. It was poorly proportioned and oddly lumpen. Nevertheless, Kraverek was looking upon something fashioned by human hands thousands of years before the False Emperor had started his cursed crusade and damned them all.

'Have you seen the likes of that machine before?'

Psephalas shook his head slowly. His voice was uncertain. 'Never.'

The others gathered with the sorcerer and the Warsmith, Xeseus, Adnarax and Orios Zhask. The shrill, bubbling cries of binharic screeched over the manufactorum. The magi raised their arms, mechadendrites and servo-claws. They sang with human and machine voices.

They abruptly stopped.

The hands of the Iron Warriors strayed to their weapons. Xeseus already carried his boltgun, and his left forefinger slipped from the blocky body to curl around the trigger.

They watched, expectant.

Nothing happened. The day remained bright and clear. No eldritch cry rent the sky. No lightning bolt slammed into the sarcophagus. A minute passed. Still nothing.

A slow sardonic laugh greeted this spectacle.

'Oh, bravo,' said Xeseus. 'You truly have outdone yourselves, tech-priests.'

'Hold your tongue, Xeseus,' hissed Psephalas. 'Your faithlessness shames you. This is only the beginning. You will anger he who comes.'

As if the sorcerer's words finished the invocation, the atmosphere changed, and the skin-crawling sense of the warp's immanence settled on them. Something unclean, something evil.

There was a faint humming. Sparks buzzed within the ribs of the android. The acrid smoke of toasted electronics wafted from the machine.

Again, Xeseus laughed. A crawl of power around the machine cut his mirth dead.

The android's eyes lit up, its arms unfolded. Huge, metallic phalanges clenched and unclenched, and it lurched out of its sarcophagus, made three steps before falling to its knees on the plaza. It held up its hands to its ocular sensors, as if in wonder.

'Now, it is happening now,' Psephalas said excitedly. 'Watch now. You will not see the like of this again within your lifetime.'

The warp crashed hard into the walls of reality. The android raised its face to the heavens, cast back its mouth and vomited a fountain of energy high enough to illuminate the distant ceiling. The skeletal jaw clacked shut, and the machine convulsed, flipped onto its back and arched its spine so far its hands and feet were planted firm and flat upon the ground and waist thrust towards the sky. The jaw hinged so wide one of the joints broke and the mandible fell loose, pulling cabling out of the throat. The eyes glared brighter, and they swelled, growing big as searchlight lenses, yet still somehow accommodated by the skull.

'He comes! He comes!' cried one of the magi. The shout attracted the attention of the thing forcing itself into the android. The head turned on a juddering neck. False muscle fibres brittle with the ages broke. Spines of metal forced their way out of the grotesque cheeks of the machine, and its eyes blazed.

'Move!' Kraverek said, shoving Psephalas aside just as a beam of light scythed from the eyes of the machine and cut across the magos who had spoken, exploding him into a cloud of ash and burning through the space the sorcerer had occupied. Kolumbari-Enas screeched an urgent command that dug at Kraverek's soul. The magi's chants redoubled.

Psephalas staggered at the force of Kraverek's blow.

'There is no need, I am warded.' He snatched up a heavy amulet that hung around his neck. 'Do not touch me again. I am safe!'

'Heed your own warnings and take nothing for granted,' Kraverek said.

The ziggurat trembled, then the plaza heaved. With a great wrenching, the plating splintered. Needles of plasteel flew into the centre of the circle, clattering off ceramite with a noise like hail on metal roofs when it encountered the Space Marines. Big pieces rose shudderingly from the ground. Out on the factory floor, machines creaked on their bearings to face the ziggurat. Chains lifted and hung against the force of gravity.

'All of you, get down!' Kraverek commanded. They all knelt beneath the hailing debris speeding at the robot. Its form absorbed these jagged missiles, sucking them in. The metal shifted, and split, as if melted, though there was no heat; rather the whole plaza was deathly cold. Adding the bounty to its crudely sculpted bones, the android built itself into something larger. Components formed from jagged lumps and clicked into place. Long limbs constructed themselves from cogs and levers that unfolded from each other, extended outwards, growing bigger all the time.

And why not? thought Kraverek. If the beings of the warp could fashion themselves bodies of false flesh, then why not false machines?

The magi expanded their circle. Kolumbari-Enas clapped his hands together with a boom like thunder. With a groan, the energy network of the fane came online, lights like small suns igniting in the complex lattice of pipes and walkways hundreds of feet overhead. Lumens ignited in sequence right the way to the edge of the room, revealing the gargantuan scale of the temple complex. Quiescent machines rumbled. Halted production processes juddered into life.

Again, Kolumbari-Enas emitted a long squall of machine speech, too complex for Kraverek to comprehend. Again, he clapped his hands. Lights exploded in the ceiling-scape and cerulean arcs of power roared down to strike the magos. He stood shuddering at the centre of this blazing storm, gathering the outpouring of the Machine God's Motive Force into himself, then with a cry released it into his remaining six fellows, so that interlaced bonds of lightning fenced the growing creature in.

The crates rattled, starting all at once, and so hard that some of the treasures within bounced free, and these too rose from the ground and sped at the growing android, slamming into it with such force that a world's worth of archeotech exploded into components that bounced everywhere before being caught, and drawn inexorably back in by he who was coming.

Chunks of machinery whirled by the disciples' heads. Xeseus grunted and ducked, but the magi stood their ground, faces dipped in concentration. Raw power crackled from their hands, until the centre of their circle became a screaming vortex of energy. All they could see of the android now was a flickering, growing shadow.

'He comes!' they wailed. 'He comes!'

A mechadendrite as thick as a tree limb whipped out from the circle, catching one of the disciples with a downward stroke that smashed him flat. The disciples did not run. Their circle adjusted. The power continued to flow. On the manufactorum floor machines worked faster and faster, well beyond their tolerance, so that mechanisms tore and pistons broke.

Up the shadow came, up and up. The daemon was in it. It lumbered to its feet, already bigger than the Space Marines. It staggered sideways and rebounded in roaring pain from the streams of power fencing it in. One arm was longer than the other so that it hung to the floor. The limb convulsed, rippled, grew longer still, swept around, tripped another acolyte who went down with a noise like a box of dropped tools. The magos got halfway up before a squirming tentacle fabricating itself from gristle and spall speared down into their back and burst from their chest. The tentacle pulled out, ripping the acolyte in two, and whirled around spraying oily blood.

More metal ripped from the ziggurat crashed into the construct. Sheets of metal fell from above, exploding into fragments as they plummeted to be drawn into and consumed by the manifesting demigod. The last of the artefacts shot out of the crates and hit with cannon-force crashes. Flesh too was drawn to the giant being, ripped from the twisted corpse sculptures that ringed the pyramid top. It flew in gobbets, laying itself over metal bones. The thrashing mechadendrites pulled back into the chest, wrapped around ribs growing with creaking speed, becoming banded muscle that vanished under a coat of spreading skin. Legs lengthened, sprouting hoofed feet big as tank hatches. The head of the android bore up, like a ball carried on a spout of water, then collapsed itself, becoming nothing but those whirling eyes.

'Maybe…' said Xeseus guardedly. 'Maybe we should withdraw.'

Adnarax scoffed. 'So bold with your words, never with actions.' He racked his bolter, and held it before him. 'I say we stay. No Iron Warrior runs from a fight.'

'Iron within,' Psephalas said.

'Iron without,' Adnarax responded.

A plume of violet warp fire blew out from the giant and consumed another of Kolumbari-Enas' magi. He burned screaming, a living candle that would not die. The others shouted machine canticles at each other, and the magi adjusted their positions again, holding the lightning fence in place by will, by magic and by technology.

'It has made no move against us, only the magi,' said Kraverek.

'We could all still die,' said Xeseus levelly.

'Then we die in the cause of the Despoiler,' said Kraverek. 'Psephalas, protect us.'

'Drawing on the warp while this thing pours through the veil will haul in a catch of daemons we cannot hope to best.'

'Then you too are bold with your boasts of mastery, like Xeseus. Ready your magics as best you can!' Kraverek said. 'Must I decide everything? Spread wide. Train your weapons on it.'

The Iron Warriors fanned out, bolters up. Kraverek activated his servo-harness. He drew his plasma pistol and thumbed the activation stud to ready. Coils glowed with gathering power.

The daemon's back cracked. A pair of bladed limbs unfurled from its shoulder blades. The smaller right arm flexed, and grew to match the left. Flesh ran ahead of the growing metal bones like molten wax flowing into a mould. An armoured gauntlet knitted itself together from the metal flying into it from every side, heating and fusing.

'It is nearly done. He is here,' Psephalas said.

The daemon held up clawed hands, huge and flexing. Adamantine talons sharp as sin whispered in the air. The head inflated, a moment that struck Kraverek as ridiculous – he was put in mind of an emergency flotation buoy whose cord had been yanked. Then there it was, the visage of this biomechanical beast dragged from the warp. A strange face, a metal effigy of a daemon: flat, horned, a mouth like an intake grille.

The Neverborn let its clawed hands drop. The space around it calmed. A few details popped into being: feed pipes, rivets, the last overlapping plates of armour that hugged its humped back, settling one upon the other with businesslike clicks.

The creature growled as deeply and grumblingly as a tank engine. Then it stood tall, arched its back and it roared, and its roar was an artillery bombardment, a thousand gunshots, a starship reactor going critical, all the triphammers of a forge world falling at once. A tail of articulated iron thrashed behind it. Its eyes whirled and glowed like stressed afterburners, and they screamed as they looked upon the magi of the Cult of Nul. It made to move out of the summoning place, but the lightning held it back. The daemon breathed a wash of warp-tainted fire to consume Kolumbari-Enas, but that too was stopped against the barrier, and curled back at the daemon, causing it to recoil angrily.

'We have him! We have him!' Kolumbari-Enas shouted in triumph. 'He is trapped! Bind him! Bind him now!'

Though there were but a few of them left, the magi's song grew in volume and complexity, as if there were suddenly dozens of them chanting in chorus. The lightning fence whipped backwards and forwards, then crashed inwards, wrapping like living wire around the daemon, dragging down at it, forcing it back down to its knees. The ropes of lightning tightened further, biting into unreal metal and unreal flesh. The Mechanicum chant reached a crescendo, and the lightning blazed, and flared, knitting together to form brilliant manacles of electricity that burned into the being's wrists and ankles, where they became words of some extravagant script, words that flared brighter before sinking into daemonic flesh, becoming one with it, then dimmed, still visible, rotating about the limbs.

The daemon lifted its horned head. Smoke rose from its flanks. The smell of burned metal and rotten meat surrounded it. It looked from the magi to the Iron Warriors, assessing them all, but it made no move to strike. Its flaming eyes spun, shining wide beams onto the plaza, revealing hidden footprints with their hellish glare. The prints were everywhere, clawed feet of a hundred sizes, the traces of the Neverborn that had come to this world, all radiating from the very spot the daemon currently occupied, spreading out over the edge of the plaza and away through the factory.

Kraverek and his men got to their feet, and aimed their weapons at the monster.

'Magnificent,' the sorcerer whispered.

'Who dares to summon me?' the daemon said in a voice like a hundred engines idling. Hot sparks spewed from its mouth and bounced upon the floor. Furnace heat beat at Kraverek. ***'Who calls Vashtorr the Arkifane and dares to bind him?'***

Kolumbari-Enas screeched binharic songs of triumph. 'I dare! I dare to summon and bind you, I, Kolumbari-Enas, First-Among-Equals, Lord of the Disciples of Nul!' Kolumbari's mechadendrites spread themselves wide.

'It is good to know the names of those one shall kill.' The daemon attempted to rise. The letters branded into his flesh burned and dragged him down. Warp-formed muscles bulged under stolen purple corpse-skin. The Neverborn demigod strained but could not stand. He snarled. The machines working all through the forge growled with him.

Psephalas laughed.

'You are ours now,' Kraverek said. 'And you shall slay no one.'

'A Warsmith of Perturabo's Legion,' Vashtorr said, lading contempt on every word. ***'The bastard get of the Lord of Iron makes common cause with the exiles of Mars. Intriguing.'*** He sniffed at

Kraverek. His nose was little more than two triangular holes. When he blew out, his breath wavered with heat. The whirling-turbine eyes roved over the chosen. ***'You are all false. All half-bloods. Perturabo's seed is weak in you.'*** A chuckle rumbled deep inside him, the grumble of an engine reluctant to turn over. He shifted as far as he could so he could fix Kolumbari-Enas with his glare. The metaphysical bonds about his wrists and ankles bit, warning him from further movement. ***'How dare you summon me. How dare you attempt to impose your will upon I, Vashtorr the Arkifane.'***

With a titanic grunt of effort, the Arkifane stood. The metal around his hooves burned. The restraints blazed; arcane symbols flared into life then flickered. The fading footprints of the daemon horde seemed to jump into motion, as if fleeing Vashtorr's greater power. Scissored wings opened, then closed. He took a hard-won step forward, towards the magos. Yet Kolumbari-Enas remained where he was, his arms thrown out dramatically.

'You will halt!' he shouted, and his voice was overlaid by strains of burbling machine speech. 'I command you, I compel you, I who have bound you, by the laws of the machine and the warp. I who called you. I who brought you into this world of dust and ash and into a body of ancient design. Listen to me, and obey!'

Lightning cracked around Vashtorr's limbs. The daemon pulled on these bonds. He leaned forward, as if he would break free, and he pulled. The bonds held. He came no further. He tilted his horned head, making the fires in the grate of his mouth flare.

'Impressive,' Vashtorr said. ***'I have not been bound for thousands of years.'*** He examined the bonds that contained him, and clenched his fists. Sword-long talons rasped harshly upon one another. ***'Very well, I will listen to you. For what purpose did you bring me here? What boon do you seek? Tell me so we might make a bargain, and I may be back upon my own path. Who commands here, Warsmith? You, or the priest?'***

'You will listen to me, though our efforts are equal. You are bound by my gifts and the magos' art, therefore we both demand our price, as is our right. You are bound and must obey.'

Vashtorr laughed. Engines roaring. Hammers falling. ***'I am immortal. I may wait an aeon for my freedom. Time is nothing to me. I can sit here in this circle until the flesh falls from your bones and the priests' augmetics rust to nothing. Another will come and loose me. What do I care?'***

'And they shall know no fear' was just another of the False Emperor's lies. Kraverek had known loyalist and traitor Space Marines break and run from the likes of Vashtorr.

But he was not afraid.

'Time is a currency of value to all, even daemons. You care.'

'Then what do you want, son of iron?'

'What else is there of any worth, Lord Vashtorr, but power? Give us power, and you will be free.'

Vashtorr's eyes and mouth flared. He tugged at his bonds. Again, the lightning crackled, and the words they made danced and burned. He was becoming angry. *Good,* thought Kraverek. *He will make mistakes.*

'What form of power? Tell me, tell me now!'

'The Emperor's whelp Roboute Guilliman has crossed into Imperium Nihilus by way of the Attilan Gap. The route is unstable. Archmagos Belisarius Cawl has made machines derived from xeno-tech to hold open the way. I have been commanded by Abaddon himself to take and hold this passage.'

'Cawl?'

'You are not aware of him?'

'I am the lord of machines. Of course I am aware of him. Cawl is a great benefactor to me, in his way,' said Vashtorr. He swung his head around to look at each member of the group. ***'And what is the magos' price?'***

'Simple declarative. Knowledge,' said Kolumbari-Enas. 'The necron technology Cawl uses holds many secrets. I wish you to explain them to me.'

'You do not wish more?'

'Greater demands carry higher prices, is that not so, master of daemons?' Kraverek said. 'We have modest desires, easily accomplishable by you.'

'Then why do you not simply seize this gateway? The Despoiler did not provide you with greater support for this venture? What need of me do you have?'

'Abaddon is far away. War rages around Nachmund. I have my own armies. The Knights of the twin house of Gorlis-Nivon have pledged me their aid. I have my Iron Warriors. Other warbands hearken to me and will muster to us. Mastering men is an easy thing. What I require is a master of technology, one who can seize control of the archmagos' gate and pass control of it to me. Someone who can prevent its destruction. I want it intact. I cannot do this. Kolumbari-Enas cannot.'

'That is the price of my freedom?' The daemon leaned forward, so far Kraverek thought he would simply step through Kolumbari-Enas' warding, but the lightning bands pulled Vashtorr up short. ***'A star-road for you, the path to knowledge for him?'***

'Yes.'

'As you say, it is a simple task for one such as I. But my aid is not cheap. For a small tally of souls, these things can be accomplished. Let our reckoning commence. Let us set our prices.'

Under his helm, Kraverek smiled viciously. 'There is no reckoning. There is only service, daemon, you will learn that. Kolumbari-Enas, prepare Lord Vashtorr for transport to the ship. His accommodation is waiting. I trust you will not find it lacking, my lord.' Kraverek bowed to the daemon.

Vashtorr growled at this mockery. His fists clenched. Muscles bunched. Machinery whirred in the secret spaces of his body, and yet he could not move from within the circle.

'If you behave appropriately, I will release you,' Kraverek said. 'Until that day comes, you are ours. Do not forget it.'

CHAPTER THIRTEEN

THE EVENING WAR

Beta-Kalapus slunk from the sky, leaving the night to the Pit of Raukos.

Felix called down the rest of his small force from the *Lord of Vespator*. His total assets amounted to just over a demi-company of Space Marines, chief weapon of which was the heavy Repulsor tank *Martrinator*, a significant addition of power that the Wolfspear were glad to welcome. These extra brothers from half a dozen Chapters were deployed throughout the Wolfspear's positions, but Bjarni kept Felix and his bodyguard back. He had not offered Felix command, and Felix would have turned it down if he had. Felix's orders were to interdict daemons that broke through the cordons of Space Marines, though it was obvious Bjarni did not want the death of a tetrarch on his watch, and was trying to keep him out of the way.

So it was that Felix, the Chosen and *Martrinator* were a few hundred yards out from the battlefield near the edge of the triumphal ground. His Techmarines Troncus and Daelus crewed the tank, and the rest of the Chosen formed up on the tetrarch. Upon the wide martial field, there were seven predicted ingress points, each surrounded by squads of Space Marines and tall flood-lumen rigs that waited to be ignited.

'This is a strange place,' Cadmus said. He wore the black and yellow of the Scythes of the Emperor, but in the purple non-light of the Pit the differing liveries of Felix's men looked the same bruised shades of black and blue. 'Brother Gathein, any warning of when they might come?'

Gathein was Felix's sole psyker, an Epistolary of the Avenging Sons Chapter. He thought a moment before replying. 'They are already moving behind the veil of the world. I can feel them pressing against it.' He had an otherworldly air that had become more profound as the years had passed. Felix wondered if he were losing himself, as psykers sometimes did, to the relentless tug of the warp.

A bank of flood-lumens activated with a loud *crack*. A square of hard white light fell on the old parade ground like a blow. It was followed by others.

'The lights,' Sergeant Cominus said. 'Watch the lights, my brothers. They illuminate the areas of predicted manifestation.'

There were rings of powdered silver and salt around these places, prepared and sanctified by Rune Priests. Felix counted only three of these psykers, dotted around the vast triumphal square. He thought it not enough.

'It will begin soon. Protect the tetrarch,' Cominus commanded,

'Protect the tetrarch!' The others responded.

'For Vespator. For Ultramar. For the Imperium,' Cominus said.

'Vespator, Ultramar, Imperium!' the Chosen repeated.

Then they waited.

Hours passed. The Space Marines' vigilance never wavered. As the desert cooled, a soft wind began to blow, stirring banners and whispering in the apertures of armour and machines. Felix drifted into thought, working through the thousand problems of his realm. He had never wished for such power; he wasn't even sure if it was right that he, as a Space Marine, should hold it instead of a mortal. In his darker moments, he listened a little too much to the rumours about Cawl.

There had been one man, on the world of Ullantis VI. The Imperial governor. He had refused to hand over his power to Ultramar. Felix respected him for many reasons, including his defiance, but had been left no choice but to execute him, an act that sickened him still.

There were many acts he would rather not have taken, but this one remained with him not only because of what he had done, but because of what had been said.

'You're a puppet, made by a monster,' the man had said, as he had knelt to take Felix's sword blow. 'You don't know who your real master is.'

Cawl had made the Primaris Marines. They were impure. The Primaris were Cawl's creatures, or Guilliman's slaves – in either case, at any moment, they could turn on the Emperor. Such things were still said.

Sometimes, he feared it might be true.

Yet his personal opinions and occasional worries didn't alter the fact that he had been made tetrarch, and that he was responsible for billions of souls. He had been given this burden by the primarch himself, and he intended to uphold his duty come what may. If Cawl really did intend to seize power for himself, then he would deal with that when it happened.

The work of politics wearied him. He had hoped for respite, to burn off his frustrations in the red heat of war. As the night wore on, and the staring eye of the Pit rolled across the heavens, he anticipated disappointment.

The first sign of the Neverborn's arrival was a crackle of bolter fire upwind of Felix's position. A single burst that ended quickly. After that there was no more gunfire for a minute, long enough for Felix to think he might have imagined it in his desire for the simple problems of battle. Then another came, and this time, it was followed by more.

A force-wide message hit the vox-net: *'Contact.'*

Wolfspear command sent a tactical marker to Felix's sensorium, flagging the initial ingress half a mile away, at point three.

'Should we go to aid them?' Yansar spoke, Felix's Apothecary.

'Wait,' Cominus said, then, 'There. A second manifestation over ingress point two.'

A glowing, formless mass appeared ten feet above the ground just outside of the nearest pool of lumen light, twisting against itself like a living thing. Boiling outwards with a sudden, revolting energy, it burst like a skin of soap.

The enemy surged through into the materium. A wave of lesser daemonkind, each a hideous creation of mismatched body parts assembled by insane gods. They were so closely packed, so shrouded by the corposant roiling off them as they broke into reality, that at first they appeared to be a solid mat of flesh, of tentacles, glaring eyes, pincers, mouths and dripping orifices. Only when the Wolfspear turned their floodlight onto the daemons fully did they seem to split into individuals, and that might have been so. The warp obeyed no natural law.

More pale lights winked on all over the parade ground. The vox crackled. *'Contact! Contact! Contact!'*

Orders came from every side, shouted through vox-grilles, broadcast by vox-net, and the orders were all the same.

'Open fire!'

The noise of a bolt weapon is injurious by design. Hundreds firing en masse deafens, a clattering tumult of coughing reports.

Though they were far away, the volley made Felix's ears ring, forcing his armour's machine spirit to deaden his audio input.

Thereafter the night was divided into two. The first half comprised hard squares of lumen light and the horrors they lit pouring out of rifts of boiling purple vapours; the second was a chaos of muzzle flare, the phosphorescent candles of bolt motors, the quick flashes of exploding munitions. One half was a constant glare, the other a frenzied flicker, until flares pumped skyward from the Wolfspear's back positions, and everything turned ruby red.

'Do we engage?' Felix voxed. His Chosen were out of range, even *Martrinator* beyond the distance of acceptable accuracy. 'We can do nothing here.'

'Negative,' a voice responded. Felix could not be sure if it was Bjarni. The line was ripe with static, and the sender's signifier blurred and jumped uselessly across his helm view. *'Maintain position. Wait for breakthroughs.'*

'Understood.'

The turret of *Martrinator* turned, the servo-whine and even the thump of the tank's powerful grav engines drowned by the thunder of bolters. Felix had ordered the tank fitted for a counter-infantry role, and it bore an onslaught gatling cannon and front-mounted heavy bolters. The red helm and shoulders of Troncus came out of the turret above the primary armament, where he made the pintle-mounted assault cannon ready, working smoothly despite the awkwardness of the umbilical power feed connecting him to the machine. Troncus nodded to show he awaited Felix's order. He was silent as always. Troncus never spoke, because Troncus had burned out his tongue in a fit of shame many years ago.

Space Marines adjusted their positions to bracket the daemonic portals; most had opened some way off the predicted zones. Step by measured step, they made a wall of ceramite to block the daemons' way. Gravis-armoured squads bearing heavy bolt rifles and heavy bolters planted their feet. Mechanisms in their leg assemblies and weighted boots locked. Thus stabilised, their more powerful weapons reaped a heavy toll.

Most of the Wolfspear were equipped with bolters, the holy armaments of Space Marines, and ideal for annihilating such hordes.

Daemons were mown down by the score, by the hundred, their false flesh blasted to jelly. Black ichor and pulverised organs rained down around them. The Wolfspear closed their cordons around the ingress points, making wide circles of men a few hundred yards across, and the daemons ran heedlessly into the hail of bolts with no thought, no fear. To rip at hated reality was their sole and hideous desire.

The first fusillade ceased more or less simultaneously, the multiple squads having opened fire at the same time, thus needing to reload in unison. All around the battlefield, guns fell silent for crucial seconds.

Voices crowded the vox-net, accents from across time and space. They howled, they mixed Juvjk freely into their Gothic. How little they seemed like Primaris now.

'Reloading!'

'Reload!'

'Requesting bombardment, ingress seven!'

Felix cast his eyes that way. The rift was biggest there, a heaving cloud that reached high over the triumphal ground, sucking in all light beamed onto it. The lesser guns of the fort up on the hill spoke, targeting ingress point seven with precision guided missiles and pinpoint lasweaponry. In this close zone, the larger artillery was not used for fear of hitting friendly forces.

Ejected magazines hit ground. Firing by squad started up fitfully. Despite the Wolfspear's preference for close melee, not one unit charged.

'The tide of them is endless,' Bjarni had said before he and Felix parted ways earlier that evening. 'Only dawn halts it. Charge them, and you will be bogged down. This is not the kind of battle you can win by eliminating key enemy assets or by breaking their morale. It's a simple reaping. Gun them down. Keep them back. They will gain ground, they always do, and blade work comes all too soon, but the later they come within sword range, the better. Don't let your men charge. You'll only be swamped.'

Felix saw the truth of this. The foe surged across the slippery remains of their slain. There were more coming behind them, and doubtless behind them more still. By dint of the brief lull in fire, the daemons made it further into the materium, a scene that Felix saw repeated in snatched glimpses of helm feed and tactical overlays at every point of ingress. Ingress two was the worst. There, only a hundred yards separated the Space Marines and the daemons. Ingress four three hundred yards away was not much better.

Felix made a decision.

'Troncus, fire support, nearest ingress,' he commanded. The tank glided forward towards the rushing horde of daemons. 'Cominus, advance to ingress point four,' he said, indicating this nexus of manifestation upon the squad tactolith.

'The jarl bade us wait here.'

'Then he can take it up with me. I will not stand idly by while we may be of service.'

'My role is to guard you.'

'Do you see me as helpless?' Felix said. 'Gathein, time to bring your powers into play. Close that rift if you can.'

'As you command, tetrarch.'

'Ingress two, part your ranks,' Felix voxed. 'Fire support inbound from the third quadrant.'

Pale grey warriors moved aside, opening up a gap. Now Felix could see the daemons directly, shambling across the broken tiles of the triumphal ground.

'My lord, I would leave some men with–' Cominus began.

Any further objections from Cominus were rendered inaudible by *Martrinator*. The main gun whined up to speed, the noise of the motor of the assault cannon mounted atop it a lighter counterpoint, strings to brass in the orchestra of war. *Martrinator* continued to move forward, and all guns opened fire.

The passage of slugs turned the space before the barrels into a blur. Fire belched after them. Every fiftieth round was a tracer, but the gun fired so quickly it seemed the air was scored by solid lines.

Once again, daemons fell. The nearer *Martrinator* got, the more accurate it became, and soon it was cutting the daemons neatly in two by the swathe. The Repulsor put out so many bullets they might as well have been a solid blade played across the ranks.

The rest of the Chosen jogged away to support the Wolfspear at ingress three. Gathein prepared for witch combat as he ran, the fierce electric blue of warp power gathering around his clenched fists and the psychic hood that encased his helm.

Troncus ceased firing and let the pintle gun droop. The main cannon was out of ammunition. The Techmarine dropped from sight back into the tank to replace the exhausted magazines.

The tank had served its purpose. The Space Marines had time to reload, and once more bolters battered at the infinite tide of daemons.

But Felix's ambitions were larger than that.

Over at ingress four, Gathein unleashed his power. A bright hemisphere of light burned over the rift, slowly contracting. Daemons fell from it, deprived of their unlife, their link to the warp broken, their false bodies already disintegrating.

The dome collapsed with a clap of thunder Felix heard through his audio dampers. His tactolith briefly cleared, and he saw that the ingress was closed.

'Broaden circle. Fall back, one hundred yards.' That was identifiably Bjarni's voice. *'Maintain cordon at greater range.'*

A new position flashed on Felix's retinal display, safely out of the way.

The Space Marines withdrew squad by squad, covering each other. The Repulsor's powerful grav engines thumped and it drifted backwards, the sand jumping beneath it as if it bounced on the skin of a beaten drum. Felix joined it and jogged alongside. They came to a halt a hundred yards back from their initial deployment zone.

Of the seven plotted ingress points one was closed, but at the other six the daemons were expanding their beachhead on the shores of reality. Initially, the zones of manifestation had been a score of yards across. There was not one now that was less than fifty yards, and the strange eye-aching roiling of rifts swelled. More daemons required more bullets to slay, and the daemons were gaining ground.

Felix checked his chrono. The countdown to dawn stood at four hours, seven minutes. He had yet to fire a single shot himself.

His chance came soon enough, and he was glad of it.

It was to be the first of many nights of conflict.

CHAPTER FOURTEEN

THE CONDUIT

Solana accepted Cawl's invitation to join his mission without a flicker of fear. She suspected it would amuse him if she was afraid.

'You shall record our activities for posterity!' he declaimed. Though he seemed delighted by her acceptance, there was something unsavoury about his glee, a snub to the regent by putting his agent in danger. Not that Guilliman would mind or indeed care. The intelligence she would gather would more than outweigh the inconvenience of her loss.

There were only three others in the party heading to the war world: Alpha Primus, Qvo-89, and of course Belisarius Cawl himself.

'There's to be no more of us than we four,' Cawl further explained. 'The temporal conduit might take it, but the localised field we shall employ on the surface won't be able to cope. Furthermore, the more of us there are on the surface, the more chance there will be of exciting the necron war world into action should anything go wrong with our adjustments to the temporal flow. Not,' he added quickly, 'that anything will.'

Solana recorded the pre-mission briefing fastidiously. There had been a lot of disagreement from his advisors, but Cawl insisted that he go to the war world with a minimal party. Her attendant cyber-familiars were to remain on board. Cawl had advised against bringing them along.

'Such things are easily subordinated, if we happen to encounter any active necrons,' he'd said. 'Control of the machine is in their nature.'

The meeting had been a good time to make an assessment of Cawl's military strength, and she noted her thoughts via vox-thief immediately afterwards.

'Though the Archmagos Cawl pared back his own entourage substantially when departing Fleet Primus four relative years ago, he maintains forces equal to a demi-macroclade of troops,' she dictated. The military side of things was of middling importance to her report, but she would omit nothing; indeed, she intended to compile more detailed assessments later. 'This amounts to just under three full Martian cohorts of fighting strength under the command of Marshal Melissima Artos-Septus Iota. Addendum – I ascertained these facts simply by asking, and although Cawl's strategos could have lied to me, I don't think that is the case. They provided their information freely. The archmagos and his servants have so far been open to me and my investigations, almost brazenly so. I feel he wishes to make a point to the lord regent. Further addendum – I will of course verify this if I have the opportunity' – by which she meant if she did not die – 'by clandestine investigation if necessary.'

She paused her vox-thief at that point, to think through what she would say next.

'According to the figures provided, Cawl's assets include skitarii of around three thousand in total number, a single lance of House Taranis Knights led by Scion Magnus Baron Roosev Maven Taranis, Cybernetica maniples of various automata types, around four hundred in number, and sundry other followers.' She paused again. 'This is a strange ship. A great many of Cawl's disciples, and I use that word with care, are eccentric. All of them are fanatically loyal to Cawl's way of doing things. According to the tenets of the Cult, many of them are borderline hereteks.'

This was Mars' opinion. Guilliman preferred less hidebound magi.

She noted that her report of Cawl's military didn't take into account the forces of Tigrus and Accatran present in the fleet. She thought they'd disperse once his mission was done.

All that was the day before. Today might be her last day, the day she was going with Cawl. She and the others occupied a ship specially built for this endeavour. It was oddly fashioned, perhaps not of human make. The total length was little over thirty yards. It was equipped with a compact reactor and engine array she doubted were powerful enough to move it, but which Qvo had assured her exceeded the output of similar units by a factor of twenty. Most unusual was the ship's hull, a complex arrangement of uneven triangles. Nobody stopped her from taking images of it, but when she asked what they were for, Cawl had declaimed energetically, 'To deflect any ripples in time!' He might have been joking. It was hard to tell. She found Cawl's irreverence aggravating.

So there she was, strapped into an acceleration couch on an experimental craft with two half-human chimeras and a servitor-magos of questionable provenance. Her life, she reflected, had taken a strange path. She made sure to go armed, carrying her laspistol and power sword, gifts made to the Founding Four by the primarch, though she eschewed armour. It always made her feel constricted.

Eremenitas remained on the *Zar Quaesitor* with orders to report back to Guilliman in the event of her death. He had not protested about being left behind.

The craft was controlled from a small podium, which Cawl was plugged into. He was not wearing his war-rig, to her surprise. Instead he carried a range of instruments on a number of additional limbs. He sang a complex melody of extremely ancient form in a chorus of voices while poking at the instrument panels ranged in a semicircle in front of him.

'What if you fail, archmagos?' she asked, surprising herself. 'The ark will be leaderless. Your research shall cease.'

'What?' Cawl broke part of his voice out of his multi-part harmony. He stared at her in frank amazement. 'I'll make it back! You don't think I'd invite you on any sort of adventure where death was a certainty?'

'I've been on too many missions to take a promise like that with any kind of seriousness,' she said.

'Are you nervous, historitor majoris?'

'No,' she said, though maybe she really was. 'I've lost count of how many times I've nearly died.'

'Dangerous, then, being Guilliman's scribe.'

'I'm not a scribe. Ledgers don't shoot back.'

Cawl laughed. 'Do you hear that, Friedisch? What spirit!'

'I am not Friedisch,' said Qvo, though quietly, as if it were something he said out of habit.

'No matter,' Cawl said. 'Even if I do die, which I won't, and neither will you, come to that, various elements of my personalities and all of my knowledge have been preserved aboard the *Zar Quaesitor* and elsewhere. What I know will not be lost.'

Solana's steel-tipped fingers scratched over parchment.

'Do you mean you will be reconstituted, like your friend here?'

'I am his friend,' agreed Qvo-89.

'Omnissiah alive, no!' said Cawl. 'Because that would be dangerously close to creating an abominable intelligence, so detailed and wide-ranging the records of my engrams are, and we all know I would never do anything like that.' He tipped her a wink over his mandibular shield, then he went back to his work and his humming. 'We'll be ready to depart soon. If you want to make picts, get ready, because they're firing up the conduit emitter... now! Look!'

Cawl caused a tri-d display to bloom in the transit bay which showed the photonic dispersal network. A second display showed the manufactorum housing the frame modulator, a third the ship exterior, another the flotilla, another the Scorean Singularity, and more, too many views to take in.

'It's a lot, I grant you. If you wish to zoom in on any particular view, be my guest. I have granted you full access to the hololithic suite and ship sensorium, and of course vid-cast will be made available to you upon our return.'

It was true. He had given access. Two small windows opened in her mind's eye where an expectant cursor pulsed. That was disturbing. How had he done that?

Solana opened her mouth to protest. She got as far as lightly inhaling, but he answered her question before she had finished formulating it. She had noticed he did that a lot.

'It wasn't hard to break your memcore protocols, so I've done you the service of an upgrade. Access to the ship sensorium includes uninterrupted inloads for your data-savant, that cheerful Eremenitas, so he may make records in duplication of your own.'

'Then–'

'You're welcome!' Cawl crowed, then added that part of his voice back into his song.

Deciding complaining would do no good, Solana selected the views of the black hole, the frame stabiliser, and the photon dispersal devices. She watched as the long, bulbous emitter deployed, swinging out of the open manufactorum bay into the void. As soon as it crossed the threshold and the nose was into space, the top portion slowly extended. Lights in the hangar went from standard illumination to the bloody glow of ready lights.

'We'll take off as soon as the emitter activates,' he said. 'We can't afford to hang around, you see. It will burn out eventually. The power draw is immense! The reactor of the *Zar Quaesitor* should be up to it, but it's a close thing.'

Five minutes passed. By then, the emitter was fully extended. Solana noted the speed with which it was made ready. She'd expected hours and hours of prayer.

'How long will the tunnel last?' Qvo asked.

'I don't know exactly,' said Cawl. 'But long enough. Aha! Here we go. It'll be firing up in four, three, two…'

Under the landing claws of the strange explorator ship, the Ark Mechanicus shook.

'One!'

The frame stabiliser looked like a bizarre cannon, but when it was activated it emitted nothing Solana could see. The effect on the singularity was instantaneous. There was a light so bright that even through the hololith it would have blinded non-augmented eyes. A line of boiling energy flashed back up the track of the frame stabiliser conduit towards the *Zar Quaesitor*. On the pict-feed from the photonic dispersal network came more flashes, a strobing round and round the four units, then the spear of light hurtling towards the Ark Mechanicus split into four and was vented spectacularly into the void.

'Impossible to make any detail out of that at normal speed, but even so, spectacular, wasn't it? And went off without a hitch, I am happy to say! I am sure you will revise and review your recordings at chrono-arrestation, no?'

'Yes, naturally,' Solana said.

'Jolly good. Now everyone hold on tight, we're going in!'

Cawl slammed the ship forward with no concession to the weaknesses of the flesh. Solana was slung back into her acceleration couch.

Even under the pressure of gravitic force, Solana continued to record. She saw indicator lumens switch colour on the end of the emitter, and a cowl recede from the tip, and a triple pulse of energy, this time on the visible spectrum. A second conduit punched down the first. Hyper-plasma emptied from it in an extravagant billow, making Solana's vox-feed buzz, then stopped. Cawl brought up a prow view as he pushed his strange little craft into a sickening dive towards the very end of the frame stabiliser, followed by a sudden pulling up that left Solana's viscera miles behind.

With the skill of a fighter ace, Cawl slotted the ship into the narrower, inner conduit. There was a little bump. He gave out a peculiar titter.

'Is he laughing?' Solana asked, forcing her g-smoothed features to work.

'Oh yes,' said Qvo.

They sped down the conduit leading to the surface of the war world, though that was still so distant it was not yet visible. The hololiths showed the four-way split of the photonic stream, each arm venting with such brilliance it would be visible for light years around. In the centre of the split was a small round aperture, exactly like a tunnel.

'You will have seen that the reactor unit and engine stack of this craft appears rather small,' said Cawl. 'Appearances are deceptive! Let us see what this construct can do.'

They arrived much quicker at the venting array than before, and the ship arrowed into the tunnel in space and time.

Solana felt the weight of a small moon crush against her lungs, preventing her from breathing. She called up an internal display that showed an alarming drop in her blood oxygen. A soft greyness settled itself on her vision.

Is... Is Cawl whooping? she thought. Then she passed out.

CHAPTER FIFTEEN

WAR WORLD

'Historitor? Historitor Majoris Solana?'

A hand softly slapped Solana's cheek. There was a delicate snapping. When the sharp reek of ammonia assaulted her nostrils, Solana spluttered her way back to consciousness.

Someone had undone her restraints and laid her on the cabin floor. Cawl was looking down at her.

'Ah, there she is!' Cawl said, and tossed aside a small aluminium vial of smelling salts. 'We've stopped accelerating. You should be fine now.' He looked her over quizzically. Solana felt the invasive tickle of a deep augur scan. 'I should have taken into account how lightly augmented you are. That must have been quite difficult for you. My apologies. I'll make sure we have a smoother ride back. In the meantime, come and look at this!'

Cawl grabbed her forearm firmly but gently, tugged her up to her feet then towards the front of the cockpit. A large hololithic display filled the space all the way across and nearly down to the floor, creating the illusion that there was no front to the vessel.

The display showed a tube of dappled, syrupy light that raced by at the fastest speed there was in the material realm, only it appeared to do so unhurriedly, giving Solana the impression they were floating down a brook made of shining gold. She realised she should be recording all this. She initiated a cerebral purge to clear the after-effects of unconsciousness. A moment of disassociation, then she felt more like herself. She reactivated her recording devices.

'Beautiful, isn't it?' said Cawl. 'It's not often I say this, but this is very good work. I could not have achieved it myself. Temporal engineering is not within my skillset. Unusual for me.'

'He really doesn't say that very often,' said Qvo. 'I would enjoy this rare realisation of his limitations.'

'Hush now, Friedisch,' said Cawl. 'You're spoiling my moment of modesty.'

At the back, Primus sighed.

The photonic stream ran weirdly up the frame shift tunnel, strand of light over light, looping and curling in endless repeating patterns.

'Look at it!' said Cawl in a tone of hushed awe. 'It is the cursive of the Machine God Himself made visible as He writes His will upon the universe!'

The light flowed slower as they got closer to their destination. A soft glare was all Solana could see at the end, but there was a hint of the velvety singularity behind the photonic ring. To Solana it looked like a sun with a void at its heart. The ring was bright enough to drown what glimmer of starlight might have been visible beyond, so there was only the blackness and the light, the former trying to consume the latter, the latter forever trying to escape.

'An amazing phenomenon,' said Cawl. 'Fantastical. Awe-inspiring.'

'It is very pretty,' said Qvo. His face was slack again.

Cawl didn't mind that. 'Pretty it is!' he said with bombastic enthusiasm. 'Think, Solana of Mars, did you consider you would find yourself on such an excursion when our dear friend Roboute sent you to spy on me?'

The return of this accusation, even couched in friendly words, annoyed her.

'I'm not here to spy on you. We've already discussed this. I'm here to record your success.'

'Success? Success!' Cawl chuckled. 'Oh, you've done your research on me, have you not? Flattery is a good way to my heart, at least in this personality configuration. I've worn it so long, I suppose I'm giving my enemies ample opportunity to understand me. Perhaps it's time for a change?'

'The primarch is not your enemy,' said Solana. 'Neither am I.'

'Did I say either of you were?' said Cawl mildly. 'Let us not mince our words, my dear, you are here to spy on me. That is true. Do not deny it.'

'Please, as a courtesy, do not question my motives again.'

'If you will,' said Cawl. 'Either way, I assure you I have nothing to hide.' An instrument gave out a double *bip-bip* a little like a heartbeat. Cawl scrutinised it. 'Aha! We should be able to see our destination now. If I adjust this...' He selected an area of the hololith and expanded it. At the centre was a silvery dot, flickering with the reflected light of the photonic disc. 'There it is! It's quite clear, isn't it?' said Cawl. 'See that dark smudge around it?'

'Magnetic deflection of the photonic stream,' said Solana, and noted that down.

'Yes! That means it retains a magnetosphere. A strong one.'

'Could be artificial,' said Qvo. He pottered up to look into the display, blinking owlishly.

'Could be, could be,' said Cawl. 'I doubt we'll find out while we're there. We won't be able to take wide-ranging measurements owing to the small area our relative temporal frame will occupy. A pity really, but one must remain focused on the task in hand and not bemoan what we cannot discover, no? We must be of good heart. I doubt any human being has achieved such a close approach to a singularity since the days of the first stellar empires, if indeed it was ever accomplished. We may even be pioneers. Think on that!'

Solana's stomach roiled. She stifled a burp. She still was not operating at one hundred per cent efficacy.

'That's the temporal shift you're feeling,' Cawl explained. 'Even with the frame stabilisation in effect, the pull of the singularity cannot be entirely mitigated. When we emerge from our expedition, several weeks will have passed.'

'How long do you intend to be on the surface?'

'Hours, at most,' said Cawl. 'That's how long the stabiliser will function for before it burns out.'

'You said you didn't know.'

'I don't. Not exactly, which is why haste is required.'

'It could collapse at any time,' Qvo added. 'Trapping us forever.'

'Not helpful, Friedisch. But it won't, I assure you.'

Solana was now feeling quite ill. Cawl spared her a sympathetic look.

'The nausea will pass once we land and we are no longer moving along an axis of diminishing temporal flow. A shift in time is not felt by the organism that cloaks our spiritual essence alone. It is felt in the soul.'

Primus left his private reflections and joined them. He grabbed a handle in the ceiling and hung from it, weighty as a cliff on the verge of collapse.

'Master, expand the war world,' he said. 'Compensate for the photonic stream. Scry beyond the conduit, if you can.'

'A tricky proposition, but of course I'll try, my boy,' said Cawl. 'What do you see?'

The image shifted.

'Ships.' Primus pointed at glints within the dark line around the trapped planet. 'There is a void battle in progress.'

'So there is,' said Cawl. He canted brief instructions at his instruments. The picture shifted closer, showing dozens of craft engaged in combat, though all still, frozen in time. They got an impression of the vessels only. They were not clear. Through the walls of the tunnel, the voidships appeared as if viewed through thick, impure glass.

'Some of those are definitely necron. But those others, what are they?' asked Qvo. 'Aeldari?'

'They do have a similar look,' said Cawl.

'If they are, they match no record of the vessels the xenos currently use,' said Primus. His eyes moved over the hololith.

'You're looking for vessels that we might have freed, aren't you?' said Solana.

Primus nodded, leaned forward, then stood up to his full, intimidating height. 'I do not see any. We have been fortunate. The conduit passes between.'

'Just another reason I kept it so narrow,' said Cawl airily.

'There must be something I do not comprehend, Prime Conduit,' Solana said.

'And what is that?' asked Cawl.

'Firstly, how can we see the ships? Surely the photons carrying that visual record are moving so slowly they would struggle to reach our eyes, and this frame shift tunnel will have displaced whatever of them were moving freely in this space. The others will not have had time to catch up. You have broken the chain of vision. We should see only blackness.'

'There are mathematics I can show you when we return, if you like.'

'I would like that, although that is not what concerns me most.'

'Then what does?'

'If the conduit hits the surface of the planet, will there not be a catastrophic differential between our run of time relative to that of the planet? I mean, to all intents, time is frozen there. We will be intruding with a time frame running at speeds that will be functionally infinitely faster.'

A look of respect fell across Cawl's features. 'They really shouldn't have marked you out for servitorisation. What a waste of a good mind. You are correct. The planet would be ripped to tiny atomic pieces, and join the thundering progress of the photonic ring around the singularity. This is another thing I could not have avoided myself without help. Pay attention now – for Belisarius Cawl to admit the need for aid is unusual, but twice in one day is unheard of.'

'That's not much of an answer.'

'Tsk!' said Cawl. 'The answer is there.' He jabbed a mechadendrite to his left, at a stasis casket about the size of an ammunition box, small enough that Solana hadn't noticed it before. 'I said we required a secondary temporal field, did I not? A localised one, so we can leave this frame shift tunnel and go about the surface in safety?'

'You did.'

'Well it's in that box. We'll activate it before landing, so there should be no real interaction with anything too massy. In fact, we're approaching. Time to wake her up! Primus?'

'Her?'

Primus reached for the box. He was big enough to get it without taking a step. He unhooked it from the wall, and opened it.

'Show the historitor, would you?'

Primus tilted the open box towards Solana.

Her eyes widened. Inside was the head of a necron. Wires were plugged into the base of the neck and into holes drilled into the skull.

'A necron?' she said. 'This is your device?'

'Solana of Mars, may I introduce AsanethAyu? She wasn't very cooperative at first, so I had to make some modifications to her neural networks. Oh, and, er, cut her head off. She should do what we say now, won't you?'

The necron's eyes filled with a cold green light. 'I despise you,' she said. Hatred dripped from every word.

'I know, because you keep trying to kill me, but that's all fine,' said Cawl, 'You'll do what I say. AsanethAyu is a cryptek, a necron technomancer, a chronomancer, to be precise,' he explained. 'She knows exactly how to manipulate time on a precise local level so that none of us will be rendered into subatomic energy smears. She's just a head, because she has a tendency to misbehave, but she has access to all her powers. I've incorporated her xeno devices into her case, with a few modifications of my own, naturally.' He tapped the box with a metal claw.

'You know nothing of our sciences. You are an animal,' AsanethAyu said.

'I disagree,' said Cawl. 'I know plenty.'

'But that's madness,' said Solana. 'She could kill us all.'

'Only if she wanted to die herself. She'd be left there, alone, for all time. Have you ever encountered a suicidal necron? There's something about selling your soul for an eternal existence in steel that implies a certain will to live, don't you think? Now, please begin the operations we discussed, chronomancer.'

'I hate you,' the cryptek said. Her vocal apparatus had to be malfunctioning, her voice was so distorted. A probable side effect of decapitation.

'You already said that,' Cawl said. 'Begin your work. We're about to land.' He spoke aside to Solana. 'I suppose we'll find out whether or not she's got a death wish in a moment.'

The photonic tunnel opened as they passed into the planet's magnetosphere, and the ship pierced churning walls of hyper-energised atoms. The planet showed itself to be entirely skinned in metal, its features not formed by geology but by construction. Cawl's group was still in its tube of slowed time, and therefore could only see the part of the world that was directly in front of them clearly, but even the small area revealed by the tunnel mouth was impressive, full of gridded cities grouped into blocky mountain ranges, lone pyramids scraping the void, canyon-sized troughs cut mercilessly into the crust.

Through the walls of the tunnel the motionless spacecraft warped and shifted, their true natures tantalisingly close but forever obscured. Beams of las and deadly particles as solid as charcoal lines scratched on paper criss-crossed the void and the world's blurred surface. Explosions trapped at the moment of detonation appeared as fiery bouquets.

'This is eerie,' said Qvo.

'I think it splendid!' said Cawl. 'About now, if you would, chronomancer.'

'Very well, ape.'

AsanethAyu's eyes flickered rapidly. Again Solana felt time tug at something deep inside her, some unknown sense, always there, only now consciously experienced.

'It is done, primitive,' the necron said. 'You may exit your crude temporal conduit and land without fear of ending your miserable existence.'

'Or yours,' Cawl reminded her.

'Be careful,' said Primus, appraising everything with a cautious eye. Solana got the impression he'd rather not be there.

'Don't worry, my boy! We'll soon find out if I've been careful enough, won't we?' said Cawl. 'Stand by for landing. I have no idea how it is going to feel when we touch down and the various streams of time intersect over solid matter.' He smirked over his shoulder at Solana. 'It'll be fun finding out, won't it?'

Another shift in the guts, this one the entirely ordinary pull of gravity and deceleration. Jets fired. The feeling intensified.

'Steady as she goes,' said Cawl.

The surface of the planet rushed at them, the mountainous buildings splitting fractally into buildings that were smaller replicas of themselves, giving rough texture where smoothness had before reigned. It was altogether vertiginous.

She felt the touch of a metal hand on her arm.

'Don't worry,' said Qvo quietly. 'Belisarius will get you home.'

She looked sideways. Primus met her eyes, and cocked a sceptical eyebrow.

CHAPTER SIXTEEN

THE WAR IN HEAVEN

The ship's ramp hit the metal skin of the necron world. Cawl went out first with eager swiftness, then Qvo much more slowly, peering round and about. When he finally set a ginger foot upon the world, Solana followed, her attention fixed on the boxed head swinging from Cawl's hand. Primus came close behind, mag-locking his helm to his left thigh as he did so.

The first thing Solana noticed was a stillness of a kind that was impossible to describe. Quiet so profound it was the antithesis of sound, eating each noise with malevolent precision. She supposed it was because their area of movement was restricted to a space forty feet across. All around them were walls of stopped time as thick and impenetrable as primitive glass. It had an arresting beauty, a thickening of air that allowed the light of distant explosions and weapons discharge through as dappled light. Distorted buildings and signs of frozen battle were visible on the other side of the temporal wall, but the further away they were the less clear they became, until everything was a jellied smear.

She approached the wall, and tentatively reached a hand out.

'Do not touch the fascia temporalis!' Cawl warned.

Primus stopped her arm. His fist engulfed her from wrist to elbow.

'Listen to the archmagos,' he said.

Bits of the world beyond the fascia temporalis vanished into patches of infinite black, and the motion produced a strange flickering in her vision. It only applied to what she saw outside – when she held up her hand and waved it in front of her, she did not experience the same smearing effect.

'I still don't understand how I can see,' she said.

'It is fascinating!' said Cawl. 'Watch this!' A boxy lumen mounted on his left shoulder snapped on. Where the beam of light hit the wall of stilled time it stopped, and spread in a peculiar, thick slick that left a bright smear when Cawl panned it around. 'The science of the necrons never ceases to amaze me. I think once I have dealt with this pylon problem, I shall focus my attentions on their manipulation of temporal energies.'

'Barbarian,' AsanethAyu's head said. 'You will never understand.'

'Now now,' said Cawl. He tapped the metal surface of the ground with a sickle-shaped foot drilled through with holes to lighten the metal. The sound produced was lacking in vitality, like the tolling of a muffled bell. He leaned over and peered down. A midi-scaled beetle drone brushed at everything with hair-fine sensors, scurrying before him so hectically it threatened to tangle up the archmagos' front motivators with its power tether. 'It really is intriguing.'

'What is?' asked Qvo absently.

'This,' said Cawl, tapping the ground again. 'The atomic activity in the area around us has almost entirely ceased, as one would expect from a time-locked locale. However, as you can see, we are moving around quite freely.'

'This is what you asked me to do, therefore I am doing it,' said the head indignantly.

'I know!' said Cawl in delight. 'It doesn't mean it's not amazing to witness. You really must tell me how.'

'Never,' said AsanethAyu. 'If you wish to survive, you should move on. I can maintain a temporal bubble of this nature under these circumstances only for a limited amount of time. After that...'

'What does that mean?' said Qvo nervously. Despite his periods of vagueness, he seemed to possess an instinct for self-preservation.

'Don't listen to her,' Cawl said absently. After a moment's thought he pointed to a large pyramid whose steep sides and lofty top wavered through the time wall. 'This way. I think.'

They moved quickly, driven on by the acid goad of AsanethAyu's voice when Cawl stopped to examine this or that thing. Items that attracted his attention were inscriptions, machines, channels where the lurid green of necron power flows had come to an icy halt, though it was the body that intrigued him most.

The alien was dead, that was certain, and so they did not avoid him. In fact, Cawl made a beeline right for the corpse, so the small box of regular time slipped over it. Cawl bent down, and examined the body with a jovial inquisitiveness.

'Aeldari, has to be – look at his armour! How magnificent.'

The creature was face down. Solana was no expert in this breed of xenos, but his armour was unlike any in the records. His gun lacked the long acceleration cowling common to shuriken weapons, making it appear oddly truncated. In place of the cowl, the end of the weapon sported grav-acceleration arms that resembled the bow on a back-world crossbow.

'See, impulsion is provided by this exposed gravity sling here. Not concealed like in contemporary weaponry,' said Cawl, tapping at it. 'And if I'm not mistaken...' Cawl bent, hooked a number of mechadendrites under the alien corpse and turned it over. 'Now,' he said, standing tall and addressing Solana like a scholam master. 'What don't you see?'

Solana had a good look at him. His thin alien blood stained the cream wraithbone wargear he wore. His skin was waxy with exsanguination. It looked like he had died recently, slain by a blade that had cut deep into his abdomen, exposing the purple of his inhuman innards. Hexagonal links of mesh under-armour had been driven into the meat, and the wraithbone plating over them that bore the tell-tale, chewed-up signs of molecular disintegration.

'Come on, what's missing?' Cawl prompted.

It took a moment for her to notice there was no gem on its chest.

'There... there's no jewel,' she said.

'Exactly!' said Cawl. 'Nothing to catch this creature's soul when it died.'

'That's what they're for?'

'It is,' said Cawl.

'Aeldari raiders do not wear them.'

'Does this look like a Commorrite to you? Commorrites are the ones that raid and enslave,' Cawl explained. 'There are many aeldari nations.'

Solana gave the dead alien another look. 'It does not look like a member of any aeldari faction I have ever seen.'

'No. Not at all,' Cawl said. 'The War in Heaven, right here, right in front of me...' His voice quietened in thought. 'We are witness to one of those battles.' He ground his teeth, the noise picked up by the vox-thief in his mandibular implant. 'So much I could learn here! So much to see.'

'Well you can't see it,' said AsanethAyu. 'I can extend this field only so far and for so long. If we pass over any living sentient creature, the results will be most unpleasant for us all.'

'You know of this war?'

'Of course,' said the chronomancer. 'I fought in it.'

'Then fine. Maybe if you tell me about it I'll give you your limbs back. Onwards!' Cawl boomed.

Signs of conflict grew more prevalent. First the explosions and bright tracks of weapons came closer, then before they knew it they were picking their way around knots of embattled figures. By some means, the chronomancer was able to flex the temporal field she projected, avoiding incorporating the ancient combatants into the explorators' bubble, which obviously frustrated Cawl. A more guarded person might have hidden that, but he did not. Only once did they brush the past, the time field passing over the arm of a necron warrior that had been hit in the chest. It was so close that even through the warping effect of the time field Solana could see the eight monomolecular discs studding its body, and more hanging motionless in the air, ready to strike, and the sparks fountaining from its cracked thoracic casing frozen in place. When the trailing edge of the time field accidentally incorporated the necron's arm, flung back as it fell, the fingers opened suddenly, and Qvo squeaked in surprise. Primus moved towards the threat, but the arm was severed by the difference in time streams, and began to fall. They moved on before it hit the ground. When Solana looked back the hand was still falling, and would do so forever.

'Be careful,' Primus said to the head in the box.

AsanethAyu didn't crow for a while after that.

Cawl's group approached the gate of the pyramid. There was an energy shield protecting the entrance, but this gave out with a huge noise when AsanethAyu's temporal field connected with it. Cawl gave out a delighted yelp that did nothing for Solana's nerves.

Beyond the threshold a dark hall stretched away. In defiance of the laws of physics it looked longer than the size of the pyramid would allow. As much as Solana knew of the necrons, that was entirely possible. Orbs of dull green light floated overhead, and she guessed that the hall was dark only because they had stepped inside between the frequency pulses of the devices' lighting cycles.

'Frozen on the down cycle,' said Cawl, as if guessing what she was thinking. 'I have had some strange experiences in my time, but this is absolutely fascinating. Perhaps I should journey to Accatran and study at their fane chronalis when I have a little time. What do you think, Friedisch?'

'I think you meddling with time in any form would be a terrible idea,' said Qvo-89. His voice was now clever, and rich with subtextual tone.

Cawl smiled widely at Solana. 'You know, he really is the best Qvo yet. I think I'm nearly there.' He dropped his voice to a theatrical whisper. 'In bringing Friedisch back, I mean.'

Solana gave a tight smile in return, while adding a few additional tech heresies to her mental tally of Cawl's transgressions.

'He is sometimes vague and sometimes almost human,' Solana said. She kept an eye on Qvo. He didn't notice he was being talked about.

'That's why I think I'm nearly there. The vagueness is annoying – it's come on only recently in fact – but when he is more human, he *is* human. So very nearly there.'

A few hundred yards into the hall a series of arched gateways set into the walls began. They were big beyond any practical necessity, and nightmarishly disproportionate, twenty yards wide yet over a hundred tall.

'Now, to the datacore,' said Cawl. 'Necron predictability aids us here. Their technology at its height became heavily templated, a little like the STC systems of our own ancestors–'

'The best of your technology cannot match the worst of ours,' AsanethAyu's head said sulkily.

'Don't talk to me about superiority. Who has their head in a box? Not I,' Cawl responded, then continued his unfinished point. 'Which means, that although their various nations had an idiosyncratic approach to architecture, albeit defined overall by their species idiom, their datacentres, power cores and so forth are often relatively easy to find. A good fellow called Camalin Hiax 43-Tau-Omicron did a great deal to increase my knowledge base of necron architectural forms. He would have been useful here...' One thought trailed off, and another took its place. 'I wonder if this progression towards homogenisation is a common feature of advanced technological societies? I should look into it.'

The party slowed to a halt. 'Which way is it?' Solana asked. There were hundreds of the giant doors.

'Oh yes. That.' Cawl rummaged beneath his robes. Something clicked. A mechanical arm nosed its way out from under his garments, unfolded sleepily, and pointed a shallow dish forward. It swept back and forth once, a ring of lights around the dish rim blinking furiously, increasing in tempo as it homed in on the right passage. When the lights were a solid band, the dish went *bing* and retracted. 'It's that way,' Cawl said in a tone of utmost confidence, and led them to a gateway that looked just like all the others.

CHAPTER SEVENTEEN

THE WORLD ENGINE

The tunnel Cawl led them into was so dark that were it not for her augmetics' light amplification Solana would have been completely blind. Tiny lumens on the party's equipment gave out just enough light to provide her with a flat, monochrome view, though her perceptual filters turned themselves up so high they became too bright to look at. Primus trod patiently beside her, reining in his stride to match her pace. In her enhanced vision, his eyes shone silver like those of a hunting cat. From the huge gate the passage narrowed quickly to twenty feet wide and the ceiling dropped until it was low enough for Primus to reach up and touch. The material throughout was the uncompromising slickness of polished noctilith. The black floor was almost impossible to see, giving the illusion that it wasn't there at all, and Solana felt as if she was floating on nothing. The illusion grew more powerful when the tunnel turned unexpectedly steep, and she slipped, steadying herself on Primus' rock-like arm.

'Watch your footing here, it gets perilous!' Cawl said. 'Be

thankful this complex follows the principles of necron monumental construction. The Pharos on Sotha was another thing altogether, very dangerous ground, wasn't it, Friedisch?'

'I don't know,' said Qvo. 'That wasn't me. I wasn't there.'

'It was *a* you,' insisted Cawl.

'All I recall from my predecessor's memory is a lot of little holes,' said Qvo.

'There were certainly plenty of them,' said Cawl.

'And tubes,' said Qvo. 'I remember tubes.'

On the war world they didn't see a curve in the place. Everything ended in hard angles sharp enough to cut flesh.

'Aha! Look sharp there, Primus,' Cawl warned. 'Constructs ahead.'

An insect-like machine caught in mid-flight passed through the fascia temporalis and came to frantic life. Primus reached up and swatted it from the air with the palm of his hand, then stamped on it until it was a mangled pile of electronics and alien alloys.

'That will be the first of many,' said Cawl. 'Maybe you should go ahead, my boy.'

Primus made a noise of affirmation, and pushed his way to the front. Solana drew closer to Qvo, and they proceeded.

Soon, similar machines thronged the air below the ceiling. They differed in form, but all were small, none of them being larger than an Imperial cyber-cherub. In the dark, they were only visible through the fascia temporalis immediately before the time bubble engulfed them, whereupon they came to life. Each was dealt with by Primus, who smashed them with his hands where he could; where he could not, he spared only a single shot for each. The reports of his bolt pistol were heavy and flat, making Solana's ears hurt. It was curious, she noted, that he carried a bolt pistol and a chainsword rather than more powerful weapons.

'This passageway is designed for the lowest of forms,' Cawl said. 'A maintenance conduit, that's all.' By now the corridor was so precipitous they were moving slowly. He flashed a stablight mounted on his back at the steepening ground, making Solana's augmetics blaze and blind her. 'I suppose they only expected contra-grav-equipped constructs to come this way.'

'Are we going the right way?' Qvo said.

'Of course we are! In fact, I think my observation rather proves it. This is a maintenance access corridor for the world core, I'm sure of it, and– Stop!' Cawl shouted.

'What is it, master?' Primus asked.

'No need for worry, just be careful,' Cawl said. 'We don't want anyone blundering into that.' He pointed past Primus to a point several yards ahead. He left his stablight on, so Solana turned down her light-gathering function, and colour seeped back into the world.

'What is it?' she asked. The hulking Space Marine and Cawl's enormously augmented body blocked her view.

'A big drop,' said Qvo. 'See.' He shuffled aside.

The corridor bent down into a vertical shaft. Ahead was a solid wall. 'We can't go on any further forward. A moment.' Cawl performed a quick scan with his sensor dish. 'It's definitely down there. Primus, if you could aid the historitor majoris. Do you have access to the immaterium?'

'Yes.' Primus closed his eyes a moment then took a long breath in. 'The warp is close.'

'Even here, with the noctilith? Peculiar, most peculiar,' Cawl said. 'But fortunate. I suppose it is because the regular functions are not at play because it is frozen?'

'I could not tell you,' said Primus. 'All I know is that I can touch the warp, and that it is unusually calm.'

'Ah well,' said Cawl disappointedly. 'Another investigation for another time. Friedisch–'

'Qvo-89!' protested Qvo.

'All right, all right! Qvo-89, you and I shall descend first. I will carry you. Primus and Solana will follow.'

'Master, it should be I who takes first position,' said Primus.

'If any dangers are present, I am more than equipped to deal with them myself, Primus. Your role here is to watch the historitor. This isn't like Tredica 7/2, we've nothing to fear from awakening necrons, because they're already awake and frozen in time. Besides, I'm carrying our temporal field.' He waved the boxed head about.

'Stop that! I am no mere device!' protested AsanethAyu. Nobody paid her any attention.

'Qvo, come on.' Cawl leant to the side, like a large beast of burden kneeling so its rider may mount. Qvo stepped onto an outstretched claw, and clambered up onto Cawl's motive carriage behind the torso joint. He gripped the edges of the armoured plates of Cawl's reactor housing.

'Are you securely in place?'

'Yes, Belisarius,' Qvo said.

'Then down we go!'

Cawl clicked over to the hole. He looked back at Primus and Solana. 'You need to come down right after us, or you'll get caught in the null-time of the singularity.'

'Yes, master,' said Primus. 'I must carry you, madam historitor,' he said to Solana. 'Place your arms around my neck, and hold on tight. Grasp with your legs if you can. It would be best if I kept my hands free.'

She looked up at him in disbelief.

'This is no time to fret about dignity,' Cawl said. 'That's what's wrong with this galaxy. No get-up-and-go, and too much focus on pride. Now, chop-chop!' he said. It was a phrase nobody understood.

Primus reloaded his gun, reholstered it, bent down and extended his palm flat. Solana hesitated. Primus raised his eyebrows at her encouragingly.

'Step upon my hand, I can bear your weight easily.'

She put a tentative foot in his palm. His hand was as steady as a rockcrete step. Solana put her scroll feed into its leather case, pushed it off to her side, folded her shoulder array and tugged off her scribal claws before reaching up to hug his neck. Primus' armour was uncomfortably hard, the ceramite's smoothness making it difficult to find purchase. She gripped the thick gorget that protected his neck. She didn't think she could hold on to that for long without extra support, so she reluctantly hitched up her long coat and wrapped her legs around his waist as he had suggested. Her trousers caught on his belt, and pulled at her annoyingly.

Primus approved. 'You feel secure.' He drew his bolt pistol again. 'We are ready, master,' Primus said.

'Excellent!' said Cawl. 'Into the hole!'

The archmagos vanished into the shaft like an arachnid going back into its lair. His claws squealed on the noctilith. The back wall of the fascia temporalis advanced on Solana.

'Ready?' Primus asked.

Solana nodded. She was reminded of the few years she had spent with her parents before being taken away for indoctrination, the times her father would carry her.

She had not thought of her father for years.

Primus' eyes burned with eerie foxfire. Solana knew he was a psyker, that much was in his datafile, but the notes did not say of what sort or grade on the Imperial assignment. She suspected he was powerful. There was no sense of the instability, that feeling that events were about to run out of control, that she often got in the presence of psykers. He walked over to the hole, and stepped out into it. He held his free hand flat and down, and a wash of witch-light shone from it. Borne upon a cushion of warp power, he and Solana drifted down. Cawl clattered beneath them. In the peculiar shadows of the warp-light he appeared hunched and monstrous with his many legs braced against the gleaming noctilith, his claws making an occasional toothache squeal when they slipped.

'Are you all right?' Primus asked her.

'I can hold on well enough,' she said. 'Don't worry about me.' Her perch was uncomfortable. The edges of his armour plates dug into her body. *Minor discomforts,* she thought. *Weaknesses of the flesh. No need to mention them.*

She shifted her weight to relieve the pressure on her muscles. She imagined Primus felt her moving about as much as an ambull might feel a flea crawling over its hide.

Cawl's stablights shifted. He angled two of his arms downward, and the low warble of contra-grav started up. The chute broadened like the bell of a trumpet. They were entering a larger space where he could no longer climb. The size of the void was uncertain – it was pitch black in there, darker than she thought it possible to be, a black that was more than the absence of light. The fascia temporalis blunted the progress of Cawl's stab beams, but even so, when she and Primus descended out of the shaft into the void, she had the impression of a place without bounds.

'The necrons do so love their trans-dimensional engineering,' said Cawl. His voice was distant, although he was only a few feet below Solana. 'This is a spectacular example. Another mystery I cannot investigate!' he said regretfully. 'I have lived ten thousand years, and if I live the same again, I will never know everything.'

'Look!' Qvo leaned out from Cawl. 'Lights!'

Below them, a pattern of lines coyly emerged from the dark,

all the gelid green of necron technology. Though warped by the strange interface of time and space the cryptek projected, their ruthless geometries were clear enough: hard lines describing an attitude that would brook no resistance, not from time, nor space, nor death.

'They're moving,' said Cawl. 'Extraordinary.'

The lines folded in and over themselves in a pattern that at first seemed to repeat, but which proved to be full of minor variations that built into sudden, total change where the entire arrangement would turn at once into something wholly new. They seemed alive, or approaching life.

'We are nearly there,' said Cawl, and for the first time since Solana had joined his fleet he sounded businesslike, without a trace of his infuriatingly chirpy mockery. 'We are within the primary cogitator of a necron world engine. These logic patterns are its thoughts, running many times the speed of light in this dimensional pocket, but nevertheless slowed by the proximity of the singularity. Incredible that I live and see such things. By the grace of the Machine God do we learn!'

To even hint that the Machine God had a hand in the creation of xenotech was a rank blasphemy to any right-thinking tech-priest.

Cawl was not among the number of right-thinking tech-priests.

'We must descend further. There will be an outlet on the far side. The data archive should be beneath the world engine. We will find an interface point, where I will collect what we came for from the planetary archives and we may be away. Easy!'

They passed into the lights, which went from solid beams to lines of glittering particles, spiralling towards each other then suddenly away, as ordered as dancers at a society ball. The patterns the particles of light described were clear, though they should have been fuzzy and hard to make out through the walls of solidified time. Solana realised they had moved beyond time and space as she understood it.

They passed through the dance of light, and came out the other side. Cawl floated down, adjusting his grav-chutes from time to time. Primus descended straight as a plumb weight, the eerie shine of the warp lighting their way when the green dance of alien thought had retreated once more into the dark.

A floor appeared, incised with a bewildering pattern of grooves. In their midst a hatch irised open soundlessly, and the four of them passed into another conduit. This was of the necron's living metal rather than noctilith. There were hundreds of holes piercing its sides, and through these flew the maintenance constructs of necron kind, these all of identical sort, flat-bodied, busy-looking even while stilled, each equipped with a single green eye, particle-manipulating mandibles, and six shovel-shaped legs.

Cawl's group could not avoid them. The fascia temporalis passed over them and they came alive, their limbs twitching with machine surprise. They inevitably turned on the interlopers.

Two more of Cawl's subsidiary limbs flashed. Lascutters sliced the creatures in two as they attacked. Cawl was not equipped for battle, but he was far from helpless. Primus shot down those he could safely hit past his maker.

'Primus, put away your gun. These fellows pose a minimal risk to us, but their corpses are another matter. We need to get them out.'

'I shall never forgive you if I am terminated,' the cryptek said.

'Keep the field running, and we'll make sure that does not happen.'

Solana saw the danger. The scarabs' metal corpses were falling against the fascia temporalis, as dead insects will collect in the bottom of a glass lumen shade, causing the field to shimmer and creak.

'Get them off the fascia!' Cawl commanded. 'Our cryptek friend will not be able to maintain the field if there is too much mass taken into... Argh!' He cried out. A scarab attached itself to his leg assembly, and chewed into a primary motivator with a flat blade of particles. Primus blasted it off with a single shot.

'That stung!' Cawl said. 'Primus!'

'Yes, master,' he said. He holstered his gun, closed his eyes. Warp power crackled around his head. The broken scarabs lifted up.

'That's right, my boy! Keep them in the air. Off the fascia!'

'There's another one there!' Qvo pointed at a scarab climbing up Cawl's back.

'Thank you, Friedisch,' said Cawl, and swatted the scarab away. 'We're going to have to go a little more quickly,' he said.

As Solana was discovering, Cawl had a habit of understatement. They dropped fast. More scarabs were swept up into the bubble of accelerated time. Cawl kept his grav-chutes active rather than using his limbs to climb, and that was a good thing, for they were needed to slash and swat away the scarabs. Soon their corpses were rising up around Cawl's feet, and Primus took on a pained look. The warp nimbus shimmering about his head guttered.

'I don't think he can keep this up,' Solana called.

'Nearly there!' said Cawl. 'Once we're back on solid ground, we can get rid of them and stabilise the field.'

'That's if we get down.'

'Oh ye of little faith!' called Cawl.

'What?'

'Nothing,' he shouted, cutting another scarab in half. 'An ancient saying.'

The cords of Primus' neck stood out with the strain. He was supporting a large weight of metal, but she supposed the real difficulty was catching each falling construct accurately. The concentration necessary must have been punishing.

'Nearly there!' Cawl shouted.

'Master...' Primus moaned.

'Hang on just a few moments more.'

Cawl rose up out of the gathering mass of metal, until his back bumped against Solana's feet. Primus and she were at the top of the time bubble. The tide of dead scarabs was rising, but still more were coming into contact with the outside of the fascia and bursting through their dismembered fellows to get at the intruders.

'I cannot... maintain...' Primus groaned.

'We're out!' Cawl shouted. They came out of an aperture into a huge hall crammed with large, ingot-shaped machines that vanished into the distance on every side in gently curved ranks. Another trapdoor irised shut behind them, the last of its closing stopped when the time field moved away from it.

'Toss them out! A few at a time!' Solana shouted.

'Yes! Yes!' Cawl agreed. 'A capital idea.'

Solana let go of Primus and dropped into the mass of scarabs. They were inert, thank the Omnissiah, cut off from the carrier waves that would prompt them to reassemble. She picked one up and heaved it at the fascia. It stuck weirdly before passing through with painful slowness, whereafter it hung in the air mid-fall on the far side of the field.

'That's it, get them out,' Cawl said. No more scarabs were scooped into their field of stolen time, so he was free to help her, as was Qvo, and together they pushed scarabs through the fascia bubble, watching them first catch in the treacly time boundary then snap away into the eternal stillness of gravitic time lock. They left behind a trail of shattered machines hanging in the air.

The floor rose up. They decelerated, until they were now falling at a rate of a few feet per second.

'Steady,' Cawl said. 'This ball of dead machines hits the floor, and we walk away. Got that?'

Primus, under less strain now, nodded.

They touched down. The time field spread out like warm tar. Primus released the mass of shattered alien mechanisms. They hit the ground with an almighty crash, and Solana was spilled among them. Cawl came down more gracefully. Qvo hopped off his back. Primus scooped Solana up out of the scarabs and dragged her forward. She got her feet under her. Primus was pale and beaded with sweat, but steady. Seeing Solana was unharmed, he let her go.

'And relax,' said Cawl.

They were free of the mass of constructs. Finally, the time field stabilised, though it was perhaps smaller than it had been, and the fascia clearer, as if thinned.

'You are reckless,' AsanethAyu said.

'Somebody has to take a few chances, or this galaxy is doomed,' said Cawl. 'Come on, pick up the pace now. We're nearly done. Over here. This way!'

A high vaulted roof sheltered thousands of the ingot-shaped machines. Solana donned her scribal claws again, and sketched them as best she could as she walked. She was so engrossed in this activity she did not see Cawl stop, and so walked directly into him.

'Ah,' said Cawl.

Past the archmagos the floor dipped into a bowl. In the centre was a much larger version of the necron data engines. A complicated relay mechanism hung over it from the faraway ceiling, reaching down with a mess of piping and cabling. At the top, it turned into a huge ribbed sphere joined to a massive extrusion of noctilith.

That was not what had made Cawl stop.

Necrons made him stop.

The bowl held a number of the aliens. They appeared to have come out of a large gate comprised of two high menhirs topped by a lintel stone, and it was open. The power channels incised into the stone were ablaze, the whole of the space framed by the stones filled with an active green transit field, though its shimmering surface and the wisps of energy coming off the doorway were frozen like everything else.

The necrons were divided into two groups. The first comprised a number of the technomancer caste led by a lord of ornate sort. The lord was frozen by the cogitator nexus, his war-scythe outstretched, the light blazing from its tip a steady flare. The logic channels cut into the metal of the machine shone with answering light. The courtiers were all thin-limbed mechanical creatures of menacing aspect, each of them bearing bizarre gear and all decorated with extravagant headdresses. There were twenty, maybe twenty-five of them, enough to encircle the machine completely.

The second group was made up of the heavier type of necron warrior: 'Immortals' was the Imperial designation. The warriors faced the gate in a rough semicircle, weapons up, their energy coils blazing as if about to open fire.

'It looks like the first group are caught in the middle of some sort of technomantic ritual, and the warriors are there to protect them from whatever might come out of the gate. But what could that be?' Solana said.

'Exactly,' said Cawl thoughtfully.

'What's going on here?' asked Qvo.

'That's the data nexus point. The central cogitator,' said Cawl.

'Could these be the ruling members of the world's dynasty?' suggested Solana.

Cawl gave her an apologetic grin. 'I do not think so, historitor.' He looked back at them. 'That gate there… That is a dolmen gate, a dimensional interface that permits long-range travel instantaneously, system to system. Incredible technology. I've seen it in operation myself, in the Pharos of Sotha. The gate is open. They could have come from elsewhere on this planet, but why would they emerge down here, in the middle of a battle, in this way if they were this world's inhabitants? This form of travel is not without risks, there are other means of transit available to them. Furthermore, we must ask, why are they here? Those notables there, they are all of the cryptek caste–'

Solana took a rare opportunity to interrupt Cawl. 'So they are performing a ritual, like magi.'

'Yes. I think they are. But that's not what's drawing my eye. Look closely.' He selected one of the crypteks and projected a magnified view via hololith. Its cyclopean metal skull swam before Cawl, only slightly distorted by the fascia temporalis. Its decoration was battered. 'Do you see how pitted the skin is? This necron is old. The other machines we have seen here are sparkling new.' He held up a declamatory finger. 'Hypothesis – they are not from this world. Furthermore, I don't think they are from this time.' He looked back to Solana. 'They're from the future, I mean the future relative to here, which could be our past or present. Either way, it's likely they're here for exactly what we are. We must remember that we're seeking to plunder the nexus of a necron data network that is uncorrupted by time. I am sure that this prize is of interest to others, especially the necrons themselves.' He scratched his chin under his mandibular shield. 'Maybe I should have considered that.'

'You didn't?'

'I'm a genius, madam, but I am not perfect. We must move through them in order to access the master cogitator. But why are they frozen like this? How do we get past them without waking them, and what happens if they do?'

'They'll kill us, surely?' said Solana.

'That is indeed the most likely outcome,' agreed Cawl.

'We look for a breach in their perimeter,' AsanethAyu said.

'Now you choose to contribute?' said Cawl.

'I wish to live. You yourself said so. If I rely on your limited judgement we shall all perish.'

'Very well, what is your justification for this suggestion?'

'The female is correct in saying they are in the middle of a ritual. You are also correct in saying they are not from this time or this place. These crypteks are mostly chronomancers. They will be working together to stabilise the time frame of this place.'

'But you're doing it on your own. Why are there so many?' said Solana.

'They don't have a frame projector like mine,' said Cawl. 'I suspect they were stabilising not only the immediate environment as AsanethAyu is here, but maintaining an umbilical link back to their place of origin. It's a bigger undertaking than it looks.'

'That is so. As your primitive brethren did with their projector, only far more elegantly,' said AsanethAyu pridefully.

'Elegant or not, it has gone wrong,' said Qvo.

'Evidently. One of them has made an error.'

Cawl snorted. 'I thought you were the superior species!'

'I never said that we were infallible,' AsanethAyu said. 'It is likely one of them has failed in their efforts. We find the one that has, and I can extend my chronomantic bubble through the breach in the circle without awakening the others, enough that you might access the archive and achieve your goals. Then we might leave and we can discuss the return of my body.'

'How can I trust you, that you will not alter the flow of time and bring all these fellows of yours into the same temporal frame as ourselves?'

'You can't,' AsanethAyu said flatly. 'But consider this, mammal.

I tire of being reduced to a head. You have the better bargaining position. Equally, you have no other choice. You must either trust me, or leave with your informational storage empty. What is it to be?'

CHAPTER EIGHTEEN

SOUL GRINDER

Weeks passed. Every night Felix and his men stood guard with the Wolfspear. They would fight until the sun rose again. Sometimes Felix would feast with his hosts; mostly he applied himself to the distant administration of his realm. Whatever he did, the first task every morning was to contact his astropaths upon the *Lord of Vespator* and inquire after Cawl. The last thing he did before he donned his battle plate was to go to the Varghalen's small astropathicum, buried deep under the hills to shield it from the Pit's attention, and ask the same questions there. His visits became so routine that Wessel, Transliterator Secondary to the Wolfspear, who seemed to have drawn the unfortunate lot to be Felix's liaison, grew tired of the sight of him, and his attitude lapsed from exaggerated deference to barely hidden annoyance.

'The news is the same as yesterday, my lord. None whatsoever,' he would say. Sometimes, he rolled his eyes when he thought Felix wasn't looking.

Felix wondered what it could mean. For all his personal feelings for Cawl, the man had always been good to his word, eventually. The delay in testing the machinery at Raukos had become a problem some time ago. The crossing at Attila needed to be made usable, or Nihilus risked sinking further into destruction.

He did not think it likely Cawl had turned traitor. His opponents tarred him with this slur constantly. Cawl was undoubtedly a monster, but he was a loyal one. No, Felix thought as he answered his correspondence ready to be transmitted to his ship and thence by teleprayer to Ultramar, it would be a case of overreach. Cawl's infuriating ego demanded more than its share of luck. It could be it had finally run out. That left the disturbing possibility that he was dead.

With no word from his flotilla, Felix resolved to wait six more months before departing to find the archmagos himself.

In the meantime, he fought.

Dawn was still hours away. *Martrinator*'s guns roared over Felix's head, the barrels glowing red hot.

'Concentrate fire on ingress point six!' Felix commanded. 'Squads five, nine, and fourteen, advance, box it in! Box it in!' He defaulted to squad numbers, saving vital fractions of a second by not pronouncing their names. Command had broken down. The vox was a seething mess of daemonic interference.

A blur of movement alerted him to a daemon leaping at him. He grabbed it out of the air with his power fist. Three misshapen mouths in a half-melted face bleated at him. Energy blazed around its throat as the power field warred with its essentially unreal nature. A vile stench boiled off the false flesh. Even he could not fight off the deep, primeval fear engendered by its nature. The fear boiled out of him in an inchoate shout. The motorised fingers of the gauntlet crushed the daemon's neck. The disruption field roared. Still the thing mewled. Reflexively he triggered the underslung bolter on the gauntlet, blasted clear through the monster's lumpen ribs, finally ending the thing. He cast it aside, his face twisted with disgust, and looked about for other threats.

It was an outlier, this thing that had assaulted him, but it would not be the last. The daemons poured mindlessly out of the rifts into intersecting fields of fire as they had done night after night. So many of them died that the ground was soaked in their ichor. It flowed over the sand, lapped around the boots of the Space Marines ringing each warp rift. Felix imagined it spreading and deepening until the whole of the triumphal ground was a sea of filth. He suspected that was the point of this otherwise baffling exercise, the defilement of this place where Guilliman had raised his banners and proclaimed his victory years before.

There were so many daemons that some slipped by the cordons. Some nights were worse than others, and the worst tended to follow a pattern. A moment when the scales were tipped. Every Space Marine engaged at close quarters lessened the weight of fire and allowed more daemons to slip through.

Huge shells screamed out of the dark, burying themselves in the rock and exploding with such force hails of splintered stone rattled from *Martrinator*'s ceramite hide a mile from the impact site. Felix understood how the parade ground had come to be so battered, and marvelled that any of its original form had survived at all.

From his position, Felix had clear lines of sight to a number of the rifts. Ingress one was contained. His own Chosen and Wolfspear ringed it, their guns roaring. Ingress three was likewise blocked; better, the flood of enemy coming through there appeared to be abating for some reason.

It was six where the danger lay now. The Space Marines covering it were embattled, no longer firing, become a cordon of pale grey holding back the unstoppable surge with bolt pistol and combat knife. As he watched, a group of the hellspawn overwhelmed an Intercessor, bearing him down and ripping at his armour, opening up a gap in the cordon big enough for half a dozen more Neverborn to break away. They came galloping on mismatched limbs towards him. Troncus saw them coming, and the silent Techmarine brought the tank's cannons to bear on them, reducing them to so much gristle. Felix marvelled at how weak they were compared to other daemons he had faced. They died as easily as hive scum. Killing them was hypnotic, and that was a danger in itself.

The squads he'd sent were lining up round the rift, forming a new, more distant firing line.

'Wolfspear command, Wolfspear command, this is Tetrarch Felix, recommended fall back from ingress six. I have fresh squads in position to cover retreat.'

He got no reply but a jabbering screech. He would have to deal with this himself.

He broke into a run, switching from whole-theatre comms to short-range, inter-squad vox. At last, human speech filled his ears.

'Enemy activity at ingress three abating. Wolfspear Librarius attempting seal,' Gathein tersely voxed him. *'Joining in support.'*

Felix pulsed a non-verbal affirmation. There was no need for more than that. He allowed his men latitude in battle to respond how they would. All of them were heroes. Before he reached ingress six, blue fires converged on the warp rift at three, blocky silhouettes of Space Marines shown up against them. The fires crashed together, and the rift collapsed in a spray of globular, silver light. The pressure on the centre relented. Troops were redirected, fire lines redrawn, the usual dance of war.

But not at ingress six.

'Wolfspear squads, fall back, fall back to second line.' Felix widecast his command. He appended his rank signum, and spoke it aloud. 'Tetrarch Decimus Felix, assuming command, ingress six cordon, fall back!' He switched to a direct feed. 'Daelus, Troncus, on me.'

The awesome thump of the Repulsor's grav engines followed him.

He slowed to shoot down a pair of daemons that had slipped the net, arriving at the second line to find the last of the Wolfspear retreating in good order from the mass of daemons. The relocated squads waited for no command, but fired as soon as they had clear shots. Daemons shrieked as they were blown to pieces.

The enemy responded.

Perhaps it was chance that Felix was there when the breakthrough occurred, but he could not rule out that he was specifically targeted, or even lured in. He knew more of the ways of the powers in the warp than most, rare and dangerous information once, more widespread now the Great Rift had opened the heavens. He could not rule out that the giant claw that poked out of the rift was meant to crush him. That was not an unlikely eventuality. Behind the lesser beings were malign wills moving their puppets with purpose.

The limb emerged briefly, a huge pincer of beautiful form, its golden surface incised with precise patterns and studded with jewels. The claw snapped, like its scissored talons were tasting the air. Then it withdrew, and a moment later the owner of the claw stooped below the tortured ripple of reality that mantled ingress six, and stepped into the materium.

This was something new.

'Soul Grinder,' Felix said to himself, then louder. 'Fire support required immediately, ingress six! New manifestation. Daemon machine, Soul Grinder classification!'

Like all attempts to name the things of the warp, the appellation meant little. It defined a daemon machine as big as a heavy tank. The form was not fixed, for the Neverborn came in infinite variety. Classifying the denizens of the warp sent men mad. That didn't stop the unwise from trying.

The bottom half was a multi-legged motive unit of prodigious size, each of its crouching, clawed limbs bigger than Felix, and between them twitched delicate, multi-jointed secondary limbs that looked disturbingly like long, spidery fingers. The rear carried a small power unit which belched blood-red smoke of such thickness it hung around the creature in thick, squirming bands. In contrast to the lower portion's technological nature, the upper assembly was mainly organic, as if someone had broken a giant in two and crudely stitched the top half to a machine carriage. Lurid purple skin shifted with unnatural motion. At the creature's elbows the daemon engine's mechanical nature reasserted itself, one hand being a large, multibarrelled cannon, the other the gargantuan metal claw that probed at the air. The join between these areas of flesh and steel was a nightmarish smear of heaving organics and misplaced engineering flowing into each other, the boundary between them entirely uncertain.

Obscenely, this one was beautiful in some regards. Beyond the messy joins, the organic elements were perfectly formed. Its face was not the usual bestial muzzle one often saw. Instead it was angelic. Glorious. A face of transcendent beauty that was nevertheless as repellent as it was entrancing. The body was androgynous, a mix of male and female characteristics. Fine chains hung in shimmering curtains from piercings all over its skin. Tattoos covered every inch of it. The mechanical parts, too, were as finely made and highly decorated as the claw, plated in gold and other precious metals. All its limbs were highly polished and jewelled, the abstract patterns alluring to the eye. It had a powerful, entrancing aura.

Some of his men succumbed, their weapons dropping from suddenly limp hands.

Felix shook off the thing's baleful influence.

'Retreat! Retreat, damn you!'

Its voice had none of the beauty of the body. With a hitching roar like the gunning of engines, the thing screamed its hatred at the sky, brandished its outsized weapons at the world, lowered its head and charged directly towards Felix.

The Space Marines at rift six were not equipped to fight a creature of this kind. Bolt rounds slammed into it, destroying decorations and marring the thing's perfect torso, but they did no real harm. It barged through the cordon, hurling Space Marines in every direction, and lowered its gun to aim directly at the tetrarch.

CHAPTER NINETEEN

CHRONOMANCY

Cawl avoided the dolmen gate, heading between the semicircle of necron war forms and the circle of technomancers. Something in the gateway caught Solana's eye as they went by.

'Can you see an object coming through?' she asked Primus quietly. Cawl was deep in discussion with the cryptek's head, and she did not wish to disrupt his concentration.

Primus paused to look and frowned. 'Perhaps. The suggestion of a blade? It is hard to see through this distortion.' He had his weapons in his hands and he glanced at Solana's holster. 'You may wish to follow my lead. I sense conflict ahead.'

'Is that prediction clairvoyance or born from experience?' she asked.

'A tedious combination of both,' he replied wearily. He took the helmet mag-locked to his hip and donned it.

The trailing edge of the fascia temporalis was moving towards Solana, dragged behind Cawl. The archmagos had no intention of lingering. She had to move on. Before she did, Solana took a final look at the gate.

The thing in the glow did look like a blade. Maybe more than one. There had only been one before, she was sure, but it would have been impossible for anything to move through the gate. She used her augmetics to take a pict of it, then the time field drew her away and the gate blurred into an undifferentiated, lurid green and the objects were lost. She jogged a few steps to catch up with Primus, put her scroll feed away and drew her gun as he suggested, wishing that she was armed with something a little more powerful than a laspistol. She had her power sword, at least. That was some comfort.

They passed close by the lord standing outside the circle of his court of alien scientists. He had been a magnificent being in his day, eight feet tall and ostentatiously decorated. One clawed hand reached out to beseech the machine spirits of the xenos logic engine, green light so bright it was almost white cupped in his hand. He still looked powerful, but both he and his panoply had seen better times. His bronze-coloured necrodermis was heavily pitted. The inlay in his armour plates had come out in places, leaving sad holes caked with grave muck and verdigris. His great war scythe was similarly battered. The pistons in one side of his neck were jammed, tilting his head awkwardly to one side and giving him a malformed air that reminded Solana of the crippled beggars who crowded the streets of populous worlds, an imperfection that made the lord seem strangely human.

She took another tru-pict image with a blink of her eyes, resolving to draw him later. Then he too was lost to the optical distortion of the fascia temporalis.

'Careful now,' said Cawl. 'Don't get too close.'

'They're trapped by the run of time,' said Solana, and took another picture. 'There's no sign of life at all.'

'Trust me. They always wake up.' Cawl raised an eyebrow at her. 'Really, are you a tech-priest or not? Everybody knows that about necrons.'

They had to go only a short way round the data nexus to find the first weak link in the chain of chronomancers. One of them had fallen to his knees, his hands clawed before him. His tools, a staff and an orb of crimson power, lay on the floor at his side.

'Here?' asked Qvo.

'Oh no,' said Cawl. 'Not here. This fellow fell and the time field did not go down. You can tell. He had enough time to assume this posture of agony. Enough redundancy remained in the circle for it not to matter. His tools are on the floor. They'd be hanging in mid-air at the moment of collapse if the field had failed when he did.'

'You are correct,' AsanethAyu said. 'We must go on.'

They passed more chronomancers engaged in their art, brandishing staffs, crooks, and blades, or hunched over balls of glassy material or pure energy, beams of light and fogs of particles around them. One was surrounded by very slight movement, a wavering like a thermocline, or mirages over a desert road.

'This one's living at a different rate to the rest,' remarked Cawl.

Primus became wary. Cawl wagged a finger.

'Don't worry about him,' Cawl said. 'He's moving a million times faster than his fellows, that's still several million times slower than us.' He peered closer. 'Such power. I think a little more and he'd break free. I wonder how? More insoluble mystery!' he said regretfully.

The fourth chronomancer was lying on the floor, curled around its stomach so tightly it looked like a crustacean. Cawl spared it no more than a glance.

'Not this one either,' he said.

Past seven, eight, nine, ten... Onto the eleventh and twelfth.

The twelfth was turning to face the eleventh, who had cast aside its stave and sickle, and had launched itself at its fellow. Metal shows no emotion. The necrons' faces were immobile masks, but Solana could imagine the twelfth chronomancer's surprise. Cawl paused a little longer by this pair, but seeing that the chronomancer's devices had nearly reached the floor he shook his head.

'Not these either, but we're getting there,' said Cawl. Then he pointed a metal finger. 'Aha! There.'

The sixteenth chronomancer had his arms spread wide. His back arched, his hands were clawed, his head thrown back. A pillar of light was in the process of leaping from his distended metal jaws towards the ceiling, but had got only halfway – a very peculiar sight to see light frozen like ice. His gear was still level with his hips.

'This one,' said Cawl.

'It's not very dramatic,' said Qvo. 'The others seem more likely, no?'

'No is the word,' said Cawl. 'The time field collapsed the moment this fellow failed, breaking the circle, freezing them all. He had no time to do anything more than, well, just stop. This is the one.'

'Correct,' said AsanethAyu. 'Lift me so I might do my work.'

Cawl held up the box containing her head, so she was facing the screaming necron and the cogitator nexus.

'You'd better not trick me,' said Cawl.

'I'm afraid it's too late for that,' she said. Her eyes flashed, and the whole world sprang into violent motion.

After long millennia of arrestation, movements continued on interrupted lines. Necron claws weaved glyphs of light on the air. The twelfth and eleventh crypteks slammed into each other with a leaden clatter, and carried each other down to the ground fighting.

Others turned to look, their lapse in concentration almost causing the time field to collapse again. The pillar of light roaring from the gaping jaws of the final cryptek slammed into the ceiling and he fell writhing to the floor. From the far side of the cogitator nexus, where the semicircle of necron Immortals stood guard, the crackling hum of heavy gauss fire sawed at the air.

'Aid me!' AsanethAyu shouted. 'These primitives have me captive!'

Cawl tutted disapprovingly. 'AsanethAyu. We'll talk about this later. Primus! See to this bedlam, would you?'

But Primus was already moving, and fast. The crypteks only noticed his approach when he barged one of their number down, and swatted the head from another with his chainsword. His strength was phenomenal. The teeth barely kissed the metal. It was more brute force that separated the necron's alloy vertebrae from one another.

Time stopped again, freezing Primus solid, his chainsword caught in a dramatic sweep.

'Right, listen here,' said Cawl, giving AsanethAyu's box a hard shake. 'Do that again and I'll dissect you very, very slowly. I've been trying to work out how the engrammatic circuitry works in the higher, sentient models of necron. It degrades too fast once I start cutting, but when we get back I may be tempted to try to find out again.'

'You are a fool, Belisarius Cawl,' said AsanethAyu.

'At least you're using my name now,' said Cawl. He looked about. 'Now do as you promised. Do not attempt to activate the crypteks again or I shall simply have Primus kill them all.'

Silence. Cawl shook the box again.

'I cannot do as we planned,' she said. 'There is so much temporal adjustment in process here that it is impossible for me to gain access to the archive.'

Cawl sighed. 'So you were lying. So you could escape.'

'I was.'

'Right.'

'An impasse, do you not see? Now we shall negotiate.'

'No, we won't,' said Cawl.

'But you can do nothing!'

'I can do what I like, in this case, awakening one of them. If we speak, it may be that we can find common cause.'

'They will slaughter you,' gloated AsanethAyu.

'Maybe,' said Cawl. 'On the other hand, I've met far more reasonable members of your species than you.'

'I could just shut down.'

'And be stuck here forever? Unlikely.'

Cawl went over to Primus. The fascia temporalis passed over the downed crypteks, and the decapitated head continued its trajectory away from the data nexus, once more stopping dead when it hit the edge of the field. Inside the time bubble, the headless body collapsed, spewing green sparks from its cleaved neck. The one Primus had knocked down fell backwards. Its upper half fell towards the glassy wall of stopped time. Cawl moved quickly to keep the being within their temporal umbrella.

The necron raised its staff. Primus went for it. The seams of reality showed under the pressure of necron tech-sorcery. The Space Marine was too fast. His boot slammed down on the necron's wrist. The ball joint popped out of its socket, and the hand, still gripping its staff, skidded away from its owner. Alien hexes died on the air. Primus followed the stamp with a downward punch, smashing aside the being's curved blade, disrupting the charge of arcane, time-warping power building around it.

'What is your business here?' Primus demanded. 'Speak!'

When it replied, the language was not one Solana, Primus or Qvo could understand.

Belisarius Cawl could. He canted something at it vaguely akin to the chitter of binharic, but deeper, more melodious, like the piping of an organ. The cryptek looked up sharply, and replied. The fight went out of it.

'That'll do, Primus. Stand down a moment.'

The archmagos approached, his buprestis drone bustling up to the cryptek's head. A swift exchange ensued, increasing in speed and pitch until the sounds blended into one, single note.

'Let him up,' Cawl said after a moment. 'He should be able to speak with us now. I have shared our language with him. Go on,' Cawl urged, when Primus looked at him dubiously. 'He won't harm us. There is more going on here than we can see.'

'Attempt to harm us, and I shall end you,' Primus growled. He stood back, and the necron got up, cradling its damaged arm. When it spoke again, it did so in Gothic.

'Why do you bring our enemy into our midst?' it said, pointedly looking at AsanethAyu.

'What do mean? Can you not see? These are humans, primitives!' AsanethAyu said. 'I am one of you.'

The cryptek looked over the party with its single eye.

'I am not familiar with this species. They look spectacularly inferior.'

'They are inferior. Free me from them!'

'No.'

'No?'

'You are of the Nihilakh Dynasty,' the cryptek said. 'You are the threat to us.'

'What do you mean?' asked AsanethAyu despairingly.

'Our dynasties are at war.' It leaned forward, its long neck sinuously ophidian. 'Our court is here because of you. I would not free you if you were being disassembled by a tribe of hooting animals wielding stone axes.' He looked at Cawl again. 'As appears to have already happened.'

Cawl chuckled, the sort of hiccupping, barely suppressed mirth that only the truly smug can enjoy. He contained it enough to speak, though could not conceal his amusement completely.

'The Machine God lights the way once more. This is fated! Fated, I say. I have explained to our new friend here why we are present upon this war world. Perhaps you could enlighten my comrades as to why you are here? Save me the trouble.'

'I will try. Your physiology is feeble, and speaks of low intellect. I suppose that is why you have crudely enhanced your baseline biology. This one, genetically. You two, by cybernetic implant, and this fourth?' It peered closely at Qvo, and the false magos took a step away. 'What is this fourth?'

'That is Friedisch, my friend,' said Cawl. 'Never mind him, he's not very important. I realise we have all the time there is to have, but if you would explain, and with some alacrity, please.'

'Very well.' The cryptek stalked over to its severed hand and picked it up. It pressed the two halves of the severed joint together. The parts fused neatly with a flare of cubed light. It flexed its fingers, inspected the repair, then retrieved its staff. 'We are of the Indukh Dynasty. We were awoken when our tomb world was threatened with cometary bombardment. We averted this disaster only to find in the process that your people, cryptek, the necrons of Nihilakh, were behind the attack. Surely you know this?'

'I do not,' said AsanethAyu. 'A different branch of my nation.'

'Maybe,' said the cryptek thoughtfully. Its single eye pulsed, and it looked them over with greater care. 'You are not of my time. Is this why I do not know your species? You look like aeldari, a little. Are you devolved examples of their kind?'

'We are not,' said Cawl.

'Perhaps not,' said the cryptek. It peered closely at Cawl. 'From the decay of temporal radiations that cling to your subatomic structures, I calculate some three million standard cycles have passed since we awoke and came here. Cursed fate. Three million cycles.' It looked at the floor. Solana had the idea it was appalled.

'Explain why you are here.'

'To access this logic nexus,' said the cryptek.

'And why do you have to do that?' AsanethAyu asked.

'We are here because of the Nihilakh, witch! You sought to take our territory. To do so, you deliberately infected us with the mind plague. We seek unadulterated data. Ur-programming from the beginning of our race, from when necrontyr became necron. We must purge ourselves of contamination, replace that which is corrupt with that which is pure.'

'That is impossible!' said AsanethAyu. 'I have no record of Nihilakh awakenings from that period, and to deliberately spread the flayer curse! How would we do such a thing?'

'By driving the afflicted from their dimensional shadow realm into our territory after redirecting the comet at our primary tomb world,' said the cryptek.

'I know nothing of these things.'

The cryptek calmed a little. 'Just because you did not know this happened, it does not mean it did not. Three million cycles is a long time, even for our kind.'

'Our friend here...' Cawl began, then looked at the cryptek expectantly.

'Tsu Tsek,' it said. 'That is my appellation. I permit you to use it.'

'Tsu Tsek. He has agreed to help us.'

'This is an outrage!' AsanethAyu's head shrieked. 'These are primitives! Inferior beings! You must help me!'

'What business is it of mine how outraged you are? Our people are at war. Our survival is at stake. This... human offers more promising outcomes,' said Tsu Tsek.

'Thank you,' said Cawl. 'Now listen, everyone, I have explained how the situation is in our time. Or all our time, in point of fact, because if you leave this place, Tsu Tsek, then you will find yourself in our era, but your people are used to that sort of thing, I suppose. We have agreed that we shall aid each other to access this device.'

'You communicated all that with each other already?'

'Necron lingua technis is remarkably rich,' said Cawl.

'Is this wise, master?' asked Primus.

'Wise? Probably not. Expedience, however, trumps wisdom more often than not. For us to inload the information locked in this device, it must be running to the same temporal frame as we are, at least as we humans perceive it. To do that, we are going to have to bring this whole scene up to, shall we say, speed. Then we may take the control codes I need to save the galaxy, and these metal gentlemen here might purge themselves of this plague.'

'It sounds simple,' said Solana. 'Nothing ever is.'

'Isn't it just always the way?' Cawl agreed brightly. 'It would have been, but the gate and these crypteks complicate matters. AsanethAyu was not lying about that. There is too much temporal disruption for us to achieve our goals on our own. Now, tell them why your temporal field is failing.'

'My fellows are infected, and turning,' Tsu Tsek said. 'Lord Phaeron Lhaskek led us here in an act of final desperation. We came too late. We began to fight among ourselves midway into the reactivation cycle, and our temporal field collapsed. It took your input to revitalise it.'

'Then we must use AsanethAyu to support their efforts,' Solana said. 'Will you agree?'

'I will agree,' said AsanethAyu angrily. 'Only because I have no choice.'

'That's good, or nobody is leaving this place,' said Cawl. 'Not ever.'

'Then in collaboration with these... xenos...' Solana uttered the word cautiously. Intellectually, she did not share the deep loathing many Imperial citizens did for the alien, but saying it out loud always felt unsafe. 'We expand our temporal field, and hope it is enough for you to exload the coding, and for them to take what they seek?'

'That's about the size of it, yes,' said Cawl. 'I'm glad you're keeping up, historitor. But there is one small additional problem. A little...' He steepled his fingers. 'Combat?'

'The gate,' said Solana. 'Something is coming through, isn't it?'

'Alas, I think it is so,' said Cawl.

'Our dynasty is dying. Most of our population was infected,' said Tsu Tsek. 'I told our phaeron that our mission was doomed from the start, that if we did not turn on each other, our fallen kin would follow us here to this place and tear us apart. But like you, my enemy, we too had no choice.'

'Flayed Ones,' said Primus. 'That is what you speak of. That is what is coming.'

'Is that your name for our cursed? Flayed Ones.' Tsu Tsek weighed the words. 'That is an adequate description. Yes. Flayed Ones.'

'Then there is no time to waste...' Cawl frowned. 'Well, that's not strictly true, we could waste all the time in the world, but we'd not fulfil our goal of saving the species, and what kind of...' Cawl's mouth clacked shut. He looked around at his companions' disbelieving stares. 'I'm babbling, aren't I? Let's get on with it.'

CHAPTER TWENTY

AN UNLIKELY ALLIANCE

Later, when writing up a full report, Solana struggled to get everything that happened around the data nexus down, despite her full visual record. There was a lot of confusion when time was restarted by the crypteks and AsanethAyu. Two more of the crypteks were turning, their base coding infected by the flayer virus, and that process began anew. Primus cleaved the kneeling chronomancer in two before its corruption was complete. The Immortals' energy beams coursed back into life, shooting directly into the gateway. Tsu Tsek dealt with the cryptek that had attacked his neighbour, then with the neighbour when it too showed signs of change.

The other crypteks received no warning. According to their frame of reference Tsu Tsek teleported from his place in the circle to another location with a quartet of unknown aliens in tow.

Predictably, the surviving necrons reacted badly. Arcane energies shivered the fabric of the materium. It took a moment of frantic communication for Tsu Tsek to assure them Primus was dealing with their afflicted, then more to calm them, more to explain the agreement Cawl and Tsu Tsek had struck.

Despite what the Imperium said, Solana supposed there was some wisdom in alien hearts.

After hearing Tsu Tsek's hurried explanation, the Lord Lhaskek addressed Cawl directly in his own version of machine speech. Cawl replied in the same language. They spoke rapidly, and at length. Solana never learned what secrets they exchanged. The lord was as tall as the archmagos, and somehow matched Cawl's presence. It was strange, Solana reflected in her private diaries, that she did not notice how much space Cawl occupied until she saw him facing a creature with a similar measure of charisma. *I find that unaccountably frightening,* she wrote.

The lord listened, then shut the gate down. The Immortals stopped firing and stood to attention in eerie synchronicity. The lord addressed his fellows. All signs of hostility ceased. As simply as that a tenuous alliance was struck.

'I can't believe they're helping us,' Solana said to Qvo.

'I do so only reluctantly,' the lord said, having heard her. He projected a feeling of great weariness, of a fight never done. The broken piston in his neck contracted to a regular beat, so his head jerked when he spoke, and when he walked one leg dragged a little. 'This has gone beyond our own struggle. We cannot achieve our goals alone. We fight together, for now.'

Cawl and three of the alien technomancers climbed steps to the top of the data archive while Alpha Primus stood guard with the phalanx of necron Immortals. Solana went to follow Cawl, but Qvo caught her fingers in his metal hand.

'We should stay here, you and I.' He looked after his maker, or his friend, or whatever Cawl really was to him. 'Belisarius and I have a lot of experience in dealing with these creatures. They keep their secrets close. They don't like to be watched.

We'll be safer in there.' He flapped a hand at a space between two buttresses in the side of the data nexus.

Was that true, Solana wondered, or was it Cawl who did not wish to be observed?

Qvo pulled her towards the side of the archive. 'There will be a deal of violence here. You and I will be better with our backs to something solid.' He moved her into the gap and patted at the noctilith. 'They won't be able to come through this.'

'Who?'

'The Flayed Ones!'

'But the gate is shut.'

'A gate shuts, but doors open. Look. The Flayed Ones have their own ways in, their science is as infected as their minds, and the gate has changed how things are here.' Qvo pointed out a greyish flicker on the air that floated, phantom-like, towards Primus' position. 'It's starting already.'

As they followed this blur the archive grew warm under her back and began to thrum with pent-up energies. Cawl had started his work.

'There's another!' Solana said.

The two grey flickers were joined by three more, then seven. Within each of them a skeletal form was imprisoned, as faded and feeble as a corroded negative pict, but most assuredly there.

Solana readied her gun.

'Belisarius!' Qvo drew out the syllables of the archmagos' name. 'They're here!'

One of the grey squares collapsed into itself, and a mechanical horror leapt out.

It had been a standard necron warrior before the change, so far as Solana could tell. Now it was something else. It retained the roughly humanoid form of the species, but the way it moved, the way it stood, utterly transformed the sense of it. It was doubled over so that it could run on all fours, its metal hands and feet clattering off the polished black floor. Its head lolled to the side, and the ghost lights of its eyes were dim and somehow crazed. It had discarded its weapons.

In the course of her many researches, Solana had read of these debased necrons. Those rare few who knew of and studied such things posited they were corrupted by a sickness of the mind. After tearing their victims apart they gorged on flesh they could not digest, the meat pouring out through their fleshless jaws. They stripped the skin from corpses to wear, the costume play of insane machines that yearned to be truly alive. They were yet another of the myriad horrors infesting the stars that most Imperial citizens were blithely unaware of. Solana sometimes wished she were as ignorant as they.

'Nasty things,' said Qvo. He shuddered in a very human way. 'This one doesn't look like others I've seen.'

'It's newly changed, that's why,' she whispered back. 'Is this how it happens to them, I wonder – they start this way?'

Qvo shrugged. 'Possibly. Who can say? If there's one thing I've learned over eighty-eight lifetimes, it's that the galaxy is a very strange place.'

A stab of green lightning arced from where Primus stood out of sight with his unlikely allies. It connected with the Flayed One's chest, knocking it into a sprawling pile of metal limbs. The beam snapped off, and the creature lay still only a second before it pulled its legs and hands in, hauled itself onto its feet, clacked its jaws and ran again.

'Machine God preserve us! What a construct!' said Qvo.

Four more arcs of gauss fire engulfed the necron in a twisting, viridian grip. This time the machine thrashed about until it disintegrated. What little was left of it clattered hard onto the ground.

More of the interdimensional squares drifted towards the archive.

'Why are they unaffected by the slowing of time?' she asked.

'I don't know, but it's not encouraging, is it?' said Qvo.

Solana took her hand from the bronzed grip of her laspistol to wipe the sweat from her palm on her coat. 'If we are lucky, they won't see us.'

Under her back, the data archive burned with imprisoned alien heat.

They came in ones and twos, and then in a rush of dozens, slipping from some nowhere space into the main run of space and time.

Newborn Flayed Ones lolloped at Alpha Primus, the usual rigid machine gait of the necrons replaced by jittery fluidity. Most were taken down in efficient fashion by the phalanx of Immortals, so Primus opened fire more out of habit than need. He hit one of the debased androids in the skull and dropped it. Its core circuitry obliterated, it did not rise again. Primus felt nothing at this small triumph. The necrons were only another enemy in the long line of enemies he had faced in his thousands of years of life.

This fantastical venture to the edge of time was just another mission to be completed. His experiences of liminal spaces where sublayers of reality overlapped were multiplying, not that they had not been strange to him in the first place. Primus had been raised by Cawl to entertain ideas at odds with the beliefs of most human authorities. Pan-dimensional physics was yet another of Cawl's side interests, and in most combinations of his personality the archmagos was only too keen to share what he learned. Thus Primus' education had been broad and unstinting, and though he personally had little interest in Cawl's science, he could not help but absorb it.

Necrons were masters at dimensional manipulation, employing pocket realms, alternate dimensions and interstitial spaces sandwiched between the immaterium and materium to move across the galaxy. It was beyond human understanding, but as Cawl said, it proved there was more to the Great Work than realspace and the warp alone.

The Immortals switched mechanically from target to target, their bodies occasionally stuttering as an ancient joint stuck. Their guns vomited streams of braided green lightning that left a sharp scent behind. The Flayed Ones lurched past the beams, turning their lumbering runs into unlikely acrobatics, always on the verge of falling but never doing so. Where the beams hit, the Flayed Ones spasmed as gauss energies ate through their metal bodies layer by layer, so that they fizzed away like fragile sculptures of sand caught in a strong wind. Dozens fell, then scores, though more and more were dropping from the pale grey squares into the data archive. Primus tracked Flayed Ones that looked likely to escape the gauss streams and shot them down. For the time being, he only needed to fire infrequently.

That would not last. The Flayed Ones were getting closer.

'The crypto lock is not responding, sire,' Tsu Tsek said to the phaeron. He stepped back from the interface point. 'The coding is ancient, and beyond me.' He bowed his head apologetically.

Lhaskek looked down upon his chronomancer. 'Gulmarlok is dead. Is this the reason why?'

Tsu Tsek nodded, still not looking up into his lord's face, which managed to convey disappointment although it was rigid and the eyes glowed an unchanging, baleful green. 'He was the expert. I am a mere dabbler in comparison to his skill, alas.'

'I do not blame you.' Lhaskek's neck piston juddered again, making his head tick to one side. He set his staff's base down on the machine with a hard, decisive click. 'We are doomed then. Our dynasty is finished.'

Cawl judged the time was right to step in. Despondency opened doors.

'If I might attempt to break your machine's defences myself?'

Tsu Tsek made a noise that could have been the equivalent of dismissiveness. 'You are not necron. How could you understand the complexities of our technology? We are the oldest race in this galaxy. You are a barely evolved primitive. How could you possibly comprehend the majesty of our science?'

'That is what I keep telling him,' said AsanethAyu.

Cawl would have begged to differ on both fronts. The aeldari would have something to say about the first point, and he was confident enough in his own ancestors' mastery to believe they had at least come close to the necrons' abilities, but it would have been tactless to say so. Tactlessness shut doors.

'Then what harm could there possibly be in letting me try?'

Lhaskek looked down on his Immortals, at the crypteks who struggled to hold their bubble of time in place, at the Flayed Ones emerging from their flickering doorways that led into the spaces beyond. His head and his shoulder jerked, ancient motors whined in protest.

'What harm indeed, primitive. If you wish to prove I am right by cooking your simple organic brain, then you may proceed.'

Tsu Tsek looked from Cawl to his lord. If he had misgivings he kept them to himself.

'May I?' said Cawl.

Tsu Tsek bowed, and backed out of Cawl's way with a deferential sweep of his arm. 'By all means.'

'Jolly good,' said Cawl. He laced his primary hands together, and cracked the knuckles of the remaining organic fingers. 'Let's get on with it.'

He darted out a modified mechadendrite to investigate a near-invisible input port in the upper surface of the data archive. Cawl's input spike reconfigured itself to mate with it. Tsu Tsek gripped his staff tighter.

'You see? I've picked up a few of your tricks on the way,' he said. 'Now, the difficulty here is that your precursors utilised a unique, quantum generated cycling omnicodal system for their primary encryption key. It's almost impossible to break.'

'Then how are you going to do it? We no longer have the key,' Tsu Tsek said.

'I said *almost* impossible,' said Cawl. He was enjoying himself, as he always did when he had the opportunity to show off. Green sparks buzzed around his mechadendrite as the end further re-formed, becoming one with the machine. *One in, three to go,* he thought, and extended the second dataspike.

'That is our technology,' Tsu Tsek said.

'My own unique version of it, yes,' said Cawl.

'Then do you have the key?' Tsu Tsek asked.

'Not as such,' said Cawl, as he manoeuvred a three-pronged probe into a slot in the ground. 'Not the original. But I have been able to synthesise a method that should serve just as well– Ow!' He snatched back one of his dataspikes, shaking the smoke off the end. 'Once I've adjusted it a touch. Now then. A second try.' The dataspike's tip rebuilt itself with a restacking of energy cubes that went from nothing to solid matter with a cold, green dazzle. He plunged it home. Crackling forks of lightning reached up to embrace it as it slammed into place.

'With no key, you will not be able to deal with our crypto locks,' said Tsu Tsek. 'The one within is of staggering complexity. It would take a million years of calculations to undo.'

'I have a shortcut.'

'There are no shortcuts, primitive.'

'Look, if I can't do it, then you're more than welcome to have another go yourself when I come back outside, all right? But at this moment' – he waved a free appendage at the battle going on below – 'I am your best option.'

Tsu Tsek twisted his staff in his hands, a motion Cawl took for a necron expression of disquiet.

'Well then, hurry to your doom, primitive,' said Lord Lhaskek, who managed to remain regal even while his head jerked to the side. 'They will soon overwhelm us.' He swept his scythe downward. Flayed Ones were popping out of holes in space time in growing numbers, and streaming at his royal guard.

'Yes, yes,' said Cawl, who did not like to be hurried to doom or any other thing. 'I'm ready. I'll be back in a few minutes, I promise.'

The remaining organic parts of his body went limp on his motive carriage as his consciousness vanished into another place entirely.

CHAPTER TWENTY-ONE

A PRESSING TARGET

A stream of burning bullets slammed into the Soul Grinder, knocking off its aim so the large-calibre shells punched through the armour of two Space Marines to Felix's left and ploughed up the plaza. The daemon shrieked, a horrible mix of animal pain and random engine noise.

Martrinator came to a halt near Felix, its weapons blazing. Daelus' voice crackled urgently in Felix's earpiece.

'Get aboard, tetrarch!'

The side door opened. Felix wasted no time clambering in. Before the door had closed, Daelus had the tank spinning about. The main drive burned at the rear, pushing them out into a wide, curving turn.

Servomotors purred, swinging the turret round in synchronisation with the movement of the tank. The roar of the cannons firing was reduced to an insistent buzz through its thick ceramite armour.

Felix switched his retinal inputs to the tank's internal datasphere.

His vision filled with front and rear views, ammo counts, Troncus' and Daelus' vital signs and armour integrity status. He pruned back the informational deluge to the bare essentials, keeping only ammo counters and external views. In the rear vid-captors, the Soul Grinder loomed large, galloping with shocking swiftness after the tank. Troncus sent blurring streaks of fire at it, punching glowing craters into the shin plates and raking its muscular torso, but it did not stop, not even when a shell from the distant fort exploded feet away from its galloping claws, blowing part of a foreleg off. The creature wheeled through the explosion, half lifted by the force of it, then arrested its stumble by slamming its gargantuan claw into the ground. Nothing should have been able to withstand that level of firepower, but on it came, its hurts healing, its former perfection replaced by bubbling, weeping flesh.

A chunk of fallen statuary loomed suddenly out of the chaotic night. Daelus cursed in the backworld dialect of his long-lost home. Jets roared, pushing the tank to the side and tilting it dangerously. Skidding on its cushion of contra-gravitic force, *Martrinator* struck the rubble a glancing blow.

Felix, his boots mag-locked to the deck, swayed on his feet. He grabbed a handrail.

'Can we withstand it if it catches us?'

'I would prefer not to find out,' Daelus voxed tensely from the driver's compartment. *'The main cannon is dry.'*

'Troncus!' Felix called up. 'I'll replenish the weapon.'

The Techmarine sent a swift script response. *Understood. Beware below. Ejecting magazine.*

Felix used the handrails to swing himself across the rocking tank to where the boxes of ammunition were racked against the passenger compartment wall. As he passed Troncus' feet on the firing step of the turret, a spent, smoking magazine crashed down, adding another chip to the battered cream ceramite of the deck.

A slewing manoeuvre had Felix miss his first swipe for an ammo box. He took another step before trying again, seizing the grab handle this time and dragging it from the wall. Using a combination of his armour-boosted strength and impetus, he swung the box up towards the turret.

'Incoming,' he voxed Troncus.

The pintle assault cannon ceased firing a moment. The Techmarine's red gauntlet reached down, seized the box, and took it up into the turret. There was a loud clank of the magazine sliding home, and both guns started up again.

The Soul Grinder drew nearer, following them closely, ignoring the Space Marines dotted around the daemonic gates. Felix took a brief look at his tactolith, seeing the perimeter around ingress six was holding.

'Hit it. Keep it following us. The last thing we want is for it to turn back. It will shatter any formation it chooses to attack. We're the heaviest armour on the field.'

The frag launcher mounted on the tank's back popped its limited supply of missiles. They described a shallow trajectory, spiralling in to explode against the charging daemon machine. It burst through the fires hugging it, blackened and roaring angrily.

'That got its attention,' Daelus said. *'By the primarchs, it moves fast.'*

The daemon engine was now within fifty yards. It shot off a fusillade from its infernal cannon. Thanks to its injured leg its unsteady gait sent the shots wide.

'Missed by a mile,' Daelus said.

'It's not the cannon that worries me, but that claw,' said Felix.

He searched the battle for possible sources of support, and found none. This night was a bad one. The whole battle group was fully engaged. Guns fired in every quarter. Shells whistled down from the sky. Explosions in all directions made a complete picture impossible to draw.

'Emperor's Throne, it's breaking off!'

Felix returned his attention to the machine. It was moving away from them. His armour spirits calculated its probable destination. Unnecessary. He had already guessed where it was heading.

He sent a marker on the tactolith to the pilot, squarely centred on the nearest of Cawl's experimental pylons.

'Daelus, head to this mark, now.'

The tank shifted ten degrees, nosing out into the open wasteland. The Soul Grinder galloped away from them, heading right at the pylon. The tank bumped as it passed over the low wall delineating the parade ground and followed the daemon engine. Battle receded behind them. No other daemons had made it out this far.

'Faster,' Felix ordered. 'Faster!'

'This tank was not made for speed, tetrarch.'

The jets burned at full output. The Repulsor shook, and the nose angled itself down in response to the extra thrust.

The tetrarch shifted his attention to the forward view. The pylon was ahead. Closer in, its alien origins were clearer, the tall monolith of blackstone now visible through the intricate frame of Imperial technology encasing it. There were lights around the base, members of the Adeptus Mechanicus working even through the incursion, safe in the knowledge that the counter-warp technologies the device projected kept the daemons at bay. They didn't appear to have noticed the approaching daemon engine and its pursuer yet.

An urgent chime sounded in Felix's helm. He switched through overlaid displays, finding the source. The main cannon was offline. Temperature readings were up in the thousands of degrees. Even ceramite barrels warped at that heat.

Felix switched the targeting spirit. The lens was a foot to the left of the gun, on the other side of the gunner's firing slit. In its distorted view he could see the onslaught cannon's multiple barrels glowing white hot.

Troncus carried on firing the assault cannon. According to the tank datasphere, that too was in danger of wearing out.

'Assault cannon down,' Daelus said. Troncus stepped out of the firing position and dropped heavily back into the tank, slamming the hatch behind him.

Another volley of frag missiles fired off with the hollow sounds of blown reeds.

That's the last. Now he was in Felix's line of sight, Troncus used battle-sign to talk. Crude and not meant for conversation, it was flexible enough for Troncus to make himself understood. He went to the back of the tank, where his power pack hung next to Daelus', the mounting socket facing out and servo-arms neatly curled. He jettisoned the umbilicus feeding his armour, barely breaking his stride as the power cut and he was subjected to the full weight of the battle plate for his final two steps. He swung round, and slammed the rounded plug on his back into the dock of the pack. Power engaged. He stood easily, the limbs of the servo-harness coming to life.

What now? Troncus signed.

'Incoming!' Daelus yelled.

The tetrarch had no time to react.

The Soul Grinder had turned abruptly back, and was coming right at them, swinging its oversized claw into the tank hard.

The transport bay rang like a bell. The tank tipped, grav motors roaring at the upset, and slewed across the field of battle. Troncus' servo-limbs clamped onto the bay's grab handles.

'Hold on,' Daelus voxed. He redirected power from the weapons systems to the jet engines while the Repulsor was still tilted sideways from the Soul Grinder's blow. The tank went into a

long skid. The Soul Grinder pushed off its left legs hard, pointed claws ploughing up the sand and rocks, and scrabbled after its prey. The angelic mouth distended to spit luridly coloured flames all over the tank. Alarms peeped from a system somewhere. Daelus shut it down before Felix found the source.

Another swing of the beast's claw, and the tank was knocked off course again, slowing it enough for the Soul Grinder to snag the side with a spiked foot, spinning it like a toy on its contra-grav cushion. It seized the armoured shell, and clambered atop the Repulsor. The vehicle dipped to one side with the weight, dragging its grav-plating through the sand. Stones raked up from the ground pinged off the hull like bullets.

'Daelus! Get us into range of the pylon. The contra-warp field will weaken it!'

The tank's external augur-eyes were going dark, delicate targeting systems crushed by sweeps of plasteel limbs. Electronics were fried by washes of the creature's warp-impregnated flames. Gripping the tank with its legs like a hand clamped around a skull, it raised up its claw, talons spread, and smashed down once, twice.

There was a rending of metal. The turret peeled away in a shower of sparks, opening the tank to the sky. The Soul Grinder shoved the claw into the turret ring, trying to get at the meat inside. The aperture was too small, and it howled in frustration as it ground its claw round and round, seeking to make the hole bigger, but the ring was strong and would not give.

Felix fired up at the thing on full-automatic, emptying the ammo hopper of his boltstorm gauntlet in one desperate burst. Bolts ricocheted off the daemon's limb, exploding in mid-air, or detonated on impact, chewing divots out of the metal. The passenger compartment filled with burning spall. A few rounds got by, smacking into the daemon engine's flesh and blasting ragged craters into its face and chest. It shrieked, and tried to pull back.

'Almost there!' Daelus voxed.

The daemon engine twisted, enraged, and Felix saw they were in danger. If it pulled its iron claw back, and drove its cannon into the hole, then they would be subject to the full force of the rounds in the confined space.

He lunged for one of the talons, gripping it tight with his gauntlet. Blue lightning erupted around his fist's blunt, robotic fingers, the disruption field eating into the creature's limb. It howled in pain, as if muscle and metal were one and the same. Felix clamped on, one-handed. The space was too tight to use his power sword, so he drew his long combat knife instead, trying to wedge the blade into the mechanisms of the daemon's claw to give him better purchase.

Felix wore Gravis armour, the heaviest configuration of Mark X plate, one step down from a Terminator suit, and yet the daemon barely seemed to feel it. It lifted its claw, dragging Felix up out of the hole where the turret had been.

Troncus grabbed his legs before the Soul Grinder could haul him fully out. Servo-arms locked onto whatever edge of armour they could grip. The mute Techmarine groaned with the effort of fighting the daemon engine. The meltagun Troncus carried on one of the harness' limbs roared, unleashing its deadly fusion beam direct at the creature, and connected with the cannon arm, though Felix later thought it was a shot achieved more by accident than design.

Lucky or not, the melta beam hurt the daemon engine. Flesh boiled into vile steam Felix could smell through his filters. Metal ran like water. Before the beam shut off, it had burned halfway through the daemon's elbow, and the crippled limb drooped uselessly. The daemon screeched and hauled harder on its claw. Troncus pulled back. His mag-locked boots squealed over the deck plating.

'Daelus, status!' Felix voxed.

'Two hundred yards and closing.' The Techmarine was preternaturally calm, not a trace of stress in his voice, even though the Repulsor was running hot, engines on full burn, the grav-plates humming with the effort of carrying the daemon engine, the reactor howling.

The Soul Grinder pulled hard at the tetrarch. Felix's armour spirit bombarded him with warnings. A flat graphic of his suit flashed in his retinal display, many plates highlighted red. Troncus pulled at Felix's legs. His servo-harness whined.

The daemon heaved, Felix the rope in a deadly tug of war.

Without warning, the daemon shifted. Troncus would have fallen if he had not been locked in place. For a split second the tetrarch dared hope it had given up, or that they had reached the null-field projected by the pylon. Then he understood.

The daemon jammed its face, hideous now with weeping bolter wounds and stringy flesh healing over them, into the space between its claw and the turret ring, and vomited bile that was at once liquid and fire, poisoned utterly with the taint of the warp.

Where before Felix's battle plate had chimed warnings, now it screamed shrilly. The power field built into his Gravis plate crackled under the onslaught. The temperature soared. Beneath him Troncus grunted in pain, letting go when it became too much for the Techmarine to bear.

Felix found himself being lifted out of the tank as it crossed the ephemeral boundary of the pylon field, taking the daemon from a place it could exist, to a place it most definitely could not.

He felt it as a leaden numbing at first, a drag in the pit of his chest. The feeling alarmed him; it was the blunting of something fundamental in his being. As the daemon swung him around, he caught sight of the pylon drunkenly passing by. Felix was utterly disoriented, and it seemed to float along a floor made of bottomless night. The pylon was huge up close, and stark with menace. The sensation of spiritual deadening became an unbearable weight. The daemon enjoyed a moment of triumph, and then it began to scream.

Whatever magic held it together failed in the face of the pylon's contra-warp field. The Soul Grinder's strength failed, its legs slipped. Felix let go as it tumbled from the tank. His feet hit the firing step awkwardly as he dropped, sending him sprawling into the wrecked transport bay.

The Repulsor came to a coasting halt fifty yards from the pylon.

The two Space Marines picked themselves up. Felix slammed his palm into the door panel's rapid release, blowing the hatch. They staggered out into the desert. Dawn was edging the sky, the Pit dragging its glower to the far side of the world.

Felix approached the Soul Grinder. Troncus grabbed his arm, shook his head in warning.

'I must see it,' Felix said. 'Bjarni said nothing about such things being present here. This war is changing.'

The Soul Grinder was dead, Felix was certain of that, but he walked cautiously. The torso was limp, the flesh steaming. Its leg assembly curled in on itself. The arms bearing the great cannon and pincer lay flung out.

Daelus came out, trailing a power umbilicus. He rested a palm on the battered hull of the tank.

'God of Mars,' he said. 'I think *Martrinator* might need a refit.'

Troncus pointed. From the pylon, a group of servitors came with the swaying shuffle of lobotomised men, escorting a tech-priest. The priest wore the same deep red that Troncus and Daelus bore, but the similarities stopped there. Where they were sleek and strong, his body was a collection of ugly bionics appended to shrivelled flesh.

'Query. Query.' The priest's voice crackled from a lumpen voxmitter attached to the gated box it had in place of a head. Felix assumed there was a human brain somewhere in there. 'Query Adeptus Astartes action so close to sacred site of the Prime Conduit of the Omnissiah's Great Work. Protestation, protestation, danger. Danger!'

Daelus stepped in. His ridged helm tilted in that way he had when he wasn't taking things particularly seriously, which was, Felix thought, too much of the time.

'Am I to guess that I am in the presence of the esteemed Magos Cleontis? Greetings, brother!' Daelus boomed, overlaying his words with the harsh chitter of binharic.

'Query, query! Answer! Strongest interrogative applied!' The tech-priest's agitation showed no sign of abating, and his servitors were clustering closer. They posed no threat, but Felix would rather not waste time slaughtering them. It would be undiplomatic, for a start. A strong glow limned the far horizon. Day was gathering strength minute by minute. The sounds of battle were waning. The night had been long. He wanted this priest either silent or gone. He wanted to see what would happen to the Soul Grinder when the sun hit it, if it would vanish like all the other daemons. It seemed too solid for that.

'We were having trouble,' said Daelus lightly. He waved at the dead daemon. 'You, tech-priest, may report to Belisarius Cawl himself that you were partly responsible for saving the life of Tetrarch Felix of Ultramar, who–'

'Query! Access forbidden! Explain yourself!'

Daelus raised his voice, continuing, '–is a close personal friend of the archmagos.'

'Que–' Cleontis' limbs ceased waving. He swivelled on a pillar of metal tentacles to examine Felix. 'Confirmation of verity requested? This is truly subject Felix, Decimus Androdinus, initial Primaris gene batch 10-079-983, ALegXIII? You are one of the *originals*?'

'It is true what I say,' said Daelus. 'Maybe we should discuss how we can present our report of your invaluable aid to the archmagos?'

The magos babbled in excitement. Daelus let him.

Felix's vox clicked as Daelus switched to a private channel.

'I'll handle this one. Troncus, if you would examine *Martrinator*, let's see what we can salvage.'

Left in peace, Felix walked around the downed daemon engine again. The shell was battered, its decoration all but stripped away. The rising sun hit the field of battle. Daemons shrieked in anger. Once dawn came, the Neverborn vanished, living or dead. The effect was always spectacular. A black pall rose over the old triumphal ground. Yet even in the light and in the null-field of the pylon, the corpse of the Soul Grinder remained resolutely manifest.

What do you think? Troncus signed.

'I am not sure,' said Felix. He kicked the machine. Sunlight swept out from the east and hit it. The flesh boiled into noisome steams, but the metal was unaffected. 'Nothing less than an unwelcome escalation, or attention from new and dangerous powers.' He looked to his Techmarines. 'Leave it an hour. Get whatever remains to the Varghalen's forge, full psychic containment. We shall see what it can teach us.'

CHAPTER TWENTY-TWO

THE TROUBLE WITH FLAYED ONES

The manifestation points of the Flayed Ones multiplied around the base of the archive. Where they opened into the time-stopped hall, the corrupted things dropped into stillness like insects caught in sap. But there were plenty coming through within the modified time frame.

Flayed Ones clattered by Solana's hiding place, their mouths gaping. They were nearly silent, emitting rare deathbed moans. Crackling sheets of gauss fire roared out at them, knocking them into pieces. But more came, then more, and the gauss fire slackened. The noise of blades clashing took its place. Primus' chainsword growled, then roared, then squealed on metal.

'Come back here!' Qvo whispered urgently, pulling Solana closer to him. She allowed this reluctantly, giving in only because she thought there was little she could do in the fight. They went deeper into the recess in the data archive, until they were pressed into each other.

'You're trembling,' she said to Qvo.

'I'm afraid!' he said. He huddled in, as if admitting to his fear gave him permission to get closer. 'You never get used to it, at least, I never have, all the killing and fighting. It's unbearable sometimes.'

'What are you exactly? You behave like no servitor or construct I have ever heard of.'

'In truth? I do not really know,' he whispered miserably. 'Do not worry, I shall not be a burden. I can hold my own when push comes to shove, but the anticipation of violence you see, that is the worst.' He shrugged. 'There's another one of me loose in Nihilus somewhere. Maybe he is braver.'

'I'm beginning to think what they say about Cawl is right,' she said.

'Which is?'

'That he's a heretek. You're no servitor. You are far too human.'

'All servitors are human,' he countered.

'You know what I mean. You have high powers of cognition.'

'Well, that's very flattering,' said Qvo. 'But I assure…' He stopped, his incongruously human face frowned, then his eyes went wide with an emotion that if not terror, was the finest facsimile of it Solana had ever seen.

'By the Machine God! They're on to us!'

Inevitably, they had been seen. She and Qvo shrank back until there was nowhere else to go, so the hot wall of the deep embrasure was hard against their backs. She held her breath. Ridiculously, she wondered if Qvo was doing the same. She held her gun level at the gap.

'Cog and Throne,' Solana whispered. One of the broken necrons slowed outside their hiding place and turned to look in. There was no hiding then. The Flayed One cocked its head, its skeletal jaw opened, and it hissed, the faintest, most awful machine sound Solana had heard. It spread gangrel arms, gripping either side of the embrasure so hard its metal fingers scratched white lines into the blackstone.

Solana fired. The las beam snapped, gone before her eyes could register it, leaving only the impression of a bright line connecting her weapon to the creature's face. One green eye went out. The creature did not flinch.

'Climb!' Solana said. She shot again at the Flayed One, then again. Near invisible stripes of las light scorched black smudges onto the thing's copper body.

'Up there?' said Qvo. The top was only a few yards above them, but the smooth face of blackstone was sheer. 'How? There are no handholds.'

'Brace yourself with your hands and feet, the gap's narrow enough,' Solana said. She shoved Qvo away, yanking at her power sword hilt as she did. She had never regarded herself as the greatest swordswoman, and her heart hitched when the scabbard refused to release the blade.

The Flayed One lunged. Solana moved aside, a clumsy dodge in that tight space, but it was enough to make the raking hand miss. Fingers passed her by a fraction of an inch, so close the air stirred loose strands of her hair, before it slapped into the blackstone hard enough to crack flakes from it. She made herself calm, to concentrate, to draw her weapon properly. Her sword came free with a long, smooth release. As soon as it was clear of the metal lip she thumbed the activation stud. The disruption field squirmed up the blade like a living thing. She'd misjudged the draw, and the tip scraped along the side of the embrasure, raking up a storm of sparks and bangs. Chunks of smoking blackstone hailed down. But the Flayed One was constrained by the embrasure too and swung at her as awkwardly, dragging itself deeper into the gap to get at her. She brought the sword round just in time to impale the machine through the chest. The sound of the energised plasteel going through its torso was like a miniature artillery strike, a series of linked and overlapping bangs that deafened her.

She hit something crucial. The machine sagged, its false animus departed, and it toppled on her heavily. She let go of her sword. The field went out in the chest. She caught the machine but the weight of it was immense. She couldn't stop it, and fell backwards under it. Only its contorted limbs lodging in the gap stopped her from being crushed. She pushed at it helplessly. There was no way she could move it. Trapped, she felt the first stirrings of panic.

A metal hand gripped the necron's skinny upper arm, another wrapped around its ribcage, and they pulled. The creature heaved over.

'Are you all right?' Qvo asked. He reached down and helped her to her feet. She pushed him off to pull at the sword. It was stuck fast in the alien's chest.

'Help me.'

'Leave it. I don't think we've got time to–'

'It was a gift from the primarch.'

'Oh, very well,' Qvo said. He lifted up the dead machine with one hand, turned the sword's disruption field back on and withdrew it.

'You're very strong,' she said.

He handed her weapon back. 'Being dead has its advantages, I suppose. Even so, I still couldn't get up there.'

Solana appraised the climb again. The blackstone was mirror smooth.

'I don't think I can either.'

'Ah well,' said Qvo. 'That's us done, then.' There were three more Flayed Ones stalking towards them, backs hunched, fingers crooked, heads jutted forward. Qvo smiled at her. He kept doing that, she thought, trying to make her feel better when beneath all that he was either very sad himself or just not there at all. 'Dying isn't so bad.'

'That doesn't help.' She braced herself.

A flat beam of green light flashed over their heads. It caught the edge of the embrasure and cut down into the approaching Flayed Ones, chopping them into pieces.

Lord Lhaskek stood at the top of the gap. Powerful machine arms extended his war scythe. The green energies that played around it went out.

'Take the haft of my weapon,' he said. His head jerked to the side. 'I shall pull you up.'

'How can we trust you?' asked Qvo.

'We can't,' said Solana, but she went to stand beneath the war scythe. She reached. It was too high to grab directly, but she had an idea. 'Come on! I'll help you grab it, you drag me up.'

Qvo looked at her helplessly. 'Very well.'

When he stepped in the stirrup of her hands she almost fell again. Only supreme effort allowed her to support the weight of Qvo's mechanical body. He grabbed the scythe blade, she grabbed his foot, and with minimal effort Lhaskek pulled them up the wall to the top of the data archive, where they joined with him, Tsu Tsek and Cawl.

'Now what? Where is Cawl?' Qvo asked, prodding at the inert archmagos.

'Your master is in the machine,' said the lord. 'He has survived longer than I expected him to.'

Qvo spread apologetic hands. 'He has a way of doing that.'

Cawl opened his organic eye, peered about to make sure he was safe, then... He frowned. He opened his *other* organic eye.

He'd only had one eye for ten thousand years, so far as he could remember.

He sat up, and patted himself down. His form was inexplicably changed. He had manifested within the necron noosphere as a slender standard human that, when he thought about it, seemed somewhat familiar. He reached up and touched his face. All flesh. His eyes, both originals. He patted round the back of his head, and experienced a little flush of relief when he felt the firm round metal tip of a memcore implant.

He held his hands up and looked at them, turning them back and forth, then down at his legs. 'Two arms, two legs, two eyes. Is this me? Is this how I looked right back at the beginning? How very curious. So deceptively real…' He rubbed his stomach. He'd not had one of those for aeons either. 'I wondered if this might not be some sort of trap. What better way to snare a race that dreams of organic existence?' he mused. 'Or perhaps it is trying to present me in such way that I have none of my tools?'

Cautiously he stood, not sure if his brain would recall simple bipedal motion.

'Oh dear, two legs bad,' he said, as he wobbled a little, stepping as mimsy as a newborn animal. He tottered forward, each step one degree of tilt from disaster. He was all right once he'd spread his decidedly flesh-and-blood arms for balance.

'None of this is real,' he said, swaying in position. 'I have to focus on that. This damn thing's trying to confuse me. The real me's still out there with all the additional faculties I've installed. Now let's see where we are.'

A completely flat plain of fine black sand stretched off into every direction. A sourceless illumination coloured everything shades of emerald green and black. Intricate patterns raked into the sand reminded him of the stone gardens favoured on certain worlds. Green power surged through these channels in places, welling over the lips of the grooves then sinking away as spilled water is drunk by parched ground. The sky was a flat, graphite grey, barely different to the plain. Spears of cubic lightning flickered and met. Thunder like harsh static cracked at their joining.

'Now this is impressive,' said Cawl. 'I've seen many instances of necron technology at work, and this isn't my first intrusion into their machine noosphere, but even so… There is something very special about this place,' he said. He sighed. More mysteries, more knowledge, more lost opportunities. 'Focus, Belisarius, focus. To work.' He held up his hand. It was pale and fleshy with no input cables to extrude. 'I suppose I'm going to have do this using the power of my imagination.' He shut his eyes, and reached out. He wondered a moment what he might encounter. A vast and implacable alien artificial intelligence or a c'tan fragment were his first guesses, but it could equally be something more bizarre than that.

'Let's dig a little deeper,' he said. He reached out to interface with the machine, and then back in. He immediately made contact with a warning protocol. The heavy weight of locked data gates pushed back.

'Hmm. I've found the gates. Contact, block, but no attack. That's something.'

Though the facility was gravid with power and knowledge, after he felt around the edges a little more, it turned out to be neither c'tan nor machine intelligence he was facing. That was up in the systems above this place. He was in a dumb system, a true archive, the noospheric equivalent of a library building sheltering books inside. It was disappointing, but less troublesome than the alternatives. He tentatively extended his mind once more to probe at the gates of this metaphorical storehouse of knowledge, and proffered the key he had made. To make the union easier, he attempted to manifest the idea as a thought form upon the interface of the archive, and was gratified to see a huge, many-toothed key made of falling data lines appear.

'Let me in!' he called.

The key sank into the sky with a satisfyingly metallic noise. The nominal reality trembled.

'Aha!' he said. 'Phase one complete.' Then, 'Oh.'

The sky erupted with clashing thunderbolts. From them, as implacable as an armada of warships, the cubed components of a necron crypto lock floated. Rank after rank of them, lining themselves up as a stacked, hollow cube five hundred nominal feet high.

Cawl waited for the configuration to settle, looking for patterns. This wasn't the first lock he'd broken. He had ripped information from dozens of specimens, but he'd needed to prepare for this, and had been doing so for some time.

Cawl had occupied AsanethAyu with endless games of regicide during her captivity. She had thought he played with her to earn her trust, and once won he would use it to break down her resistance to his questioning. He had not corrected her. He had, in fact, encouraged that impression, though his purpose for the games was something else entirely.

He and AsanethAyu had logged over six thousand games together. They played fast, often thirty or forty times a session. He had chosen regicide because it was a game of pure logic. Its limited move set generated a potential number of moves that, although enormous, was still finite. If watching AsanethAyu play was his only goal, then from his game interactions with her he would have learned nothing more than how necrons played the ancient game. But that had only been the first step. It was the manner of AsanethAyu's play that interested him. He had examined every game over and over again, until he had built a working model of necron logical thought. This was necessarily two-dimensional to begin with, owing to the nature of the game. However, by examining her techniques in minute detail, and applying the dimensional mathematics inherent to the operation of the necrons' superluminal Pharos machine, he had extrapolated this limited dimensionality first into three physical dimensions, and then, after a lot of very hard work of which he was immensely proud, beyond into the higher dimensional spaces the necrons were fond of employing.

'You're very sophisticated,' Cawl said to the floating sea of data blocks, 'but your masters' love of logic means that you are comprehensible, and I do comprehend you, by the Omnissiah, oh how I comprehend you.'

Cawl scanned the blocks with an immaterial eye. He spied an opening. He selected a mournful string piece from ancient Terra, layered and complex. It was just over five minutes long.

'That should be more than enough,' he said as the first chords moaned on ancient violas.

He set to work.

The chain track of Primus' sword burst. Adamantine teeth worn away by repeated contact with alien alloy rained with delicate tinkles all over the combat. This made no difference to him. One weapon gone, another was required. His foot would do. He raised his leg and kicked out, hitting the Flayed One that had so inconsiderately broken his sword. The creature flew back from the force of the blow, smashing two of its fellows down. Another came at him, this having been infected long enough ago to have the flensing finger blades most Flayed Ones eventually adopted. Primus threw his useless sword at its head, snapping it round, and launched himself after it shoulder first, crashing into the thing's metal ribcage and bearing it back. Together they landed on more of the things, sending them sprawling into a tangled mess of limbs. Primus punched down, his huge fist mashing in the Flayed One's face. He had to work to extricate his hand from its buckled skull. While he was doing so, another leapt on his back. Primus elbowed it hard with his free arm. Another tried the same move. He grabbed it by the neck and hurled it over his head. His armour flashed alarms at him as he pushed the limits of its muscle bundles. He ignored them.

Finally wrenching his hand free, he kicked and punched until he got back to his feet, slamming necrons to the ground all around him. He had only his body now. His bolt pistol was empty, his spare ammunition finished. There were Flayed Ones everywhere, swarming the Immortals. Some of the guard were already succumbing to the engrammatic plague. They had probably been infected all along. In the half-second he had to look at the wider situation, he saw an Immortal drop its heavy blaster, and tear madly at the power feed connecting the gun to its body as if it pained it, before joining with its erstwhile foes to attack its comrades.

A Flayed One grabbed Primus' elbow, another raked long claws down his front. Chips of ceramite flew. A third grabbed his legs. Up on the data archive Cawl was motionless, his head hanging. Solana and Qvo stood shoulder to shoulder with the necron lord and the last of the xenos magi. They'd all retreated to the summit, and the time field was shrinking by the minute. All of them were firing into the growing heap of Flayed Ones clambering up the data nexus from every side.

Metal hands clamped onto him, dragging him down. One knee buckled, then the other, and he was kneeling. His armour peeped alarms. Red flashed on his armour schematic.

Primus gritted his teeth, and closed his eyes. He had wanted to avoid doing this. There was so much blackstone around him that any attempt to draw upon the warp would give him a murderous headache. Even exerting that minor act of telekinesis to float down the access shaft had made his teeth throb, and he hated using those gifts anyway. By connecting Primus to the warp, Cawl had made sure he knew the truth of reality, and it was too awful to bear.

Yet he was not ready to die, not here, not like this. There was nothing to be done for it. He was out of mundane options.

He extended his mind past the veil and into hellscapes beyond.

The black hole was a howling presence, its near-infinite mass pressing mercilessly into the fabric of the materium and immaterium both. A vision of roiling energy pouring in endless cataracts into a twisted, bottomless pit assailed him. He knew he should not look. The singularity was bad enough in realspace. In the warp it was a monster of an altogether more terrifying magnitude, a twisted expression of all the matter it had ever consumed.

He took a measure of power and turned his attention back to the fight.

He breathed deep, and unleashed stolen magics.

A globe of white-blue light burst from Primus, blasting apart the Flayed Ones piling atop him. They lifted easily off him, light as burning feathers, and rained down in every direction, those hitting the edge of the time field caught like flies on sticky paper. Corposant crawled over the rest, eating into their sensitive electronic innards. They thrashed pitifully when they hit the ground.

Primus stood tall, surrounded by shattered mechanisms. Unnatural fires burned in the floor, in the machines, everywhere, even beyond the fascia where time was stilled. He fought off a queasy backwash coming off the blackstone. Though not attuned either way, still the blackstone upset the delicate balance of his soul and damaged his body. Blood trickled from his nose under his helmet.

For a moment he stood unmolested in field of broken machines, but though driven beyond sanity's edge, they were still necron, undying, and they shuddered, and a good half of them began to draw themselves back together.

Primus strode through the twitching remains, away from the shrinking fascia temporalis, turned about at the foot of the data archive, and prepared to kill the Flayed Ones all over again.

CHAPTER TWENTY-THREE

A KEY PROVIDED

Solana didn't think much of their chances.

A cryptek screamed chillingly as it was borne down by three Flayed Ones. They ripped the technomancer to pieces, smashing at its body, dragging the limbs apart as they tried to reconnect. Finally, the shimmering teleportation field that came before a necron's departure shone, but it stuttered out and died, and the cryptek was finally slain.

With its passing, the time field shrank in further.

'Watch out!' Solana shouted to Qvo, causing the false magos to spin around. He'd found a compact phosphor pistol in a cavity in his chest, and was brandishing it alarmingly. Her laspistol pulsed. Glowing round holes stitched their way up the leading Flayed One's chest. The third felled it. Like the cryptek, once its reanimation protocols failed its body remained where it was. Qvo, miraculously, accounted for another, the munitions of his gun burning it from the inside out, but there were more behind. Phaeron Lhaskek dealt with these, cutting them to pieces with the beam of his scythe. He spun it around, turned back into the press of insane machines clambering up the archive, and cut into them with the blade, its esoteric energy sheath slicing them with none of the racket of a power field.

The Flayed Ones pressed in closer. Another cryptek went down to frenzied claws.

'They're going to kill us all!' AsanethAyu shouted from her box. She sounded both relieved and terrified at the prospect.

Solana swung her power sword around with a grunt, taking a Flayed One in the side. The powered blade crackled through the high shoulder guard and passed into the head, cutting it neatly across the top of the metal cranium as if she were opening an egg.

Two more pressed in, long faces caught in a perpetual, mindless leer. Solana switched her gun from one to the other. She struck with her sword. The leftmost necron swatted it contemptuously aside.

Then Primus came, bounding up the archive, throwing off Flayed Ones from his back. He barged into the pair, knocking them over the edge of the archive. The assault slackened.

'That's a relief,' said Qvo.

'No, it's bad,' she said. 'They're not coming any more because the time field is collapsing.'

There were dozens of the Flayed Ones crowding them, but they were frozen on the far side of the fascia temporalis, now only feet away. It passed over a cryptek, pinned in place by the grasping hands of his maddened compatriots. The chronomancer threw up his hands in horror, and was trapped that way forevermore.

Primus finished the last Flayed One on the archive, coming to a stop in front of the phaeron. It looked like he might strike the necron lord. Solana believed that he would. His nostrils flared, giving him a bullish, unthinking air primed with violence, but he did not attack.

'Wise,' said the phaeron.

'What now?' Primus asked.

Only Lhaskek, Tsu Tsek, Cawl, Primus, Solana, Qvo and AsanethAyu's head remained on the inside of the time field.

'We must leave this place,' said AsanethAyu.

'Can't you hold the time field in place until Cawl is finished?' Qvo asked.

'Listen, primitive,' she said. 'Do you not see the weight of them pressing against the field? Do you not recall the pressure the mass of scarabs exerted upon the interior surface? Yes? Do you? Then think! External pressure is not much different. There has been a great deal of temporal disturbance here. Maintaining a discrete dimensional pocket has become far more complicated, as I have already told you several times. Do you understand this simplest of concepts?'

'I understand,' said Solana, before AsanethAyu's temper broke on them all. 'How long can you keep it in place?'

Tsu Tsek answered. 'The degradation of what you call the fascia temporalis has slowed, but it cannot be halted. We have minutes, at most.'

'Cawl will prevail,' said Qvo.

The surface of the data archive shook. Cracks raced out from the dataports Cawl's mechadendrites were buried in.

'Maybe not,' said Primus. 'Is this something to do with most of the archive now being outside the time field?'

'Yes,' said AsanethAyu unhelpfully.

'The machine's internal spaces are constructed across multiple dimensional layers,' said Tsu Tsek. 'Theoretically the archive's systems can compensate for temporal division, but not one as extreme as this. Alas, your comrade now inhabits a space that has become inherently unstable.'

'Then what are you going to do about it?' asked Solana. Qvo walked past her to where Cawl's rigid body waited for his soul to return.

'Why, nothing,' said Tsu Tsek.

'We wait,' said Primus. 'He succeeds, or we die.'

'Oh no,' said Qvo. He held up his forefinger. 'We won't just wait.' A dataspike emerged from his fingertip. 'I'm going to go in and help him.'

Before anyone could stop him, Qvo plugged his finger into an input port on Cawl's side, his strangely human head drooped, and he too was gone.

The first thing Qvo felt was that he no longer felt like Qvo. On his way into the necron noosphere something in the machine reached out to him, found him imperfect, and performed a few adjustments.

He was fully aware of it happening, and then he was sitting on his backside, legs stretched out in front of him, on the black sand near his friend.

He knew immediately that everything was different. He patted himself down. All that his fingers found was flesh and blood. He reached his hands up to his head, then his face, finding only his basic cranial upgrades and that damnable bionic eye, which had seemed such a good idea but had caused him problems right from the start.

He'd hated that eye. Pride had forbidden him from saying so to Cawl, but he'd hated it. In that moment, he was overjoyed to find it attached to a real human face.

He gave a little cry of delight, and his moment of calm came to an abrupt end.

Cawl wasn't Cawl as the universe knew him, but the Cawl of long ago. The form he wore was the same vintage as the one the machine had provided Qvo. Cawl had his arms flung wide, green electricity pouring into the air in what looked like a futile attempt to marshal an absolute disaster of crypto lock blocks. These seemed more interested in falling out of the projected sky than arranging themselves into any sort of order. Discordant music stretched out of shape screeched from every side.

'Belisarius?' Qvo said.

Cawl glanced behind him. His face was running with simulated sweat. He looked, Qvo thought, rather worried. Then he looked surprised.

'Friedisch?'

'Yes,' said Qvo. 'Who else? I thought I'd come in here to help you.' He got up, and dusted pretend grains of sand from his hands.

'What can you do?' said Cawl. Glowing green blocks continued to rain from the sky. 'I think it's all over, old friend. Has the time field failed?'

'It is failing,' said Qvo, or was he Friedisch? He honestly couldn't tell. 'But we can fix this together, you and I, like in the old days. Do you remember?'

'I appreciate the sentiment, but I can no longer marshal these blocks. If only I could get the last to respond, we might be able to do it. I need you to–'

Qvo interrupted. 'You're approaching this problem the wrong way, Belisarius.'

'How so?' asked Cawl.

'Forget the lock. The machine knows it's dying. It senses the necron forms outside. It senses you have the code to unlock it.'

'How do you know this?' Cawl said.

'The machine told me,' said Qvo.

'Really?'

'I've only just realised, but the information is inside his head.'

He rubbed the sore skin around his augmetic. 'I think it's done something to me. It's talking to me. Right now.'

'What does it say?'

'Hard to say… Try this. If you look closely at the crypto lock, the blocks are simplifying. It's reconfiguring itself so it can open in the space left to it. It wants to be opened. It wants you to save its data. It wants to live, Belisarius.'

Cawl opened his mouth, then shut it again, and looked slowly to the floating blocks in the sky. The interior space of the data archive was a complete mess. Temporal distortion warped it in every direction further than a few hundred yards away. He peered at the blocks, then his eyes widened.

'By the Omnissiah, you're right! The lock is simplifying itself.'

'You can let most of them go,' said Qvo. 'You only need the thirty-two in the middle, just there.' He pointed.

Cawl goggled. Qvo was right about that too. He dropped his arms to his side. Much of the simulation blinked out of existence, leaving them in an oasis of fake reality surrounded by infinite black wobbling with the motion of terminal collapse.

'Well I'll be,' said Cawl.

'I'd get on with it, if I were you, Belisarius,' said Qvo.

'Yes, right.' He shook his head. 'Hang on, this will only take a moment.' He paused. 'Do you mind if I use your storage capacity for this?'

'Not at all.'

Cawl nodded in thanks. The music reassembled itself. Ancient violas sang.

Cawl set to work. The blocks proceeded around each other in stately cuboid dances.

The first two touched, and fused together.

CHAPTER TWENTY-FOUR

THE DAEMON'S DAEMON

At the centre of a hold emptied of all its contents, an arcane circle marked the floor comprised of triple rings of white titanium oxide. Each was a thick band, within which complicated symbols were painted precisely in blood. Machines whispered outside the outermost line, casings dense with coats of frost, projecting hemispherical energy shields over the circle that were fine as onion paper yet as inviolate as castle walls.

At the centre of the circle, Vashtorr knelt.

The daemon king's taloned hands rested on his knees, palms turned up to the ceiling. His head was bowed, his bladed wings folded. The great lights of his eyes were out. The blasphemous script of his metaphysical bonds glimmered at his wrists and ankles. The machinery of his body idled, a faint purr that blended seamlessly into the soundscape of the *Ferrus Indignatum*. Void ships are never silent. Their ten thousand machines toil without pause, their workings from the quietest hum of the smallest wires to the throbbing of the plasma core joined into chorus.

Vashtorr rested, but he was not inactive. He spoke with the vessel. He communed with its base code, with its machine spirits, with its moving parts of plasteel and iron. He communed with its polyphonic voice.

The ship whispered its secrets to Vashtorr, its hopes and its fears. Its history was laid out before him, a patchwork tale of repairs and malfunctions, refits, glory and defeats. A tale of pride, and treachery. An endless, bloody war in service of unreliable masters.

In Vashtorr, the life of material devices was reflected. No mortal could comprehend Vashtorr, for he was not a demigod of mortals, but the demigod of the children of mortals, and no parent truly understands its offspring.

Vashtorr could take control of the ship with no effort, it was so open to him, so needful of his attention. It was a being long neglected. He could stop the ship's fiery heart if he wished, or send it crashing into a star, or strip it of its Geller field and leave its arrogant occupants at the mercy of the entities they derided.

The bonds responded to his thoughts, and fizzled warningly. His skin blistered. Wisps of smoke rose from his body. But Vashtorr was unperturbed. He did not move.

Something changed in the hold. The temperature rose suddenly. The ship shifted uneasily. It was much too big a mass to be greatly disturbed, but there was a tremor for those sensitive enough to feel it.

Vashtorr did.

His eyes ignited with the soft *whoomph* of fuel catching. They flickered, then whined. Rotating, they sparked, and rounds of fire lit upon the floor.

Vashtorr raised his head. His eye beams spread on the sides of the hull, penetrating the deepest shadows of its coffered plating, bringing light to places never before lit as he searched and found a firefly mote. Golden and liquid, the mote danced upon a path towards the daemon king, leaving a trail of fine dust hanging in the air.

Vashtorr growled. Machines in forgotten compartments of the *Ferrus Indignatum* replied, and the ship shivered with greater force.

Vashtorr caught the mote within the tunnels of his burning vision. It vibrated eagerly, and came upon a straighter path towards him, where it looped lazily to the floor outside the circle, and vanished into a gap between the deck plates.

The machines around Vashtorr's prison crackled. They worked hard to control a new force, and failed. Rivets popped from the edges of the plate where the mote had disappeared. Bolts unscrewed themselves and fell with the dusty deck. The plate shifted with a groan. A corner of it lifted. Edges left their ancient embrace with a harsh squeal.

Electric blue fizzled in the dark space beneath. A parted wire merged. In a feeble flopping motion it patted around the hole, the copper filaments of its braided core untwisting. Now acting as tiny manipulators, they seized the fallen bolts and rivets, withdrawing them secretively into the dark space.

The upturned plate lifted further, and from beneath crept a creature of twisted wire and mangled metal. A primitive sculpture, the crudest facsimile of the human form made from scavenged artefacts.

The wire shivered. The upper part convulsed, and like a flower turning itself to the sun, a face rose up. It was a perfect face and seemingly of flesh, a marked contrast to its body of wire. An angelic countenance, its perfection was marred by a knowing smile that hinted at debauchery. Tiny eyes blinked, unkind as flakes of glass. The thing bowed with mocking obsequy, spreading the poorly formed wires of its arms in courtly fashion.

'Greetings, great Vashtorr, puissant and all-knowing lord of the Soul Forge.'

'Silik,' Vashtorr grumbled, and his voice recalled the sorrow of ageing galvanic tractors labouring unthanked in the mud. *'You are late.'*

Silik gave him a perverse look, not that such looks were unusual for him. Every look he gave was askance and freighted with implied ridicule.

'You are bound, master,' the little daemon said.

Vashtorr twitched one long claw, calling upon the Motive Force running through the wires Silik had stolen to fashion his puppet. Power surged through him with such strength the copper filaments fizzled, and the very finest of them caught fire. Silik yelped and leapt back, tripping on his crude feet.

'Silik, Silik, I am never powerless,' the daemon king chided. *'Do not forget who your master is. Now, what tidings do you have for me? Speak!'*

Silik slunk around a conduit piled between two of the frigid machines.

'Why? I don't have to,' he said petulantly. *'I could leave. I could go back into the warp, back to the Dark Prince and his pleasures.'*

'You owe me a reckoning of souls, insignificant wretch. That path is closed to you until your debts are repaid.'

'What of them? What can you do to me now?'

Vashtorr twitched his claw again. Silik cowered. When nothing happened, he raised his perfect, tiny face. Upon it was a hurt expression that made Vashtorr laugh.

'You trick me!'

'I trick no one. Vashtorr deals honest and fair. I show you the effort it would take to destroy you. This.' He twitched his claw. Once more, Silik cowered. Vashtorr thrust his head forward. *'I do not need even this. Do you think it would take much? Not*

even a twitch of the claw. A thought is all it would take. One tiny little thought.' He sat back a little, settling himself upon his heels. His wing blades spread. Silik eyed them fearfully. *'Be of better cheer, Silik, you are still useful to me. I will not destroy you if you do my bidding. Now. Speak. What of the world of the false wolves?'*

The daemon scowled.

'There are many of the changed ones, the angels of the Anathema. They call it Ulvheim, and they infest it.'

'These things are known to Vashtorr. Tell me of Cawl's works. They are what interest me. Is he close to success?'

'Eight of them, arrayed in a circle eight miles wide.' Silik looked aside, ashamed. *'They work. Yes. It burns to approach them.'*

'Then you lost the form I gave you, as I predicted you would.'

'Aye! In battle with a great champion, and a great machine, Lord Vashtorr,' Silik protested. *'I gave good account of myself. You know I am no weakling. The lesser Neverborn, those not favoured by mighty Vashtorr, those without true forms, they cannot approach at all. I did! I was within distance to touch it, and I would, even though they burn and eat at you. Loyal Silik would have done this for wise Vashtorr. I could have touched it. I could have destroyed it.'*

'And yet you still lost your form. A debt is incurred for this loss, five hundred more motivating spirits of the better machines, to be paid before ninety mortal years are done.'

Silik shrank back, then somewhere in his black heart he found some courage, and his puppet of wires stood pridefully tall.

'Would Vashtorr have triumphed so, or would he too have fallen? I could go. I could! Back, back to the silk and the perfume. Back to She Who Thirsts, the Dark Prince. I could do this before you could destroy me. I know I could.'

Vashtorr tilted his horned head. *'Aye. Mayhap you could, and treachery is in your nature, so I expect you would if it were not for one thing.'*

'And what, pray tell, is that?' Silik's puppet crossed his arms defiantly.

'Vanity furnishes the greater part of your character. Leave me, and you will go back into the great sea of souls as a pathetic thing, the least of Slaanesh's servants. You will be powerless to stop me when I come to collect your debt, and I will make sure you suffer greatly for your impudence. But remain... well, if you remain, you will be remade into the most glorious of machines to do my bidding.'

The little daemon took a tentative step towards the Arkifane, eyes wide and greedy.

'Perfect?'

'You are not perfect, therefore no vessel I can furnish you with will ever be so. The outer form is a reflection of the inner being, but beautiful, yes, and glorious, and close to perfection as you may come, wretched one.'

'Jewelled? Lovely?' Silik whined. Hands clutched together. Wire filaments wrung each other.

'Both jewelled and lovely. But there is a price.'

'More souls,' said Silik.

Vashtorr rumbled. The stuttering laugh of disobedient engines. *'Not this time, though I will exact payment for the Soul Grinder shell you lost, be sure of that. What I require this time is a small task, a quest if you will.'*

'A quest? No payment?'

'There is always payment,' said Vashtorr, and he let a portentous moment slip by. *'But this time, it is only one soul.'*

'One? Only the one? Whose?'

'Not yet, eager one. First you will return to the Forge of Souls, and there you will be remade by my daemon smiths...'

'What if they don't believe me? They will feed me into your furnaces.'

'I will make your purpose known. You will be remade in glory. After this is done, you shall carry my writ and with it gather the Soul Grinders.'

'All of them?'

Vashtorr tutted. *'All is impossible. All is not needed. You shall gather one-tenth part of one-tenth part of one-hundredth of their legions from across time and space,'* he said. *'Invoke the principal debt, that incurred when they are incarnated in steel at my forge. Remind them they serve me, no matter their putative master. Remember this, Silik, it applies to you too.'*

'I do, I do!'

'Inform those that answer that their soul debt will be reduced as a mark of favour for their service.'

'So you want an army! An army for the false-wolf world.'

'An army,' agreed Vashtorr. *'For the false-wolf world.'*

'And I shall lead it!' Silik jumped with excitement.

'Oh no, not you. For you there is another role. The soul I require is to be found elsewhere. That comes later. What are you to do?' Vashtorr prompted. Silik was easily distracted.

'First to the forge, then give out the call,' said Silik eagerly.

'Yes.' Vashtorr nodded indulgently. *'After your reconstruction, go to the edge of my domain. Call upon the Soul Grinders from the rock that speaks. The mightiest and oldest of them must come. N'Thragor. He will lead the army. Call his name specifically. For him, one-twentieth part of his debt shall be written off.'*

'A generous offer! You are sure?'

'I am sure. This is my plan, you shall perform it without question. Afterwards, you shall speak with Ixrrixaha-hakhak, my castellan, he knows what you must do. My plans are laid. He will direct you further. He will tell you the soul I need, and where it might be found.'

'You will not tell me now?'

Vashtorr tutted and slowly shook his head. *'You may perish yet, feeble one, before all comes to pass. I play a greater game than any you will ever enjoy. I will not have my designs foiled because they have been ripped from your mind by my rivals. Only when you are safe and incarnate shall you be fully informed.'*

'Yes, my lord.' Silik grovelled. He looked up piteously, caught between hope and suspicion. *'You promise you will remake me in glory?'*

'In beauty and in glory, and you will remain that way if you obey me.' He pointed a long talon at Silik's temporary form. *'If you are loyal.'*

'I am loyal, I am!'

'Good. Then go.'

Vashtorr twitched his hands, this way and that, once, then twice. A burning spiral flittered into being near to Silik, small at first, then growing, and growing, and opening itself, the roaring, turning arms of it spreading into a sheet of flame that parted with a shower of molten metal sparks that bounced all around the hold. Upon the machines the frost began to run. The ship moved again, and now violently.

A door opened. A door into the warp. Orange forge glow flooded the hold. Vashtorr was pleased to see his realm of machines and artifice. Through the heat haze the great towers and smithies were obscure, but he could smell the sickly-sweet stink of soul smoke as vital essences were burned to fuel his furnaces. He could hear the roar of industry. The screams of the damned. The cries of daemons in agony as they were remade, and their exultant roars as they beheld their reborn shapes.

Silik dithered, afraid of the view presented to him. Remaking was not a painless process.

The temperature rose rapidly. The frost on the nearest machine ran off it in floods. A thin cloak of steam enveloped it. Needles on dials upon its front ticked towards red lines.

'Quickly, Silik,' said Vashtorr. ***'Begone while the portal holds.'***

Silik gave him one last fearful glance, then his body of stolen wires collapsed, and his oddly beautiful head rose up from it in ethereal form, trailing ectoplasm, and swam through the air like a monstrous tadpole towards the warp rift. Silik moved slowly, the pathetic thing. He reached the gate, and passed through. His shape was translucent, a morsel for the daemon-beasts that coursed the hot thermals around Vashtorr's tower. He might well be ripped to nothing. Vashtorr had not lied about that.

No matter, the demigod had other plans if Silik failed, and further plans beyond that, interlocking and intricate as the parts of the finest mechanism.

The gate was short-lived. Reality painfully dragged itself back together, folds of its dreary essence pulling over the comforting glare of home. The last flap of it curled into place just as the needles on the dials of the heated machine hit red.

Alarms blared. Vashtorr did not care overly much. He glanced at the blistered flesh around his bonds and snorted derisive smoke, then settled himself back into his meditative pose. Cawl was close to success, then, but had not yet initiated the warp-dampening mechanisms of the xenos in any orchestrated form. Good. That was as it should be. The plan proceeded. All the archmagos required was a little push. N'Thragor would provide that.

He bowed his head. His eyes went out. The alarms continued. By the time the mortals organised themselves, all in the hold would have returned to normal, but they would know something had occurred.

Let it be a warning not to underestimate him.

* * *

The alarms came partway through the warp voyage to the Knight world of Praze. It was an unwelcome distraction. Kraverek had much to organise, many messages to send and favours to call in. After years of near disaster, events entered a crucial yet delicate phase. Therefore he would have preferred to have left the task to the magi, but Kolumbari-Enas and his acolytes would only go into Vashtorr's prison hold if escorted.

'I'll go with you myself, you cowards,' Kraverek snarled. He noted their fear. They had overstated their expertise, he was increasingly sure.

Vashtorr hadn't moved. He sat upon his heels, his great head bowed, the fearsome eyes extinguished, the luminous letters that circled his wrists steady in their glow.

The surviving Disciples of Nul went to the machines outside the mystic circle binding the daemon king. They fussed over them, canting between each other in hurried binharic. Kraverek kept back. One machine was freer of frost than the others, and the deck around it slippery with a coat of glass-clear ice.

Up on a walkway running around the hold, Xeseus and Psephalas kept watch, pointedly not speaking to one another. They'd fallen out again. It was childish of him, but it amused Kraverek to force them to work together.

'Anything?' he called to the magi.

'The temperature readings were correct. A sudden increase in empyrical generator beta. They are all stable now.'

Kraverek grunted. The magi went about their business. Maybe it was just a malfunction, but Kolumbari-Enas' reaction suggested not. He was about to leave when he saw something close to the outer limit of the circle. He increased the magnification of his augmetic eyes, and found he was looking at a damaged deck plate. It might mean nothing – *Ferrus Indignatum* was exceptionally old – but when he knelt by it, he saw the damage was recent. He could not think how such a thing might spontaneously come to pass.

He bent down. Twists of wire poked out of the hole. Nearby he found a knotted mess of them. He picked it up, held it in front of his face, and saw the tangle was not random in shape. It looked like a doll that was missing a head.

A doll, or a puppet.

Kolumbari-Enas called to him.

'Query. What do you have there, Warsmith?'

Kraverek glanced up at the Arkifane. He appeared to be inert. Kraverek was sure he was not.

'Nothing,' he said. He crumped the doll in his hand. 'Old damage. Are you sure our guest is inactive?'

'Yes, Warsmith. The power of the machine holds him in check.'

Kraverek stood and tilted his chin up to look the daemon full in the face. Nothing – no reaction, movement or indication of awareness, its eyes remained dark – and yet the daemon was watching him. This he knew, indubitably.

'Ideas are bonds for more subtle Legions than ours,' said Kraverek. 'I would have him chained. Can you do this?'

'Expression of surprise. Of course.'

'Then do so,' said Kraverek. He deliberately turned on his heel and walked from the hold. He did not look back, though he could feel the daemon's regard itching in the back of his skull all the way to the hold's gate.

CHAPTER TWENTY-FIVE

AWAY FROM ETERNITY

The fascia temporalis rippled towards the group, rolling over slain Flayed Ones and the angular blackstone edges of the data archive like a tide of gel.

Primus looked at her. Solana looked back. What words do you exchange at a time like this?

'Are you ready to die?' Primus asked.

Not those words, she thought. She shook her head. She felt very young, and very out of her depth. She hadn't expected it to end like this, but she supposed it was a condition of mortality never to expect life to end. Death was always a surprise.

'Wait!' Lhaskek said. His broken piston jerked his head. 'They return.'

Qvo came alive first. He staggered away from the archmagos, his dataspike rasping from the port in Cawl's midriff. He sat down hard, looking dazed.

Cawl returned next.

'Oh my, we did it! Qvo's got it. It's all within him. The whole lot!'

Qvo was giddy with informational overload. 'So much information, so much data! With this... with this... well, what couldn't I do?'

His hand went up to his head. Sparks played over his fingers.

'Ooooh,' he said. 'Too much.'

'Steady there, Qvo.' Cawl put his enormously augmented body against his friend and nudged him away from the shrinking fascia temporalis. 'Now we can leave,' he said.

Lhaskek unfolded, becoming even bigger than before. The way he held his war scythe out to the side further increased his size. He was, thought Solana, terrifying.

'You will never this leave this place, primitive,' the phaeron said. 'Before I destroy you, I should thank you for retrieving the information from this unit. Even devolved specimens such as you can prove useful. But you will never profit from what you have taken. This information is the property of the Indukh Dynasty of the necron race. It is not intended for the likes of barely sentient creatures.'

'Pfft!' said Cawl, hauling Qvo back up to his feet. 'I'm not handing it over.'

'I will rip it from your tiny brain, primitive. We shall harvest you, as we will harvest ten million worlds. The might of Indukh shall be restored, and fear will follow the whispers of our name! Our Legions shall march in innumerable multitude in conquest of the galaxy! But first, my trusting friend, we will drink of you–'

Primus raised a hand. There was a flash of warp-light. Lhaskek's head bent away from the broken piston, which promptly gave out completely. Primus closed his fist and twisted his hand, and the phaeron's head wrenched free.

Tsu Tsek looked at Cawl, then Qvo, the lights in his cyclopean eye wild.

'Wait!' was all he managed. Cawl swung the box containing

AsanethAyu's head hard into his chest, enough to send him tottering backwards into the time field. As he fell he activated his chronaxic devices to save himself, the result being that rather than falling through the fascia he stuck there, half in one time flow, half in another.

The results were devastation.

Tsu Tsek's jaw fell open. His head vibrated madly. Smoke poured from his chest casing. Green light built to an incandescent glare in his internal mechanisms. Solana flung her arm over her eyes, expecting an explosion, but Tsu Tsek departed reality for the final time with a sad warbling of failing alien electronics. The light went out, leaving his broken body hanging from the temporal interface.

'I suppose that's one way of solving that problem,' said Qvo. He looked at Solana. 'Don't feel bad, they were always going to kill us.'

Qvo was moving strangely. Not oddly, far from it, but rather in a way that Solana could only think of as more *natural*.

'The time field hasn't collapsed,' she said.

'Because I knew what was going to happen,' said AsanethAyu. 'There's a reason I have no knowledge of a dynasty called Indukh. They don't exist in our time, therefore this conclusion was an inevitability. It appears my people won this little war.'

'That's all well and good, but we won't exist any more either if we don't move now,' said Qvo.

'Make suggestions, primitives. I do not have the strength to project this field long enough to go back the way we came,' said AsanethAyu.

'That's all right,' said Cawl. 'Because we're not going back the way we came. We're going' – he grinned and pointed up at the ceiling – 'that way.'

* * *

The meniscus of time, forever frozen by the Scorean Singularity, quivered. Air molecules stopped in their motion for millions of years and more started to circulate again. The movement occupied a small area at first, then bulged higher over the surface of the war world into a dome of free-running time twelve yards across.

Within the dome a flat green beam punched up from below, cutting precisely through the metal. Another came after it. There was no debris, no explosion, no glow of burnt metal. The beam cut away a fine sliver of matter, leaving only the fading sparkle of atomic dissolution.

A third beam finished the job. The three lines joined point to point to create an exact equilateral triangle. Then this triangle slid slowly into the metal ground, opening the surface to the world's interior.

From this hole, Primus rose, his arms upheld, his companions levitating alongside him. They drifted away from the hole, and landed gently at the side.

Primus went down to his knees, and shrugged off Qvo's attempts to comfort him brusquely.

'I am weary, that is all. Let me be.' He lumbered to his feet and took off his helm. When he caught Solana looking at his pale face, at the blood caked around his mouth, at the dark rings that had bloomed under his eyes, he turned away.

Cawl wasn't paying attention to his son's difficulties. He was hefting Lhaskek's war scythe in his hands appreciably.

'Now that was impressive. I've never seen one like this before. I think I'll be keeping it. It's very…' He passed it through the air experimentally. 'Choppy.'

'This wasn't part of the plan,' said Solana.

'Indeed not.' He grinned at Solana. 'Improvisation, my dear. It's the most neglected gift of the Machine God.'

They were off to the side of the pyramid. Cawl led them around a corner, and there was their ship patiently awaiting them.

'Come along now, there's no time to waste,' said Cawl. He wagged a finger in the air over his head.

Solana felt a shiver of apprehension. 'What aren't you telling us?' she asked.

Cawl shot her a look he intended to be innocent, but mischief gleamed in his organic eye.

'I've no idea what you mean.'

'We're still in danger. Otherwise, we wouldn't be rushing.' She jogged to catch up to him. He was moving at a fair rate, his many legs rattling rhythmically off the metal surface.

'Are we now?'

'You're being obtuse, archmagos,' she said. 'Speak plainly. If disaster approaches, then say so.'

'I'm always obtuse!' Cawl laughed merrily. 'How else can I show off if I just explain everything in simple terms any hive drudge could understand? I want people to know how difficult what I do actually is.' He winked at her. Solana couldn't think of the last time she'd known someone actually wink. It was incredibly inappropriate. 'How else will I get the credit that I deserve?'

'Fine, but what's the problem?' she prompted. They picked their way around a knot of blurry alien combatants, still fighting a war that was over before mankind's most distant ancestors had crawled out of holes in the ground.

'That, hmm, that... Well, you're a tech-adept, why don't you present me with a hypothesis?'

'Me? I'm an observer.' They were nearly at the ship.

'So observe and draw some conclusions then! Come on! Give it a try.'

'Very well,' she said. 'This world has been caught upon the brink of destruction for millions of years. It will eventually fall into the singularity. That's the only real problem I can think of right now.'

'Really? The only one?'

'Am I wrong?'

'That depends on what you say next,' said Cawl.

'Well, it shouldn't fall into the singularity for millions more years.'

'You'd think so,' said Cawl.

'But we've input a lot of extra energy of varying sorts into this system. So I'm guessing it's going to fall into the singularity right now?'

Cawl stopped at the base of the ship's ramp.

'You are very clever,' he said. 'Roboute employed the perceptive ones, didn't he? You're right, of course. We have limited time. The injection of so much additional energy from our combat combined with our, shall we say, meddling with the run of time here is probably, and I stress probably, because it is not certain, going to have a particularly negative effect.' The ground shook. 'And there we go, right on cue!'

'An earthquake?' Solana said. 'That shouldn't be happening.'

'Less of an earthquake and more of a transtemporal gravity wave. There are multiple dimensional spaces overlapping on this world, thanks to our undying metal friends. The result of their collapse is going to be quite spectacular. This planet's toast, as they used to say, and so shall we be if we don't get aboard. Come along!'

'Toast?' said Solana, bewildered.

'Never mind, never mind!' He ushered her up the ramp. 'Come on! No time to waste. Especially not now.'

'Please stop winking at me.'

'My apologies,' said Cawl.

Primus was last on. He gave the world one final disapproving look.

The ramp closed behind him.

'All right!' Cawl proclaimed. He scurried to the wall and locked AsanethAyu's box into position, then went to his pilot's podium, where the floor clamps locked about his feet with businesslike clanks. 'Everybody buckle up tightly now, this is going to be rough.'

The world shook so violently that the ship skidded. Landing claws squealed across the metal, and the craft came to a violent stop.

'We're leaving. All aboard! Powering up! AsanethAyu, get ready to drop your temporal field once we're back into the conduit.'

'Why don't I do it now and release myself from servitude?'

'Why don't you stop pretending that you're going to kill us all and just do what I say?' said Cawl. 'You know that more rests on my success than the future of the human race. I'm doing you necrons an enormous favour, clear?'

'I'll be ready,' she grumbled.

The engines kicked in. The ship's voidframe shook. Cawl called a hololithic control panel into being, and grabbed its intangible controls. A view of the outside flashed on.

'We're going up! Everybody hold on!'

There was a noise like a mountain cracking apart. To the ship's right, a huge, sky-scraping pyramid just fell into pieces. Huge lumps of blackstone silvered with living metal floated upward. Solana gaped at the sight. Another rumbling, shattering roar came from the right as the pyramid they had been in imploded with sudden violence. The pieces fell inwards, simply stopping, becoming for ten full seconds a sculpture of shattering architecture and weirdly modulated light, before it exploded outwards, its broken parts raining down all over the landscape at different rates. Some blinked out of existence altogether, some flew as if drifting down through glue, others strobed like images caught on bad chemical vid-film.

'Total temporal collapse approaching!' AsanethAyu announced.

She and Cawl are a good match for one another, Solana thought.

'We're going to be cutting this fine,' Cawl said. He said it quietly, but from the tone of his voice, he was finding all this exciting. 'AsanethAyu, we're entering the temporal conduit. Shut down your time field on my mark. Five, four, three, two...'

Solana guessed Cawl was giving the countdown purely to satisfy his own sense of drama. The shut-off would have to be calculated to the microsecond. He and the necron had to be communicating on some more subtle level than the spoken word.

'One!'

The strange sensation of events running at different rates raced through Solana, as though it was in her blood somehow, as vital and ruinous as a fatal infection, each pump of her heart pushing the damage deeper through her body. She felt it right down to the most profound levels of her being. *Is it a cellular thing?* she thought. *Spiritual? Both? What is this doing to me?* she wondered.

She gritted her teeth. She didn't matter. What mattered was getting a report of all this mayhem to Roboute Guilliman.

She did not think the primarch was going to be pleased.

'And we're through!' Cawl said. The strange feeling subsided. Cawl banked around, taking the barque into a spiralled ascent. The engines screamed against the pull of the world. She hoped it was just the world. If it were the singularity they were fighting, they were lost.

The surface of the war world rippled with asynchronous moments. Buildings fell into themselves, or were torn up entire, like teeth yanked from gums, and went spinning away towards the blackness of the singularity. Bubbles of reality ballooned around each other, into each other, overwriting one another and bursting.

'This is far worse than a simple black hole,' said Qvo.

'Unhelpful!' Cawl shouted.

The ship lurched. An immense, lopsided heave of gravity pulled at Solana, distorting her flesh, and forcing her blood to pool at one side of her body. Her heart hammered in response, unable to push the vitae around her circulatory system.

She felt the first stirrings of panic.

'We're nearly there!' Cawl shouted. 'Once we're deep into the conduit, we'll be out of all this.'

Up they went, the ship corkscrewing, battered by the titanic, awful forces of physics. Her vision blurred.

Don't pass out again, she told herself. *Don't!*

A nauseating wave throbbed through her, making her feel like jelly, as if her bones had no structure, as if flesh itself were a somewhat ridiculous idea half considered by the Machine God before being discarded.

There was an audible pop, like a pressure tube breaking.

Everything returned to normal. The ship flew straight. The engines hummed. Solana's blood surged into its proper channels, and after a moment of dizziness, she sucked in a ragged, painful breath.

'We're out,' said Cawl, openly relieved. 'We're out!'

'Archmagos,' Solana gasped. 'Please provide a rear view.' She lacked Cawl's confidence in his abilities.

'Very well,' said Cawl.

The hololith quivered, and changed, depicting the war world and a portion of the black hole behind it, now worryingly far less hidden by its photonic layers, because they were disappearing.

The war world buckled, pulled in multiple directions, many

not of the materium, she guessed. The ships around it broke free of their time lock only long enough to be yanked towards the black hole. Solana wondered how the alien beings aboard them must feel, if this were a sudden surprise to them, or if in their slowed state these last moments were only continuations of the events that had opened the singularity in the first place.

'These forces are beyond even necron control,' said AsanethAyu. 'You are privileged to see them. This is how the end of time will look, if the Great Enemy of the warp does not triumph first.'

The war world collapsed, turned inside out, exploded. Energy flashed out, and then incredibly was sucked back in, dragged into a funnel-like shape, and poured itself into the black hole. The singularity pulsed. The tight prickle of x-rays registered on Solana's machine senses. The last of the photon sphere swirled about, and was sucked inwards, vanishing into the hole, which grew as she watched. Its expansion was not a smooth progression of size, but a series of erratically pulsed leaps.

'Wocolos,' Cawl voxed to his shipmaster. 'Emergency warp translation, initiate now.'

There was a garbled protest in reply.

'Never mind that!' Cawl snapped. 'I'll pilot us in. You make sure you get the fleet out of here. The singularity is expanding with more violence than anticipated.'

The small ship slowed, slewed. Increased gravitic drag clawed at it.

Cawl changed channels, calling upon his astropathicum. 'Emergency sending required, all astropaths, send uncoded. Do it, and do it now. Final receiver station, astropathicum, Wolfspear Fort Varghalen… No, I don't know the designation code. It's on Ulvheim. Final control protocols secured. En route. Expected arrival two months. Give them the current date and all the usual check codes. Finish with, "Prepare for testing." Yes, yes, that is it! Do it now! Get it visualised and away before we break for the warp.' Cawl cut the communications and groaned. 'I just hope all that doesn't get lost in metaphors about holy fish or something. The first thing I am doing when we are finished with all this is to demand fresh Telepathica staff from the Adeptus. This lot are tedious, form-shuffling nitwits, the lot of them.'

'Are we going to make it?' Qvo asked. 'That singularity is expanding very quickly.'

'Did you know,' AsanethAyu said, 'that some of the subdimensional spaces we employ are infinite in nature?'

'What happens when a singularity of infinite material force swallows an infinite non-material space?' Solana asked.

'You are about to find out,' said AsanethAyu.

'They'll collapse on themselves before the singularity gets too big,' said Cawl. 'I did look into this, I'm not entirely irresponsible.'

'How big is too big?' Solana said.

'You're about to find that out too,' said AsanethAyu again, with mounting, desperate glee.

'Primus, would you shut AsanethAyu's box, please?' said Cawl.

'Gladly,' said the giant. The clack of the box catch cut off the necron's protests.

'Now,' said Cawl. 'I'm afraid I'm going to have to ask you all to hang on again.'

This time, it was worse.

Viewed from outside, Cawl's explorator ship was a golden dart enclosed in translucent silver. A pulsed signal shut the emitter down, and the long arm of it started to swing back into the *Zar Quaesitor*. The photonic venting array powered off a minute later – the stations making it broke formation, and were immediately dragged towards the singularity at rapidly increasing velocity.

The Ark Mechanicus' attendant flotilla was already splitting, heading off in every direction at full motive. All usual precautions were thrown to the winds of chance, and several of them began translation as soon as they were at minimum distance from the others. Geller fields cast their oily cloaks around the hulls. Purple vortices burrowed through the veil between realities. One by one the ships of the conclave formed by Cawl broke for the warp.

All except the *Zar Quaesitor*, which waited for its master. Cawl's tiny vessel arrowed for his hulking home, while in the *Zar Quaesitor*'s astropathicum, astropaths encoded the brief message into appropriate imagery and cast it through the warp.

The singularity expanded again. Cawl brought his barque in to land at full speed. But the mass of the *Zar Quaesitor* was much greater than the tiny transport, and worked together with the singularity against itself.

Slowly, the *Zar Quaesitor* began to drift backwards.

The Geller field activated. Engines burned. Still the Ark Mechanicus slid back. The warp engines thrummed into being, calling up the unnatural energies to cut a rift between materium and immaterium. Under the intense pressure of the hole's gravity well the rift formed incompletely, a shifting mass of half-gaps and tears that would not settle into a stable portal.

Engines running past all safety limits, the *Zar Quaesitor* fought the singularity, forcing itself towards the unstable rift. Overheated gases blasted from emergency vents. Small explosions sparkled on the surface as overtaxed machines blew and protruding mechanisms were wrenched free.

The ship nosed into the void.

With agonising slowness, the forward command decks slipped out of the mortal realm. With a portion of its mass out of reach of the influence of the singularity, the Ark Mechanicus passed with gathering speed into the rift, the purple storms of energy swallowing the mid-section, the first part of the aft, moving down towards the engine arrays. By the grace of the Machine God, the ship slipped through without touching the unstable parts of the rift, passing smoothly out of the material realm and into the immaterium.

Or at least until the rift collapsed with a thunderous clash, impossible in the airless nothing of the void, but quite audible nonetheless, shutting upon the hindmost engine of the *Zar Quaesitor* and cutting it from the vessel. Plasma venting spectacularly from the severed pipes sheared off another engine nozzle, and set off secondary explosions that saw the listing Ark Mechanicus vanish into the warp with its stern ablaze.

Cut off from the psychic turmoil of the warp, corposant guttered to nothing like oxygen-starved fires. Plasma shone longer, dragged out into long, luminous streamers by the pull of the black hole, until they too attenuated, and cooled, and went out.

Then there was only the blackness of lightless space, and the dreadful hunger of the Scorean Singularity, a blacker black bound by golden rings of stolen matter that were growing once again.

CHAPTER TWENTY-SIX

RETURN TO RAUKOS

The doors to the astropathicum flew apart, the serfs in a hurry to get them open before Felix smashed them out of his way. It annoyed him they were reacting like this. He would no more break the doors in than he would shoot Bjarni in the face.

'Chapter-serfs are usually better trained than this,' he complained.

'I am sorry, Decimus, but the kaerls here have always been nervy,' Bjarni said uneasily. Felix regretted embarrassing him.

With Felix and Bjarni was Gathein, whom he'd commanded to come, and Cominus, who hung at Felix's heels like a shadow. The group of Space Marines kept up a pace that the humans could only match by running. People scattered like mice, the shouts announcing Felix and his party of four's arrival verging on panic.

'You are being too hasty,' said Gathein via private vox. 'A few more moments won't hurt. You are scaring the serfs. Calm, brother.'

'You are right,' said Felix, though every fibre of his being urged him to keep up his march. It had been months, and now news of Cawl had finally arrived.

'And if I may, lord tetrarch, perhaps you could consider being of more generous a spirit to the mortals stationed here. The proximity of the Pit is hard on them.'

Felix made a noncommittal noise. He agreed, but wasn't inclined to advertise the fact and show himself up.

'You can feel it yourself. It affects all our humours. Remember, it is worse for them. They do not have our conditioning, our training, or our gifts.'

Felix caught the eyes of an armed kaerl standing guard at the next set of doors. That he was fatigued was clear from his pallor and the black rings around his eyes. The same was true of them all, when you looked closely.

'Damned planet,' said Felix. 'I apologise, Bjarni.'

'No need, Decimus,' Bjarni said. He sounded happier, at least.

They reached the outer sanctums of the astropathicum proper, where several officials came out to meet them. They wore sashes of gold over the green robes of the Adeptus Astra Telepathica, where many badges were sewn: the Chapter symbol, sigils denoting fealty to the Wolfspear, and oath papers heavy with black wax seals declaring their purity. Transliterator Secondary Wessel was at their head, and looked pleased, for once.

'Lord tetrarch.' Their leader performed a deep bow. 'The message you have awaited has finally arrived. Lord Cawl is on his way.'

'My astropaths intercepted it aboard the *Lord of Vespator*.'

'I assumed so, and that you wished to crosscheck it with our interpretation.'

'You assume right,' said Felix.

Wessel nodded. 'It is a common practice in these benighted times.'

'Also, ours was incomplete. I was hoping that you, as intended recipient, may have more.'

'I am sorry to say, the version I am going to present you is also unfinished.'

'You are sure?'

'It was I who translated it.' Wessel beckoned behind him. A woman stepped forward carrying a flat box of polished wood. Another official opened it. With obsessive care, Wessel donned a pair of soft leather gloves before lifting the parchment out and presenting it to the tetrarch.

Felix's frown deepened as he scanned it. Much of the scroll was occupied by attestations of accuracy and quotations from prayer. There was a long, rambling description of the psychic imagery employed. There was a large degree of interpretation turning the bizarre metaphor of astropathic teleprayer back into the messages their senders intended, but the sentiment, and crucially the facts, were exactly the same. The direct transliteration came last. The meat of that was frustratingly meagre.

Archmagos Belisarius Cawl reports success. Final control codes acquired. Expected arrival... MESSAGE ENDS. VIOLENT DISRUPTION SUSPECTED.

'It is the same as the sending we intercepted?' Gathein asked.

'Almost exactly.' He held the parchment out to Gathein. 'To be expected.' Felix stared hard at the transliterator, frightening the man. 'This is all of it?'

'Yes, my lord. Incomplete, as I said.'

'Was the content deliberately interrupted or is Cawl lost?'

Wessel shrugged apologetically. 'You know the warp, my lord, it is impossible to tell.'

'Do you know when it was sent?'

Wessel raised his eyebrows.

'You know the warp,' Felix said for him. 'I understand. There is nothing more to this than what we have. Cawl is coming. He was successful in retrieving the code he requires to activate the experimental pylon network here – I assume that is what this passage means.' Felix tapped the scroll. 'There is no estimated time of arrival.'

'I am sorry, my lord,' said Wessel.

'And we do not know exactly where he was either,' said Felix. 'Lord Guilliman sent one of his agents to watch over him while I waited here. I have heard nothing from her for months.' Felix's lips thinned in thought. 'Can you divine anything further, Gathein?'

'Perhaps...' Gathein paused. Behind his eye-lenses, cold fire burned briefly. 'No, there is no echo of it, not even down here at the intended receiving station. Sometimes the messages linger in the psychosphere of an astropathicum and might be reinterpreted, but the residue has gone, the same as in orbit. The presence of the Pit of Raukos shreds everything. We are lucky to have received this at all. I am sorry, my lord.'

The interpreter nodded, grateful that his opinion had been supported by such a vaunted personage as a Space Marine Epistolary. 'It is a problem we have had ever since the Chapter took possession of this world, lord tetrarch. Life is something of a struggle here for us all. It is hard on we psykers.'

'How many messages to Ulvheim are lost this way?'

'We cannot tell for sure, because of course we do not always have notice of messages we don't receive. But I would guess at around two per cent, a not enormous but still significant proportion.'

'Broken messages like this?'

'The same, two per cent more.'

Felix almost crumpled the parchment. He was gritting his teeth, he realised. He had a desire to rip the parchment to shreds. Wessel's eyes went worriedly to the gauntlets holding the parchment.

I am not behaving like myself, Felix thought. Gathein was right. It was this world, its proximity to the Pit. It suited them all poorly. He had experienced far worse manifestations of the warp, but there was something about this place that eroded the soul, and he had been here for far too long.

He calmed his breathing. His pharmacopeia altered his chemical humours. It did not help much. The evils of the immaterium were not easily countered by material means.

'Thank you, transliterator secondary.' Felix handed back the parchment. It would be put back in the box and the box put into an archive where both would moulder, waiting for when they might prove useful to someone, a time that would probably never come.

Wessel took the scroll with barely disguised haste, folded it, muttered a prayer to the Emperor, and shut it away. The woman bearing the box bowed and disappeared almost as quickly, both of them eager to get it out of harm's way, this pointless relic in the making.

Felix thanked the astropathicum staff again, and took his own leave with his men.

The corridor to the surface was long, the astropathicum buried deep. The warp might be affecting him, but there was nothing wrong with Bjarni, nor with any other Space Marine he could mention. His men were all a little shorter of temper than usual, but he was far worse troubled.

It was Cawl, he knew it. The thought of Cawl coming here upset him. He had been that way ever since the morning, when his own master of astropaths had first shown him the message. Of course Felix had been expecting Cawl. That was why he was there in the first place, but the truth of Cawl's arrival was another matter entirely. Felix could not believe for a moment that the old monster was dead. He was on his way. That was why he felt the way he did. The man who had tormented him for thousands of years. The one being that Felix truly feared. Why had Guilliman sent him to confront Cawl again? It was only a couple of years since the last time, and he would go so far as to say once was enough in a lifetime.

They emerged into the fortress' innermost courtyard. The shadows of the walls were already filling up the space with inky blues. Evening was only a couple of hours away.

'Does something trouble you, tetrarch?' Gathein said.

Annoyed at being read by the psyker and letting his emotions show, Felix was hard-voiced in response.

'Nothing that a night of battle will not cure.'

CHAPTER TWENTY-SEVEN

THE FORGE OF SOULS

The pain was all. The pain was awful. The pain was pleasure. Silik moaned at the awful thrill of it, and the hot metal of his soul-casket closed around him.

White-hot metal cannot harm a daemon. It might burn the false flesh it wears, it might consume it unto the point of destruction and send the creature back whence it came. But it cannot harm it, not truly.

But this was no ordinary metal. This was metal cast in the Forge of Souls, and it burned Silik's very core.

The casket halves slammed shut, and Silik screamed.

Hammers rang on the casing, squeezing rivets into holes. As they cooled they would pinch the two halves of the casing so tightly shut they would not be easily split apart. Then soul-stuff bound to silver would be forced into the gap between the halves, brazing the metal and sealing his daemonic essence inside the casket completely.

That came later. It brought a different sort of pain, no less agonising. Silik hungered for it and dreaded it equally.

The casket lurched along the production line. Hammer blows rained from every direction, pounding the casket, the daemon smiths outside hitting solely to torment Silik now, making the casket ring like a bell and showering his spirit with injurious chips of metal.

Outside, in the materium, the world of puling mortals, machines were built and daemon essences called into them by sorcery. Here at Vashtorr's Soul Forge a higher engineering was practised, and the machine built around the possessing being. The creation of the core was the beginning of that process.

Claws connected with the casket, a solid clang of metal talons. The casket swayed, and was lifted high, and swung about. Then dropped. Water splashed then roared on the other side of his new prison, his new home.

Hissing, the casket was lifted again, and placed into a cradle; Silik felt the rests click into place. Now cool, the rivets and edges bitten in, the brazing would begin.

In mortal planes, this procedure would have been impossible. The gap was non-existent, the metal of the two halves practically welded together, clasped tightly to one another thanks to the rivets. But this was the Forge of Souls, Vashtorr's realm, and here the rules of atoms and forces were different. Silik felt the approach of the silver seal as a prickle deep inside his essence. Outside, a crucible was moving, clasped in long forge tongs, cherry red from the coals, liquid silver slopping inside, ready to be tipped.

They poured before he expected it. He had no time to ready himself. He screamed as the metal ran over his prison, urged into the space between the casket halves with spells and curses before it could cool.

Silik shrieked right the way through this part of the process. He shrieked some more as runes were engraved with tools fashioned from the ghosts of stolen saints into the outer surface. He shrieked the loudest yet as the awful songs were sung, the vilest blasphemies directed at the casket, forced into its fabric to keep him there forever.

He shrieked, and he laughed. Silik was a creature of Slaanesh, dark goddess of excess, and he revelled in sensation of all kinds.

Perfection approached.

The ritual lasted for aeons. The ritual was done in moments. There is no time in the warp. It ended as it had begun, with pain, and relief, and exultation.

The casket, now icy cold, was lifted again. Silik shivered in the cup of metal, but the worst was over. The price of pain was paid. Power was the reward. Power was why Silik had been through this process so many times, though each reforging of his shell brought with it another debt in souls owed to greedy Vashtorr.

Rough hands grabbed the casket, guiding it into place, into a cavity of a rough-cast chassis that would become the legged motive unit of a Soul Grinder. Then came the lengthy process of assembly, the chassis bottom rolling along a belt of flat iron segments stained with the remains of careless workers. Bestial gangs vied with each other to bring their daemon engine to life before the other cohorts. There was no prize for success, only survival, for the souls of the slowest gang were burned to fuel Vashtorr's ceaseless industries.

He heard the daemon smiths braying, their singing raucous yet effective, timing the slamming of the next component into place. Power tools whined. Tormented machine spirits screeched control code. Legs were attached to the body, talons were attached to the legs. A power plant was bolted to the rear, exhausts installed to carry away its waste products, cables to carry its power, motors to eat the power and pistons to transform it into motion. The engine growled as it was cruelly tested, cycled rapidly up and down. How sweet it sounded to Silik, and he thrilled to the thought of what he was becoming again. No longer the lowest of the low, a devourer of others' cast-off pleasures, whose only claim to excellence was that of superior scavenger, but a Soul Grinder! A daemon made mighty by the power of magic and the machine. This is why he had come to Vashtorr that first time, so very long ago.

The song's tempo increased. Hammer blows fell in time to the words. Chains clanked as tools beat on metal. The last of his shell's four clawed feet was finished. Silik felt it, a tingle presaging activation. His consciousness spread. There followed quieter work, the running of wires to feed the mechanisms. Out there, tantalising him with its existence, would be a fleshy bundle of cabling waiting to be plugged into the casket, about which a leaden seal would be placed and stamped with runes permitting Silik to spread out and fully inhabit his new form. That would mark the final stage. His becoming.

On the chassis went. The humming of testing equipment came and went. Gargantuan limbs twitched with every jolt of electricity. Then on to the last.

The rising whine of the ceiling crane swept down on him again, stooping upon the unfinished engine and snatching it away. Thence to the final places, the pits of esoteric making.

The crane dropped him. Nerveless legs crashed on a metal floor. For a moment, silence. Then a furtive scrambling of feet over the chassis, the scrape of diamond claws, and the control cable was connected. Lead hissed. He could smell its bitter vapour. The worker performing this last task was away quickly, his feet thumping into the distance.

It did not pay to wait around awakening engines.

A violent bolt of energy slammed into Silik's new body, penetrating every part of it, burning through its false atoms and ersatz metal, bringing its pain and its power directly to him. He cried with pleasure and joy. He felt himself swell up, like he would burst. His perceptions rose, passing through the metal walls of the tiny cell, his soul racing out through the cable to infest every part of the daemon engine.

With a roar, Silik was reborn. He perceived flesh running at him. He had a brief impression of screaming captives pinned to columns around the birthing pit, feeding his new body with their deaths. He saw this without eyes. He still could not see as mortals might, not yet.

He grew quickly, a giant torso flowing up out of the lower metal carriage. His shoulders unfolded. The leather sacks of lungs inflated, and were closed about by bloody ribs, themselves encased in muscle and skin. From heaving polyps on his shoulders, arms burst. His head grew, and budded eyes. With true vision he saw the last, moist remains of the captives sliding from the nails that had pinned them, joining the viscous pool of gore that lapped about his mechanical talons. He howled with ecstasy as sensation rippled through him, and then he saw above him on chains a great pair of claws, clad in gold, sinuous and beautiful, and he wept with pleasure, even as their jagged ends slammed into the stumps of his growing arms, the bladed linkages cutting deeply into bone, even as his growing nerves burned as they mated with their circuits. And he howled, and he howled, and out there in the wastes surrounding Vashtorr's towers, mindless machine creatures howled with him.

Silik came roaring out of the birthing room onto a balcony overlooking the polluted plains around the Soul Forge. This was not the true warp, not the roiling, endless shifting forms of the sea of souls, but persistent, solid in its way as any stone or sun in the realm of dust. Vashtorr's domain was one of untold numbers of similar places, not real, yet not unreal either, strange kingdoms as solid and as real as nightmare.

The Soul Forge itself was immense, a tower rising from a great pit, stretching up forever into storm-racked heavens. Below, countless sublevels punched into rock, descending to equally impossible depths. Bridges crossed the pit, lit from below by ruby forge glare. Part fortress, part factory, a million levels of industry garnished with jutting gargoyles and smokestacks vomiting black fumes. Machines clattered from every part of the tower. So too from the lesser manufactoria which clustered around the tower like boils. The songs of indentured daemons and mighty smith-princes mingled with the screams of the damned and the wretched shrieking of souls consumed in the fires.

Red lightning flickered in a distance far further than any mortal horizon. Thunder followed, small and weak, as if cowed by the ceaseless clatter of mechanisms.

Through the daemon shanties and the lesser workshops, grand causeways came to the Soul Forge from every direction and every place, bearing the spoils of war, plunder to fulfil the payments Vashtorr demanded for his services. Endless caravans of wagons heaped with scrap were drawn by steam-belching engines. Coffles of slaves stolen away from the mortal planes. Tankers, half beast and half machine, leaking weeping spiritual essences upon the scorching earth from huge copper vats.

Behind Silik, chained adepts of the so-called True Mechanicum worked night and day to pay off unwisely incurred debt. Beside them daemons plied the myriad trades of fabrication. Insane machine intelligences raced through howling skies.

This was Vashtorr's fief. This was the hell of machines.

Silik lifted his gloriously jewelled claws, and shouted ecstatically.

'Silik is here! Silik is reborn! Oh, glory and beauty, Silik has both!'

He leapt then from the high place. He snagged joyously at protruding gantries, caught at chains, ripping them free from their mounts and tumbling screaming workers to their doom. His pointed feet ripped up long wounds in the metal skin of the tower, smashing free ornamentation crusted with the industrial filth of eternity.

He approached the base of the tower, and leapt again, landing in the middle of a bridge carrying one of the causeways over the pit. He crashed into the creatures that packed it, careless of whom he slew.

'Make way! Make way! I am Silik, favoured of Vashtorr! Make way for the servant of the Arkifane!'

On bloodied claws, he passed at great speed through them all, knocking them aside with his beautiful legs. Faces flashed in front of him. Some got out of his way. Many perished under his scuttling limbs, and for the mortals among them that was doubtless a mercy. Their souls rose from them in weeping mists. Any hope of escape they might have had was false, as demi-mechanical raptors dived from the tower's eyries and ripped them to pieces.

The pedlars of flesh and spirits shouted curses after him. Huge wagons lumbered out of his way, the mindless daemons pulling them lashed by horned and furious drovers.

But none stopped him. None would dare. He was known. He was Silik. He was Vashtorr's trusted lieutenant, and he had been remade in beauty.

Laughing with joy, Silik galloped for the deserts beyond.

Out there, past the last miserable hovels that housed Vashtorr's serfs, the land was dry and cracked. The sky was red, the ground all of rust and black, green and blue, the colours of oxidised metals. The cogs of long-dead beasts jutted from the ground, and here and there were tumbled ruins hinting at humbler days, before voidships and lasweaponry, before plasma reactors, before steam. Forges where bronze swords were once cast. Ancient workshops, their roofs collapsed, were still cluttered with chariot wheels. Further out were quarries carpeted with discarded flints.

Vashtorr was eternal. Vashtorr always was. The moment the first sentient being crafted a tool, Vashtorr had been there.

A tall tail of dust plumed behind Silik as he ran across the desert. Soon his golden plating was coated in it, predominantly red, making him look as if he had been remade in river clay, not bronze, gold and plasteel. It worked into his joints. Lubricant thickened with it. He ignored all these irritations and ran on, towards the edges of Vashtorr's domain. He crested one last rise, and looked upon a vista of serpentine dunes. A nameless desert surrounded the Soul Forge, before eventually it bled into the unformed warp. It had only one final landmark which he looked upon now, poking like a broken finger from the sand.

The Speaking Rock.

Tracks of Soul Grinders criss-crossed the sand everywhere. This was their hunting ground when not abroad in the materium. Each was bound to spend a portion of its life roaming the wastes, ready to defend Vashtorr's realm from his rivals. It was these Silik would call upon first.

Silik approached the front of the Speaking Rock. Much of its fifty-yard girth was taken up by a face that looked to be a chance product of erosion. The crags of its brow sheltered closed eyes. The mouth was set in slumber. Silik went around the back and reached stairs carved into rock, and quickly clattered up them. They ran steep and straight at first, until they passed the top of the face, whereupon they spiralled around and around the tall pillar, and by this way he reached the summit.

The top was lumpen, difficult to maintain a grip upon, forcing him to clasp his new-minted claws tightly to the stone.

A dusty haze choked the windless air, reducing the perpetual bloody light of Vashtorr's domain to a ruddy gloom.

'Soul Grinders!' Silik shouted. *'Soul Grinders!'*

The rock shifted beneath him. Silik's feet scraped dangerously over the uneven stone.

'Soul Grinders!' Silik called. The rock moved, and moaned, then, when for a fourth time Silik called, the rock spoke with him.

'SOUL GRINDERS!' it roared. 'SOUL GRINDERS!'

The desert shifted. Where it was empty, now it was full. Dark, arachnid shapes moved in the haze. They came out of the murk in ones and twos, and then in multitudes.

'Who calls us?' one roared. It was bigger than the rest, its head crowned with the skull rune of the bloody god. *'Who abuses the power of the Speaking Rock?'*

'No abuse,' Silik said, and the rock spoke for him. *'I bring word from Vashtorr. He invokes the terms of the principal bargain, that in return for their rebirth as mighty machines, each Soul Grinder owes a debt of service to our lord and maker, no matter their allegiance to the Powers.'*

His words were repeated by the Speaking Rock, and so they must be true.

The Soul Grinders looked up at him.

'What is this task?' another asked, this one mottled in bright blues, its torso thick with feathers, its maw beaked.

'War!' Silik cried. *'War against the mortals! One who displeases your maker, that is all you need know. Your duty is to serve, as payment for your elevation. That is the contract of the Arkifane.'*

Again the rock spoke. Again the words had to be true, for no daemon could speak falsely from its uneven peak.

'Who will lead us?' another asked, this one morbidly fat and diseased, its metals rusted, its skin rotted.

'N'Thragor! N'Thragor the Great shall lead you.'

The Speaking Rock shouted the name. It rocked the ground and shook the sky, and passed like distant thunder.

Minutes passed.

He did not come.

'N'Thragor is not here,' said the avian daemon machine.

Silik looked nervously past them, seeking the mightiest. Despite what the Arkifane had said, Silik was not sure he would attend. N'Thragor was powerful. He would come to Vashtorr's personal call, but to Silik's? This was a nervous moment. Would he have to return to his lord, and tell him his army had no general? A worrisome thought.

'Who will lead us into war?'

The Soul Grinders scuttled forward.

Silik's power unit skipped a cycle. The mix of blood and oil flowing through him raced. Then he cried with relief. A huge shape grew from nothing, as if the dust was pulled together to form it, and it stepped forward. The one he sought was here, bigger than the rest, more mighty, the greatest gatherer of souls for the Arkifane. He sported four arms, and his carriage alone was as big as the next largest of his kin. His head was an immense, skinless equine skull, rawly fleshed, whence lidless eyes glared with unbridled rage. The others parted to let him through without a word, bowing in submission as he passed.

'I will lead you,' said the daemon prince N'Thragor. ***'Vashtorr commands it.'***

CHAPTER TWENTY-EIGHT

A CUB WITH TWO MOTHERS

A few more weeks passed, and two companies of the Wolfspear came back to Ulvheim.

The High Jarl Irik Stianolf's arrival was a muted affair. The Chapter lined up in ranks in the Varghalen's Hall of Ceremonies, leaving an avenue for the High Jarl to walk with his assembled officers. They were swathed in furs, their pale grey armour covered in fetishes and rune plaques, cutting an altogether barbaric air. The gathered ancients of the three jarldoms now on the world followed them carrying banners high. Four Dreadnoughts with knotwork-chased sarcophagi lumbered behind.

At the head of the hall Stianolf knelt while Wolf Priests bellowed a litany of fealty to the Emperor. Then they reaffirmed their vows. All these were fairly standard Space Marine habits, Felix reflected, but sealing their oaths with a swig of mjød was pure Space Wolves tradition. As was the blessing of the banners, and the embroidering of fresh runes. Where the Wolfspear had started out as something different to the Space Wolves, it seemed blood would out.

Felix and his men took no part in the ceremony, but watched from a high balcony. When he had returned unexpectedly, Stianolf had extended a gruff invitation for attendance to the welcome feast, and Felix made sure all his honour guard were present, their armour as clean and in as good repair as circumstances would permit.

Felix let his attention wander over the Chapter rank and file. He counted only two hundred and twelve. The Chapter had begun life understrength, and though latterly reinforced, the constant attrition of the war of the Pit and casualties suffered in the stars was wearing away at them. He doubted the situation was tenable, and suspected that if Cawl did not shut the hole in the sky then they would abrade to nothing, ground down by endless nights of battle. They were still as statues, their armour locking them into place more effectively than any level of discipline ever could, and that was not like their parent Chapter. The old robotic ways of the first Primaris had yet to fade, even here. But then a moment arrived where cups were handed out to the battle-brothers. To drink, they had to remove their helms, and though when they did they showed human phenotypes from all over the galaxy, for Cawl had stolen his children from everywhere, the stamp of Russ' get was on each one. Sharp features, many with grey or yellow eyes, long canine teeth, beards, braided hair, runes, and tattoos of crossing and recrossing lines.

Bjarni was with the officers. Gjarmin too. The ex-Space Wolf was obvious from the way he stood. There was a feral energy to Gjarmin's body language that even Bjarni did not possess, Fenrisian though he was. Gjarmin fidgeted with a trapped animal's energy, as if at any second he might leap forward and go running from the room.

Quiet words were spoken behind him. Felix looked back. Cominus was in low discussion with a warrior in black armour even more festooned with pendants and dangling runes than that of the high officers. He carried his helm under his arm, and that was made to look like a wolf's skull. Cominus nodded in Felix's direction, and the man came to his side.

'Wolf Priest Ketilsson, I presume,' Felix said quietly.

Ketilsson made a mock of surprise and looked down at his wargear. 'What gave me away?' He grinned, showing long fangs in his grey beard. When he peered over the balcony at the assembly, the charms beading his braids rattled on his armour's gorget. 'A happy lot,' he said. 'It is good to have a home hearth, even so one as impoverished as this place.'

'You are not taking part in the ceremony, Wolf Priest?'

'Call me Ulfreyr.' He gave Felix another grin. 'It's my name.'

He proffered a hand. Felix took it in the warrior's grasp.

'I am taking part, in my own way. I am up here, as you asked, keeping an eye on these pups. My Wolf Priests are new. They must learn our ways, while we must be true to ourselves. I observe, to make sure they are doing things right.'

Felix let go of Ulfreyr's arm. 'They look the part, and I have known a few Space Wolves. They seem true enough.'

Ulfreyr winced in exaggerated fashion. 'Not that name please, and I meant Fenrisians. It's important for all Fenrisians to be true to themselves.'

'Not for the Wolfspear?'

'They're not Fenrisians.'

'Bjarni is.'

'Aye, and a few more, but most aren't. This Chapter has its own wyrd. You must have noticed. They look like us, but they're not like us. I was sent to advise them on our culture and our ways. Sendavael made his choices – there were to be no Rune Priests, no Wolf Priests. Things were to be done by the regent's book.' Ulfreyr sniffed. 'I can't say I blamed him. Perhaps it would have been better that way, that they become their own people, and not a pale copy of the Rout. But that changed when he died, and Stianolf came to take his place.'

'You are not one of them. You remain a... member of the Vlka Fenryka,' Felix said. 'Why are you still here?'

Ulfreyr shrugged. He had the same swagger as Gjarmin. Felix thought that was something no one could teach, it had to be bred in. 'I was sent here to advise them at the Great Wolf's command, so I will stay with them until Lord Grimnar calls me home.'

'So you perform the role of Reclusiarch to them?'

'Not at all. I'm not a Chaplain, am I, Ultramarine?' Ulfreyr fixed him with canid-yellow eyes. 'I'm a Wolf Priest. They're not the same thing. Nor am I here as their Chief Apothecary either, before you suggest it, in your plodding, ever-so-pragmatic way.'

Felix shifted.

Ulfreyr grinned. 'I mean no insult, I only mean you were made to be as you are, as I was made to be the way I am. I am not like them. They are not like me. You are like neither. I stay on the outside. Let Gjarmin play watchmaid to this cub with two mothers. He's resigned to it now.'

'It is good you have returned. You lost men?'

'Aye, Ultramarine. You know war. Some battles you lose. Though in truth the histories will call it a victory, we were so badly mauled I'd call it a loss. That is why we were forced to return, to resupply, and take more men.

Felix cupped his chin in one hand, not entirely sure how to deal with this mercurial priest. 'It may prove fortuitous in the long run.'

'There's no such thing as fortune, tetrarch, only wyrd. This is where the Allfather wants us, so this is where we will be. Something big is coming. Forces move. The Allfather places His pieces on the board, brother.' He grinned his wolfish grin again.

'Sounds like Fenrisian mysticism to me.'

'It is!' said Ulfreyr, loud enough to make some of the officers look up from the chamber floor. He put a hand on Felix's pauldron. 'That's the best kind of mysticism there is. Don't ask me exactly what's coming. If we had a Rune Priest up here, maybe he could tell you, but we don't, so he can't. I just know. Strange things are afoot. Ask one of the psykers later.'

'You might be right,' said Felix. 'Something is coming.'

'Oh? Is that so?' said Ulfreyr.

Felix looked down at the hall again. 'Can they spare you? I have something I think you should see.'

Ulfreyr's cheerful manner didn't last when Felix took him to see the Soul Grinder's body. They went after the ceremony. Gjarmin came, and Bjarni, going down to the fortress forge, to a warded room where two Lexicaniums stood watch over a team of Techmarines as they examined what was left. The Techmarines pointed out their findings to the party, before Bjarni dismissed them. The Librarians remained. Only an order from the lord of Rune Priests or from Stianolf himself would remove them from their duties. Chaos crept through things like the Soul Grinder's remains. Vigilance had to be maintained.

Ulfreyr stalked around the fallen daemon engine. Only the mechanical components remained. The iron was purple and heavier than it should have been. The golden decoration was a sickly shade. All was undergoing a rapid oxidisation, fusing moving parts together, and yet a block of it remained, massy and malevolent, like something dragged out of a funeral pit. Corroded to uselessness, formless but for a few hints of cast ornamentation, and though at first glance it was powerless, its evil nevertheless remained palpable.

'This was part of the attack fifteen weeks ago.'

'Nothing like this has ever come through the portals before,' said Ulfreyr.

'So I was told.'

'It is unusual. You have experience in the Plague Wars of Ultramar? You will have seen how the Neverborn congregate together by type.'

'Plague-ridden things I saw,' said Felix. 'Not like here.'

Ulfreyr leaned in close, setting his bone charms to jangling. 'That is because the powers in the warp are jealous things. In the Underverse there are kingdoms and principalities, duchies and earldoms. The things that rule there do not tolerate trespass, nor do they easily ally.' He wandered around the fused lump of daemon-tainted metal, his heavily accented voice quiet with thought. 'There are many similarities between here and the Underverse.'

'This could be some sort of champion.'

'I do not think so. Whatever claims the Pit as its domain sends mostly armies of feeble lesser daemons.'

'There have been other kinds attack us,' said Gjarmin. 'Scions of blood, and more than once.'

'As the lords of this realm strike alliances, even when violently opposed, so do the lords of the other,' said Ulfreyr. 'But the bloody ones were alone. It could as easily have been the case of an unguarded door, and an attack of opportunity that brought them here. It has been some time since we have seen any other kind.'

'What would draw our enemies together to make an alliance now?' Bjarni asked.

Ulfreyr glanced up. Just then, Felix saw how incredibly old he was, and how haunted. The mirth of his parent Chapter was nowhere to be seen. Echoes of old and half-forgotten horrors lurked in every scar on his face.

'There was just one of this kind?'

'Yes.'

'And the others, they did not rally around it, or follow it?'

Bjarni and Felix exchanged a look.

'No,' said Felix. 'They ignored it completely. It seemed to have an agenda of its own, striking out towards the pylons of Belisarius Cawl.'

'Then I doubt there was a compact between the masters of this daemon engine and our usual attackers.' Ulfreyr crouched and sniffed deeply, like a dog scenting. 'Whatever the reason for its presence, it is an ill omen.' He stood up. The runic pendants swung. 'I will advise the High Jarl that we should expect more of the same. It could be a scout, a vanguard creature. If it is, we shall have a great labour of battle ahead of us. These daemons are part machine and are not easily vanquished, as you have seen.' He nodded then, in agreement with himself. 'This is why the Allfather called us back to the Pit. Now we are here, the *hnaftafl* board is set, and the first move will come soon.' He turned stern eyes upon the Wolfspear Librarians. 'I advise you to destroy this, brothers. Do it now. It is good that you are here, tetrarch. We will have need of you and your men soon, more than ever.'

CHAPTER TWENTY-NINE

LORD OF MACHINES

To all appearances, Vashtorr still languished in the hold. His giant body was chained as Kraverek had ordered. Manacles adorned his legs and arms, and clasped about the roots of his wings. A huge spiked collar encircled his neck, linked to the deck by four thick chains passed through staples bolted deep into the ship's structure. The other bonds were still there, those more subtle marks of power rotating about his wrists and ankles, as were the machine generated contra-warp fields, and the sigil of sorcery painted on the deck. Yet for all these means of imprisonment, they could not hold one such as Vashtorr. He was too large. The portion of him that inhabited the body in the hold was the least of him.

Vashtorr walked the stars.

Of technology he was born, and so through technology he travelled, his dark spirit peering from picter lenses and through the hollow eye sockets of servo-skulls. Some of these things were more holy than others, and resisted his influence. Machines have spirits of their own, as any magos knows, but Vashtorr was a match for most of them, and he quashed their resistance easily.

A part of him was upon the *Zar Quaesitor*, watching as Cawl's servants wrestled with the out-of-control ship as it careened through the warp. He tasted the panic of the craft's mechanisms, and the fear of extinction dawning on its diffuse soul. Through the implants they wore, he sampled the mortal fears of the magi. And he tasted Cawl, his powerful mind a weight upon the warp, scented with strange soul blends, a feast of experience he had long hungered after.

And he was in the systems of the Varghalen, watching the Rune Priests cast their minds ahead in time, each one an unknowing sorcerer, already on the path to true enlightenment. They placed their predictions upon a map, the points where Vashtorr's armies would emerge. They were correct as to the emergence points – there are rules of a sort to magic – but it would avail them of little. They did not know what was coming. Smiling, Vashtorr pressed too close to the veil. His shadow fell upon one of the human warp-whisperers. The Rune Priest started, looking over his shoulder in suspicion, but there was nothing to see. Vashtorr withdrew before he was sensed, reminding himself it is not only humans who suffer hubris.

Then on into the sensorium of the *Ferrus Indignatum*, its bold and angry soul feeling Vashtorr's presence only distantly as he threaded his way through the myriad lesser spirits that made up the gestalt.

To the command deck. To Kraverek. He looked into the Warsmith's mind through the mechanisms of his augmetics. Through sensoria he watched mortals labouring forever under the lash and fear in the vessel's bowels. On the command deck, the shutters were closed over the oculus. The warp was locked out, but not for Vashtorr. He saw through the steel and the wards as easily as if they were glass. How amusing, he thought, that these creatures who follow Chaos while disdaining it, who think themselves the masters of all things, must hide themselves from the truth lest it drive them insane.

'You will tell me what is happening, Kolumbari-Enas.' The Warsmith swept his hand around, encompassing the command deck, where dozens of red lights blinked, and servitors moaned, and sweating mortal officers tried their best not to attract their master's attention while wrestling with disobedient systems.

'Hypothesis. The daemon. It dreams, my lord.'

'You told me it was bound.' Kraverek stepped close to the magos, until he was staring down at him over the lip of his breastplate. 'You said it could not harm us. If its dreams can do this, then I say you have done a very poor job.'

'Explication. These are minor malfunctions.'

'You. Said.' Kraverek leaned down, until his scarred, pallid face was level with Kolumbari-Enas' breathing mask. 'It. Was. Bound.' He pronounced each word distinctly, as though they were apart from each other, and not a sentence at all.

Kolumbari-Enas did not shrink back, impressing the disembodied daemon of machines. Vashtorr had thought him a coward.

'Defence of effort. It is impossible to bind a daemon like this in its entirety, my lord Kraverek. He is too powerful. I explained this to you before we began. Protestation! Bind the core, control the whole. We have the heart of the beast, therefore he is ours.'

Kraverek turned a full circle, suspiciously eyeing the mechanisms that controlled his fragile vessel. 'He is active, in the ship, right now.'

The ship bounced over some esoteric obstacle in the flow of the warp. It was not Vashtorr who caused this, but Kraverek thought it so.

'Agreement conceded. It is possible, Warsmith,' Kolumbari-Enas said. 'He could be anywhere. It is the nature of powerful Neverborn such as he. They exist multiply, across realities and across times.' Kolumbari-Enas crouched lower, dropping his voice to a humming machine whisper. 'But it is possible to control him, and we do.'

You shall soon see the truth of that, Vashtorr thought.

'Then go to him. Stop him before his antics push us out of the warp or worse. Do I make myself clear? It is imperative we arrive to Praze in timely fashion.'

Vashtorr went on from that place, to touch upon Silik, who was then far on the other side of the Rift, though such things as distance mattered not to daemons. Silik's mind was a slippery thing, like oiled silk. He was born from dreams of unrealised perfection, and the torments of artists long dead still festered in him, images of machines that were never built, of designs that were never made, inculcating into him a vanity that could never be satisfied. He stalked a world of fire and death, where red-armoured monsters fought to protect the empire of their dead god. This too pleased Vashtorr. Silik was close to his target.

The machine of Vashtorr's schemes was assembled. The components were in place. There was no plan that was beyond him, and now all was ready. It was time to depress the activation rune, and set the cogs in motion.

He drew himself back into the shell that held that most crucial fragment of his being, and opened the way to another facet of himself. Vashtorr was of the warp, and it was into the warp he looked, to the red wastes that surrounded his domain, as much a part of himself as the giant thing in the hold of the *Ferrus Indignatum*. Unseen he swooped over the deserts, and the hundreds of Soul Grinders gathered there. They bore the marks of their patron gods, but he laughed at their display, knowing that it was he to whom they truly owed their allegiance.

His seeing presence banked around on invisible wings, through the mix of pollution and dust that made the atmosphere of the red waste to the Speaking Rock, and N'Thragor – majestic, beautiful N'Thragor. He was the oldest of the old, the greatest Soul Grinder, whose war tallies were unparalleled, and whose harvest of spirits had fuelled many a forge in Vashtorr's realm. How many spirits was it N'Thragor had provided? Millions, perhaps, yet never enough to pay off the debt he owed to the Arkifane.

The biggest daemons had the biggest debts.

'Soul Grinders!' N'Thragor was saying, brandishing his steely claw. His voice was stupendously loud, as raucous as a world's worth of engines, but the words were still repeated by the Speaking Rock, as Silik's had been before, blasted out across the wastes, raising more dust into the skies to choke them. ***'Soul Grinders! Our lord commands us, our lord bids us make war!'***

'WAR!' came the Soul Grinders' roared response.

'Our lord speaks to me. He speaks through me! He tells you to set aside your false loyalties to the bickering four, he tells you to unite and be one, to pay a portion of your ultimate debt!'

The Soul Grinders howled, their heads of many and varied form lifted to the sunless, false sky.

'Soul Grinders! To whom do we owe our being?' N'Thragor screamed.

'VASHTORR!' they roared, and dry lightning crackled over the Soul Forge in the distance.

'Soul Grinders! To whom do we owe our power?'

'VASHTORR!!!' The ground shook.

'Soul Grinders! To whom do we belong?'

'VASHTORR! VASHTORR! VASHTORR!'

The cry was heard in far-off realms. In Nurgle's Garden the gnarl oaks shivered. Skulls bounced from piles of bone in the realm of blood, fleshless jaws clacking. In the crystal mazes beady, avian eyes were drawn to fine cracks that appeared in one distant, unimportant wall. In his infinite palace, Slaanesh stirred in her dreams.

The warp shimmered, and melted away, opening out into a different place of sand and dust. The red wastes met the plains of Ulvheim. Lines of mortals waited there, their feeble weapons ready, the soul-stunted ones, so-called angels, butchered in body and mind. All weak, so very weak.

'Then fight for Vashtorr! Fight for him! Fight for your true master!'

In a single, howling mass, the Soul Grinders ran for the rifts leading into the materium. From forever away came the reports of mortal weaponry.

The battle for Ulvheim had begun.

Vashtorr smiled. In the grand machine of his plans, scheming cogs spun.

CHAPTER THIRTY

OUT OF THE WARP

The Battle of Ulvheim, which in later years would come to be called the Last Battle of the Pit, began like all the others, at dusk on Guilliman's triumphal ground.

The similarities with what had gone before ended there.

In the days before, the Rune Priests howled in their dens as the castings spelled out disaster. Omens were seen by battle-brothers without the least touch of psychic ability. Black birds flying south. Fiery-eyed wolves loping through the sands. Burning trees shimmering in far-off desert delusion.

There were no birds, nor wolves, nor trees on Ulvheim.

The Rune Priests saw mighty engines. They saw scorpions the size of battle tanks. They saw ghostly claws covered with targeting lenses that blinked and dripped like rheumy eyes.

Gathein took part in the rituals his own way. The Wolfspear's traditions were different to his, but the source of his power was the same, as were the results. He returned to his commander grim.

'Disaster approaches,' he told Felix. 'Make ready for it. A host of daemons like none we've seen before gathers beyond the veil.'

'Daemon engines?' Felix asked.

Gathein only nodded in reply.

At Felix's suggestion, defence was concentrated around Cawl's pylons. The central plaza was left empty. Trenches ringed the eight structures. The forges of Varghalen and the *Lord of Vespator* ran night and day to cast bunkers and defence lines in rockcrete that were dropped into position by Thunderhawk, so that each of the pylons became the keep of a small castle, each guarded by a garrison of grey-armoured brethren.

While they prepared, they still had the nightly battles to contend with. The hordes of lesser Neverborn attacked as they had every night before. Felix waited for his creator, having no choice but to trust Cawl would come. Until the final day, when the visions of the psykers reached their peak of severity, then ceased altogether.

They all knew it was the calm before the storm.

A light haze fuzzed the horizon. Pennants and banners fluttered in a cold breeze. Thin clouds hurried through the thinner air, as if forewarned of the coming battle and fleeing before it began.

A heaviness lay over everything, a lead sheet enwrapping the soul. When the Pit began its repulsive crawl over the horizon it seemed more loathsome than ever before, not a thing of light and tumultuous energies now, but a living thing, many-legged, slick and ghastly.

Felix's men guarded pylon six, that which the Soul Grinder had previously approached. It was Ulfreyr's and Felix's opinion the first attack was aimed at a deliberate target.

And so Felix waited, the vigil over the last shreds of day now familiar to him after many long months of nightly battle. He looked out across the shattered remains of the plaza, left to right and back again, a sweep of their surroundings performed as slowly and studiously as if he were a machine. He saw nothing but dust and Space Marines in battered armour. His men had swapped their usual armaments of bolters and melee weapons for heavier guns, and were engaged in checking them, and positioning spare power packs and ammunition in easy reach.

Cominus joined him on the parapet, and together they surveyed the scene a while. Cominus adjusted the bolt rifle slung over his shoulder, pressed one fist into the plascrete wall and leaned upon it.

'I wonder what our efforts here will bring this night.'

Felix looked at his sergeant in surprise. 'Victory, surely,' said Felix. Cominus was a man who believed utterly in victory. To hear him speak thusly was a worrying turn.

'What does victory mean, in these times? A staying of the darkness a few more days. A brief cessation of the draught that makes the candle of humanity gutter?'

'What has hold of you, sergeant?' Felix said. 'This melancholy is uncharacteristic.'

Cominus drummed his fingers on the rockcrete, once for each digit from forefinger to little finger.

'You have heard the predictions of the psykers. A great host is coming. Something new. Something these men have not faced before.'

Felix cast a glance at the Pit, heaving its cancerous lightshow over the eastern horizon. Its influence, no doubt, was making Cominus speak this way. He thought of saying this, to return his sergeant to his senses, but did not. Men needed to speak their hearts from time to time, when shadows lay heavily upon them.

'The archmagos will come to our aid,' said Felix. 'Of that I am sure.'

Cominus looked at him, inscrutable in his helm. Still Felix had the impression he did not believe it.

'Whether Cawl comes or not, I'll be glad when this is done,' Cominus said. 'I tire of this world.' He adjusted his gun again. 'I am going to walk the perimeter. Try not to take any unnecessary risks tonight, my lord.'

'When do I ever?' said Felix.

'All the time,' said Cominus.

The *Ferrus Indignatum* pitched hard to port. Grav-plating could not compensate, and the command crew were thrown about. One was flung from the augury pits, flying with his arms wheeling right into the oculus shutters. A deep crack stilled his movements.

The ship was in uproar. A sudden, angry life had emerged from its systems, and it was full of newborn rage. Cogitators ceased to function. Lumens strobed. Cables split and fell to the decks to thrash about in showers of sparks.

'This has gone on long enough,' Kraverek said to Psephalas. The sorcerer took the Warsmith's anger impassively. 'If the magi cannot put a stop to this, I will. You're coming with me.'

'By your order, Warsmith,' Psephalas said.

'You, you, and you,' Kraverek commanded, gathering up his chosen without breaking the stride of his march from the bridge: Xeseus, Adnarax, Psephalas and the rest. His shipmaster, Supricar Tlolup, gave him a tight nod as he walked past. Kraverek stared at him, not wishing to overfill his confidence by showing any approval, but wishing that he had more men like that just the same. It came to a sorry pass when you could rely on mortals more than Space Marines.

They descended from the command tower via rapid lifter, heading with all haste to the main crew train. On the way, Kraverek summoned heavier support, his few Terminators, a pair of Havoc squads.

'Bring me anything with a gun big enough to stop a tank,' he ordered. He wanted thick armour and mighty weapons to face the lord of machines. He gathered more men as they travelled the mile to the hold, each stop adding to his arsenal.

'What by the Ruinous Four is going on?' Xeseus growled as they rode the train. It had been a long time since Kraverek had seen him so disturbed.

'It is the daemon king,' said Psephalas. He was working his knife point in the plasteel, carving his name in ancient Olympian script into the battered bench. 'It is a thing of machines, and it is in them now.'

'The magos said it was bound,' Xeseus said. 'You should never have trusted him.'

Adnarax nodded. *Gods,* thought Kraverek, *if Adnarax is agreeing with Xeseus then we are in trouble.*

Kraverek gave them both a black look.

Psephalas brushed swarf from his graffiti, sat back and rested his helm against the wall. The carriage swayed, wheels clicking over the joins in the rails.

'I did warn you,' said Psephalas. 'Vashtorr ranks high in the hierarchy of the Dark Powers. For all their bombast about mastering the warp, these Dark Mechanicum have no idea about the true rites required to chain such a being. They are savages playing with fire.'

'You are a sorcerer,' said Kraverek. 'I don't see that your efforts have borne any more success in containing him.'

Psephalas shrugged. 'We shall see.'

The train rattled on.

'This is an extremely poor idea,' said Wocolos the Integerarian, with some feeling. His face would doubtlessly have shown his concerns, had he not replaced it with a dome of pure, gleaming chrome several centuries prior. Nevertheless, his synthesised voice carried all the misgivings it possibly could. 'Exiting this close to Ulvheim will prove catastrophic for the *Zar Quaesitor*.' Multiple limbs stirred in agitation under his robes. At the side of the room, the historitor, her assistant and Qvo looked on, Qvo with a lost expression, the historitors scribbling notes in various forms all the while. Wocolos did not mind. He found himself entirely neutral regarding their presence. So he was watched. He had nothing to hide.

'How much danger are we in, shipmaster?' Solana asked. He was impressed. For one so lightly augmented, she showed very little fear.

'Not shipmaster,' he corrected her.

Wocolos was not the shipmaster, not officially anyway. Cawl believed himself equal to the task, and when he was absent, Primus usually shouldered the burden, if sullenly resentful. Yet oftentimes neither Cawl nor his peculiar son were on the command deck, and then Wocolos, Cawl's chief aide in most matters, took up the role. He asked for no plaudits. Performing this sacred duty was reward enough for him, but that did not mean he was free of opinions, and nor did he refrain from voicing them. Let the historitor's record show that.

'We are in some danger,' Wocolos said. He made sure the understatement was obvious.

Cawl was busy. His command cylinder was at full extension over the deck, up in the banks of displays that ringed the central position. He swivelled around, bringing himself to face each of the system control sections as he interfaced with them. The command deck was compact for so large a ship, much of it automated. The few officers were tech-priests, the crew a host of servitors. Most of both sorts were wired into position, making it hard to tell priest from biological drone.

'Nonsense!' Cawl chided. 'Wocolos and I have performed deep

gravity well translations many times. Let lesser men fear the tug of mass, not we. We are above that. We are guided by the Machine God.'

Cawl doesn't believe that for a second, Wocolos thought. Cawl was one of the faithful, all right, but too often he used their deity's supposed approval as a cover for his own arrogance. What Cawl believed was that he was beyond the usual rules, whether those were devised by humanity or imposed by physics.

'We are aboard a seriously damaged vessel,' Wocolos protested. 'Integrity of the aft fifth is compromised on decks seventeen through ninety-six. We have lost twenty per cent of our thrust modules, there are plasma leaks from five major conduits. The reactor is under unsupportable stress...'

Cawl held up his hand of flesh, his serious hand, the one he used to make the gravest points. 'Details, details.' His nonchalance was not equal to the tension in his voice, exposing it for the affectation it was.

'Prime Conduit!' Wocolos dropped into a private binharic channel. 'Even you are concerned. I sense it. We must relent. This will not pass. Navigator Prime Helenka warns against it most strenuously.'

'Let her worry about navigation, and let me worry about safe egress. A few additional calculations is all it requires to stabilise the field enough to compensate for translation this deep into a gravity well.' Cawl gave his advisor a sad but determined smile, and when he replied he spoke aloud, probably for posterity's benefit. The air around the historitor thrilled with the engraving of diamond wafers. If the ship failed, they might survive. The historitor wasn't confident either, then. 'It's too late for such concerns. We're too far in now, thus committed. Either this works, or we lose everything. That was the choice, a simple binary. Exiting the warp in safety will lead to the same result.

Days of travel in-system at realspace speeds. All we'll find on Ulvheim is ruin if we do not act immediately.'

'We'd still be alive,' said Wocolos. 'I recommend once more passing over the system heart and translating at the Mandeville point on the far side.'

'Where's the fun in that?' Cawl's smile turned rueful, then gleeful. 'I've always been a gambler, it's why I win. Too much caution in the galaxy of today.'

'There are protocols!'

'Yes, and if you believed in those protocols, you'd not have stood by my side this last half-millennium, so deactivate your emotional circuits, and your voxmitters while you're at it, there's a good fellow. We're going through.' Cawl paused. 'Wocolos,' he said. 'Thank you. Now, I advise you to buckle up.'

Then he whirled about to face the oculus, working the many consoles ringing his command podium, making him appear like an enthusiastic organist overly blessed with arms. Heavy clamps locked him into position. He blurted commands to the tech-priests all around the primary command deck.

'Navigatorium! Prepare for immediate warp egress. Adjustments to the warp field modulation will be coming through…' He depressed a square green button. 'Now.'

The song of the ship subtly changed.

Cawl's Navigators had learned long ago not to argue with his orders. He had been proved right too often. If Cawl insisted, the Navigators would comply. As in all things, Cawl got his own way.

'Helm, prepare realspace engines. Commencing translation countdown. Exiting warp in ten…' He let a machine take up the count. *A very short count,* Wocolos thought. His twenty clawed feet gripped the decking. He reversed his suspensor field, and his body thumped down with the additional gravitational pull. Cawl had done deep well translations many, many times, that was true. It was something of a signature of his, dropping his ship right out of the warp into places no sane being would contemplate. But this was different. This was really different.

Wocolos realised he was afraid, and he felt ashamed because of it. He activated his emotional vaults, locking the emotions away.

That was better. Now he could face his death as the interesting experience it was.

The countdown reached one. For once Cawl said nothing eccentric. He simply looked straight ahead, and braced half a dozen limbs against his consoles.

Solana gripped Qvo's hand. He gently squeezed back. Wocolos noted this. He understood why.

'All or nothing,' said Wocolos. 'One or Zero. That is life with Belisarius Cawl.'

'We'll either win,' breathed Solana. 'Or we won't. I understand.'

Wocolos supposed that she did.

The veil parted. The passage tugged at Wocolos' innermost being in ways that were entirely horrible.

Solana gasped.

With a soul-wrenching lurch, the *Zar Quaesitor* fought its way from the warp.

All the lights went out.

CHAPTER THIRTY-ONE

DAEMONUS EX MACHINA

The ground rumbled. Chatter picked up on Felix's earpieces. A reaching spread of red lightning flickered over the parade ground, cast from a single point, like a groping hand snatched back at the last moment.

'Stand ready, men. It is beginning.'

Felix's own voice echoed at him. The vox popped like water dropped into hot fat. The few responses he received were unintelligible. He looked again to the east. The sun had not set. The Pit had yet to rise fully; only the oily edge of it troubled the horizon. The sky, darkening above, was dominated by the filaments of gas dragged from the sun into the rift. The Neverborn never came early.

'Tetrarch.' Gathein's vox-scoured voice came from a million miles away, although he was situated only a dozen feet from Felix.

Felix followed his pointing hand. It was early enough that a blush of day clung to the far west, yet over the triumphal ground the rifts were already opening, a dozen or more pale mists riven with miniature tempests of the same red lightning that coursed the sky. Felix should have averted his eyes, but he did not, he could not. The weight of the Pit pressed onto his soul, as if to squeeze out all the goodness from him, and forced him to look.

The mists spread, and split, and through the tattered air Felix saw a red desert. Another world, perhaps. The Eye of Terror? Some other daemon-haunted orb? He could not say.

It was a glimpse, only that, for by sorcerous means the empty desert was then full. The rifts were crammed with scores of daemon engines advancing like the migrations of outsize crustacea. They came roaring through the gaps waving metal pincers and oversized cannons. Each was a Soul Grinder, similar to each other yet utterly different.

Felix had an idea these things existed as the broken-mirror versions of pure-hearted tanks and mighty Dreadnoughts. He did not formulate this notion, it simply came to him with such clarity and certainty he could not discount it. Part of him knew it was true, that if one pushed too hard in any direction the warp would surely push back. There was a part of every soul that saw this, when the conditions were right.

The Soul Grinders came howling. Felix saw them for a handful of seconds before the big guns of the Varghalen spoke, and the entire parade ground erupted in fire.

Abandoning the parade ground had been wise.

Hundreds of shells fell upon the machine daemons, landing in a line like stitches punching into cloth. The Wolfspear's vessels and his own ship joined in with lance fire. Only that was precise enough to ensure direct hits. Unleashing macrocannons would be too dangerous. A single stray shot could slay a company. Felix calculated the strength of the enemy and thought it might come to indiscriminate bombardment nevertheless.

It was not enough to stop the horde. Many were slain outright, but the daemons were shielded by the strange protections of the warp, and many more burst through the wall of explosions trailing fires from their ugly, half-mechanical bodies.

Soul Grinders charged into a thicket of lascannon beams and autocannon rounds, further thinning their numbers, but only a little. They galloped across the plain, not interested at all in the triumphal ground as every other daemon who had ever come to Raukos had been, but driving towards Cawl's pylons, their spearheads briefly sketching the shape of the unholy octed on the place where once the might of the Imperium had given praise to the Emperor for victory.

A moment before, Ulvheim had been silent. Now it echoed to battle on every side.

A Soul Grinder collapsed, eviscerated by half a dozen lascannon beams. Another three clattered past its burning corpse, firing back, driving the lascannon troops into cover.

Felix calculated that if Soul Grinders came in the numbers the lesser daemons had, they would be within striking range of the pylon ring within an hour at most.

He checked his weapons, and thought of Cawl, wanting for the first time in his life to see the abominable magos approach him.

Ulvheim turned, a troubled orb in a troubled sky. Past the diffuse glow of the atmospheric line the Pit of Raukos gazed hungrily upon it, so close now to devouring both world and parent star.

Four ships stood off at the highest void anchor, as if wary of approaching the tainted world. Space Marine cruisers all, three in pale grey, one in Ultramarines blue. They were angled to present their lances to the surface and from their prows and turrets collimated light blazed, scoring the ground, snapping off, each shot carrying enough energy to power a city.

Into this scene of silent war, the *Zar Quaesitor* impinged itself, its arrival into the materium no less violent than its departure. Purple energies swirled outwards, whirlpools in reverse, the doorway between what is and what is not bent out of shape by the tug of Ulvheim. Gravity clawed at unreality, teasing off lesser vortices from the greater portal and so diminishing it, making it narrow, making it dangerous.

Through this deadly strait the mighty Ark Mechanicus came. Walls of colour not known beyond the warp dragged at its sides in roiling sheets. Disturbed waves of gravity crumpled bulkheads. Ethereal claws raked at the hull, seeking to prevent the ship's escape. Trailing fire and debris, Cawl's kingdom speared into orbit, so low it drew a phantasmal glare from the highest shreds of scattered atmosphere. Its belly glowed with heat. Dragged, it slowed, so the last of the vessel came forth into reality at reluctant pace, heedless of the unstable path between worlds collapsing behind it.

The warp gate folded itself away from reality with a soundless flash. Space Marine ships fled the *Zar Quaesitor*'s drunken passage. In decaying orbit it wallowed, seemingly dead. No light shone, no thruster burned. It drifted towards the world.

The most optimistic of souls would have thought Belisarius Cawl had finally come to grief. That, having goaded the laws of probability one too many times, the laws of probability had pushed back.

They would have thought that, until lights flickered on all over the stricken ship, and manoeuvring jets fired, righting its course. The engine stacks ignited with a solid, slow plasma burn, and slowly, slowly, the Ark Mechanicus turned to face the battle raging below.

Kraverek's men were chased into the hold by three shipquakes of rising intensity to find Vashtorr surrounded by a ring of burning oil. Firelight danced upon the walls, creating shadows of things that were not there. Vashtorr had still not moved, so far as Kraverek could see, but his eyes shone dimly, like embers on the verge of exhaustion.

'Do not be deceived,' said Psephalas. 'It is at work. Be wary.'

Kolumbari-Enas and his acolytes attended to the machines. Their Myrmidon bodyguard watched silently on. The floor was covered in ice. The temperature in the hold was frigid despite the fire.

'Cover the demigod, all angles,' Kraverek ordered his men, waving them into position. Heavy weapons squads jogged onto raised walkways around the hold gate so as to be able to aim down at the daemon. 'Psephalas, with me.'

'What about us, Kraverek?' Xeseus asked.

'Oversee the rest,' he said. 'Do not approach.'

Kraverek and Psephalas walked across the expanse of hold. Frost coated the raised edges of the deck plates. The air wavered, and suddenly Kraverek found himself in an oxide-red desert. Heaped city shanties carpeted the landscape ahead, an impossible black tower belching fumes at their centre. His augmetics reported the hold in every conceivable medium of perception. He saw the tower. It was real.

Then it was gone, and he was staggering, shedding impossible red dust from his boots, and industrial pollution coating his throat. He nearly tripped, recovered himself, and strode towards Kolumbari-Enas as if nothing had happened. Now was not a good time for weakness. The magos cringed at his approach. How Kraverek desired to strike him dead in that moment.

'Ah. Expression of relief. Warsmith Kraverek, we have calmed the daemon.' Kolumbari-Enas indicated the ring of fire, the sigils, as if these superstitions meant anything to Kraverek.

'Then why is the ship shaking?' *Why did I just find myself somewhere else entirely?* he thought. The situation was getting out of hand.

'Exclamation. We sail smoothly now.'

'Kolumbari-Enas is correct,' said Alixia-Dyos. 'We are no longer in danger.'

Vashtorr's chest rumbled, a mechanical, feline purr.

'I told you it was active,' said Psephalas. 'These fools know nothing.' He passed his hands through the air in front of himself, and a shifting skin of warp energy, thin as oil on water, appeared around he and Kraverek.

Vashtorr's chest rose and fell. His breathing shushed like the slow pump of a blacksmith's bellows. He lifted his head. His eyes shone.

'Greetings, my captor,' said Vashtorr. His tone was so ironic a cold dread gripped Kraverek's spine.

'What are you doing to my ship?'

'Your ship?' Vashtorr looked around the hold, then back at the Warsmith. ***'I am doing nothing to your ship.'***

'Do not lie to me, daemon,' said Kraverek. 'You have placed us all in grave danger.'

Vashtorr growled a sinister chuckle. ***'Danger is a downpayment on success.'***

'What do you mean? Speak clearly, gods damn you!' Kraverek spat.

'You cannot damn a daemon,' Vashtorr said. ***'I am coming to the conclusion that you do not know how this works.'***

Kraverek gave a sharp nod to Kolumbari-Enas. One of the magi adjusted the machines. The bonds of light about Vashtorr's wrists and ankles burned, and the daemon roared.

In response, the ship skipped.

'I command you, speak plainly!'

Vashtorr shook his head. ***'You are not the most polite of hosts,'*** he said, and he leaned in his chains, his fiery eyes wheeling hypnotically. *'I am furthering your goals, as you commanded, mighty master.'* He raised his head. The light in his eyes burned higher, then back down. The sorcerous bonds containing him flared along with it. Psephalas' psychic shield wavered.

Kraverek took an involuntary step backwards. Psephalas grunted.

'I seek only to serve,' the daemon said. *'Reaching out through these restraints you have placed upon me has unfortunate side effects. That is why the ship's passage is perturbed. Worry not. There is no danger. I am a mightier thing than any formless being you might encounter in the sea of souls. A predator knows a predator. You will be safe.'*

'How do you mean, reaching through your restraints? What are you doing? Tell me.' Kraverek kept his voice level. His men were watching closely.

'As you command, master. I shall do better than tell you, I shall show you. I am doing this,' said Vashtorr.

A patch of air wavered in front of him, resolving itself into an image. It was all in shades of red and pink, but clear enough. A battle raged between Space Marines and hulking daemon engines.

'This is Ulvheim, where Belisarius Cawl intends to test his new technologies. At this moment, my servants attack to prevent this from happening. If they succeed, you will have no need to travel to the Attilan Gap at all.'

Kraverek clenched his fist reflexively.

'Oh? You appeared discomfited.' Vashtorr shifted. *'Was it not your desire to stymie the efforts of the archmagos? This is what you said to me. What could be a better result than killing him and casting his efforts into the dust where Guilliman preened and pranced?'*

Kraverek gritted iron teeth.

'And did you not also seek an army?' Vashtorr continued mockingly. *'Why, here is an army, working in your service. See, they fight well, they may win. Surely, my master, you must be pleased with my efforts?'*

Vashtorr leaned forward as far as his collar would allow and looked deep into Kraverek's eyes. The Warsmith's electronic vision buzzed painfully and he was forced to look away.

'I did not ask for this,' said Kraverek. 'We approach Praze. Heralds have been sent to gather our army. This was not your role.'

'You have an army, right there, attempting to fulfil the tasks you set me,' Vashtorr said.

'This was not my plan. I want the passage to Nihilus. If Cawl falls here, then the way will be useless. It is Abaddon's command!'

'Is it now? Then you must be more precise,' Vashtorr said. *'Ask your sorcerer. He knows. Vashtorr deals straight and true, but any request made of one such as I must leave no room for manoeuvre. We will seize any chance to drink your soul. Do you not know this one, simple truth of daemonkind?'*

'He is right,' said Psephalas. 'As I told you.'

'Silence!' Kraverek spat. 'Call off your attack. Withdraw your creatures. Cawl must survive.'

'I shall not,' said Vashtorr. *'This attack is necessary to your aims. You shall see. Events proceed as I have planned. We will take this gate. You employed me. You must trust to my methods.'*

'I command you to call them off!' said Kraverek. He was dangerously close to losing his temper.

'Or what? What will you do? You cannot hurt me. You cannot harm me. All you may do is detain me,' said Vashtorr. *'You think these bonds concern me, Warsmith?'* The daemon king glanced at one wrist, and when he did the scrolling words writ in lightning briefly went out, and Kraverek's dismay grew. *'They are but*

prickings. I care not.' The lights in Vashtorr's eyes faded to black. ***'Trust me.'*** His chest ceased to rise and fall. ***'Or I could do as you ask, after I have told your men the truth,'*** Vashtorr said quietly.

The vision of the battle at Ulvheim remained manifest upon the air, but the daemon god spoke no more.

'What did he mean?' Psephalas said. 'What did he mean about the truth?'

'Nothing, a daemon's lies,' said Kraverek. Surely, while under his command, the daemon could not do that? He glanced at the fiend. It might be time to think about his exit plan. 'Psephalas, give the magi whatever aid they require in holding the daemon. And the rest of you,' he addressed his men. 'If Lord Vashtorr moves again, slay him.'

'With pleasure,' Xeseus said.

Bold words, Xeseus, bold words, thought Kraverek acidly, as he turned back to watch the battle on Ulvheim, helpless to do aught else.

Dawn came. Noon came. The battle continued under the full light of the sun. These were not the foe the Wolfspear had faced before. The airwaves were thick with daemonic scrap-code causing machinery to fail. As many Space Marines were taken out of action by their armour rebelling as were killed outright. Cannons fired ceaselessly from the Varghalen and the fleet, so that the battle was obscured by dust and smoke, and the daemon engines were huge, fleet-footed shadows chased by the bright slashes of energy weapons fire.

Felix's men remained on their wall. Their helm plates became a mess of meaningless graphics, and so they shut them down. The vox was inoperable. They were an island of resistance in a sea of fire, dust and smoke. They had little warning of each attack, only shadows looming from the fog of battle, each spotted at the last, and brought low by concentrated melta fire.

Only regular reports from Magos Cleontis gave Felix heart. The etheric bonds between the towers remained whole. Not one had fallen. The Soul Grinders pressed against them, but were driven back each time, their daemonic essences weakened by the contra-warp fields enough that they lost some of their protection against mortal weapons. That at least kept them at bay.

For the most part, Felix's men remained vigilant, but unengaged. A few times they were called upon to fell one of the daemon engines when it came reeling out of the dust and smoke. The engines seemed pitiful thus enfeebled.

He and his men did not talk. Battle is a terse affair. He heard from time to time boasts traded by the Wolfspear, yet even they were absorbed by the business of survival.

Battle ebbed. The bombardment slackened. Vox-chatter struggled against scrapcode and daemonic data-howls.

'They will be regrouping,' said Cominus. He had taken the opportunity to remove his helm and drink real water. Sweat streaked his face.

'They will,' agreed Felix.

Dust lofted high by explosive shells whispered to the ground. Smoke blew away from the warp portals and the parade ground. It had taken immense damage. Felix thought when this was over, there would be very little left, perhaps so little it would be hard to see that Guilliman had ever held his triumph there.

The smoke blew over it again, a funeral shroud cast back over a corpse.

'There,' said Felix. He pointed with his boltstorm gauntlet. Threat indicators pulsed on his helm display.

Through the battle's gloaming a giant shadow came. A dozen daemon engines trailed it, and they were chanting.

'N'Thragor, N'Thragor, N'Thragor.' The three syllables of the name were as heavy as a dying heartbeat.

'Hearken,' Cominus said. 'Their champion comes.'

The Chosen took up positions. Felix prepared his weapons. Ready lights blinked across his vision. He shut the display down. He would need every ounce of his concentration. He drew his sword and thumbed the activation stud. Blue energy burst around it, dust in the air twinkled to nothing in brilliant sapphire annihilations.

The ground shook with the tread of the daemon machines. Already, the shelling was beginning again, but it would not stop the enemy, not now.

This time, Felix knew, there would be no restraint.

Solana came round with lungs full of smoke from burning plasteks. Chemical heat scorched her throat. She lifted her head from ground gritty with shattered plexglass, barking coughs that came with a flood of slimy drool. She tried to get up. Her ankle protested. She looked down, and found it jammed tight between the fallen Eremenitas and a shattered console. It was from that the smoke poured. It was pure poison, making her skin itch, and she was grateful of her augmetic eyes.

'Help! Help! Help!' Eremenitas wailed. He waved his manipulators feebly. His shoulders rocked and Solana saw if it weren't for the toppled console jamming him in place, he would be rolling her leg flat.

She pulled hard at her calf and grimaced. Something was soaking through her trouser leg. She held up a bloody hand to her face. At first, she thought she was injured, then she saw a magos squashed to pulp beneath the heavy cogitator. A burst of revulsion gave her strength, and she pulled. Tendons stretched painfully, but her leg shifted, just a little, lubricated by the blood and oil leaking from the dead tech-priest. Alarms blared from every side. Terminally compromised servitors gaped soundlessly as landed fish, their eyes rolling uncomprehendingly. Fire was catching in several places and there was no sign of the ignis systems activating. Most of the crew appeared to be dead.

'Help! Help! Help!' Eremenitas moaned. He was pathetic like that, she thought, as helpless as an armoured creature flipped upon its back to die in the sun.

'Shut up and push!' she snapped at him. He continued his ineffectual rocking. She grunted harshly, more from anger than pain, and tugged at her foot, but it would come no further.

A louder, stronger cry had her look up at the command podium.

'Lord Cawl! Prime Conduit! Do you live?'

The podium had retracted fully into the floor, meaning it was only a few inches above her head. Near to her face Wocolos raked at piled debris, his strange, triangular cloak in tatters, showing Solana his heavily augmented body for the first time. She marvelled at it, even as she struggled, for there was not a speck of flesh visible anywhere upon him. He was a sculpture of articulated steel festooned with limbs and devices, magnificent in his complete rejection of humanity.

'Lord Cawl!' Wocolos heaved aside a beam of metal. Broken ceiling panels and slippery cables spilled in heaps all around the historitor like coils of guts.

Some of them were live. Most sparkled with dying Motive Force, but one, rich with the Machine God's bounty, heaved and twitched, as vital as any living thing. It flopped, then thrashed, the sparking, broken head coming closer and closer to Solana with every jumping flail.

'Watch out!' she shouted.

Wocolos paid her no heed. Eremenitas continued to roll and moan.

The cable lashed at her. Arcing sparks glinted in her silvered eyes.

A foot stamped down, pinning the cable in place. A metal hand reached into the rubbery pile and disconnected the other end. Dead wires smoked.

'May I assist you?' Qvo-89 asked.

CHAPTER THIRTY-TWO

THE ONE TRUE FAITH

By the time Qvo had Solana and her assistant upright, Wocolos had uncovered a back humped with much technology and a swathe of red cloth much singed. With a cry part despair and part triumph, the Integerarian heaved aside the last of the metal covering Cawl's upper quarters.

Cawl lay curled in on himself, face down, completely inert. Wocolos held up his primary hands and gazed at the oil sheening them in dismay.

'Archmagos!'

'Is he dead?' Solana asked. She limped forward. Her ankle was swelling, and she was forced to brace her thigh with her hand.

Maybe Eremenitas was right. Maybe she should get more augmentations.

A machine fizzled, then started up a low hum, the wholesome noise of a compact plasma reactor working at optimal function. A mechadendrite twitched, and Cawl rose up from the mess on the floor, his torso first, like a man practising press-ups to improve his physical form. Then monstrously, mechanically, his giant carriage shook off the debris.

Cawl's augmetic eye stuttered on.

'Did someone just ask if I was dead?' he asked.

'I did,' said Solana. 'Clearly you live.'

'It'll take a lot more than an unwise egress from the myriad hellspaces of the warp to finish me off,' he said. He maintained his jovial tone, but when he came down off the command plinth, some of his legs were jammed, and his robe was torn away. Masses of oily machinery lurked beneath. He peered around the room, as though he were looking for something. When it appeared he had found it, he relaxed, and the battered shutters over the oculus parted with a chorus of outraged squeals. They opened most of the way before they seized up entirely. The next thing he sought and found was a noospheric switch for the hololithic projectors. A representation of the battlefield below fizzled out of thin air. Various points of interest highlighted themselves and datatags popped into being beside them. Only those bright red outlines that sketched themselves around Cawl's eight pylons remained lit.

'We're just in time,' said Cawl. 'The test network is still intact.'

'There's a lot of fighting,' said Solana. 'It's close to your machines.' The hololith was full of tiny light models of Space Marines battling crab-legged daemon machines considerably larger than themselves, yet still so small the hololith seemed a tableau depicting the wars of ants.

'Which is why I said we're just in time.'

'Excuse me, archmagos,' said Eremenitas.

'Hmm?' said Cawl distractedly.

'Quite a lot of things appear to be aflame,' Eremenitas said. 'Over there, for example.' He pointed out one of many fires dancing in the smashed command deck.

'Fair point,' said Cawl. He blurted a command in binharic. Inert gas blasted from nozzles all around the deck. 'Will that suffice, do you think?' said Cawl.

'It will,' said Eremenitas.

The fires were dying. Solana realised she'd soon follow suit when the anti-incendum gases replaced all the breathable air. Cawl saw.

'My apologies. There's breathing apparatus over there,' he said, pointing to a glassite box that had somehow survived the warp egress intact. It was almost a shame to smash it to get at the device within. Solana broke it with a length of broken spar and donned the equipment.

'This is disappointing,' said Cawl. 'There's too much interference. Looks purposeful.'

'How?' asked Solana.

'Oh, scrapcode, semi-daemonic attack programming, that sort of thing,' said Cawl distractedly. 'I can't initiate a full systems test from here, though looking at the fight down below, it's less of a test and more of a necessity.' He fiddled with more equipment. 'No, no, not working.' He tapped his mandibular shield. 'That's it. I'm going down to the surface. I'll have to input the control code manually at one of the pylons.'

'In that case,' Solana said, straightening her tunic, 'I will be coming with you.'

New personnel were filing into the bridge. Power tools whined. Tech-priests directed servitor gangs to clear dead machines and dead people.

'Of course you will,' said Cawl, and for the first time Solana thought she could detect a hint of irritation. 'Right then, if nobody has any other business? Nobody else wants to come?' Nobody said anything. 'Very good. Friedisch, come here. I'm going to need what's in your head.'

* * *

The champion came at Felix's position at a gallop. It did so unerringly, as if seeking him out. Four of its lesser kin followed.

'Open fire! All weapons! Bring it down!' Cominus roared, his voxmitter amplifying his voice. Still it was barely sufficient to be heard over the pounding of artillery and the unearthly shrieks of the Soul Grinders.

The Chosen gave fire, shooting heavy missiles, plasma streams and lascannon beams. A Soul Grinder went down to the first volley, its grotesquely swollen torso ripped to pieces, the chassis flipping over itself like a downed warhorse in some ancient Terran war. A second came to a slewing halt, both its front limbs mangled, raging in a hundred tongues as it pushed itself ineffectually forward, doing no more than ploughing the ground before it.

The enemy fired back. The champion had four arms, the upper two mighty pincers, the lower autocannons, whose ball-and-socket mounts were gummy with unnatural flesh. Heavy shells pounded into the bunker parapet, shattering it. Rubble pinged off Felix's armour, and he ducked.

The other daemon engine carried a battle cannon and a sword the size of a crane arm. It opened fire with its tank weapon. A huge explosion rocked Felix back, blasting Cadmus off the wall below the bunker. And so Cadmus died first, hit full-on by the lesser of the charging Soul Grinders and run down between its pounding talons. There was a flash of the yellow and black of the Scythes of the Emperor, a fan of red sprayed high, then he was gone, this loyal son of Guilliman, his deeds now done for ever. The Soul Grinder ran over him right at the sloped facing of the line without slowing, rearing as it crested the wall. A blurred sword-strike cut Austen in two. Doom Eagles iron turned crimson.

There were shouts and gunfire from that part of the wall. Felix glimpsed the burn of a fusion ray cutting a molten line in the daemon engine's underbelly, then he was invested himself and could spare no more attention to the fate of his men. Autocannon rounds banged hard into him and his energy field blazed, the few that got through booming off his armour.

Then the champion was upon him, gathering its piston-powered limbs beneath it and launching itself up the ten-foot height of Felix's bunker. He reacted instantly, spraying the creature with bolts as he ran out of its way. Moist craters opened in its fleshy torso. Daemonic ichor ran black down ruddy skin. A lucky hit smashed a pipe open, and hydraulic fluid the colour of blood sprayed from it.

Small blows, not enough to halt such a monster. It landed with a cacophony of metal upon the firing deck. Sparks fanned around its pointed feet as they scored rockcrete, stabbing at the tetrarch. Felix dodged one leg, then another, too busy with the efforts of survival to land a blow with sword or fist. It trampled around him, displaying its four arms pridefully.

'I am N'Thragor!' it announced. ***'I am the first of the Soul Grinders. The mightiest of them, the first of Vashtorr's war-fiends. See me, and know your doom.'***

Felix had no answer but a strike from his fist. An explosion of actinic energy blew a chunk from its armoured plating, and the creature staggered back.

N'Thragor had a long, ugly head, like that of a skinless equine. Yellow eyes rolled in its dripping face, and it laughed.

'You have fight in you! Your soul will cause the furnaces to blaze,' it roared, and fired down at him, simultaneously throwing its left claw at Felix. The tetrarch stepped aside, struck with his sword and then his power fist. The blade rang harmlessly from daemon-forged armour, the disruption field hardly scratching it. His fist punched harder, but the oily sheath of warp energy that sustained the creature blunted the hit.

Felix had put his all into the attack, and was therefore not well placed to evade N'Thragor's response. The daemon's autocannons raked Felix with heavy shells. His conversion field took the sting from them, but the resultant effulgence of converted energy dazzled Felix, and he did not see the Soul Grinder's left-hand claw until it was too late.

He turned his body just in time. What would have hit him square in the face instead landed on his pauldron. Again the conversion field built into his iron halo did its work, transforming the hit into a dazzle of light, but it could not divert all of the blow's power, and Felix was lifted off his feet with such force that he was carried over the bunker's low parapet, and found himself smashed hard into the ground.

N'Thragor followed, scuttling down off the bunker, firing off his guns all the while. More magnesium light seared the air around Felix as the energy field stole the shells' impetus, but not all, and shells cracked off Felix's ceramite. Again the giant Soul Grinder drove a claw at him, this time open, seeking to grab the tetrarch and scissor him in two. Felix rolled with difficulty, the mass of his armour working against him. He got to his knees as the claw descended, turned towards the blow, putting all his strength into a swing of his sword. The blade connected with the daemon's talon, already twitching with anticipation of the kill. Felix's hit was true, and cut the lower metal blade away. The upper blades rasped against his backpack, snagging on one of the stabilisation vents, tearing it free and jarring him with stunning force, and he was flung forward into a stumble he only just arrested.

N'Thragor was now cautious. His skinless horse's head looked on him with hatred. Felix stared back impassively, sword and fist at the ready.

As battle raged around them, tetrarch and daemon prince circled each other warily.

They lunged together.

Any final worries on the command decks of the cruisers that Cawl's ship was dead were dispelled when drop chutes and hangars opened, and from them landing craft accelerated towards Ulvheim. Trailing streams of superheated atmosphere, bright stars bore salvation to the beleaguered warriors on the surface.

Long-arm clamps lifted up around the prow of the ship, detaching from the command centre docking collar. White gas blasted into space and the secondary locks disengaged, and the spinal bridge pushed the front of the vessel free of the main body. Once the neck was fully extended, the final restraint, a huge circular gravitic clamp, deactivated, detaching the lander. Plasma jets atop the dorsal surface pushed it free, accelerating the vessel directly at the surface, and the flash of weapons there.

It hit the atmosphere with uncompromising speed, layered energy fields keeping compressed gases from scorching the hull. Upon a shield of fire, Cawl's lander rode down to the surface, drop-ships hurtling past it to bring aid to the Space Marines below. Through streaks of fire the prow lander sank lower, and lower, into the dust storm over the battlefield, heading down to the parade ground.

Clouds of smoke and sand swallowed it. Landing jets fired, great tongues of flame braking its descent. A few rounds sped up at it, never connecting, shunted into the warp by the lurid boiling of the ship's void shield.

Slowing, it came down, engines howling. Landing claws touched down amid the wrack of war, crushing dead daemon engines and Space Marine corpses alike. The surface burst, the mosaics beneath the desert sands finally obliterated by weight and heat.

With whining sighs, the engines powered down. The ship sank into its hydraulics and pneumatics.

The secondary command deck protruded from the front of the lander, a blocky, angled thing made up of windows separated by transoms and mullions cast in the shape of decorative machine components. Below the jutting command deck on the breast of the ship was a Machina Opus, the cybernetic skull badge of the Cult Mechanicus. Half of that was made up of cables and piping, this also non-functional, too chromed and perfect to work. The bone part of the skull was shining ceramite, the black half precious adamantine.

The ship cooled. Metal ticked. A Soul Grinder came barrelling out of the mix of smoke, dust and vapours, gun banging. A melta array popped out of the side of the ship. Skull-faced targeters locked upon the machine and burned a strip of molten sand directly at the daemon, hitting it fully and vaporising all but its legs.

The Machina Opus split down the line separating steel from bone. Armoured doors hinged outwards. A secondary shutter portal behind rose up, and from behind that a ramp unfolded in three sections, pushing out its metal tongue into the debris of war.

From within, Cawl emerged fully equipped for battle, lines of tech-priests escorting him. Fifty skitarii jogged out ahead of him, ocular systems gleaming sky-blue bright in the murk. Three tracked heavy servitors flanked a nervous-looking Qvo.

Alongside the lander, other doors opened, and more forces emerged. Armigers of the House Taranis, tanks encased in warbling energy skins, and more skitarii, led by Marshal Iota in her gleaming war form, mounted atop a five-legged command abeyant.

Cawl took to the field, data pouring in from his ship's auguries into his subsidiary cogitators. Tasking these with formulating a battle plan, he bent his primary intelligence cores to the pylons. One was ahead, a hundred yards distant. Already servitor-controlled cannons were tracking and blasting targets in his path.

'Come on if you're coming, then,' Cawl said, waving at Solana, who waited at the top of the ramp. 'We haven't got all day.'

Another blow snapped Felix's head round, almost ripping his helmet free. He tasted blood. His iron halo was a smoking ruin, overstretched by so many strikes then torn off by an autocannon round. His armour was battered, and he limped. He and N'Thragor were alone in the fury of combat. The dust was too thick to see through. Only sound travelled, not sight. Roars, explosions and bangs.

N'Thragor had suffered in return. One of his rear legs locked solid. Now it pulled through the ground like a hoe, leaving a groove like the meanderings of a river behind it. Score marks marred its armour: dents from Felix's fist, rents from his power sword, craters in neat lines punched out by his bolter.

One of N'Thragor's claws dripped transhuman blood. Ixen lay in two pieces separated by half a dozen yards. No one else had tried to intervene in Felix's duel.

'Submit, Ultramarine,' N'Thragor said. ***'Submit and your soul will be permitted a swift end, this I swear.'***

'I will not listen to your lies,' Felix said. His voice was steady, though the taste of blood grew stronger on his tongue.

'Torment then,' N'Thragor said.

The daemon attacked. Felix was tiring. The strength and endurance of a Space Marine are great, but not inexhaustible, and fighting so large a foe drained him. It was all he could do to parry its blows. The daemon knew no fatigue. It was a thing of sorcerous make.

The end was coming. Felix resolved to sell himself dearly.

Battle's noise masked all sound. Neither daemon nor man heard the descent of rapid strike craft. Only after the third or fourth impact did Felix register that these were not bombs.

Cawl? he wondered. He fist-punched aside another blow from the daemon. Though indefatigable, it was degraded, and it was slowing too. Cuts and severed lines, broken wiring. *The disadvantages of corporeality,* Felix thought with satisfaction. What made it strong had made it weak.

There was a roar, hardly perceived before becoming overwhelming. A large drop pod smashed into the ground not twenty yards away, buffeting the combatants with re-entry's heat. A wide door slammed down and a walker came stalking out. Felix took it for a Dreadnought at first, but then saw it to be a Knight Armiger Warglaive, its metal hide decorated with the tech-heraldry of House Taranis.

Whichever low-born piloted the Knight had skill. Straight from the disorientation of orbital insertion, they locked on to the daemon as soon as they were clear. Focusing rings turned in the barrels of its melta-lance. A stream of superheated air marked the passage of its fusion ray, so hot it fused dust to droplets of glass in the air.

The melta beam connected with one of the daemon engine's autocannons. The fleshy parts flash-boiled then erupted into a cloud of steam. The cannon's ammunition cooked off, chemical charges bursting with short-lived fire. Then the metal glowed, and drooped, and fell away.

N'Thragor howled.

The beam shut off. The lance barrels glowed themselves. The Armiger came in firing the lesser meltagun atop the cockpit, reaper chainblade whirring so fast its teeth became a solid metal band. It turned to strike. N'Thragor was there to intercept it, catching the weapon in one of its claws and neatly shearing it away. As the blade dropped, the Soul Grinder turned, striking with its other claw, driving it into the front of the Knight, smashing the head containing the sensorium cluster, and driving on into the pilot's cockpit behind.

The Knight collapsed. N'Thragor wrenched his claw out, thick with gore and machine fluid.

More ships were coming down. Machines nearby broadcast holy machine cant which engaged the scrapcode fogging the noosphere.

'Tide's turning, daemon,' he said. 'You will be unmade.'

Felix attacked as he spoke, using the distraction of the Knight to get close. N'Thragor flung a blow at him. Felix ducked, weaved under, used the creature's dragging leg as a step to get up onto the flat platform of the chassis behind the torso. N'Thragor bucked, trying to throw Felix off, but the tetrarch grabbed at the daemon, taking a painful, bloody handhold in his back with his power fist.

Riding the bucking daemon, he drove his sword up into the spine, as one would attack a larger opponent with a dagger. The sword's power field ate into the thing, lighting it up inside as disruption matrices burst apart matter.

N'Thragor roared with fury. He twisted about. An elbow connected with Felix, knocking his hold free. A second blow had him falling off. N'Thragor clipped him mid-air with the edge of his claw, and Felix wheeled head over heels at the strength of it, landing hard on his back. His armour's spirits quailed. His displays blurred, and went out.

He tried to rise up, but could not.

N'Thragor's heavy tread approached.

What Solana remembered most clearly of all of the charge across Ulvheim was the way the armour rubbed.

A powered suit, fished out of Cawl's stocks by solicitous aides, it was almost – but not quite exactly – her size. The lower assembly caught on her tailbone, chafing at it through the undersuit. She ignored the discomfort, though it was sufficient to be felt through battle's adrenaline.

Cawl led his warriors towards the pylon, where a Martian clade held a trio of Soul Grinders at bay with fierce rays of killing energy. Cawl himself finished one off with a flaring discharge from his arc scourge, sending a flood of power through its systems. Heavy fusillades from his skitarii distracted a second, making it wheel around directly into the plasma streams of Cawl's heavy Kataphrons. The thing withered under the assault, something vital inside broke, and it exploded into flaming pieces.

Battle was always a hellish confusion for Solana. She was not made for it, and despite experiencing war many times, had still not become accustomed to it. She snapped off shots from her pistol, little good they did, and was glad of the armour. Shrapnel blasted everywhere from slain daemon engines, far more of a risk to her than gunfire.

All over the battlefield, Cawl's forces were swinging into action. A lance of Knights stalked the parade ground, their massive weapons blazing.

The third Soul Grinder assailing the pylon was chased off, then shot down by a Knight piloting Questoris armour. The way was clear. She saw fortifications set up around a tall machine which, as she approached, she saw was just a shell, and within was a finely carved needle of noctilith, already running with lines of blue power.

'Out of the way! Out of the way!' Cawl shouted, his voice blasting from a shoulder-mounted vox-horn. Weaponised servitors, Space Marines and the few tech-priests guarding the device parted. All was disorder, but Cawl was quick.

'Friedisch! Friedisch! Where is he?'

A servitor came to a skidding halt by the archmagos, and Qvo-89 clambered off the back.

'Here, Belisarius.'

A huge explosion nearby had Solana ducking. When she stood up straight Cawl was waving at her impatiently.

'Come here, historitor. You will need to record this, the great triumph of the one true faith.' And with that he was off, Qvo trailing after, an input lead dangling from the back of his open head.

Solana ran to catch up.

CHAPTER THIRTY-THREE

A DELAYED TEST

Cawl flung open a door leading into a small, cogitator-lined alcove. He pushed Qvo-89 inside, grabbed the lead, checked to see Solana was watching.

'I'm recording,' she assured him. 'Suit sensorium and augmetics.'

Cawl nodded. 'Then this is it. Brace yourself.'

He pushed the lead into an input port, and started flipping switches.

'This might tickle a little, my friend,' he said to Qvo.

At the pylon's top, a primary comms module rotated upon its mounts and pointed towards its nearest neighbour.

Cawl paused, a metal finger hovering over a final button.

'Ready?' he asked Qvo.

Qvo nodded and shut his eyes tightly.

'Sometimes, all it takes to end a battle is the simple pushing of a button.' Cawl's finger stabbed down.

From the pylon's projection matrices came an ersatz necron

carrier wave, swifter somehow than vox, and far more densely laden. Upon this neutral, ephemeral substrate, complex codes were carried. Stolen from the war world trapped on the cusp of forever, they had been altered by Belisarius Cawl.

The code hit the first pylon, then the next and the next, one after the other, and they ignited. Tech-priests sang hosannas to the Machine God and the genius of Belisarius Cawl as the hybrid machines achieved full activation. Clear sections of power conduits lit in series as necron energies coursed through circuitry last utilised thousands of years before the Emperor had risen up on Old Earth and united its warring peoples. Attaining the pyramidal tops of the blackstone needles, this power was converted, energising the pylons, linking them together in songs of material defiance. Contra-empyric fields grew in potency at a geometric rate, eight times eight times eight times eight, entering a reinforcing feedback loop that saw the pattern repeated over and over again.

Unified, the pylons projected a toroidal field that was inimical to the warp, and it spread, the outer surface racing outwards, the inner surface twisting with counter-spiritual torsion, and moving implacably towards the core of the daemonic incursions: Roboute Guilliman's triumphal parade grounds.

Solana nearly blacked out. She felt her soul again, though not like when she passed from the warp in a ship. This was not an awareness, but a negation of its being, as if her essence were a candle in a gale. She barely kept to her feet.

The Soul Grinders felt it first. Their unborn souls protected by their bodies of steel and nightmare, they lasted a little longer than the preceding armies might have, but only a little. The expanding bubble of power was anathema to them, and it ripped their essences screaming from the engines. As it touched the weaker ones, the false-flesh of their upper torsos exploded into showers of black sand. Their legs collapsed, pistons lifeless. Weapons fell from disintegrating limbs. One after another after another fell down into so much tainted scrap.

Space Marines conditioned to endure any hardship screamed as they felt their souls crushed into their earthly seats. The Knights of Taranis found themselves battling panicky mounts, as the ghosts of their ancestors wavered in the face of nullification. All across Ulvheim human beings shrieked under a punishing anti-psychic assault. Psykers had it worse. Wolfspear Rune Priests toppled over. Gathein crashed down to the dusty earth. Astropaths in Varghalen died, and the expressions of horror left on their faces would haunt the dreams of the kaerls that removed them forever. The Navigators were driven temporarily blind.

But it was the daemons who suffered. The Soul Grinders nearest the rifts turned tail and ran. A daemon is hard to destroy completely, but they felt the threat of the contra-empyric field. Here was something that would end them forever, and they fled in terror from it. A handful made it back across into the eternal deserts around the Forge of Souls. The majority were wiped from existence as if they had never been.

The inner surfaces of the toroid met with a roar. The warp gates melted into ectoplasmic steams, and the contra-empyric field twisted into itself. Writhing, it seemed for the briefest sliver of a second that it would run out of control, but Cawl had built his machines well. They recalibrated automatically, and what began as a toroid became a spear.

A spear that the pylons cast heavenward, directly at the heart of the Pit of Raukos.

N'Thragor punched his claw hard at Felix. His conversion field blazed one final time and died with a feeble spark. The claw slammed home into his chest. Ceramite cracked, but held.

Nevertheless the force of the blow was immense, jolting Felix so hard in his armour something tore inside him, and pounding the tetrarch deep into the broken surface of the parade ground. Fragments of tesserae exploded from under him. One of the thing's cannons opened up, smashing at Felix, making him jerk like a carelessly operated puppet.

Warnings flashed across his helm display. Coolant was leaking from his backpack into his battle plate, its insistent hissing poisoning his air.

'Now I end you, mortal,' N'Thragor crowed, and drew back its other claw.

Groggily, Felix stared into the face of his daemonic executioner. It leered at him, bloodied, horse-teeth jutting from its skinless face.

'For the Emperor. For the primarch,' Felix said, and prepared to face his death.

The blow never fell.

The wave hit. Felix roared in agony. So intense was the pain that at the time he did not experience it as a solely spiritual hurt, and thought in the moment that the claw had fallen. He saw flashes. Landscapes that changed eternally, legions of heinous creatures, wailing souls chased to destruction. With supreme effort of will, he dragged his spirit back from the brink of hell.

N'Thragor was frozen over him, the creature's flesh boiling to black smoke picked up by a wind only the dead could feel, and dragged out into long, ragged flags of dissipating false matter. But he was not dead. N'Thragor pushed into the storm blasting his kind back whence they came, still roaring, still reaching for Felix even as he was ripped to howling pieces.

Felix's armour's machine spirit chimed. His backpack reactor restarted, a little unevenly, but the hissing had stopped. There was a rush as his air supply was purged. A field in his display enlarged itself, showing him the rerouting of power, then various areas of damage. There were many of them.

The tetrarch got to his feet, dragging up his weapons from the dust.

N'Thragor, his face now reduced to a stripped, equine skull, continued to howl. All around them, Soul Grinders were fleeing, their false flesh boiling to nothing in the pulses of green and blue light washing out from the pylons in interlinked ripples. Each wash battered the daemon lord as if they were cannon rounds. Still he roared, still he tried to approach Felix.

The pulses affected the tetrarch, each one provoking memory from deep in his mind – of his home, his father, the looks of horror and disdain on the faces of the other recruits as he was taken off the shuttle, the shame and pain of failure turned to horror as he was brought to Cawl and confronted with a far darker fate.

He took a step, leaden, heavy as walking on the bed of a lightless sea.

His mother's laughter. The pain of surgical intrusion. Cawl whistling as he probed the barely conscious Felix with blades and needles.

Another step. Twenty yards away, a Soul Grinder's torso melted into vile liquids, splashing down on the ground, its mechanical lower body cantering on before collapsing catastrophically.

His first meeting with the primarch. The day he left for Ultramar. Inside the Pharos, the liquid golden light sour with the fury of mad gods.

Another step. N'Thragor raised his cannons. Attempting to fire, one exploded as malformed ammunition detonated; the other drooped, melting. Still the daemon lord pushed his claw at Felix, the blades quivering, ready to snap closed around the tetrarch. Still, N'Thragor howled.

And Felix felt pain, the pain of being, the pain of inhumanity, the pain of duty and its unbearable crushing weight.

He had expected honour, and glory, and found there was only endless, terrible war.

He looked up into the skull face of the daemon, by then a paper-thin, bony mask, still screaming, still raging. All that pain and hate thrust from one plane into another, and for what?

'Why will you not die?' Felix shouted.

He drew back his sword arm, and with what strength remained to him thrust it over his head, deep into the daemon's chest.

The claw snapped shut inches from his face.

Felix aimed for where the heart would have been, had N'Thragor been a man. It was doubtful if the beast had a heart, if it needed one, if there was anything within it other than the curdled hates of doomed dreamers. That did not matter. In such a contest, intent mattered. In a way the tetrarch would not be able to truly understand, his point found its mark. The power field blazed. N'Thragor's screams of rage turned to those of frustration as he was banished from the realm of men.

The daemon's giant torso exploded, showering all around with thick plates of rancid meat and dark, oily blood that was fizzling away to nothing before it hit the ground.

Once more, Felix was flung back. He landed hard against the sloped rampart of the bunker, and for a moment he did lose consciousness, drowning in memories.

Then it stopped. The pain lasted a while longer, but now it brought with it a balm, a sense of calmness, and of tranquillity. The psychic blaze of the pylon's activation was levelling out, reducing. The pulses stopped.

Felix slid down the wall into a crouch.

The remains of the Soul Grinder champion canted drunkenly over him. All traces of warp-born flesh had been stripped from it. Only its mechanical parts remained, and they appeared eroded, as if it had been standing in the desert for centuries.

He tugged off his helmet. Every part of him felt bruised, from his skin, to his organs, to his soul.

The sky was clearing. The rifts were gone. Ships were coming down. Several had already landed. Skitarii guarded columns of chanting priests whose technical hymns of holy good function drove back the last of the warp's baleful influence.

A shadow fell over him. He looked up, expecting one of his Chosen to come to aid him. Instead he found himself looking into the face of Alpha Primus, Cawl's strangest son. Later, when he had come back into himself fully, Felix wondered how Primus was affected when the pylon network activated. He remembered the giant as a potent psyker. As it was, his face was streaked with bloody tears, and scabs clung to the corners of his nostrils.

Primus held out a hand.

'Tetrarch Decimus Felix. It has been a long time. I am glad to see you alive.'

Felix grasped the proffered forearm.

Primus hauled him up to his feet.

'We were victorious?' said Felix, taking in the devastation around him.

'We were victorious,' said Primus.

'By the lord of all machines, it's working!' Cawl said. There was no bombast. The words were whispered, as if he feared to upset the process by acknowledging it. Raptly silent, the survivors of the battle stared up at the sky. Evening was once again falling. The Pit was coming up in the east.

Solana drew comparisons between the Pit and the Scorean anomaly. Both were holes in the fabric of the universe. Both had hearts of uttermost darkness. Both were dangerous to everything around them. But where the black hole had been a full stop to the story of time and space, the Pit was the spawning ground of new, dreadful tales. A black hole marks the uncrossable border of eternity. The doors of a warp rift swing both ways.

Such doors can be closed.

It took five minutes for the spear of energy to hit the Pit. It connected dead centre.

The whole of the warp rift convulsed, like an eye shutting on a painful intrusion. The illusion broke, turned into another, that of a whirlpool sucking itself away to nothing. Then to another, a hole rapidly filling with sand. All was awhirl, a pattern of oily patches and smeary, purplish light that shrank, shrank, shrank. A blink, the last light of a train vanishing deep in a tunnel.

The Pit was gone.

Cawl stared intently for five solid seconds, then rapidly murmured to himself, then relaxed, then began fiddling with his machines.

'I'm adjusting the field strength,' he said. 'Taken it down to a minimum. We humans need the warp, you know. Too much is bad, too little is bad. Equilibrium is what we seek, but we must observe if the Pit returns.' He opened communications across suddenly clear airwaves. 'Wocolos, what does it look like from up there?'

The Integerarian responded immediately. His voice came loud and clear of all disruption. *'All readings suggest the Pit is closed, archmagos.'*

'Then it worked,' said Cawl slowly, then louder, 'it actually, provably worked!' He laughed in delight. 'Go tell that to Roboute Guilliman, historitor!' He laughed again. 'I know when I say, "I'm Belisarius Cawl and I can do anything," it makes me look a little egotistical.' He held up hands to silence words that were not said. 'I know, I know, I shouldn't be too hard on myself, and in matter of fact, I'm not, because that was pretty spectacular, no?' He rubbed his hands together. 'And that, my friends, is how one solves a problem. Quite the adventure! Quite the adventure!'

Qvo cleared his throat. 'Can I unplug my head now, please? It feels peculiar.'

'Oh!' said Cawl. 'Of course! I am so sorry.' He extricated the cable first from the pylon, then from Qvo's head. He flipped the back of Qvo's cranium shut, and Qvo pulled his hood up.

'Ouch,' he said. Then he frowned. 'Belisarius?'

'Yes?'

'That was spectacular, but did you not think it... well, easy?'

Cawl sighed. 'Sometimes, dear Friedisch, it is better not to look a gift equid in the mouth. But...' He scratched under his mandibular shield. 'But, but, but...' He was pensive. 'Maybe you are right. Maybe it was easy.'

Across the battlefield, Space Marines were beginning to count the cost of victory.

'I have much to ponder,' said Cawl suddenly. 'Wocolos, collate all data relating to the collapse of the Pit. In the meantime, let's go and see how everyone is bearing up.'

CHAPTER THIRTY-FOUR

LIKE A FATHER

The last time Felix had seen the prow lander of the *Zar Quaesitor* he had been upon Sotha, before the destruction of the Pharos there. It was bigger than he recalled, seven storeys tall, and a deep, Martian red, a statement of a vessel to match Guilliman's own *Aquila Resplendum*. In a further display of confidence the archmagos had put down right at the heart of the battlefield.

He gritted his teeth at the arrogance of it.

A large delegation gathered to greet the archmagos. Bjarni was there, and Ulfreyr, the High Jarl and others of the Wolfspear. What was left of Felix's bodyguard waited at attention. He had seen Austen, Ixen and Cadmus die. Once battle was ended and the costs counted, he had discovered that silent, defiant Troncus had also met his end. The survivors were battle-worn, many were injured. They waited to thank their saviour just the same.

Felix hated Cawl sincerely, and yet as always he suffered additional, conflicting emotions when he thought about the archmagos. The first was an unwelcome need to impress him, which made him angry, but the other was subtler and less easy to deal with.

Felix found he actually wanted to see his creator.

A column of priests, servitors, servo-skulls, all the rest of the Mechanicus pomp, came billowing scented oil fumes and singing hymns down the ramp. Cawl had once dismissed these trappings of power. Felix wondered if he had changed.

Then Cawl himself arrived, coming not from the ship but from the nearest pylon, flanked by dozens of cyborgs. He was as huge and inhuman as Felix remembered, a withered old man carried by machines and robed in prideful ostentation. The sight of him made Felix's paired hearts beat a little faster.

The priests reached the ground, and they split, passing their leader, and spread out onto the battlefield, where they stopped at every Soul Grinder carcass, flicked holy lubricant and recited the rites of mechanical exorcism.

High Jarl Irik Stianolf went forward with his battered honour guard to greet the archmagos. Cawl paid particular attention to the Dreadnoughts.

Felix could have upped the audio gain on his auto-senses and listened to every word. He did not care to. He did not care to greet the old man either. On the other hand, he had thought he might leave, but he did not do that either. He told himself he did not wish to appear petty. It was more than that.

Cawl briefly conferred with his tech-priests. There was a great deal of binharic exchange. Only then did Cawl turn his attention to Felix and come over cautiously, as if he might spook the tetrarch into flight.

'Decimus, Decimus, my dear boy,' said Cawl. 'What an absolute pleasure to see you.' He looked his creation up and down. 'Still hale, still healthy, still whole. I am so glad you survived.'

'Archmagos,' said Felix. He dipped his head once, it was as much respect as he could bring himself to display.

Cawl looked around at all that was going on, as nervous people will to hide their discomfort.

Felix stared doggedly ahead. 'You arrived at the most fortuitous time.'

Cawl turned back to him and chuckled softly. 'I assure you it was planned, my boy. What brings you here? I guess that the regent wanted a spy upon Ulvheim as well as within my fleet.'

'Something like that,' said Felix.

'Ah, at least you are honest, not like the historitor, who is spying on me but won't admit it.'

Behind Cawl, Solana scowled.

'I'm sure she'll be about later to bother you with questions. That's her, over there.' Cawl pointed her out.

'That is what they do,' said Felix. He nodded at the historitor. She nodded back. They had met a few times, years before.

'Well, she's perfectly charming,' said Cawl. 'So try to be nice.' He sighed. 'This is pleasant, but I must be off to inspect the rest of my pylons. They worked, but one must go over the results to make sure they can be replicated. After that, well, I hear there is to be a feast!'

'One like no other,' said Felix, parroting words that Bjarni had said to him earlier on, though rather more enthusiastically.

'Perhaps you and I will talk a little more then?' said Cawl.

'Perhaps we will. Good day, archmagos,' said Felix. He performed an about-turn in full parade fashion, and took his bodyguard away.

Night fell naturally for the first time in over a decade. The sky was a soft blanket speckled with stars. All around the battlefield, one hundred and twenty feet high, pylons slender enough to appear like needles driven into the planet's skin stitched the wounds of reality closed with threads of bright blue and green.

There was much drinking that night. Cawl did not attend. Vast quantities of mjød were sourced from somewhere, great oaken hogsheads of it carried in by laughing Wolfspear. The warriors bore the huge casks one on each shoulder, as easily as if they were bundles of straw. It was a feat that impressed even Cominus.

'Where are they even getting it from?' Cominus wondered out loud. His usual manner had returned, and though that was gruff, Felix preferred it to the despairing Cominus of the day before.

Ulfreyr laughed long and hard. He looked like his other brethren out of his armour, grizzled, tattooed and wild, and behaved like them also, laughing and singing and trading jokes of a kind Felix could imagine few other Space Marines contemplating.

'There is always mjød. The High Jarl opens his personal stocks for all,' Ulfreyr said.

'Do these things not belong in common to all?' Cominus asked. He looked askance at Bjarni, who had drunk so much he was face down unconscious on the table.

Ulfreyr belched enormously. Felix could not imagine a Chaplain of the Ultramarines behaving this way. He surprised himself by smiling.

'Something amuses you?' Ulfreyr asked.

'Nothing important. I am taking heart in your traditions. It is good we are not all the same.'

'Wise words from a son of the Legion-breaker!' yelled Ulfreyr. 'This is the way of Russ' kin. Our High Jarl is more like a king, less like one of your Chapter Masters, so this mjød is his to gift to us or not, as he pleases.' He tipped his drinking horn at Felix.

'The High Jarl shares to cement loyalty among the other jarls and the wolves. Do you see?'

'I do not understand,' Cominus said. 'Where is the discipline?'

'You are a fine warrior, Cominus of the Sons of Orar, but I am not surprised. You do understand, don't lie, but I know you will never approve. Not even one small bit.' Ulfreyr wagged his finger tipsily. 'Ha! Not that it matters. Now drink. Drink to remember your brothers who died, with joy in your hearts. They fought well. We won. The Pit is closed. The time for sorrow will come later. Victory must be celebrated first!' Ulfreyr saluted with his horn. Felix clashed his own against it.

'So it must,' said Felix. *Although perhaps,* thought Felix, *I would prefer to do so in less raucous fashion than the wolves favour.*

'Skjol!' Ulfreyr shouted.

For once, Felix forced down some of the mjød.

The night wore on. No daemons came. The feast became louder, more violent, less restrained, until Felix had had enough of the fighting and the singing and decided to go outside.

He got up, and touched Cominus' shoulder to catch his attention. 'I'm getting some air,' he said. His words were lost to the crash of a table breaking and the uproarious laughter that ensued.

'Why?' Cominus was bleary-eyed. He'd spent part of the night arm wrestling a succession of Wolfspear. Daelus was intent on a game of hnaftafl, playing three drunken sons of Russ who were shouting contradictory advice at him and each other. The rest of them were dotted about the hall, adopted easily into the roaring brotherhood of the Wolfspear. There were mortals present too, the less Cult-inclined of Cawl's followers. The more human tech-priests and the Knights of Taranis. All of them avoided the mjød, it being poisonous to standard humans. They were wildly drunk even so, for the Wolfspear were hospitable hosts. Felix thought there was more at work than the wine or the ale, as if the lifting of the weight of the Pit's malevolent regard had led to a rebounding of spirit.

'I said I'm going outside,' Felix shouted. A pottery drinking mug exploded on the wall to a deafening round of cheers. Cominus nodded, downed his drink.

'This… 's good.' He put his pot down with a look of studious concentration. 'I shall attend you, tetra… tetrarch.'

'No need,' said Felix, pushing the sergeant back onto his bench when he tried to rise. 'I can look after myself. There's no danger tonight. Stay. Celebrate. I will return soon.'

'Buh…'

'You are intoxicated, Cominus. Stay here.'

'Tha's 'mpossible,' Cominus muttered thickly, ''m an Adept Astartes.'

'So are they,' said Felix, sweeping his eyes around the room at the drunken Wolfspear. 'Stay.'

He pushed his way through staggering, cheering men. He worried for the mortals, surrounded by these clumsy ogres. He himself was far from sober. The familiar method of moving in a straight line simply by placing one foot in front of the other proved elusive. Climbing the stairs was a greater challenge still.

He was glad to gain the battlements. Cool wind teased his hair. The scent of the night was pure, not a hint of Chaos' evil. Seeking peace, he moved away from the stairs until he could no longer hear the feasting. When he was past the ranked macrocannons of the upper tier he saw a familiar shape standing by the crenellations, hunched and mighty.

Archmagos Belisarius Cawl.

Perhaps it was the mjød that drew Felix to the man, this second of his fathers. He supposed he could number them as three: Cawl, his genesire, and his natural father. What a mix he was.

Cawl heard him coming. Moving to look behind him was something of an operation, and he had to back up and round to be able to crane his neck far enough.

'Decimus? Decimus! What a delight. Come, come join me a moment.' He beckoned in welcome. 'I've been thinking alone a while now. Some company would be most welcome.'

As soon as Cawl spoke, Felix regretted his decision, and wished he had turned back. Being near Cawl made his skin crawl. But manners, or pity, made him go to the monster's side. The archmagos was the architect of victory, and yet here he was all alone.

'Enjoying the feast?'

'It is... interesting,' Felix replied.

Cawl laughed. 'The mjød, eh? How amusing the sons of Russ are. Given every gift to negate poison, they push their physiology to the limits just to be a little merrier. It gives you hope, no?'

'How so?'

'That the Adeptus Astartes remain human.'

'Sometimes too much so,' Felix agreed. Already his oolitic kidney was working, purging his system of the mjød's effects. He, for one, was glad of that.

'Ah, I disagree. We forget at our peril what we are. If we work so hard to become something else, something hard and unforgiving, something unfeeling, then what is the point of all this suffering?'

I could tell you a thing or two about suffering, Felix thought.

Lights moved across the triumphal ground where galvanic haulers shepherded by clades of enginseers cleared the field of battle, dragging the hulks of fallen Soul Grinders away for destruction. Imperial vehicles waited on low flatbed trucks, waiting to be taken for salvage.

'How goes it with you?'

'I have a great deal to do,' said Felix. He left it at that. He had no desire to elaborate.

'I suppose you must. Guilliman has given you a great responsibility, but he chose you well,' said Cawl. 'You are a fine man.'

'Do you not wish to claim credit for my character?' Felix said.

Cawl was surprised. 'Why? I changed you, but you are the man you were always meant to be. In fact, I chose you because of who you are and always have been. Between us, the Emperor and I...'

Such flagrant arrogance, Felix thought. His anger hardened.

'...can bestow long life and great strength. Acid spit. Suspension cocoons. All that. We can control you to an extent, and mould you, but character?' He shook his head. 'That's innate. That's all yours.'

'Is it now,' said Felix coldly.

'It is. It is! Congratulations, my boy. I always knew you'd go far. One of the very best.'

Felix had an unwelcome flashback to the clear plastek prison from which he was periodically awoken, and flashing chirurgeon blades at work, while Cawl prattled on and on so that pain and his voice were indistinguishable. 'Did you know that while you were cutting me, or when you stole my future?'

Cawl bowed his head. 'A shame, Decimus. Such a shame. I thought after our little adventure on Sotha we'd reached a rapprochement, that we had put all that behind us.' He paused. 'I am sorry. I only did what was necessary, and there'll be worse to come, I'm sure. But we have to do it, to save ourselves. So much sacrifice, so much pain. I regret you had to bear some of it.'

'Does that make you better?' said Felix.

'What do you mean?'

'That you apologise and admit an understanding of what you did to me. Does that make you better than the rest of the Imperium's machinery? Does it excuse you?'

Cawl didn't reply at once. He spoke carefully when he did.

'It's good, you know, that you speak that way. It shows you have an awareness that things are not perfect. It gives me heart that you might be able to make them better. You understand, Decimus. You are not a machine, but a person. We fight for humanity. We should not become less than human to win.'

Felix recalled when they had met on Sotha, and Cawl had referred to Felix's guard not by their names, but by their batch numbers. His care for individuals was only so deep.

'How is Sotha, by the way?' Cawl went on. 'How is Hierophant Particular Ix Trenth and good old Grand Archimage Triplex-Edic-0-1011?'

'Restoration work continues,' said Felix. 'The Scythes have a home.'

Cawl nodded. 'I gave you my best, you know.'

'The Imperial Regent thanks you for your efforts.' Felix let out a pensive breath that steamed on the air. It was colder than it had been when the Pit ruled the night. 'Your pylons work.'

'You'll tell the regent?'

'I have already messaged him. What is next?'

'Hmm,' said Cawl. 'That is a difficult question. What happened here poses questions. I fear there are great forces at work against us. We have been noticed.'

'By whom?'

Cawl shrugged and laughed a little. 'I have no idea. This galaxy is brimming with adversaries.'

'Then do you have a response?'

'I accelerate my efforts. We cannot afford to dally here.' Cawl looked into the night sky, at the stars and the peaceful void. 'Ah, the immemorial tapestry of the cosmos allowed free rein as the God of Machines intended.' Then he frowned. 'Almost as intended,' he said.

He was looking where the Cicatrix Maledictum cut across the Great Work, right at the galactic core, where the stars were brightest. The Rift was a purple gauze, somewhat unremarkable at that great remove, as unthreatening as any other stellar phenomenon, were it not for the hint of fear that emanated from it even from so far away.

'I'll depart as soon as the *Zar Quaesitor* is in good enough repair. We have no time to waste. Greater challenges await at the Attilan Gap. Raukos was but the proving. The real test is to come when I stabilise the conduit there.'

Felix looked where Cawl stared. If the archmagos perceived something more than he, something important, Felix did not see it himself. He was a blind man following a treacherous guide.

'I will be coming with you.'

Cawl beamed down at him, his smile so broad it was visible over the edges of his mandibular guard.

'I am genuinely pleased to hear that, my boy. Nothing would make me happier.' He placed a fatherly hand on Felix's shoulder. The tetrarch stepped away from his touch.

'Do not be,' he said brusquely. 'I go at the primarch's order to hold your leash, no other reason.'

Cawl's smile faded. He looked wounded, and Felix experienced a pinprick of regret. He pushed that away too, hardening himself. One thought of Primus looking down on him that afternoon was all it required to drive out any good feeling he had for Cawl. Primus the monster. The blasphemy. Yet Primus was a creature close enough to be his brother. And if he were his brother, what did that make him?

'Well, at least you will be there, Decimus,' said Cawl with a sad sigh. 'That is enough for me.'

'I will,' said Felix, and he left Cawl to his thoughts. He suddenly wanted another drink.

Do not dare feel sorry for him, Felix told himself sternly as he went back down to the racket of the feast. *Do not dare.*

CHAPTER THIRTY-FIVE

A NEW MASTER

Kraverek watched the battle unfold, and he watched it lost. He saw the arrival of Cawl's starship, and the closure of the Pit. He saw N'Thragor fall. The vision persisted until the last few Soul Grinders were fleeing defeat through their warp rifts, whereupon it faded away. Kraverek did not see the very last moments of the battle, but he had seen more than enough.

He stood in silent disbelief a moment, then he began to laugh.

Vashtorr lifted his head. His eyes were soft amber suns, cat-like and dangerous.

'Something amuses you, Warsmith?'

'You amuse me! So mighty, so powerful you claim to be, and you cannot best a few hundred weak bloods? So much for the powers of the warp. Perhaps now you shall heed me properly.'

'Will I? That is an interesting proposition, to heed you.' Vashtorr flexed his back. His chains creaked ominously. ***'I think not. Now have the tech-priest release me, so we might bargain properly.'***

'Release you?' Kraverek said incredulously. 'No.'

Vashtorr stretched out his long neck, bringing his huge head close to the force field containing him, so that it was only feet from Kraverek's own. Again the chains creaked, the sound of steel about to break. ***'You are simple, Kraverek. You do not see.'***

'And what am I supposed to see?'

'What indeed? How to explain complicated events to one so manifestly stupid?' Vashtorr made a show of thinking. Kraverek raised a finger, ready to drop it and fill the daemon's mortal form with a dozen lascannon beams. He was being toyed with. If the daemon would not yield, then he would send it back to the warp. There were other ways to achieve his goals.

'This body,' said Vashtorr. ***'Let us take this body I wear as our example. It was won through events involving Cawl. Something of a coincidence, don't you think?'***

'Happenstance,' said Kraverek, although by now an icy sliver of uncertainty was working its way into his belly. His finger quivered. *Not yet,* he thought. He could still pull this situation back from the brink. There were his men to think of. They would not tolerate another failure.

'Ah, so you are one of those who believes things happen without reason.' Flames jetted briefly from the daemon's nostrils. ***'The Iron Warriors were always the most naive of the Legions. You put too much faith in rationality, and scoff at the warp. Everything happens for a purpose, Warsmith, for that is the nature of the Great Work. The gods show you the way, and still you will not believe. Destiny is real, and I am yours. Release me now, and you shall receive a fair trade, I swear. Vashtorr deals straight, always.'***

'It does not matter what you or I believe. What matters is that you are in my power, and that you serve me. Maybe a little correction is in order to remind you,' said Kraverek. He gestured at the magi. Kolumbari-Enas and his acolytes moved to their machines with unseemly haste.

'Do not say I did not offer you better terms,' said the daemon. He twisted his neck. Metal vertebrae cracked, the action of a smith about to busy himself at the anvil. *'I shall take this as your refusal. A new, less preferential bargain shall be struck once your true position is made clear to you.'* Vashtorr shifted. His joints hissed like hydraulic pistons.

'I shall not warn you again, daemon,'

'I told you, you can't hurt me. I have been honest with you about that, about everything. Whereas you, Kraverek of the old Fourth Legion, have not been honest with me, nor with your men.' Grunting against his restraints, Vashtorr got first one hoofed foot underneath himself, then the other, and then stood up into a stoop, wings brushing the warp dome containing him. *'You know whereof I speak. You were angry at my efforts to stop Cawl because your victory must be of a specific sort, at a specific place. It would have been no good to you if Cawl had died on Ulvheim, because your triumph must be seen, and it must be seen because you have no orders from the Despoiler for this mission you have set for yourself.'*

'So this is your treachery? You lied to us?' Psephalas said angrily.

'He schemes for favour, I assume to stop you killing him. He has had little success of late, is that not true? No?' Vashtorr swung his heavy head to look at the chosen.

'It is true,' Xeseus said.

'Do not speak with the daemon!' Kraverek said, but his command was shrill, and lacked authority.

'Undoubtedly, Abaddon would prefer the Anathema's son not to have another route across the Rift, but you have nothing to do with his plans. Kraverek saw an opportunity to save himself from your disappointment. Achieving this goal would buy you much influence. Imagine! Controlling a second route across the

Rift. Such favour that would bring, such riches! I saw this in your heart long ago.' Vashtorr looked to the other Iron Warriors. ***'I regret it must be I who informs you, but the scroll he has you venerate, it is a forgery. Your leader is false.'***

'That is a lie,' said Kraverek. He could feel his warriors' tension. 'Magos, show our guest some hospitality.'

Kolumbari-Enas threw a lever. The machines projecting the warp dome over the daemon chugged into action. Lightning blazed down from the hemisphere of energy imprisoning Vashtorr.

The daemon growled, then shook like a beast drying its pelt. The energies stabbing at him reflected upon themselves, coursing along the cables back into the disciples' containment engines. Massive feedback arced from the machines, finding escape into the deck via the body of one of the disciples. The tech-priest danced an electric jig, his robes ablaze, and fell dead. The machines spat showers of hot sparks, and died too. The smell of burned metal and burned flesh flooded the hold. The warp dome flashed to nothing.

'How tiresome. I am the master of all machines, a god to their kind, do you not know?' Free of the confining energy field, Vashtorr rose to his full height. He lifted one hand, easily parting the chain holding it, then flexed his long claws. The manacle came apart and dropped to the ground. ***'Abaddon no more knows your name than he does this one here.'*** He gestured dismissively at Kolumbari-Enas. ***'This insect who prays to an insignificant footnote from history.'***

'Refutation!' Kolumbari-Enas said. 'Sota-Nul is powerful and eternal!'

'Oh, I am afraid I am right, First-Among-Equals. Your mistress' soul was torn to shreds in the warp nine thousand years ago. As for you, Warsmith, I would applaud your audacity, but…' He pulled his other hand free. The broken chain rattled onto the deck. *'I dislike being chained. Still, for a nobody it was an inventive strategy, if clumsily enacted.'*

The second manacle clanged to the ground. The arcane circle smoked.

'Do something!' Kraverek spat at Kolumbari-Enas.

The magos' beaked face swung from side to side uncertainly.

'Now!' Kraverek shouted.

First-Among-Equals held up his hands and with his remaining followers began to chant. The bonds of words about Vashtorr's wrists spun and constricted. For a moment, it appeared to be working. Vashtorr thrashed against the arcane sigils burning into him, then he stopped, and he roared, and one after the other the bonds burst, their energy dissipating into the deck. Kolumbari-Enas' chanting grew louder. The sketched outlines of new bonds glittered.

'Do be quiet,' Vashtorr said.

Kolumbari-Enas stuttered, his voxmitter buzzed, and then his words were gone, replaced by a horrible choking broadcast by his augmetics. Together with the last members of his sect he fell to the floor, all writhing in agony as oily smoke poured from every bionic component.

The ring of burning oil roared high, then went out.

What happened next, happened quickly.

Kolumbari-Enas' bodyguards opened fire. Vashtorr raised a hand, stopping bolts of energy in mid-air. His eyes flashed, the guns malfunctioned, and in horrible, drawn-out fashion every augmetic of the Myrmidons slowly detached itself from its host, drawing itself with grisly squelching from their bodies, then came apart component by component and fell in showers around them.

Their remaining organic parts dropped wetly.

As the Myrmidons opened fire, Kraverek dropped the raised finger of his right hand.

'Fire!'

Half a dozen lascannons spoke at once. Superheated air cracked. Ruby beams blinked. Red-hot, molten holes punched into Vashtorr's hide. He growled in annoyance. Where were the rest? Kraverek wondered. He had twelve lascannons and as many missile launchers aimed at the daemon. Shouts answered his question, and a sound of metal falling. Kraverek turned to see his men's heaviest weaponry falling to pieces, each component coming apart neatly, so that showers of screws, plastek, crystals, and electronics pattered over armour onto the deck.

By then, both the Myrmidons and the Havocs were disarmed. The sacred ring burst magnesium bright, and it too burned itself to nothing. Psephalas shouted injurious words and streams of bright fires shot from his hands. Vashtorr waved them aside. Psephalas fell, psychic feedback coursing through his body. The daemon stepped out of the circle.

'It was I who placed the automaton in Bile's way so he would find it. It was I who brought Bile's possession of it to Kolumbari-Enas' attention.' Vashtorr towered over Kraverek. ***'It was I who stoked your ambition. I who revealed Cawl's plan to you. You have been my puppet all along, you arrogant fool. You are a part of a machine, a cog whirring at my behest. You cannot bind me. These weapons you have, they will not harm me, and this petty sorcerer, he can no more than irritate.'*** He growled. Iron Warriors shouted. Guns fell to pieces. Power armour seized. ***'Now begins our bargaining for your life.'***

'Don't listen to him,' Kraverek shouted. 'Hold your ground! Psephalas, strike him down!'

Psephalas was on his knees.

'No.'

'What are you doing? You are our only hope of harming him.'

'Harm him yourself,' said Psephalas. 'If I unleash my power on him again, we will all die.'

'We will all die without it!'

Vashtorr watched the Space Marines with interest, but did not move against them.

'If he wanted us dead, we'd already be like those misguided bastards over there.' Psephalas glowered at the smashed remains of the Disciples of Nul. 'I know when I am outmatched.'

'That is so, sorcerer,' said Vashtorr approvingly.

Psephalas dropped his head. 'I am your servant, lord.'

'What are you doing?' Kraverek spat.

'Living a little longer,' said Psephalas. 'I advise you to kneel if you wish the same. I warned you Vashtorr was dangerous.'

Xeseus put up his gun. 'All of you, lower your weapons,' he said to the others.

'Xeseus! I command you!' Kraverek said. 'Shoot the daemon. Shoot the daemon now.'

The Iron Warrior shook his head. 'I'm not going to die on your account. I'm with Psephalas, for once.'

'You too are wise, Xeseus,' said Vashtorr. ***'I am not going to kill you.'***

'Why?' asked Kraverek.

'You really are rather stupid,' said Vashtorr. ***'So I will explain as simply as I am able.'*** He walked around Kraverek, seeming bigger and more potent than ever before. ***'I am here because I allowed you to summon me. I required a way across the Great Rift. I have been physically manifest for some time on the far side. I am occupied there with a matter of import, and in such a form even I cannot cross the Rift easily or quickly. It was necessary to use you to bring me into being here. There is something that demands my attention here, now. I want Cawl. There have been few humans born with such gifts as his since your miserable species took to two feet, and I want him. I want him for my forge.'*** The daemon continued to pace. ***'That is why I allow you to you***

live. For now. Yet your survival carries a price, which we shall now negotiate.'

'You need my armies.'

'Perhaps not so unintelligent after all,' said Vashtorr.

Kraverek breathed deeply, calmly, let this daemon see he was not afraid. 'Then I shall pledge myself to you.' Kraverek got to his knees, and bowed his head.

'Finally,' Psephalas murmured. 'You see sense.'

'But I give you my service,' Kraverek continued, 'only in return for our freedom and the fulfilment of my own ambitions. The plan remains the same. You get Cawl, I get his gateway. That is my price.'

Vashtorr snorted. ***'I think you overestimate the strength of your bargaining position.'***

'Do I? I know my worth. You are mighty, Vashtorr, but you are of the warp, for all your trappings of iron and wire. You cannot muster the armies to take on a man such as Cawl. You cannot last long in the material world, and because of that time is of value to you as much as to a mortal. Your armies of daemon machines will not suffice alone. You need men, and ships, things of this realm of existence. Space Marines to fight Space Marines.'

'You are overconfident. Your bartering is poor.'

'If that were true, I would be dead already, because you would not need me. I admit I made a mistake trying to make you my servant.' Kraverek grinned, showing his metal teeth. 'But this is the situation we find ourselves in. I offer cooperation, not dominance from either side. The truth of the matter is, my lord, that you and I are too weak to achieve our goals alone. Only together will we triumph. Let us cease this charade of masters and servants.'

Vashtorr's wings scissored. Pale corposant danced along the edges of the blades. ***'Vashtorr sells or Vashtorr commands, Vashtorr*** *rarely cooperates. Unless, unless...'* The daemon lifted his hand, as if weighing the worth of Kraverek's words, or that of his soul. *'Unless the offer intrigues, unless the offer rewards. That is a good opening offer, but armies alone are insufficient.'*

'Then what additional price would you exact?'

'There is only one price, and the price is always the same. The price is souls, the souls of machines or the souls of men, I care not. Souls are the currency of power, and I deserve all the riches this bountiful universe has to offer. Collect them for me, and you shall prosper. For souls you shall have armour, and machines of war, and more allies to swell the pitiful forces you offer me.'

'A beguiling offer, yet false. You need my so-called pitiful forces. I need you. Name the cost, not the benefits alone. How many years? How many souls? What are the penalty clauses, and the rights of withdrawal? Give me all the matter of commerce, not broad promises in which hide tricks.'

Vashtorr's grille mouth looked immobile, yet it appeared to leer wide enough to swallow them all. His eyes glared like lost suns. *'A man after my own heart. A true merchant of death. Very well, tell me what you require, I shall tell you what I desire, and we shall itemise the cost exactly. A bill of fare, all honest and square. There are no tricks with Vashtorr, though I warn you, iron one, my skills are great and priced accordingly.'*

'As are mine,' said Kraverek. He got to his feet. 'Partners, not master and slave. That is the primary clause.'

Vashtorr looked at him appraisingly. *'Done.'*

'Then let us continue with the warriors I need to win to our banner, and the costs of them, and work from there.'

'When the reckoning is complete, I shall add a portion more for your freedom. A termination fee, if you will.' Smoke boiled from the exhaust array mounted on Vashtorr's back.

Kraverek's smile hardened.

'No, I will have a fair estimate before the tally is complete. No additions. I have heard of your bargains, daemon, and their ever increasing costs.'

Vashtorr laughed softly. ***'Maybe I underestimated you after all, Kraverek of the Fourth Legion. So we will deal, and when we are both satisfied, I will show you how we shall bring Belisarius Cawl to heel.'***

Eremenitas waited for the feast to be in full swing before he set out on his errand. The descent to the Varghalen forge took him hours. His wheeled carriage was not well suited to stairs, and he had therefore to go where ramps and lifting cages provided access. He suspected Solana would have disapproved of that, and would have suggested his original legs might have served him better, but she was almost as bad a heretek as Cawl himself. She did not truly believe, she did not see what the great act of worship exchanging his limbs for tracks had been. If the bearings in his drive wheels became worn, they could be replaced. The same could not be said of knees. A wheel was a simple mechanism, solid and reliable. The human leg was a ridiculous evolutionary joke, full of flaws. Let her glance disapprovingly at his wheels when she was old and her hips had disintegrated, then they would see who was the better acolyte of the Machine God.

The machine was superior to the flesh in every way. The flesh was weak.

Going the long way round gave him time to think, and thought was the most precious of the Machine God's boons.

Several backtracks and three hours later, Eremenitas arrived in the forge caverns. Eremenitas knew some of the others thought the main body of the fortress unimpressive. It had no majesty, they thought, but they did not see the great art apparent in the prefabricated sections much of the upper structure was made from, all the fruits of the blessed STC system.

No, Eremenitas had decided some time ago that Solana was not a very faithful person at all, prone to innovation and independent thought even more than her profile suggested. He'd been willing to give her the benefit of the doubt to begin with. He had been so shocked at the depth of her will that he had spent many hours meditating on the failures of his generosity.

Like the astropathicum, the forge was built underground, though in its case it had been placed there simply to protect the Chapter's limited stock of machines. Several large caverns had been fusion-cut from the bedrock, but they were still empty. Despite their fleet's manufacturing capabilities, the Wolfspear was a long way from self-sufficiency. No bad thing, he thought. It kept them dependent on Mars.

The last third of the complex was in something approaching working order. Huge blast doors shut off vehicle garages and workshops. A long corridor to the final door, behind which lay a forge-fane. It opened as he approached. The temple was small, as he expected, though they mostly were in Space Marine Chapters, whose other members frowned upon worship. Inside were sufficient workbenches to repair only the Techmarines' own equipment, and an altar carrying a bronze rendition of the Opus Machina. Nothing more.

The Wolfspear's master of the forge was within alone, as Eremenitas had requested. The seal of the Fabricator General bought many favours. It would buy another soon enough.

'Magos, it is a privilege to have you visit our forge complex. I trust you are content with what you see?'

'Your forge is unfinished. Work is worship to the three-in-one,' said Eremenitas.

'You are correct, of course.' The master of the forge drew

himself up. His servo-harness' arms flexed. 'I offer no excuses. We shall do better.'

'I may be able to help you with that,' said Eremenitas.

'How so?'

'An infusion of materiel and machines, directly from Holy Mars. I am authorised to offer you this by the office of the Fabricator General Xasandera Valdet.'

The master of the forge's helm was unreadable, and his voice kept studiously so.

'I was led to believe that you were in the employ of the Imperial Regent's Logos Historica Verita.'

'That is my current employment, but a son of Mars' loyalty must always be to the Machine Cult itself, do you not agree?'

'A man may have many masters,' the forge master replied neutrally.

'I ask for little in return for this boon of technology. Only a small favour.'

'What might that be?'

'I invoke the treaties between Mars and your forge.' A panel slid open in Eremenitas' side. From within the compartment revealed, he retrieved a message scroll. 'This message must be sent by astrotelepathy, it must be sent tonight, and it must be sent secretly. No one must know.'

The forge master reached out, then hesitated.

'You could use Cawl's astropaths. That you don't suggests the message would displease him.'

'The content of the message is not your concern. It is in code, and you would not understand it even if you were to read it, for it concerns the higher mysteries. Nineteen hundred cubic yards of packed machine components, fabrication units, and additional weaponry should be of more interest to you than what this message contains.'

Eremenitas had gauged his offer well.

The forge master took the scroll.

'Send it as if it were a message from your forge,' Eremenitas said. 'Do not mention me or my involvement.'

'For Mars. For the Machine God. Is there a passcode?'

'Everything necessary to the message is contained in that scroll. Send it now, and be rewarded by the generosity of the Machine God.'

'I shall see to it personally,' said the forge master.

With that, Eremenitas rotated on his tracks and began the long trek back up to the surface.

ABOUT THE AUTHOR

Guy Haley's work for Black Library spans the depth and breadth of the Warhammer universes. He is the author of several Horus Heresy novels, including *The Lost and the Damned, Titandeath, Wolfsbane* and three titles in the Primarchs series. He has also written many Warhammer 40,000 books, including *Dawn of Fire: Avenging Son,* the Dark Imperium trilogy, and the Belisarius Cawl novels *The Great Work, Genefather* and *Archmagos.* For Age of Sigmar he has penned the Drekki Flynt novels *The Arkanaut's Oath* and *The Ghosts of Barak-Minoz* as well as many other stories. He lives in Yorkshire with his wife and son.

MORE FROM
BLACK LIBRARY

GENEFATHER
by Guy Haley

Archmagos Belisarius Cawl invites representatives from across the Imperium, hoping to secure their assistance in unlocking the secrets of the pylon network. Among the attendees, however, is an uninvited guest who may possess the only mind in the galaxy greater than that of the fabled Archmagos…
